The Boy-Bishop's Glovemaker

MICHAEL JECKS

The Boy-Bishop's Glovemaker

**SIMON &
SCHUSTER**

London · New York · Sydney · Toronto · New Delhi

A CBS COMPANY

First published in 2000 by Headline Books Publishing

This edition published in Great Britain in 2013 by Simon & Schuster UK Ltd
A CBS COMPANY

1 3 5 7 9 10 8 6 4 2

Simon & Schuster UK Ltd
1st Floor
222 Gray's Inn Road
London
WC1X 8HB

www.simonandschuster.co.uk

Simon & Schuster Australia, Sydney

Simon & Schuster India, New Delhi

A CIP catalogue copy for this book is available
from the British Library.

ISBN: 978-1-47112-629-1
eBook ISBN: 978-1-47112-630-7

Printed and bound in Great Britain by CPI Group UK Ltd, Croydon CR0 4YY

For Spike, Cathy, Jordan and Kristen, because without their help (and printer) I'd never have got started.

It's also for Fred Storm, the Blues Brother who lives on.

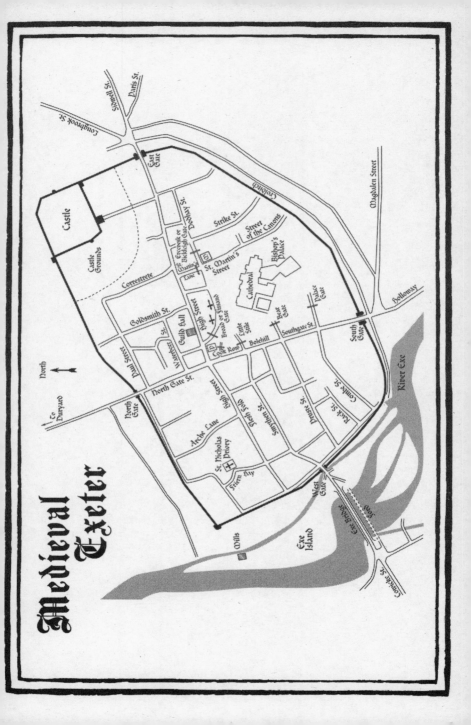

ACKNOWLEDGEMENTS

I have to thank too many people for their help in researching this book for me to be able to list them all, but some stand out for their specific assistance:

My wife Jane, who patiently proofread this, like so many of my other books, and pointed out all the little details I'd missed.

Margaret Cash, who has helped me greatly with this work. I have her to thank for the translation (from Latin) of Grandisson's *Regulations for the Boy-Bishop* which appears on page 7.

The librarians at the Devon and Exeter Institution, who scratched their heads doubtfully when I asked about ancient maps, ancient pictures, ancient names, and especially, ancient ceremonies. Yet each time they were able to recall specific documents or books, and if they couldn't give me the references directly, they always managed to point me in the direction of the authors or works which could.

MICHAEL JECKS

The people of North Dartmoor who have gone out of their way to make my research fun, who have given me fresh ideas for my stories, and who still take me to see new places where horrible things could have happened!

GLOSSARY

Annuellar   Sometimes also called Annivellars in Exeter, these were the priests who served the Chantries. They were appointed by the Dean and Chapter of the Cathedral to service a specific Chantry and to participate in the choral services along with other minor clergy. Annuellars were paid by an annual stipend and lived alone in rented chambers in the Close. They were paid some £2-£4 each year, from which they had to pay rent and buy their own food. Some had private means.

Canon   There were twenty-four Canons in Exeter, men who had chosen to live together bound by the Church's rules. They controlled the income of the Cathedral in common and mostly lived in the Close in their own houses. The more senior Canons were also expected to look after a Secondary and a Chorister, providing them with meals and offering other patronage.

Chantry
A popular way for people to protect their souls was to found a Chantry. This was a Mass held at set times or days to pray for the founder's soul. The Mass itself was the Chantry, although prayers for members of the founder's family were sometimes added. Chantries could be expensive since they often involved funding an altar, chapel, or part of a church, as well as providing sufficient money to pay for priests to service it. Exeter had many such Chantries.

Chapter
Exeter Cathedral had a large Chapter comprising twenty-four Canons. This body was ruled by the Dignitories. Among the Canons were the Archbishops of Barnstaple, Cornwall, Exeter and Totnes. Only the Dignitories possessed separate endowments.

Choir
The full body of men who served the Cathedral, comprising the Chapter and the Minor Clergy. However, the area of the Cathedral in which their stalls were placed was also termed the 'choir' of the church.

Choristers
To assist with the singing there were fourteen Choristers, who were appointed

by the Precentor and held their posts until their voices broke.

Custors   These were the custodians of the buildings, furnishings and gates. In the Cathedral, four Custors looked after lights, ornaments and vestments under the supervision of a sub-Treasurer. Similarly other Custors rang the bells and kept order.

Dignitories   This was the ruling body of the Cathedral. It comprised the Treasurer, Chancellor, Precentor and, at the head, the Dean.

Minor Clergy   There were four groups which are lumped together as Minor Clergy: the Vicars Choral, the Secondaries, the Choristers and the Annuellars. During the early 1300s there were some twenty-four Vicars, twelve Secondaries and fourteen Choristers. The Minor Clergy had a pleasant, sociable life. They had more personal freedom than a monk or friar, not to mention the potential for enjoying the varied amusements available in a city.

Minor Officers   Many of the routine tasks were undertaken by independent clergy with no other employment. They included the Custors, various administrative clerks, the Bailiff of the City, who collected rents, and the Succentor.

Punctators   These behaved like school prefects, noting down who had (or rather had not) attended services. The Vicars, Annuellars and Secondaries were supposed to attend all services unless ill, on pilgrimage, or granted special leave of absence, and Punctators kept records, checking off those who arrived against their lists.

Rulers   At special ceremonies, those which the Canons couldn't be expected to remember since they only happened once a year, Rulers would be positioned in front of the choir on revolving stools. They would prompt the choir, singing the first notes of each part of the service to remind the rest of the order of service.

Secondaries   These were appointed by the Dean himself. Generally they were adolescents and youths aged between seventeen and twenty-four. Several were admitted at puberty because they were Choristers whose voices had broken. Sadly it seems that many failed to gain higher offices and remained tonsured clerks or acolytes in order to keep open the opportunity of some form of career in their adulthood.

Succentor   This man was responsible for the music and the rituals within the Cathedral. He controlled which songs and prayers would be used.

Vicars Choral   Originally the Vicars were personal servants for the Canons, and thus there were twenty-four, one to match each Canon.

Each was appointed by his own Canon,
to whom he rendered personal services in
exchange for benefits. He had lodgings in
the Canon's house, meals at his table, and
accompanied his Canon to the Cathedral.
In 1300 they were paid some £2-£3 per
annum in cash, but of course lived with
free board and lodging.

*The Regulations for the Boy-Bishop at Exeter
Cathedral after Bishop Grandisson c. 1330
(translated from the Latin by Margaret Cash)*

To the Mayor and Commonality of the City of Exeter

1. No wine or cake should be made available on the eve of
St Thomas the Apostle at Kalandarhay.
2. No breakfast shall be made on the Feast Day of St Thomas
the Apostle in the room of the Chorister-Bishop, but the
Bishop together with the Choristers and servants of the
Canons at the house of their master, as they are accustomed on other days.
3. Distribution of gloves within the Close shall be done by two
or three of the Choir, and in the city and its vicinity by two,
three or four from the servants of the Canons of the Master
Bishop, according to the discretion of the said master.
4. The Bishop shall give no regard to his brother Choristers
on Holy Innocents' Day.
5. None shall be called to lunch on Holy Innocents' Day, at
the expense of the Bishop, at the house of his master,

7

unless they be special friends of the said Bishop, and then not beyond the number of six persons. The Bishop shall pay to his Canon master, should he wish to receive it, four pence for whatever lunch is taken. And the Bishop shall consider himself content with his master's service.

6. On Holy Innocents' Day there shall be prepared and arranged a pennyweight of bread, a pottle with a narrow neck, and two or three pennyweights of meat or one of cheese and butter, to be carried to the Bishop's room and carried by the Bishop and his brother Choristers, and he shall go down to the Priory of St Nicholas, provided that the expense of the said breakfast shall not exceed the sum of four or six pennies.

7. It is ordered that the said Bishop and his crosier, on the days after the said feast of the Holy Innocents, shall use dancing and leisure like the rest of the Choristers; and that afterwards they shall not run about through the church nor other places with the gloves, except when the County Court or Sessions of the Peace of Exeter is held, or certain respectable outsiders happen to approach the church or house of any Canon within the aforesaid precinct. And this with the licence of the Precentor or Succentor or the Clerk of the Chapel of St Mary.

Item, that the offering of money to the Bishop on Holy Innocents' Day shall be counted openly within the church before a clerk of the treasury or other respectable priest of the Choir and then shall be offered by one of the Bishop's friends.

CAST OF CHARACTERS

Sir Baldwin de Furnshill Keeper of the King's Peace of Crediton in Devon, Sir Baldwin was once a Knight Templar, but after the destruction of his Order he managed to return to his ancestral home. He is known to be an astute investigator of crimes.

Lady Jeanne Furnshill The widow of a coarse and brutal knight, Jeanne finally married Sir Baldwin earlier in the year after a protracted wooing.

Edgar Sir Baldwin's servant was once his Sergeant in the Knights Templar. When the Order was destroyed he chose to remain at

	his knight's side and became Sir Baldwin's trusted steward.
Simon Puttock	An old friend of Sir Baldwin's, Simon is Bailiff to the Warden of the Stannaries, based in Lydford. He and Baldwin have often investigated crimes together.
Ralph	The glover from Correstrete, Ralph was a cheerful, generous soul, whose murder has shocked the whole city. Especially since it appears to have been committed by his own apprentice.
Elias	Scarcely into his twenties, the horrified Elias has been arrested for the murder of his master, Ralph.
Mary Skinner	Elias's girlfriend, the daughter of a baker.
Henry	One of the Choristers, Henry has been elected to become the boy-Bishop when the Cathedral celebrates the Feast of the Holy Innocents.
Luke Soth	The leading Chorister, Luke had expected to be elected to the bishopric and was hurt and offended when his companions chose Henry instead.
Adam	One of the many Secondaries in the Cathedral, Adam is

waiting for a suitable position to appear so that he can be promoted from his minor clerical jobs.

Gervase
As Succentor, Gervase is responsible for the Choristers. The boys must be taught how to sing, but likewise they have to learn Latin, reading and writing.

Stephen
The Canon responsible for the Treasury, Stephen is also responsible for Luke and Adam, both of whom dine at his table.

Peter Golloc
A young Secondary who works in the Treasury and lives with Jolinde Bolle.

Jolinde Bolle
Although Jolinde showed some promise as a Chorister, he has fallen prey to the attractions of the city, especially those of a young woman.

Claricia Cornisshe
A serving woman in one of the taverns and Jolinde's girlfriend.

Vincent le Berwe
Vincent is a successful merchant who owns several properties and makes a good living from his trading. He has recently been elevated to one of the more senior posts in the city, that of Receiver.

11

Hawisia le Berwe
Vincent's wife, a bright young woman who is proud of his success.

Nicholas Karvinel
A merchant and associate of Vincent. He also knew Ralph well and took over much of his business when Ralph died.

Juliana Karvinel
The wife of Nicholas, a woman from Winchester.

John Coppe
Often to be found begging by the Fissand Gate, Coppe was crippled during a sea-fight.

Sir Thomas of Exmouth
Once an honourable knight, Sir Thomas has lost everything and now leads a small band of outlaws not far from Exeter.

Jen of Whyteslegh
When Sir Thomas first met Jen he was very taken with her. Later, when her parents died, she agreed to live with him.

Hob of Whyteslegh
Born witless, all through his life Hob has been looked down upon, and he has no regrets about leaving the vill where he was born. Now he lives with Sir Thomas and Jen.

Roger de Gidleigh
As Coroner, Roger must investigate any sudden deaths.

William de Lappeford
The Bailiff of the City, reporting to the Coroner.

AUTHOR'S NOTE

When I first began writing, I read *Pleasures and Pastimes in Medieval England* by Compton Reeves, and was struck by the insights it gave. One in particular caught my fancy: his description of a medieval Christmas. I was fascinated by it, and decided there and then that one day, I would write a mystery story set at Christmas-time.

The aspect which intrigued me most was the curious detail of the boy-Bishop. Only later did I realise that Exeter Cathedral annually elected a boy-Bishop – and as soon as I realised that, I knew I had to incorporate one into my story. At last, five years later, here he is.

There appears to be a direct link between the boy-Bishops of the Middle Ages and the Roman celebration of Saturnalia. This was a strange feast during which everything became topsy-turvy; social and moral constraints went by-the-by.

Boy-Bishops existed all over the country. Cathedrals, canonical churches and colleges had their own customs but were generally consistent: the boy would have been elected by his fellow Choristers on 21 December, Feast Day of St Thomas the Apostle, and would come into his bishopric at some time after Christmas, usually ending with the last service on Holy Innocents' Day, 28 December.

In Exeter the boy-Bishop took control at the last service on 27 December, and held power for twenty-four hours. During his reign he would have a fabulous time compared with normal: a Chorister in those days would have spent long hours singing in a draughty, cold cathedral, and even longer hours sitting learning Latin or writing. There would have been few breaks, and none designed for play.

Instead, on this one day, he would take breakfast with his Canon – a meal to which he could invite his friends – afterwards marching in procession to St Nicholas's Priory near the river, where the Prior would give him a sum of money and more food. Following this, he would be able to wander about the city with his friends and participate in all sorts of mayhem. As Nicholas Orme says in his excellent book *Exeter Cathedral As It Was 1050-1550*, 28 December was one day when the clergy could relax. Sometimes things went a bit too far – or at least, Bishop Grandisson certainly thought so, because he wrote scathingly of Canons whose minds were off in the marketplace, the street or even still in bed, while their bodies were present in church. Orme points out that, just as modern-day office workers enjoy Christmas parties with the associated revelry, drinking and (if only in the minds of the hopeful) casual sex, clerical staff in the early 1300s could also let their hair down for a short period each year.

In the middle of all this, there would be a gift of gloves to leading members of the city's institutions. The precise significance of these gloves has eluded me. Clearly, though, they were considered recognition for acts of kindness or patronage, and thus I feel justified in awarding them to my friends in this story.

As an entity, the Church was wholly separate from the state. The Church had its own lands and was self-sufficient, producing stores of food and drink. Sometimes it bought in goods from outside, such as wines, but these were exempt from customs and duties. The Church was not under the King's rule.

For example, if a cleric was thought guilty of a crime, he could not be convicted in one of the King's courts; instead, he enjoyed *Benefit of Clergy*. This meant that he could walk free from the city's courts and could only be tried in a clerical one. This system had wonderful advantages for the culprit. For a start, penalties were more lenient. Priests and clerics could hope to escape with a severe penance, a restricted diet and a lengthy period on their knees begging for forgiveness, while a secular criminal could anticipate a stay in gaol waiting for the King's Justices to arrive, followed by a hanging. Clerical folk had protection – no matter what their crime.

I should digress here to point out that there was a difference between a clergyman demanding Benefit of Clergy and being tried in a church court, and a secular felon being tried in the Bishop's court; the Bishop's court wasn't a cushy number. A felon would be hanged as quickly by, for example, the Abbot of Tavistock's court as he would by the King's own; indeed, it is recorded that a thief was hanged by the Abbot of Tavistock in 1322.

Yet while the clergy were theoretically living a separate life, they mixed continually with people from the city.

The Church was the social service of the age. Members of the clergy nagged and exhorted congregations to look after those less well off, using the teachings of Christ to show how men ought to behave. Throughout society, in every wealthy household, alms-dishes were circulated to collect food from diners. These would later be deposited at the door, or an almoner would distribute it among the poor.

There was no state aid for those who were hardest off, only occasional tax exemptions, but the Church ensured that all those who needed it would receive food. Theologically the Church had problems with the idea of rich people being morally acceptable – after all, Jesus had said something about a camel and a needle's eye – but after a while it was decided that wealth in itself wasn't bad, provided that the wealthy man concerned was pious and generous. If he displayed the courtly attribute of 'largesse', giving away freely from his wealth, he could go to Heaven – but woe-betide the grasping lord who gave little. At a time when the people largely believed in the reality of Heaven and the life to come, this was a powerful incentive.

Everyone had to pay tithes to the local parish church. From the total, one third was redistributed to the local poor and needy. The Church taught that surplus – any profit over and above what was actually needed for the family – should be given away. This was not charity, it was *justice*. In the flawed world which had been formed from Original Sin and the Fall of Man, there was no fair allocation of the nation's resources. Wealth was inequitably shared out and it was the duty of men to balance the availability of necessities. True charity was giving up *more* than one's surplus and depriving oneself. That was real Christian love and mercy.

All poor relief was in the hands of the clergy, who looked after widows, orphans, lepers and cripples with more concern to the means of the individuals than a specific disability. Thus a widowed woman who had plenty of money would not receive much, while a crippled man with no means of earning a living would be helped a great deal.

Religious organisations gave away food, money, clothing, and shelter. They maintained leper hospitals, homes for the injured and even looked after the aged in their retirement. Some may think they did a better job serving the needy than we do today.

I have often been asked what happened to convicted felons once they had been found guilty. Some have questioned my descriptions of hangings.

The worst excesses of judicial brutality had not yet occurred in Britain. Refined tortures were the invention of future generations, especially the Tudors. Under the Plantagenets there was only one punishment – hanging – although drawing and quartering were used occasionally for treason and peculiarly heinous crimes, and lords could be honoured by beheading instead.

This may not sound much of a concession, but these hangings took place in the days prior to scientific(-ish) executions: the victim would be turned off a ladder or a cart, or sometimes simply lifted off his or her feet by a rope.

MICHAEL JECKS

Invariably they died slowly, throttled as all air was cut off. Friends and relatives would pull on the victim's legs or thump the chest to try to end the suffering, because the process could take anything from five minutes to three-quarters of an hour, according to Reverend Samuel Haughton, a Victorian polymath who tried to use scientific principles to end villains' lives more efficiently. Later, the British developed the 'long drop' method of execution which broke the neck and killed almost instantaneously, but the medieval age was not so inventive.

So it's easy to understand that a lord would prefer to have his head removed, rather than 'dance the Tyburn jig'. A good, strong arm with a battle-axe could take off a head with one quick sweep. Sadly, life – or death, in this case – isn't always that easy, and executioners were often incompetent. Take the example of Jack Ketch. During his attempt to execute Lord William Russell in 1683, it took him four blows of his axe to remove the head; the Duke of Monmouth in 1685 had to endure five attempts, before Ketch resorted to his knife.

Of course, many people who were accused and convicted of crimes never made it to the gallows. All too often the poor devils died in gaol. The English have always had a sense of fair play, and if a gaoler caused the death of his inmates by too harsh a regime, he could be arrested as a homicide himself. Every death in prison resulted in an inquest, we are assured. So, for example, when we look at a two-month period in Wallingford Gaol in 1316, during which time twenty-eight people died as a result of cold, disease, hunger, thirst or *peine fort et dure* – literally 'severe and hard punishment' (*OED*), which meant, among other things, a starvation diet – one is reassured to read that the gaoler was attached and an inquest held.

It is less reassuring to see the conclusion that all the deaths were from 'natural causes' and that the gaoler himself was exonerated!

Exeter suffered badly during the Second World War. Many of the fine old buildings were destroyed, but I am glad to say that some remain. The Cathedral is still there, as are many of the tunnels, and there are guided tours of both. If you visit, go and see the Guildhall too; it is a wonderful, ancient building.

For me it was an enormous pleasure to sit in the sun on the Green and imagine the people who used to walk along there: the Canons in their unrelenting black, their Vicars following them, Choristers and Secondaries at their heels, all hurrying to the summons of the bells that ordered their lives, while the city people milled about the nave, meeting and greeting, making deals and haggling, or stamping documents with their seals in the Guildhall.

I hope this novel will give you some idea of how the city was. Rough and ready, stinking, crowded, smog-filled – but also exuberant, lively and rich with teeming humanity. As always, I have researched all aspects of the period as carefully as I can and any inaccuracies are my own fault. That aside, I hope you enjoy this story.

Michael Jecks
Dartmoor
January 2000

CHAPTER ONE

The first of the murders which so shook the Cathedral passed with little comment. Those who knew most about it thought it was a mere robbery. The murdered man's body was found stabbed, in his shop with all of his jewels and cash missing. There was nothing at first to connect his murder to the later deaths since he was not discovered in the Cathedral and the obvious culprit was captured so swiftly.

It took Sir Baldwin de Furnshill, the knight investigating the crime, to show that this victim was only one in the dreadful series of killings that spread such alarm and fear throughout the whole of Exeter.

The victim's name was Ralph Glover, and he felt as though his heart would burst with contentment when he threw open his shutters in the grey half-light before dawn on the Feast Day of St Thomas the Apostle, twenty-first December in the year of our Lord 1321. He adored the winter-time, especially

21

when there was a fire and hot food indoors, and this fine, crisp morning struck him as perfect. A pair of clouds floated overhead; apart from them the sky was clear in the east. All was clean and pure and when he inhaled, it felt as though he was drinking in air as fresh as the water from a Dartmoor spring, with none of the sting of wood- and coal-smoke which would later pollute it.

Leaving the house in response to the summons of the Cathedral bell, he saw that there was a light frost riming the timbers of the house opposite. The water puddled in the mud of the roadway had turned to ice and he had to mind his step if he didn't want to fall; he must also take care to avoid the piles of excrement that lay frozen like small cobbles in the gutter running down the middle of the road. This road was fortunate enough to be fed from its own spring and the stream usually washed the gutter clean, but today it too had frozen.

People were already up and about. Hawkers were making their way along the streets, maids and servants were busily sweeping dirt from the houses, innkeepers standing in the doorways watching for their first customers. All were swaddled in thick coats or cloaks against the chill breeze. At one corner Ralph passed a few poorer folk huddled round a brazier of charcoal. In the glover's opinion they looked little better than heathens, standing with their hands outstretched to the flames like priests worshipping fire, but when he saw a beggar nearby, Ralph gave him a coin.

Ralph was a cheery soul with a prominent belly and, in this cold weather, his cheeks were so red they might have been painted. Small blue eyes glittered in a fat jowly face, and his mouth was invariably fixed in a wide grin. Even in the foulest of weather he could be seen striding through the city, his great staff in one hand, clad in a cheap tunic of tatty wool, scratched and torn hose covering his legs, a heavy black cloak to exclude the worst of the weather, a simple felt hat to keep the rain from his face and scuffed, stained boots on his feet.

Despite his shabby appearance, Ralph often gave money to the poor and needy; he was rich enough from the proceeds of his glovemaking and mercantile ventures, but as a pious man he disliked flaunting his wealth. That seemed to him disgraceful. If God gave a man skills and abilities to make money, that was God's benevolence. There was nothing for the recipient of His kindness to brag about. To some extent that was why Ralph tended not to mix with other members of the Freedom of the City. He privately thought most of them were too irreligious for their own good. There were too many who sought all their rewards here on earth and Ralph felt faintly uneasy in their presence – worried that by associating with such people he might himself become tainted. The new Receiver of the City, Vincent le Berwe, was one such. Ralph couldn't like him. He was too greedy, quite prepared to tread upon those who were weaker in his quest for personal wealth. Nick Karvinel, another glovemaker, used to be the same, until he fell on hard times. Nick had shown almost intolerable greed until recently; strangely, once his fortunes were lost he hardly appeared to care.

As a member of the Freedom, Ralph was one of the most senior men in the city now he had won the Wardenship of the Bridge, but that didn't make him feel differently and he still had no desire to mix with rich people. He harboured a suspicion that a certain member of the Freedom was guilty of corruption, and he wanted as little to do with such people as possible.

23

Ralph was happier mingling with ordinary folk; like a friar he often went among the poor. On this, his last day, he behaved as he did on every other: walking up the High Street towards Cook Row he exchanged quips and jokes with the whores touting for business near the Bickleigh Gate, gave money to the poor at St Martin's Lane, silently dropped a few coins into a leper's bowl near St Petrock's Church. He always asserted that it was the duty of every man to help his fellow, and he demonstrated his conviction by liberality on a level that in others would have been called foolhardiness – or, more probably, lunacy.

He knew how people spoke about him, but didn't care. Ralph's outlook was as simple as his clothing: Christ told men to give away their money to help those poorer than themselves; the poor would most easily find the keys to the Kingdom of Heaven, and Ralph intended to do the Good Lord's bidding. That was why he held feasts through the year to which he invited the indigent, giving them food and drink and gifts of clothing. There was little else for him to spend his money on. He had no family to worry him, only his apprentice Elias, who was old enough to leave Ralph's service now; he was certainly qualified.

Ralph slipped and almost fell on a patch of ice, but he only chuckled at his clumsiness and continued past St Petrock's Church and down Cook Row. He stopped at a stall and took a pie for a few pennies, chewing slowly before returning up the road to enter the Close via the Fissand Gate.

He adored this season: he loved to see frost liming the trees, icicles dangling dangerously from roofs and upper storeys. In his cheap clothing the cold could penetrate and chill his skin, but he didn't care. Wherever he went there were fires, in houses and in the streets. And even as the flesh of his belly was chilled, his chortle of delight remained unabated. Everyone was happy at this time of year, laughing and joking, for it was almost Christmas, and all would celebrate.

It wasn't only the religious connotation of the season that gave him pleasure; he took a keen delight in the cold, ice and snow. He loved the starkness of the landscape, the bare trees, fields empty and brown, while the water solidified and stopped in the stream-beds. All the world appeared to pause and take stock, waiting for God's renewal, just as the whole of mankind would soon be forced to stop in its mad onward rush and consider its position as the Day of Judgement approached. Winter reminded him that before too long, God willing, he would be able to join his wife in Heaven. As was his wont, he glanced upwards at the thought and murmured a short but devout prayer before continuing on his way.

Which is why he wasn't looking where he was going and accidentally got in the path of a cleric who was running full pelt towards him.

'Oh, I'm . . .' There was a squeak of shock, and the cleric fled.

The collision was so forceful, Ralph was winded. He staggered backwards into a man behind him, and had to grasp the stranger's shoulder to save himself from falling.

'Clumsy damned fool,' the man growled in a deep voice as the figure in clerical garb hared off towards the Fissand Gate and darted into the Close.

'The enthusiasm of youth, I fear, friend,' Ralph gasped. He stood a while with a hand on his heart and caught his breath. 'I am easy to stumble into, I'm afraid,' he continued with a better humour. 'It'd be different if I were a young maiden with tits out to here and a saucy smile, but I'm just a fat old man with a belly like a hog's. Let me release you, I must be straining your shoulder. I assure you I'm better now.'

'Are you sure, Master Glover? You lost all the air in your lungs for a while there.'

Ralph recognised the voice and squinted at the man. Years of careful, close work had made it difficult for him to focus, but he was sure that he knew him. 'My lord?'

'Don't fear, Ralph. It is I, Canon Stephen. My Heavens, he must have hit you hard! Did you see who it was?'

'No,' Ralph lied, smiling. He had no intention of having a youthful cleric like poor Peter the Secondary reprimanded for a minor accident – especially when it was largely Ralph's own fault for not looking where he was going. In addition, Ralph knew that even the lowest groups of clerics lived within the Cathedral's grounds, and yet here was Peter outside before full light: he had probably been tempted by a girl with a pleasing smile, or maybe had fallen asleep before a fire with a belly full of ale. Whatever the reason, Ralph had no wish to see the lad punished. With a polite bow and a smiling 'Godspeed,' Ralph left the unsettling Canon to continue on his way. Ralph himself turned back so that he need not enter with the Canon.

The Bear Gate was open as always and Ralph passed beneath the great gatehouse into the large triangular yard beyond, slowly plodding up the shallow gradient until he stood in front of the huge western doors of the Cathedral.

Ralph knew he was a simple man. Many of his friends and competitors in the city thought him almost idiotic in his

straightforward belief, but he didn't care about their snig-
gers. To Ralph, the proof of his faith was here, in the massive
building still being rebuilt, where the Canons, Vicars,
Annuellars and Choristers gathered each day to sing the
praises of the Lord God.

Inside, the silence assailed his ears; it was a great void
into which any sound was swallowed. This early in the morning there were only a few Secondaries around, for the most
part ex-Choristers whose voices had broken and were hoping
to find some new occupation. They were often to be found
performing minor tasks about the place and today Ralph
could see three of them lighting candles up near the altar as
he walked in. Apart from them there were few people in the
nave this early in the morning. Ralph didn't spot his own
murderer, who had watched his entrance and now stood in
the shadow of one of the huge pillars.

It was wonderful: the broad, spacious area before the door
was empty as if to remind the viewer how minuscule he was
in God's creation, while beyond, columns towered up on
either side. It was larger than any great hall Ralph had ever
seen, a glorious space lighted by the coloured glass in the
windows. Later this place would be filled with men talking,
making deals, praying or gossiping, carrying on the daily
round of hard work and business which kept the city of
Exeter profitable. Soon Master Thomas of Witney, the architect, would be heard fussily ordering his workmen outside
and up at the eastern end.

The fact that the Cathedral was being rebuilt detracted
somewhat from its magnificence, but Ralph absorbed the
sanctity of the place, gazing at the painted walls with their
pictures representing God's works on earth, showing how

men could prepare themselves for the afterlife and help to save the souls already passed on. No amount of builder's rubble and dust could detract from these, he thought.

Soon others entered, and a little crowd of the city's most devout people gathered to witness the first Mass celebrated by two chantry priests. These Annuellars were paid by a bequest to celebrate Mass for the soul of its founder, Henry Bratton, at St Mary's altar. While the two went through their daily ritual, the crowd tried desperately not to shuffle or make too much noise, but the cold was biting. Their breath steamed in the air, adding to the smoke left by the censer and creating a grey misty dampness.

Ralph didn't care. He swayed in time to the music as he listened to the cadences of the priests, but then his expression hardened a little. It was difficult to imagine someone defrauding the Cathedral. By so doing they were defrauding God Himself. Looking about him, Ralph tried to understand how anyone could dare risk the wrath of God for money. It was beyond him. And yet he was sure that he had evidence of just that; he had seen it with his own eyes in the Guildhall on the day Karvinel was robbed. He prayed for advice, but his course of action was already decided. The Bailiff of the City would be at his house later, and Ralph would tell him all he knew. If the Bailiff refused to act, Ralph had no alternative: he must go to the Dean and inform him.

At the end of the Mass he joined the other members of the early-morning congregation trooping out from the Cathedral, but while the others moved towards one of the seven gates which gave on to the city outside the Cathedral precinct, Ralph loitered.

The sun was in the sky now, dangling over the roofs of the buildings surrounding the Cathedral. Eastwards was the row of houses owned by the Canons themselves, and Ralph stood contemplating them for a short while, admiring their lime-washed walls and timbers. Smoke rose like columns in the clear, still air and from the breadhouse next to the north tower came the odour of baking bread, a delicious scent that set Ralph's mouth watering, especially when he caught a whiff of spiced wine. Outside the bakery were several Annuellars and Secondaries, all collecting their daily loaf. Others wandered among them: beggars and the poor who depended upon the Cathedral for their food, but there was also a sprinkling of richer folk who gave good donations to the Cathedral and in payment were occasionally permitted to buy some of the Cathedral's better quality breads.

Ralph saw the Receiver's wife at the side of a Secondary, the young lad called Adam; he smiled and bowed to her. She acknowledged his courtesy ungraciously, but then, as Ralph knew, he was her husband's greatest enemy and competitor for advancement. Nick Karvinel was someone else she openly despised. In a way, he could sympathise, Ralph thought. There were few people in the city whom he actively disliked, but Nick Karvinel the glovemaker and dealmaker was one.

But enough of such sour topics. 'Time to return home,' he grunted, and turned to make his way up to St Martin's Gate. About to pass the conduit, he stopped to watch two Choristers running up from the Street of the Canons. One appeared to be chasing the other; they leaped the low fence to the cemetery, one straining ahead while the other panted curses and stretched out a hand to grab his victim.

The two hared off around the charnel chapel, then over the roadway and out of sight behind the Church of St Mary Major, and Ralph followed them with his eyes, grinning and shaking his head. There had once been a time when he too could have chased a friend around a churchyard – but that time was long gone, he told himself ruefully as he stomped heavily through the cemetery and out via the gate to the High Street, a genial fellow in faded and shabby clothing.

Afterwards John Coppe, a cripple begging at the gate, and Janekyn Beyvyn, the porter for the Cathedral Close, both recalled seeing Ralph shamble up towards the gatehouse.

Coppe was squatting in his usual place at the Fissand Gate, sheltered a little from the wind that gusted up the High Street, holding his hands to the brazier lighted by Janekyn to warm them both. As Coppe would later tell the Coroner, he saw the glover walking away just after Henry the Chorister had rushed past the gate's entrance, laughing fit to burst, fleeing his brother-Chorister Luke. Later Coppe heard that Henry had been forced to flee after dropping a beetle down the other's neck as they set off for the Cathedral.

When the Coroner questioned him, Janekyn admitted he had been supping a warmed, liquid breakfast of spiced ale standing near the charcoal brazier, peering towards the Bishop's Palace, from whose kitchen rose heavy grey smoke, proving, if proof were needed, that the Bishop's men were preparing their bread and food. He was looking forward to the arrival of his loaf of bread so that he too could break his fast, but Adam was late as usual.

Janekyn noticed Ralph as the glover passed the small charnel chapel. Ralph had been walking slowly at his usual speed, up towards St Martin's. For all Janekyn knew, Ralph might have gone out by that gate, but he didn't see him do so. Janekyn was a thin, slightly deaf cleric of some fifty years, with a grey complexion and feeble constitution. He hadn't stood rooted to the spot, gawping at other folk while his hands went blue; no, he had concentrated on his brazier, gripping his pot of hot ale and trying to persuade some warmth into his emaciated frame. In any case, he had been distracted by the two boys.

The sight had made Janekyn give a wheezing chuckle. Henry had reappeared, apparently fresh and ready for a longer chase, but Luke pounded along with a determined glower. Darting to one side, Henry bent and picked up a fresh lump of horse-dung, flinging it at his pursuer. It hit Luke's shoulder, and Henry sped away again, giggling, while the other stood horrified, gazing down at the brown mess smearing the white perfection of his clothes. Then, with a renewed fury, he chased off after his tormentor.

Luke set his mouth in a line of determination as he chased Henry, his most loathed and despised enemy. Henry was a ... 'a whoreson buggering Godless sinner'. Luke had heard a hawker shout that after an urchin in the street and he thought it described Henry perfectly.

The open grassed space led around the walls of the cloister, and here there was a wider area. Before him was the plain leading off, in the distance, to the city wall, while on his left was a clearing bounded by the Chapter House, the Cathedral and the Bishop's Palace, each with lean-to sheds accommodating tools and workmen involved in the rebuilding works. There was nowhere for Henry to have escaped to.

On the right, Luke would have seen him running over the clearing down towards the Palace Gate, and left were the shacks, each of which should have been locked, and yet Henry was nowhere to be seen.

Half-heartedly Luke went along the line of sheds, tugging at a door here or there. This part was all off-limits to the Choristers, but Luke was unwilling to go without attempting to find his enemy.

There was a noise, a creaking as a door slowly opened, and Luke grinned with the quick satisfaction of the hunter. His quarry was at hand! He crouched, taking up a handful of thick, glutinous mud, and readied himself. There was a crack as a door was thrust wide, the leather hinges complaining, and then Luke swiftly dropped his weapon.

It wasn't Henry but Jolinde Bolle, the Secondary, who came into the light with a leather-wrapped parcel which he thrust under his shirt before, blinking in the sun, he made off towards his chamber.

As Ralph walked through the gate and into the High Street, he was followed. All along the High Street and left along the Correstrete beneath the castle to his own door.

Glovers never earned much money, but Ralph was comfortably off as a result of his mercantile ventures. Not that he had need of money. His wants were few and he was not an acquisitive man. The only things he craved he could *not* buy: his wife and child. Both were dead. Tragically, they had died in the same accident when a cart overturned on them, but Ralph consoled himself with his faith, content in the knowledge that he would see them again in Heaven, God willing.

His house was one of the smaller premises, but it was adequate for him and his apprentice. There were two doors to the street; the one on the right opened straight into his shop, while the lefthand one gave onto a passage which bypassed his place of business and led behind to his little hall. Inside the hall, a ladder propped against a wall led up to the chamber above where Ralph and his apprentice slept while the scullery and kitchen lay at the rear and had their own back door to the garden.

Ralph opened the door on the left – he rarely locked his house door – and walked down the passageway into his hall. Puffing slightly, he heaved himself up the ladder to his chamber, where he threw off his cloak and pulled on a thick woollen jack which made him feel a little warmer. Then he went to his money chest, as was his wont when returning, unlocked it and peered inside to check the contents. He nodded to himself and was about to close it, when he noticed a small sack that lay within.

He had never seen it before. Baffled, he picked it up and hefted it. When he opened it, a collection of gemstones and coins fell into his hand. Mystified, he could only stare. They were not his; he had no idea where they could have come from.

Then an explanation dawned. Each year the Cathedral commissioned pairs of gloves to be presented after Christmas to honour those who had helped the Cathedral over the year. Stitched from the finest pigskin and studded with jewels, they were valuable – and expensive to make.

This year Ralph had been asked to provide the gloves for the ceremony, but he had been surprised to find that there had been less money than agreed – and fewer gemstones. The Secondary,

Jolinde Bolle, who delivered them with Peter, had haughtily pointed out that if he didn't want the commission, Karvinel would happily take it over. Bolle said that Canon Stephen, the Treasurer, didn't think it necessary to spend so much on gloves this year. With the cost of the Cathedral's rebuilding stretching their resources, economies must be made.

Ralph had accepted the money and jewels, but it had seemed odd. He had agreed the quality and the price with the Dean when he was asked to make the gloves; but if the Treasurer had decided that the price was too high, who was he, Ralph, to argue?

That was back in the first week of December, on the Feast of St Nicholas, sixth December. Now Ralph counted the gems and money and beamed. Someone had changed his mind: the sack made up the shortfall! That must be it: the Treasurer had decided to revert to the original arrangement. Strange he didn't mention it this morning, but he must have sent someone to drop off this money and Elias had put it in the strongbox for safekeeping.

Where was he? The lad should be back by now, but he had a ridiculous infatuation with Mary Skinner, the baker's daughter, and was probably idling his time away with her. It was a pity, for Ralph was convinced that Elias was wasting his time. She was too flighty for a stolid fellow like Elias. Perhaps it was a good thing; there were times when her face was harsh and unkind, even when she was smiling at Elias. Not like his own dear wife Alice. Ralph allowed himself a moment's quiet pleasure, recalling her gentle smile, her calm grey eyes and soft hair, like finest spun gold . . .

The knock at his door broke into his reverie and startled him. It was early for a client. Most people wouldn't be about for some time, which was why he and his apprentice tended to eat their breakfast at this hour. Then he remembered his invitation to the City Bailiff, asking him to call to discuss a sensitive matter. He must do his duty and explain what he had discovered in the Guildhall: an attempt to defraud the Cathedral.

Bracing himself, Ralph went to answer his door but it was no client who had knocked: only death stood waiting for him.

CHAPTER TWO

After Ralph left the Cathedral grounds, the religious day continued. Every moment was spent in praise of God and no man was free from the great task. Each had his own duty. While Ralph passed through St Martin's Gate, other Annuellars had already arrived at their altars up and down the Cathedral; at the same time fourteen Vicars appeared with some Choristers to sing the morning round of services: Matins, Lauds and the other Hours of Our Lady before beginning the Lady Mass in Her honour.

And while they sang, the bells pealed for Prime, the first of the daytime services. For this all the Canons and their Vicars were on duty; all should attend.

Dressed in his white surplice covered with the loose-fitting black cloak and cap, Canon Stephen cleared his mind of all the petty financial troubles involving the rebuilding works and prepared to leave his house to attend Mass.

With him were his household, all in black with the occasional flash of white where a surplice showed. Stephen cast an eye over them all. Young Luke didn't live with Stephen, of course, but he had come over from the Choristers' Hall to join his Canon on the walk to the Cathedral, and Stephen was disgusted to see filth on Luke's cheek and a muddy mark on his shoulder. Stephen was tempted to send him off to wash and change, but he knew that the clean laundry hadn't been delivered yet and he swallowed his angry words. Instead he went over to Luke and, taking up the hem of his cloak, spat upon it and rubbed at the sullen face.

Luke was still simmering with rage. Henry had teased and tormented him for years, but this latest trick was too much! If he had caught Henry, Luke would have beaten him to a pulp. He would have sat on his chest and battered Henry's face until the bastard pleaded for mercy, but he wouldn't have got any. Not from Luke. Not after all the things he'd done to him. It wasn't fair! Henry seemed to think he could get away with murder. Well, he couldn't. He'd see. When Luke was installed as boy-Bishop, he'd make Henry regret his actions. He'd make Henry apologise for dropping the beetle down his neck when he was singing, for throwing mud and horseshit at him, for catcalling and tipping water over him when he was asleep in bed. For all these indignities and more, Henry would have to pay.

But Henry had escaped him *again* – as he always did. Luke wondered where his enemy could have hidden. Could he have discovered a secret way through to the Chapter House? Or had he found a shed to hide in – or maybe a storeroom with a dodgy lock. Wherever it was, Luke was determined to find it and punish Henry at the first opportunity.

'Keep still, boy!' Stephen snarled and Luke returned to the present. 'Do you think you can insult God by arriving in His house with all this muck on your face? My God, you stink! I don't know what's the matter with you today. You're a disgrace to the Cathedral!'

Satisfied at last, Stephen stood back and surveyed his work. The little devil was certainly not perfect, but he was greatly improved.

Stephen nodded to his bottler at the door, who pulled it open, and the Canon and his household emerged into the chill morning air. Stephen went first, walking with his head sunk down meditatively, preparing himself for the service to come. After him came his Vicar Choral, a pleasant fellow, Arthur Hingstone, whom Stephen had appointed some few years before. Unfortunately, Stephen had been assigned a Secondary, and not allowed to choose his own. The Canon preferred bookish, considerate youths, but instead the Dean had foisted Adam upon him – an incompetent reader, a worse writer, with the eating manners of a pig. Stephen was convinced that Adam's presence at his table was the result of the Dean's sense of humour, but then the thought that the Dean possessed so human a trait made Stephen grin sardonically.

Behind Adam was the last of his choral retinue, Luke. The Choristers were selected by the Precentor, and Luke at least had the merit of being the best of the current crop, to Stephen's mind. Luke was generally quiet, well-mannered and educated. Miraculous when one considered his father, Stephen considered wryly. All in all, Luke should win the election later today. He would become the next boy-Bishop.

After Luke came the other clerics of his household. Stephen was wealthy enough in his own right and he was able to fund a goodly sized establishment. It went against the concept of shared possessions that the Canons were supposed to espouse, but more often than not, that rule was waived nowadays. Things had to move with the times, even in Cathedrals, and money mattered; as Treasurer, Stephen knew that only too well. Patronage was as important here in Exeter's small Cathedral as it was elsewhere.

His servants followed along behind the clerical staff. His bottler, cook, ushers and others trailed behind him, he knew, like a dark shadow, all with their heads lowered and hands clasped. He had no need to look to make sure of their obvious reverence, for they were all being exposed to a tight scrutiny. On all sides similar lines of religious men were converging at a slow and thoughtful pace to a point just before the great western doors of the Cathedral. It was the same each day and just as Stephen could observe each of the men in his colleagues' retinues, they would at the same time be watching his own. Any lapse on the part of the lowliest kitchen attendant or bottler, let alone Chorister, would be noticed and be cause for restrained chuckles later. There was no escape from the Canons. Well, not yet, Stephen amended, thinking of the Feast of the Holy Innocents. But that day was different.

He reached the door, entered, bowed to the altar, then to the Dean. The Bishop was away once more. He spent much of his time away now. Stephen wondered what interest the outside world of politics could hold for a man who was supposed to be dedicated to God, but quashed the thought. It wasn't for him to wonder at the motivations of others, and

Bishop Stapledon, Walter II of Exeter, was a most honourable man, spending time with his far-flung manors and priests,
ensuring that the souls in his See were being ministered to
and assisting any religious men by helping them find a place
in his school or a seat at Oxford University, no matter how
poor they might be. The meanest villein in a rustic manor
could apply to him for education and perhaps professional
training, if they showed that God had granted them the
necessary intelligence.

Walking past the Punctators, Stephen made his way to his
own stall, his household separating behind him, the servants
standing in the great, freezing nave, the Chorister moving
forward to the centre of the choir, Adam the Secondary
taking his place behind the choirboys, the Vicar standing a
little to Stephen's right in the rearmost rank.

Stephen bowed his head and uttered a prayer. Finishing,
he looked about him idly. Two Punctators stood near the
northern door, cross-checking each other's lists. It was the
duty of the Punctators to note who turned up and who did not
for the services, and from the frown on their faces Stephen
correctly surmised that someone was missing. No one would
worry too much, he thought. The weather was cold, and
many younger clerics would be celebrating the onset of
Christmas.

There was a loud slapping of feet on the cobbles outside,
and the two Punctators turned, eyebrows raised, as the
Secondary Jolinde appeared panting in the doorway. He
marched in, head down, almost forgot to bow to the altar,
and when he inclined his head respectfully to the Dean,
Stephen saw the lad was red-faced, as if he had run a long
distance.

Stephen watched the youth shuffle along the stalls until he reached his own, next to the Secondary Peter Golloc. Stephen studied the two. Jolinde would be in for a reprimand later, he thought. The fellow should have risen earlier: from the look of him he had been drinking heavily last night. His appearance was scruffy, his complexion feverish, like a man who had been up until late in a tavern and whose sole desire now was to return to his bed.

Next to him, Peter looked even worse. His face was pale, almost waxen, his lips grey, as if he was suffering from some kind of mental torment. Stephen sighed. The lad should be in the infirmary if he was unwell. There was no benefit to God in having a cleric collapse. An ill man was better advised to visit the infirmarer and make sure he got better. At that moment Jolinde jerked forward, and Stephen's attention whipped back to him. The boy was carrying something under his robes – something he was concealing, Stephen was sure. Jolinde had half-dropped it.

But before Stephen could consider the matter further, the calm, clear voice of the Succentor led the choir in the first song and the Canon forgot all about the incident.

Ralph's apprentice, Elias of Iddesleigh, tore along the alleys on his way home. Mary had made him delay his return to his master's rooms, coquettishly offering him a kiss and then insisting that he should sit with her a while before returning home.

'Mary, I can't! I've got to get back with Ralph's bread.'

'You don't care for me at all,' she pouted. 'Won't even spare me a few moments before rushing off to your precious master.'

41

'I have to,' he protested, seeing her sullen expression. 'But when I am free and can call myself a craftsman in my own right . . .'

'By then I may have found another,' she said tersely and flicked her hair from her eyes with a practised jerk of her head. It had taken him an age to soothe her with promises of his infatuation and ever-lasting devotion and now he was late. Very late.

When he arrived at Ralph the Glover's front door, Elias was surprised to find it locked against him. His master rarely locked his door. He always said, 'If someone is so desperate that they would steal my rubbish, good luck to them – they're welcome to it!' All knew Ralph had few enough possessions, and the poor would be given money for food by asking, so the glover had not been burgled in all the time Elias had lived with him. That was why he frowned to find the door of the house locked. His own keys, he recalled with a sinking heart, were still by his bed. He had thrown them there after hurrying to answer the door to Peter, earlier. Walking to the shop-front, he tried the handle but that too was secured and he stood there a while, baffled.

'Master?' he called. There was no answer.

Ralph, he knew, was set in his ways. The glover's day was normally as predictable as the passage of the sun through the Heavens. He would rise before dawn, drink a little watered wine, wash his face, and as the bell tolled for the opening of the Cathedral's gates and the first service, he would make his way to it via a cookshop, returning as soon as the service was ended to break his fast properly with the loaf which Elias should by then have bought. Recently Elias had taken to returning later and later from his assignations with Mary, but his jovial and tolerant master had never minded that. He merely chuckled indulgently when Elias eventually arrived, but that didn't mean Elias was happy to let his master down. If anything, he felt all the more guilty when he failed in his duties.

Elias had no idea anything could be seriously wrong. He was only annoyed to think that the fire which he had eventually managed to light might well have gone out by now. It made him click his tongue but there was nothing he could do. Usually he would grab his keys before he hared off to see his Mary, but not today. He had woken late when Peter knocked, and left all his keys tied together with a thong lying on the floor near his truckle bed next to his knife.

He was a slow thinker and it was some little while before he bestirred himself to consider the entrance round at the back of the house.

Gervase the Succentor glanced sidelong at the Choristers below him. He could see from here that the young devils were still at it: every so often the boys in front jerked and cast suspicious looks over their shoulders.

Little fiends! Gervase tried to extend his neck without being too conspicuous and distracting the Archbishop of Totnes at his side. Peering down and a little to his left he saw that the main perpetrator was Adam. While smiling seraphically and singing as best he could (since his voice had dropped he was a sad embarrassment on occasion) he was casually tilting his candle and letting gobbets of hot wax fall on the boys in front. Gervase was not surprised. Adam was a nasty piece of work; he was jealous of the Choristers now his own voice had failed him and he was relegated to the ranks of the Secondaries. One or two Secondaries could hope for promotion provided that they kept their heads down, worked, and demonstrated intelligence sufficient for their calling, but Adam was patently not bright enough when set against that measure, Gervase reckoned. He privately thought the boy would have to leave the Cathedral. His scholarship was not up to standard.

That thought made him look farther along the line of boys. There, up at the end nearest the Dean were Luke and Henry. Two more causes of friction.

Henry and Luke were always at loggerheads; each detested the other. They must grow out of it, and the sooner the better, because for all that Luke could draw and paint and sing so well, Henry was sharper and usually got the better of him in their exchanges. At least today Luke should be all right, Gervase thought, because the election of the boy-Bishop was due to take place – and Luke would win that.

Gervase had never paused to wonder where the tradition started. It was irrelevant: the election was an annual event, as important as Christmas itself to many of the Choristers and clergy. Each year, on twenty-first December, the Feast of St Thomas the Apostle, the Choristers would vote one of their number to become the Bishop, and for one day, on twenty-eighth December, the Feast of the Holy Innocents, which recalled Herod's slaughter of the boy-children of the Jews just after Christ's birth, the elected boy would become the city's Bishop. For those twenty-four hours, the order of the city would be turned upon its head: the Choristers would become the Canons and the church hierarchy would be upside-down. For that one day in the year, children were permitted to behave as children. All sorts of tomfoolery were allowed.

Of course, only the best-educated and most scholarly could win the election. The boy-Bishop had to be someone bright, mannerly and well-versed in the services. And Gervase would have to see to it that the Bishop knew what to do and say, but that shouldn't be hard. Luke had an excellent memory.

The foul brats – Gervase was responsible for the discipline and teaching of the Choristers so he felt entirely justified in his choice of language – would recognise that. They must vote for Luke because he was the better of the two: the better singer, the better writer, the better scholar, the better behaved generally, and easily the better born. He came from the Soth family, which was connected to John Soth, who had been Mayor of Exeter some years ago. In every way, Luke was the right choice.

Henry was only the son of a widow woman who was little more than a peasant. He had shown some promise, certainly, when he was younger, but Gervase knew how boys who showed promise at an early stage could change later on. Boys in their early teens were like different people – or, rather, animals. The sods became argumentative – worse still, the cleverer ones learned to dispute. That was when they caught the sharp end of Gervase's tongue or felt the lash of his rope's end. If they wished to remain in the choir, they must learn obedience to their master and not answer back.

Henry was of the latter type. Wilful for his ten years, he had an insolent manner and invariably questioned the validity of any command. More often than any other he had felt the full force of Gervase's rope, but still he remained unruly, disputatious and a disruptive influence on his peers.

Gervase sighed as he leaned back against the small shelf of the *misericorde*. It was many years since he himself had been ten years old, but through living with so many youngsters he could recall his own feelings with alarming clarity: the rebellious determination to behave as he wished, the desire to kick out at an unheeding, remote and aloof Authority. In his heart of hearts, Gervase had a fear that Henry might be behaving as badly as Gervase himself would have liked to, had he dared, when he was younger.

Yes: when Gervase considered the other children at the Cathedral he had to reflect that it was fortunate that Luke would become the Bishop.

John Coppe would not have disagreed with his choice. Coppe sat at the side of Fissand Gate, plaintively calling out to passers-by, his bowl in his hand. He had been a sailor for most of his life, working for merchants in the city, convinced in his nautical optimism that he would one day return home rich. Instead his sanguine nature had led to him spending all his money in taverns and whore-houses before his final disaster when he was crippled. During a vicious attack at the hands of French pirates, he had had a leg cut from under him and received an axe-stroke full in his face. Now he was a beggar.

Coppe was not like the other beggars. Many – indeed most – were bitter, tortured men and women who wheedled and pleaded, then resorted to hurling abuse at the backs of passers-by who ignored them. They thought that God had marked them out for special punishment because of the sins of their parents or some appalling offence of their own, and the knowledge gnawed at them, turning them either into whining, fawning wretches who craved the society of ordinary people or, more commonly, into crabbed, twisted souls who despised all other people.

Their avowed loathing for mankind while at the same time desiring above all things to be able to join in with ordinary life, Coppe found sad. And silly. As far as he was concerned, he had been marked out by God, it was true, but he retained the conviction that God would reward him in Heaven. When Coppe died, he knew he would be taken up before all the richest in the city, and would be fed and watered with as much ale as he could drink. That was what the friars told him, and he saw no reason to disbelieve them. As far as he was concerned, he was almost privileged.

He was given money regularly by folk who passed along the road, often by the women who averted their eyes from his dreadful, twisted visage with revulsion, but because Coppe was always polite, always ducked his head respectfully and smiled as best he could with his face so wrecked where the blade had smashed through jaw, cheekbone and eyesocket, he won their sympathy as well as their money.

And although it was cold, wet and miserable in the winter, Coppe knew that when the weather grew foul, Janekyn the porter would mutter and grumble, but would still drag a brazier out here for the beggars. Usually he would bring a small pot of spiced wine, or a tankard of ale for the old sailor. Coppe knew that Janekyn himself had been a fighter in the King's host and didn't grudge Coppe a sup, knowing that their rôles could so easily have been reversed.

No, Coppe wasn't the kind of man to be introspective and question his place in the world. As far as he was concerned, he was harmed, but there was nothing he could do about it.

Railing and complaining was pointless. It wouldn't alter his position.

Coppe was content. He could talk to the people who passed by here – especially the priests. Most of them were happy to stop for a moment to talk to him. Of course, not everyone was like that. Lots turned from him. Some would meet his eye or chat, but more commonly folk would smile nervously, realising that what had so ruined Coppe's life could affect any of them. He was a living reminder of the brutality men could show to each other. Some women would stop and talk to him gently.

He frowned a little at that thought. Usually *she* would stop to talk to him, but today she had run past with her head averted, as if ashamed.

Or scared.

CHAPTER THREE

'Master Ralph, are you there?' Elias called hesitantly at the back door. There was no answer. He had been here for several minutes, jiggling the handle up and down as he tried to loosen the wooden peg that locked the latch, but it wouldn't shift.

He stood there, the bread cooling in his arm as he stared up at the house in consternation. His master should be back by now, but if he wasn't, the fire would be sure to have gone out after being left untended for so long. Elias felt the guilt lying upon him. Ralph was an old man now. In this weather he needed a warm hall and a good fire. Elias didn't fear a beating from his master, but the idea that he should have let down the kindly gentleman was nearly as painful as a blow from a cudgel.

While he stood there undecided, he heard a movement indoors. Then there was the sound of a door slamming, and he felt himself relax a moment. His master was back! Almost immediately he felt the trepidation return. If his master was back, he would notice that Elias was *not*, and even the kindliest, most generous master would be sure to be irritable with an apprentice who had forgotten to take his keys with him. It wouldn't have mattered normally: it was Ralph's own lateness that had forced Elias to wait outside. Not that that was an excuse.

Hurriedly, Elias darted back down the long, narrow garden, past the raised beds filled with cabbages and kale, carrots and alexanders, past the herbs and the fruit trees that lay further down near the wall, then out of the gate, slamming it behind him and running round to the front of the house. Here, panting, he pushed at the door, kicking it shut behind him and walking down the corridor.

'Master?' he called. 'I was locked out, I'm afraid. I'm sorry, Master, but I have the bread for your breakfast.'

He entered the hall. The table was against the wall, with Ralph's chair at one side, Elias's stool at the other. The cupboard with Ralph's small collection of pewter stood in one corner, the large chest with Ralph's belongings was opposite, near the outer wall. Elias stared about him. The fire was crackling merrily in the middle of the floor, letting a thin, sweet-smelling smoke rise to the roof high overhead. A sudden spark glittered upwards, rising up to Elias's eye-level before gradually fading out and falling away as ash. Elias walked through to the service room behind, but here again there was no one. He touched the backdoor latch gently. The peg had been thrust through the latch to lock it in place, and he pulled it free, opening the door with a frown of confusion. No one there.

'Master?'

The only other place to look was the chamber, and he went to it, climbing up the ladder. There was still no sign of his master, however. He went to the small chest by Ralph's bed and tentatively checked the lock. It was a relief to see that the chest was still there, but to his surprise the clasp yielded to his hand; it wasn't locked. He began to lift the lid, but let it fall shut when he heard something. It sounded like someone downstairs, but not in the hall, in the shop. He listened and soon was rewarded with the squeaking of a cart with a bad wheel. He must have misheard things: it was just a fellow in the street.

Elias returned and lifted the lid once more and then his face went blank with dismay. It was empty; all Ralph's money was gone. 'Oh, oh!' Elias wailed and bit at his lip. Somebody had robbed his master. What would Ralph say when he got back? Mostly that he had employed a fool, a cretin, as an apprentice.

'Ralph? Ralph, where are you? Elias? Are you here? Where's your master?' came a voice from the hall as the door slammed again. Elias was pleased to recognise the voice as that of William de Lappeford, the Bailiff of the City.

Slipping hurriedly down the ladder, Elias gave the tall, stern-looking Bailiff a nervous smile. 'I don't know,' he admitted. 'I got here after fetching bread for his breakfast, but he's not back yet.'

William glanced about him. 'Is he late? I thought he was a regular man in his habits.'

'Oh, I expect he decided to go out to another shop when I didn't turn up,' Elias said. 'But I couldn't get in. I'd left my key behind. And his money has been stolen!'

'Strange,' William said. He was a large man, as a Bailiff must be if he is expected to fetch rents from rougher areas of town, solid, with a deceptively slow manner of moving. Dark Celtic features gave him a harsh appearance, but his bright blue eyes were often crinkled at the edges. There was no humour in them now. 'He asked me to come and see him today. He was worried about something – said he thought he'd discovered a theft.'

Elias gaped. 'A theft? But it's only just happened!' William nodded slowly, eyeing him with a sharp expression and Elias suddenly felt a cold sweat break out upon his brow. 'What is it?'

'Who else would a man suspect of theft but his own servant?' William asked.

'I wouldn't steal from my master!' Elias squeaked. 'He's been good to me, better than I should have expected, and . . .'

The Bailiff ignored him. He had walked out to the back room while Elias spoke and was slowly climbing the ladder to the upper chambers. Elias trailed after him, plaintively declaring his innocence and his complete bafflement as to where Ralph could have gone. The Bailiff stood a long while staring down at Ralph's open chest.

'I opened it in case someone could have robbed him,' Elias explained, his voice breaking.

The Bailiff had a blank expression, as if all his thoughts and suspicions were secured inside until he should choose to release them. 'The lock wasn't forced,' he said. He studied Elias silently for a moment, then turned away and went to the ladder, slipping down to the ground with an agility that looked out-of-place in a man with such a large body.

'I told you he wasn't here,' Elias said sulkily.

'What about the shop?'

'It's locked. Wait a moment, I'll get my key,' Elias said and scampered back upstairs. He went straight to the truckle bed in his chamber and put his hand to where his bunch of keys should have been, but there was nothing there. His heart lurched in his chest like a wild animal trying to fly, and he scrabbled about urgently for it: gone! And with it, his knife. His knife should have been here! While he searched, he heard the door open and shut as William left to stand in the street. Elias stopped and listened with every nerve in his body.

He heard the Bailiff's steps, the shuffle as the man tried to peer between the shutters into the room, the tentative rattle of the latch. With a lurch in his gut he heard the door to the shop open. Panicking, he went to the ladder and slid downstairs, bolting for the front door even as the Bailiff appeared, blocking it. His face was white and in his hand he held Elias's knife.

Elias could not help but stare at it. The blade was smeared with a thin oil-like layer of blood.

'Get out here, you shit,' William snarled.

John Coppe, squatting on his haunches outside the Cathedral grounds, was the first to announce the news of the death to the porter and, through him, the rest of the Cathedral precinct.

Janekyn Beyvyn was in his small room by the gate when he heard the excited murmur outside. A youngster, scarcely twelve years old, came scampering down the street cheerily declaring the news, but his voice was too high and his enthusiasm too great for Janekyn to understand him clearly. By the time Janekyn had left his porter's lodge and got out to the roadway, the lad had disappeared, pelting along at speed to tell his friends the news.

'It's a terrible world,' John Coppe declared grimly, 'when you think how those who are evil can yet prosper, and a poor soul like Ralph is destroyed. It's a cruel, terrible world.' And so it was, he told himself. There were not many who could be relied upon every morning to give a penny to a beggar at Fissand Gate. Enough for food and drink for a day if you were careful and went to Joan's alehouse. He shook his head with regret at his personal loss, tinged with compassion for the man whom he had personally considered kindly and generous.

'Eh?' Janekyn demanded, squinting. 'What's happened?'

John Coppe peered up at the older man. 'It's the glover,' he began.

'Which bugger?'

'Not bugger, *glover*! You know, Ralph – the fat man, always threw me a coin or two.'

There was a spark of understanding. 'Ah, him. What of him?'

'Dead, Porter. Murdered! His own apprentice slew him.'

Old Jankeyn shrugged. It was none of his concern that some foolish trader had chosen an apprentice with murderous tendencies. If anything, he was most aware of that special satisfaction which the old feel upon hearing of the death of others younger than themselves. Then reality hit him like a cudgel and he gaped. 'Gracious God! The poor man. And what will happen to his goods now?'

'The Good Lord only knows – but at least the city will have a good hanging. A servant killing his own master – that is treason of the worst sort! He'll have to be hanged. I hope he thought it was worth it.' Coppe felt he could afford to be jocular about it. True, he had lost a friend, but Ralph was not his only friend.

Janekyn wasn't listening. He turned sharply and went to the small lodge by the gate, where he spoke shortly to the cleric warming himself at the brazier. Soon the young man was running full tilt to the Treasurer's offices.

The Dean, a quiet and contemplative man in his early sixties, with a sparse fringe of white hair above an almost perfectly circular face, was today forced to wear a most unhabitual frown of concern. His wonted expression was one of mildly confused happiness, his smile that of a man to whom the world was a neverending source of wonder, as if he was convinced that there was a greater, logical plan to all the mayhem and lunacy if only he could understand it. But not today. Today his grimace owed more to his discontent at the failings of men than contentment with God's works.

Brother Stephen usually found his gentle, muddled demeanour intensely irritating, and the change from mildly befuddled Dean to bemused and annoyed Dean was no improvement. 'The apprentice murdered him, Dean.'

'But why?' the Dean demanded earnestly. 'Were all the apprentices to kill their masters, where should we be, hmm? In a world of madness, that is where.'

'This is more important than you appreciate, Dean,' Brother Stephen said, watching narrowly as Dean Alfred stood and walked to the window.

The other man waved a hand petulantly. 'But what can be more important than this? That a youth, almost a boy, should murder his master? It is an outrage against the natural order.

Why, one could expect to see a Canon's own Vicar killing him if this kind of hideous incident were tolerated. It would be horrible. No one would be safe. My Heavens, what could be worse, hmm?'

His mannerisms, many and varied as they were, all grated on Brother Stephen, but this, the mild, enquiring clearing of the throat, was by far and away the worst. Brother Stephen gritted his teeth. 'Dean, you will recall that we are shortly to celebrate Christmas,' he murmured silkily.

'Well naturally, Brother. It is December. In only . . . my Heavens! Can it really be only four days to Christmas? It seems only an instant ago that we were celebrating the Feast of Holy Innocents last year.'

'Nonetheless, it will soon be Christmas, and a short while thereafter we shall be celebrating Holy Innocents again. And for that we need the gloves.'

'I am sure you have them in hand,' the Dean muttered, smiling gently at the pun. He was peering from the window out over the cloisters, his hands clasped behind his back. Why wouldn't Brother Stephen leave him alone, he thought. Always had his nose in other people's affairs as if he was trying to conceal his own failings. And he did have much to hide from other Brothers. That was why Stephen kept himself aloof. But it was also his value and importance. His shame had ensured that he was among the most committed of all the Chapter, which was why the Dean had entrusted Adam, to his care.

The Brother's next words made him forget his musings about the Canon.

'Dean, I speak of the gloves which shall be given to the leading folk of the city. Those for the Burgesses are already prepared, but there are others . . .?' He let his voice trail away on a vague note of enquiry.

'Others?' Dean Alfred repeated, but then he slowly turned to face the Canon. 'You mean that the *other* gloves are not ready?'

'Dean, I do not know!'

The Dean snapped his fingers in annoyance. 'Hmm. My dear fellow, you are usually so full of bright ideas. Why not go and enquire?'

'I am a competent manager of money, Dean; I am not a Bailiff!'

'Hmm. Um. I did not mean to imply that you were. Yet we must have someone search for the gloves. Ahmm – were they all finished? Perhaps they are waiting at the glover's house?'

'I do not know.'

'Perhaps you could speak to the City Bailiff? He should know.'

'I think you should go yourself. This is Chapter business, after all.'

'Oh, ha! No, I don't think so,' said the Dean, smiling quickly. He ducked his head, then stuck a finger in his ear and dug around, while Brother Stephen sat fuming. 'No, you go and enquire and we shall soon find out what's happened, I am sure. I have complete faith in you.'

Brother Stephen drew breath to argue against the Dean's proposal, but the Dean nodded encouragingly, backing away towards the door, and before the angry Canon could rally his thoughts Dean Alfred had passed into the next room, his private chamber.

*   *   *

MICHAEL JECKS

Brother Gervase walked back to his hall with a sour smile catching at his lips. Little sods! They'd really done it this time.

The election was supposed to be a formality. Gervase knew as well as any cleric in the Cathedral that the freedom granted to the Choristers was so risk-filled that the boys needed direction ... guidance. They had to be advised to select the one from within their ranks who would be best able to conduct services, who could act as a suitable ambassador for the Cathedral and who could be relied upon not to cause too much upset in the city when he proceeded along the roads with his retinue. Luke had the carriage, the education, the courteous manners, the suave accent. He was perfect.

Gervase reached his hall and entered, pushing the door shut and leaning against the worn timbers.

But the monsters had picked Henry. It was no surprise really, not if, like Gervase, you knew the boys. As he often told himself, boys of this age could be contrary little brutes at the best of times. Perhaps that was why they had elected Henry. The Choristers had ignored the clear and obvious wishes of the Canons; they wanted a leader who could make their day of freedom *fun*.

It was also possible that Henry had offered them bribes. Gervase recalled whispered conversations between Henry and others over the last few weeks. However, Gervase was more persuaded by the argument that his charges had selected a candidate with the sole intention of putting the collective noses of the Canons out of joint.

Children today just weren't as well-behaved as they had been in his youth, he told himself sadly. God alone knew what horrors they would get up to on Holy Innocents' Day. He pictured Henry: tousled, scruffy, trying to look innocent while holding his hands behind his back to conceal a sling, a beetle, or something equally repellent. Gervase tried to put that grubby figure into the silk robes of the boy-Bishop. It wasn't easy. The child would ruin the fine clothes. And as for what he could get up to as the Bishop, well! Gervase's mind boggled.

And then, unaccountably, he felt himself start to chuckle.

THE BOY-BISHOP'S GLOVEMAKER

CHAPTER FOUR

It was two days later, on twenty-third December, that Sir Baldwin de Furnshill drew near to the city. Sitting on his favourite rounsey, he gave his wife a twisted smile and then returned to surveying the River Exe on their left side and warily eyeing the trees on their right. He was always looking for danger. Outlaws were everywhere nowadays.

'I know, my love. And I am glad, too, that we shall not be forced to remain here overly long,' he said.

His wife gave a longsuffering sigh. 'All I said was, I am glad it was not *my* fault we were invited, Baldwin. It should be enjoyable – I don't understand why you are so glum.'

'I do not like to have to travel. Especially over the feast of Christmas. It is a time to be at home, to celebrate in our own church.'

The knight had travelled extensively when he was one of the Poor Fellow Soldiers of Christ and the Temple of Solomon – a Knight Templar – but since settling once more

in his family's estate at Furnshill near Cadbury and marrying
Lady Jeanne de Liddinstone, the tall, grave man had thought
that he would no longer be forced nor expected to journey far
and wide.

Sir Baldwin was Keeper of the King's Peace in Crediton,
a job with some responsibility, but which required limited
effort since few crimes plagued the small country town, and
those that did were not generally violent in nature. He rarely
suffered the difficulties of enquiring after murders and when
there was such a case, it could normally be speedily resolved,
since the perpetrator was commonly still standing over the
victim with a knife or rope in his hand when the Hue and Cry
arrived. Many criminals surrendered themselves quietly,
accepting that they had done wrong and must pay. Since
becoming the King's Keeper of the Peace five years ago,
Baldwin had only been forced to seek four murderers in
Crediton itself.

But this was not Crediton, Sir Baldwin told himself, looking past the weir towards the stonework of the city of Exeter.

The small city was a pretty red sandstone marker in the
green of the fields all about. There were few solid buildings
outside the walls, for all those who could afford to would
buy a small house within their safety. Only a few timber
buildings leaned against the outside of the walls. Looming
over all was the castle, a solid-looking fortress built on the
highest ground. Beneath it Baldwin could see the great mass
of St Peter's, the Cathedral, with its pair of tall spires mark-
ing the two towers of the crossing.

Away from the city were a few sparse settlements which
stood out in this smoothly rolling countryside. There were
any number of church spires and towers: to the north lay St

David's, ahead of him, over beyond the South Gate was the small leper hospital of St Magdalen, while he knew that St Thomas's was almost dead ahead on the Cowick Street, not that the church could be seen from here. There were too many trees blocking the view.

Still, Sir Baldwin confessed to himself that it was a pretty enough little city; not so busy and hectic as London or Paris, not so scruffy as York, nor so unbearably humid and noisome as Limassol. It lay sheltered above a great sweep of the River Exe, quiet and serene in the clear wintry light.

The trouble was, he had another reason to wish to be at home. He did not want to travel all the way to Exeter for Christmas – especially not with his wife.

'Well, you may remain as gloomy as you wish; I for one intend to enjoy myself,' Jeanne said tartly.

He grinned at her. Jeanne and he had been married only since the springtime and he had never known such happiness. Even now, with her face betraying her truculence, he adored her. Never shrewish, usually calm and contented, she was a source of pleasure. Right now she was unhappy, rolling in the coach with each jolt as the wheels thundered over the rough roadway, registering her displeasure at every jarring crash, yet he could only see her beauty. Lady Jeanne was a tall, slender woman with red-gold hair and the clearest blue eyes he had ever seen. Her face was regular, if a little round; her nose short, perhaps too small; her mouth over-wide with a full upper lip that gave her a stubborn appearance; her forehead was maybe too broad – but to Baldwin she was perfection.

Except her temper had fluctuated recently since she had learned that she was pregnant.

It wasn't that she was temperamental – Baldwin would hesitate to use such a perjorative term to describe his wife – but she had become a little more peppery since becoming pregnant. She responded badly to his well-intentioned suggestions designed to ensure her comfort. This was Baldwin's first child and he intended guaranteeing that his wife remained healthy and that their unborn baby was cosseted and protected. Riding all the way to Exeter in the middle of winter did not strike him as the best way to protect either Jeanne or her baby, which was why, against her wishes, he had insisted that she should ride in comfort in the wagon.

'Not too far now, my Lady,' he said encouragingly.

In answer she gave a snort of disgust. 'Good. Oh, this damned road!'

He grinned and she lifted her chin in haughty contempt, but his bellowed laughter made her give a fleeting smirk. Feigning annoyance, she turned from him and pulled her furs more tightly about her. It was hard not to giggle with him when he relaxed in this way. Just then a triple hammering jerk almost knocked her sideways, and she swore viciously under her breath.

She adored her husband. He was considerate, kind, intelligent and serious. She loved his dark complexion, his almost-black eyes, his grizzled hair which contrasted so strongly with his black beard and eyebrows, as if his head had been caught in a heavy frost. Even the scar which ran from his temple almost to his jaw was, to her, an endearing mark, a proof of his martial past, evidence of his chivalry – but that didn't change the fact that he was being too overprotective because she was pregnant.

After many years of wanting children and not being able to conceive with her first husband, she had fallen with Baldwin very soon after the summer – a profound relief, because she had wondered whether she was barren as her first husband had told her – yet Baldwin's constant anxiety was wearing. Other women gave birth naturally. It was a normal event in any woman's life, as natural as breathing or making love or dying.

Earlier in the year Jeanne had seen one of Baldwin's peasants going out to harvest turnips, a short woman with a massive belly. In one hand she carried a wicker basket. Later that afternoon, the woman returned, a basket full of vegetables on her hip with, on the top, a contented baby swaddled expertly against the cold. When Jeanne asked her how she had coped, the woman shrugged evasively, unsure how to answer her mistress. Eventually, when pressed, she muttered that she had given birth to seven others, all in the field while she worked. There was nothing special about this one, she said.

And yet here Jeanne was, forced to ride in an open coach like royalty, because her husband was concerned that she might strain something riding on her mare. 'More risk of straining something in this damned wagon,' she spat as the coach thudded heavily into another rut.

At least here the route was downhill. Up was worse because then the wagon lumbered more heavily. Going down was easier, faster and more comfortable. As she thought that, another deep hole made the wagon rattle and creak and Jeanne struck her head on a stanchion supporting the roof. Cursing quietly to herself, a hand at her bruised temple, she tottered to the front of the coach and sat on the board beside

the driver, Edgar, Baldwin's steward and loyal servant for
many years.

Peering ahead she could see the city, its great bridge
reaching out over Exe Island, where a growing number of
houses were springing up, most on the island where there
were many businesses, but quite a few on the bridge itself.

'It's pretty enough, isn't it?' she commented, shading her
eyes against the morning's sun which lay low in the sky so
late in the year.

Edgar nodded, hunched in his seat and staring at the road
ahead. He grunted his agreement as Baldwin rode up to their
side, a troubled expression on his face. 'Shouldn't you be
resting, my Lady?'

Jeanne looked at him coldly without comment.

The bridge led to the great western gate of the city, which
gave onto a broad roadway running up the hill towards
Carfoix, where the northern, southern, eastern and western
roads all met in the city centre.

Soon Baldwin and his small entourage were rattling
slowly up the incline. Gardens, orchards and fields lay on
either side between or behind houses; pigs squealed and
rootled among piles of leaves and rubbish while dogs
snapped at each other as they scavenged. A cock crowed and
horses neighed or whinnied on all sides. It was not as noisy
and unpleasant as some places, Baldwin told himself, but
there was still proof that crime occurred. A man lolled in the
pillory, blood dripping from a gash in his forehead where a
rock had been hurled. Nearby, a man's body hung from a
beam lashed between two trees, his hands bound behind his
back, his madly staring eyes gazing all about him as his

corpse swung gently, turning from left to right as the breeze blew up the hill.

Jeanne peered at them. 'I wonder what his crime was?' she murmured.

'God Himself knows,' Baldwin said with a shrug. Perhaps he was a murderer. In a city the size of Exeter with many thousands of citizens, there would be several murders each month. 'None of my concern anyway,' he added airily and, as he would soon learn, inaccurately.

'Someone should make sure he's all right,' Jeanne said. She saw her husband give a quick smile. 'What is it?'

'I assumed you were talking about the corpse. It never occurred to me that you meant the man in the pillory.'

She glanced back at the dangling man. 'I think it's a little late for anyone to worry about *him*.' As she said these words, she shivered and pulled the furs up to her neck. Later she would remember those words and realise she had been wrong.

Their destination was near the Guildhall in the middle of the city, at the house of Vincent le Berwe. In a vain attempt to distract herself from the discomfort of the journey, Jeanne brought the powerful merchant to mind. Luckily Baldwin trusted her and valued her judgement, so he often discussed the men he must deal with, seeking her comments and advice.

Vincent was a successful merchant, a rich man who was well regarded among the ruling group who controlled the city of Exeter. It had not always been so. He had married foolishly when younger, a pretty, vivacious girl who was only some fourteen years old. She died giving birth to their first child, and many of the city-folk looked at him askance after that. They were religious in Exeter, and unimpressed with a man who took so young a wife. Her early death heralded dark mutterings about Vincent himself and many of his clients had left him. It had almost ruined him, although now he had been able to renew his fortunes, helped with the diplomatic skills of his new wife, Hawisia.

She was reputed to be a clever young woman: intelligent, cultured, well-reared and courteous. Since marrying her, Vincent's wealth had increased greatly. Baldwin thought she had given him the stability and comfort which he craved. Baldwin had said this with an expression of pensive under-standing, which had made Jeanne smile and put her arm through his. She knew he was considering the parallel between his own life and Vincent's: Jeanne had filled a void in his life just as Hawisia had in Vincent's. Secretly Jeanne was convinced that he would have been perfectly capable of continuing his existence without ever meeting her, provided he had his hounds, hawks and horses. That was not the case for her. If she had not met Baldwin, Jeanne would have become a crusty, embittered old widow, always regretting the fact that she had never given life to a child. And now she was pregnant.

It was with an inner feeling of relief that she noticed the Guildhall ahead. She had no wish to contemplate how much her life was about to be altered with a baby in her house, nor how truly maternal she would turn out to be when a squalling child was placed in her arms by the midwife.

The wagon stopped and Baldwin nodded to Edgar. 'Go and tell Sir Vincent that we are here,' he said, but before his servant could obey, the door opened and the man himself appeared.

'Sir Baldwin – and Lady Jeanne, too! God's blessings upon you both!'

The lookout dropped from his tree and picked up his axe which rested against the tree's trunk. 'He's coming,' he said.

All at once there was a general movement. Two men at Hob's side hurried back past him and went out to their positions nearer the entrance to the clearing, while another lifted a leather bucket to douse the fire, but Sir Thomas of Exmouth shook his head and barked, 'Stop that! There's no point. We don't want to freeze when he's gone. Leave it.'

They didn't have to wait for long. The dark figure, cloaked and hooded, appeared in the shadows among the trees, walking slowly, muttering as the dragging cloak snagged on brambles and twigs.

To him the clearing was a scene of fearsome danger, and not only from the outlaws themselves; if he was found here, he could easily be accused of conspiring with felons. Conversely, if the outlaws decided he posed a threat they might execute him no matter what their leader told them.

He stepped out boldly enough. If they had wanted to kill him, they could have done so – perhaps still would do so – and there was no point in his waiting and skulking anxiously. An arrow to the throat, a knife to the heart – there were many ways of killing a man, and these vicious bastards knew most of them.

The clearing was a rough oval carved out of the old woods. It did not appear to be a regularly used base, for there were no huts or tents, only a single log fire burning with a clean, smokeless flame. Above it dangled a large metal cauldron, in which bubbled a thick pottage. One man knelt at the side, stirring. He wore the innocent expression of the idiotic. His slack mouth dribbled and one corner twitched upwards into a smile, but without conviction. There was a nervousness in his features, as if he was used to being beaten and half-expected to be treated like a cur.

Behind him stood Sir Thomas of Exmouth, a more danger-ous man by far. His face was swarthy and narrow, his eyes glittering under a low forehead. He wore russets and greens, a thick woollen cloak and hose, a leather jack and a dangling hood – nothing to betray his true background as a knight: no gilt spurs, no mail, no insignia of chivalry. He had rejected his past and was now a mere outlaw. The only incongruous feature was the knightly riding sword which dangled from a richly enamelled belt at his side.

'Come on over here, please. Take a seat. Wine?' he said, and his visitor gave him a humourless grin as he approached the fire.

'I received your message. There's no need to pretend that we are on friendly terms.'

'But at least we do not need to be enemies.' The outlaw beck-oned. A young woman appeared between the trees and poured out wine for them, and when she was done he continued, 'I thank you for your prompt appearance. It is better, I always think, to get these things resolved as quickly as possible.'

'I don't know what you want from me.'

'I think you do. First, I want information. My friend Hamond, is he . . .?'

'Hamond was hanged yesterday morning. If you want his body, the hangman will cut it loose tomorrow. Send someone for it.'

'That is a shame, a great shame.' The outlaw held his gaze for a moment, then turned his bitter, shining eyes to the fire. He was silent a while and then drained his goblet and held it out to the girl. She refilled it silently and held the jug up for the other, who shook his head.

'He was captured after ambushing a merchant,' the newcomer said heavily. 'Not only did he not run from his offence, he had the foolishness to go ahead of the merchant into the city and drink a pot of ale at the Nobles Inn when the merchant passed.'

'He was a good friend. Headstrong, but good,' Sir Thomas growled. 'Still, he will be with God now. That's that.' He motioned to the girl. 'Enough, Jen. Leave us.'

As she walked back to the shade under the trees, he watched her go. Indeed, he was so intent upon her slender figure that he appeared to have forgotten his guest, who stirred and cleared his throat. Sir Thomas bowed apologetically. 'Ah, yes. My apologies. I was forgetting. Now, Master, I think you can help me – and I may be able to help you as well.'

'*You* help *me*?'

The outlaw stood more straight and his left hand rested upon the hilt of his sword as he raised an eyebrow. 'You may live a privileged life in the city but any man at need would be grateful of the assistance of a knight.'

'You think so?' came the sneering reply. 'What sort of assistance could an outlaw knight like you provide?'

'Your sarcasm does you a disservice.'

'How can I not be sarcastic when you have only ever sought favours from me?' came the sharp rejoinder.

Sir Thomas looked away. After a moment, he said, 'I agree that I have misused you, but perhaps I could offer money to . . .'

'Money stolen from another church? Do you mean to insult me?' the other snapped.

'All I want is justice! Hamond has been hanged – but was he guilty of the crime?'

The other said impatiently, 'He was with your gang, wasn't he?'

'Listen to me, you fool! Hamond had nothing to do with it – he was with me in the city when the ambush was supposed to have happened. I sent him to the tavern myself to fetch some wine, and it was while he was there that he was pointed out and captured. So tell me – *how did he commit this ambush, how did he get recognised by a merchant as an outlaw who had robbed him, when all the time he was with me?*'

To which his brother, Canon Stephen Soth of Exeter Cathedral, had no answer.

CHAPTER FIVE

'Come in and be seated, Lady Jeanne. Sir Baldwin, a cup of wine with you, sir?' Vincent le Berwe was effusive as he waved Lady Jeanne inside and directed her to a large chair near a hearth of roaring logs while Baldwin sent Edgar off to the Talbot's Inn in Paul Street where le Berwe had arranged a room for them.

It was a good-sized property, Jeanne thought, looking around. Situated on the High Street itself, with a shop at the front where Vincent sold his furs, it had a large undercroft, a basement area, in which Vincent stored his wines and cloths ready for selling. Here in the hall there was as much space as Baldwin had in his entire house. The hall was open all the way to the ceiling, where a thin haze of woodsmoke drifted from the fresh logs which had been thrown on the fire. Above the shop was a small chamber reached by a staircase in which Vincent and his wife slept. All was highly decorated, with ivy and holly dangling in readiness for Christmas. Red berries glistened and twinkled in the light of the guttering candles set about the room.

Vincent himself was the picture of a successful merchant. His face was florid and jowly, his belly so expansive that he must lean back to balance his weight like a pregnant woman; it billowed out voluminously above his belt, dragging it down. His hair was grizzled like Baldwin's, but his eyebrows were of a paler colour. From looking at his face Jeanne felt sure that Vincent was considerably younger than Baldwin, but worry had prematurely aged him.

Jeanne had to remind herself that her husband and she were here not for pleasure, but because Sir Baldwin was to be rewarded with gloves. Baldwin's friend Walter Stapledon, the present Bishop, had insisted that Baldwin should be rewarded for his work earlier in the year when he had helped save Belstone's convent from shame. The knight had protested against it long and hard, pointing out that his friend Simon Puttock, Bailiff of Lydford Castle, had in fact solved the mystery such as it was, but the Bishop had replied that someone who suffered while serving his See deserved a reward. Thus Sir Baldwin had been summoned to the city against his wishes, and Jeanne had refused to remain at home while her husband was being so signally honoured.

She was surprised by Vincent's wife, Hawisia. Where she had expected a sharp, strong-willed woman with a solid grasp of politics, she found a rather vapid blonde with pale, chubby features, and a dumpy frame. In her company Jeanne felt a sense of smug superiority, a feeling she was at pains to conceal.

Hawisia motioned to the bottler to pass drinks and ensured that Baldwin and Jeanne were given pots of wine. Then she tried to engage Jeanne in conversation. It was hard going, for Jeanne did not know any of those about whom Hawisia spoke, nor did she have any interest in the doings of the various dignitaries of the city. Hawisia, Jeanne decided, was one of those women whose experience, life and interest revolved about her husband. There was no time left for her to have developed her own character.

Vincent de Berwe had been elected as one of the four stewards of the city last Michaelmas, and Hawisia apparently went in awe of him and the men with whom he had dealings. It was a natural reaction in one reasonably young, but Jeanne found it annoying in a woman of some twenty-four summers like Hawisia, just as she was irritated by Hawisia's fawning attitude towards Jeanne herself. The other woman appeared painfully aware of her duties as the wife of an important man: she complimented Jeanne on her dress, politely enquired after the manor and expressed her joy on hearing that Jeanne was pregnant. Hawisia told her that she had borne a daughter herself two years before, but the girl had died in the summer when the people of the city were affected by a strange affliction. Jeanne felt a little unsettled to hear about the baby's death. Such things happened, she knew, but there was no need for Hawisia to remind her that the city was unhealthy. Jeanne glanced down uncomfortably at her belly.

After that, Jeanne found conversation difficult. These days, she found herself suffering foolishness with less patience than before. She wanted to talk to someone with more fire to them. The only times Hawisia showed any vivacity was when she discussed her dead child or her successful husband. Her pride in his achievements was at least unfeigned.

Jeanne told herself that the young woman must be very deeply in love and tried to like her, but she found herself speaking snappishly, as if to a child who would not be silent but insisted upon interrupting. To her relief, the two men had a short break in their conversation and she took the opportunity to turn to Vincent and ask, 'Tell me, we saw a hanged man in the roadway. Was he guilty of a very terrible crime?'

'Hamond?' Vincent chuckled genially. He was feeling affable now, after two large pots of wine. He belched surreptitiously and made a sweeping gesture with his mazer, a silver-chased bowl of maple that gleamed as it caught the light. 'They strung him up yesterday. It's good to see a felon swing, isn't it? Yes, the murderous sodomite was one of a small band of outlaws who robbed a merchant only a short distance from the city walls on the feast of the Conception of the Virgin, eighth December. When the man escaped and fled back to the city to raise the Hue and Cry, whom should he see but that very fellow, young Hamond, sitting in a tavern and lifting his ale in salute. Poor Nicholas . . .'

'Nicholas?' Jeanne enquired.

'Nicholas Karvinel, the merchant.' Vincent gulped at his wine. He had spoken rather hastily . . . but there was no need for embarrassment. The Keeper of the King's Peace was bright enough, but there was nothing to connect Vincent to Nicholas so far as he knew. Nothing except the fact that both were merchants and both had aspired to the same position in the City: Receiver. The thought made him smile still more broadly.

'Well, Nick was angry to see the man flaunting himself like that, so he shouted out and raised the Hue and Cry,

catching the fellow himself. It wasn't only his money that
was stolen, but a substantial sum from the Cathedral as well.
In fact, that's why Nick launched himself upon the felon, he
told me. He was never the bravest man in the city, but seeing
that scum sitting and drinking his own and the Cathedral's
money made him see red. The crook himself seemed so
astonished to be caught that he didn't even run. Brazen fool
tried to convince everyone he hadn't been near Nick all
afternoon, not that it got him anywhere. All felons deny their
crimes, of course, but he was persuasive. It wasn't until
Nick's clerk Peter identified him that the jury was happy to
indict him. He was hanged, although what happened to
Nick's money, God only knows. This Hamond only had a
few coins on him. Probably it was left with the rest of his
gang.'

'Strange that he should have gone straight to the city after
committing a robbery,' Baldwin mused.

Vincent eyed him genially. Perhaps this Keeper wasn't
such a hot investigator after all. 'In my experience, Sir
Baldwin, it's all too often the way such fools behave. They
perform their evil acts, then think that they are immune to
danger. If they can escape with their booty, they don't
consider the consequences, they simply head for the
fleshpots.'

'And the tavern in which he was discovered was such a
place?'

'Well, no, the Noble's Inn is a pleasant tavern. I have used
it myself,' Vincent grudgingly agreed. 'But that fellow probably didn't realise.'

'He was new to the area?'

'No, his family are from around here,' Vincent admitted.

'Ah.'

A trace of asperity entered Vincent's voice. The Keeper's noncommittal grunt needled him. 'So what? He went somewhere for ale, just as they all do; he had money in his pocket and bought a drink. Hereabouts he was quite well-known. His family has long had an ill reputation: it was this very soul who was found one night carrying weapons within the city walls after dark.'

'So the jury would have known he was guilty,' Baldwin said. 'If a man commits one crime he is likely to commit another.'

'Absolutely!' Vincent agreed heartily, but as soon as he spoke he saw the knight's expression. There was a cynical glint in Baldwin's eye. Vincent chose to ignore his sarcasm and continued, 'It's not Nick's only piece of bad luck this year.'

'What else has happened to him?' asked Jeanne.

'What *hasn't* happened to him?' Vincent chuckled unkindly. 'He's an interest in several local and overseas trades but this year I doubt whether he's made any profit at all. He had a share in a ship that was caught by French pirates five-odd years ago, then a man who owed him money died and his widow is refusing to pay back the debt, and in the summer his house was burgled and all his plate taken. Only a few weeks later someone else broke in and not only took all his new plate and spare money, but also set fire to the place. Luckily a neighbour saw the flames and called for help, but much of his hall was damaged and he can scarcely afford to have it repaired. And recently, to add to the injury, a glover to whom he'd loaned money was murdered and left nothing. His apprentice stabbed him to death, then took all his money, so Nicholas won't see that sum returned either.'

'The poor fellow,' said Baldwin, shaking his head. 'As you say, it's astonishing bad luck.'

'I personally feel that a man makes his own good fortune,' Vincent said with a trace of smugness as he contemplated his mazer. 'Nicholas, poor bastard, has the smell of failure about him, God Bless! What can you do with someone who invariably fails, eh? Nothing. That's why he didn't win the position of Steward as he was expecting.'

'He was up for a Stewardship?' Baldwin said.

Vincent gulped down the remains of his mazer. 'He was in the race against me but when his fortune seemed to slide his friends wouldn't give up. They asked for him to be granted the Wardenship of the Bridge, which would have put him in charge of the rents on the houses and shops on the bridge apart from everything else – but the Freemen wouldn't allow it. The city can't afford to have someone that unlucky as Warden. No, they all voted for another man in the end. Someone more reliable.'

Jeanne had moved to their side. She wasn't sure that she liked Vincent; he seemed too bullish and proud, almost amused at the disasters which had struck this man Nicholas Karvinel. Now she interrupted, saying, 'Who would that be?'

He smiled, but then allowed a frown to pass over his brow as if realising that his levity was out of place. 'It was Ralph – the glover who died.'

Peter Golloc, Secondary cleric and sometime clerk to Nicholas Karvinel, returned to his room with leaden steps.

He felt like an old man, as if he had aged years in the last week. His face was puffy from weeping at night and exhaustion threatened to force him to doze even during the services. He felt awful. His bowels were loose, and when he went to the privy, he had severe diarrhoea. His belly was on fire after every meal or drink, to the extent that he hadn't been able to eat yet today. Every time he swallowed water he nearly retched – and wine was unthinkable. He had drunk some with Jolinde at the tavern earlier, but it had turned his stomach even before he saw Karvinel.

It wasn't unknown for a malaise to strike a man like this, of course. People put it down to meat which had been off, or inhaling foul air, a miasma, on his way to the Cathedral but from all he had heard, such evil vapours only struck during hot, humid summers, and in any case, if the air had been that revolting, why hadn't anyone else been struck down by it? Come to that, why hadn't he smelled it himself? With a shuddering sigh he accepted his fate. He knew the cause of his illness and it filled him with self-loathing – and despair.

Only with an effort could he acknowledge other people in the precinct: the Secondary Adam chatting to a Canon; behind them a couple of idle choirboys scuffing their feet in the dirt; a cripple who waited hopefully at the bakery door. Peter smiled sadly at this last and reminded himself that others suffered more than him.

At his house he pushed open the door and, dragging his feet, crossed to a stool where he could sit. As he sank onto it with relief, he grabbed at his belly again, but forced himself to relax. It wasn't now that his ailment would attack but later, when he was ready for church. He knew the symptoms only too well.

It was an end – he knew that. He had hoped to earn some money to go away, to find a place at university so that he could learn his clerking properly, so that he could devote himself to useful studies and teaching. Maybe the Bishop, who had been enormously generous to others, might give him the money: Bishop Walter II had done as much for clerks all over his See. But now Peter's guilt and the resulting disease of his soul made all that impossible. He could not go to a university with a clear conscience; he dare not confess to his malady and gain a cure.

The door slammed and another cleric came in, whistling.

'Hello, Jolly,' Peter said, smiling weakly.

'Peter. Here, catch!' He threw a small joint of beef at his friend, then a great round loaf of bread.

Peter caught the joint, but the bread slipped from his grasp. His fingers were too feeble even to grip a loaf of bread. He felt the breath catch in his throat, making him sob with despair.

Jolinde's mouth fell open and he paused, pulling his cloak from his back. 'What in God's name . . .? You look terrible!'

'I feel it,' Peter said with a feeble gesture. He looked at the food.

'Take it, Peter. You need it.'

'Where did it come from?'

Jolinde Bolle sighed, but faced his friend. 'Look, I didn't steal it, all right? The meat I bought with some money from my father. The bread came from him too.'

Peter gave a wan smile. 'Well . . . thanks, then.'

'Least I can do. *You* can't afford it,' Jolinde said, taking the bread and meat and setting them on the table.

Jolinde and Peter had been sharing their rooms since the year when their voices had broken. Like Adam they had failed to proceed to the lower orders, but both were allowed to remain with the Dean and Chapter, helping with the essential work of the Cathedral in the hope that they might be able to advance themselves.

Peter closed his eyes. They hurt, even with the poor light here in their chamber, and he heard Jolinde fetch a cloak. 'Here, put this on. It'll keep you warm,' he said, passing it over Peter's shoulders.

'Thank you. Yes, that feels a little better,' Peter murmured.

'You must see the infirmarer.'

Peter shook his head. 'No, I won't see him. There's no point.'

'What do you mean, "no point"? He might be able to cure you. A barber to let out a little of your blood . . .'

'I won't,' Peter declared stubbornly. Jolinde had brought him a small pot of wine, and he sipped at it now, wincing as he felt the queasiness return to his belly. 'Ugh, no, I can't.'

'Peter, you have to see someone. I know an apothecary in the city, won't you consult him? Or someone else who's trained in medicine?'

'Look, for God's sake, just leave the subject, will you!'

'No, I won't,' Jolinde approached him and, kneeling before him, he peered up into Peter's eyes with an anxious expression on his face. 'Look, you have to see a physician. I've never seen you look so unwell. Your skin is pasty, your hair is lank . . . and you look so skinny. Have you not been eating?'

Peter looked away, and Jolinde stood up with a swift intake of breath. 'That's it, isn't it? You've not been able to

81

eat for days, and now you won't see a doctor because you're convinced you're going to die. Oh, Peter. God's body! This is stupid. Let me go and fetch the infirmarer now.'

'No, not now. Let me wait until the morning. See how I feel then,' Peter begged. 'If it's so serious I die in the night, there's nothing he could do now to save me, is there? If I'm going to die, I'd rather do so quietly, making my peace with God, than in the infirmary with a load of old men coughing and hacking through the night. Is that so strange?'

'You're scared that he might tell you you are about to die,' Jolinde said softly. 'It is not a sin to fear the pain of death, Peter. Why don't we both go now, and ask the infirmarer to examine you? Come! I shall stay by your side.'

Peter wearily turned his face to the fire. 'Oh, why don't you listen? I don't want to go.' The roiling began in his belly once more and he clenched his teeth. Behind his eyes he felt the prickling of tears at the horror of it all. He could have wept under the burden of his appalling secret. 'I prefer to wait. One night can't hurt. And if it is food poisoning, I shall be fine by morning, I am certain.' It was his own secret. He couldn't tell anyone. Even Jolly would hate him if he knew the truth.

He looked up and saw Jolinde nod. If he could have, Peter would have turned to him, begged for help, but he couldn't. His secret was so terrible that he couldn't seek the help of any other man. He hated even to see the sympathy in Jolinde's eyes as his companion watched him rise.

'Where are you going?' Jolinde asked.

'I've got to get some air. You stay here. I need solitude . . . to think.'

Taking the cup of wine which Jolinde had given him, and the loaf which the other pressed upon him, Peter went out into the cold air.

It was almost oppressive, it was so still. Animals appeared to have fled the area, seeking a warm chamber or stable. Only a human could be out in this, Peter told himself. He shuddered as another spasm shook his body, but resolutely forced himself on. Perhaps the cold would help him. He sipped wine and broke off a piece of bread, chewing it slowly and swallowing it with more wine. It hurt his stomach and almost made him heave, but that was all part of his disease. If he could eat at least half of the loaf, then he would have a little strength, could combat the evil within him.

With a series of cries, Choristers burst from the Cathedral, released from their final singing practice. Most scampered or pelted along the paths, heading for their hall and a last drink of hot wine before bed.

He watched them wistfully, recalling a time when he had been carefree and happy. Before he had been lured into evil and had been taken over. A violent clenching made him clutch at his belly.

'Sir, are you all right?'

Looking down, Peter saw Luke peering up at him with an expression of concern. 'I am fine,' Peter told him. 'I just have this pain. If it hasn't gone by morning, I'll see the infirmarer. You are on the way to your hall?'

'Yes. Are you?'

Peter smiled faintly. 'No, I came out for a walk.'

'With your supper?'

Looking down, Peter realised he was still gripping his bread. 'I'd forgotten it.'

MICHAEL JECKS

Luke gave him a vague smile. *He* wouldn't have forgotten a whole loaf of bread. Like the other Choristers, Luke lived in a state of perpetual hunger. No matter how much he ate, there was always a corner of his stomach that felt just a little empty. Not that the Secondaries were all that different, he thought. All, Secondaries and Choristers, depended upon their Canons for their food and some were more frugal with their servings than others. Luke's Canon was Stephen, a man who carried his thrifty habits with him from the Treasury into his own home. It was rare for Luke not to be hungry of an evening.

Peter was still gazing at the loaf. The sight of it made his stomach churn anew. Glancing at Luke, he smiled. 'I remember that when I was a Chorister, my Canon considered that if a few loaves and fishes could feed a crowd, a Chorister should be grateful for the same share. He was a most religious man.'

Luke giggled. It was rare for a Chorister to be treated as a human by a Secondary, and he rather liked it. Peter was known as one of the few Secondaries who would act with generosity towards the Choristers, but his next act surprised Luke.

'Here!' he said, breaking the loaf in two and passing one half to Luke. 'Keep it for the moment when you need a little extra to eat.'

'Thank you . . . Thanks very much,' Luke stammered, holding the gift tightly. He watched as the Secondary slowly walked away, then looked down, thinking, He's mad.

It was a view with which Peter would have entirely agreed. He stumbled as he walked, trying to ignore his aches and pains. It was not easy. He chewed methodically at the bread, his mouth dry, washing it down with slurps of wine.

'Oh, God,' he moaned to himself as he felt the queasiness attack his belly again. 'God, please help me! *Save* me!'

CHAPTER SIX

Jeanne and her husband left Vincent le Berwe's house just as the sun was sinking. Here in the city there was a curious twilight as the sun hid behind the houses and city wall; at their home in Furnshill, the sun concealed herself behind the woods, leaving the sky illuminated from within by a golden-pink torch, then swiftly extinguishing herself. Here there was none of that healthful, glowing ruddiness. The air was filled with the smoke from a thousand fires and down towards the river, west of them, the tanners and dyers sent up plumes of yellow and black smoke from their coal furnaces. It coloured the sun's dying rays with greyness and filth.

It was the kind of impression that filled Baldwin with longing for his own manor. He was out of place here, among the bustling hordes, and yearned for the clean, fresh air of Cadbury, a good rounsey beneath him, a hunting dog at his side and a quarry before him. That was life. Not this mean existence in narrow alleys and streets filled with the refuse of other men, of rotting carcasses of cats and dogs, of scuttling rats and the all-pervasive reek of excrement.

A drunk walked towards them and Baldwin took his wife's arm above the elbow, guiding her gently towards the wall where she would be safe. The drunk saw his movement and belched uncomprehendingly, then staggered on, bouncing off a wall and swearing at it.

Baldwin sighed. They were still in the High Street, but now he turned northwards along Goldsmith's Street. It was quiet now as the sun disappeared. Fine gold and silverwork could not be produced by candlelight, so the smiths were all shutting their shopfronts, lifting up the shutters and bolting them inside. A short way along the street lay the crossroads. The left turning led to the Talbot's Inn, and Baldwin was about to turn this way when he happened to glance right.

A few yards from him stood a pleasantly appointed house and shop. Limewashed timbers and plaster showed that it had been looked after, but now there was an air of sadness about it. A cross had been painted upon the door, and a small bunch of flowers lay on the doorstep. Nearby stood a lone figure, a one-legged cripple resting uncomfortably on a crutch. He was staring up at the house. Recalling Vincent's words, Baldwin guessed that this must be the house of the dead glover: Ralph.

Vincent had said that it was the apprentice who had killed him. Probably a dispute over how much the apprentice was being paid, or an argument over whom the apprentice was seeing. Masters were sometimes short with their boys, especially when their charges discovered the sweet delights of the opposite sex, although it was extremely rare for an apprentice to murder his master.

Baldwin had never heard of such an event in all his years in Crediton as Keeper of the King's Peace. The idea that a servant could murder his master was terrible – incomprehensible. It was surely caused by the evil nature of life in a city, he thought. Not much worse than Vincent's tale of the robbed man and his robber, Hamond, someone who already had an evil reputation. Anyone who had once been thought guilty would inevitably be assumed to be the perpetrator when another offence was committed. Why look for another felon when the whole town knew of one already? was the attitude of many. Especially when confirmed by the evidence of the merchant and his clerk.

When the Knights Templar had been destroyed, Sir Baldwin was horrified. He knew his friends and comrades were all men who had chosen to dedicate their lives to God, to obey His will, to swear the threefold oaths of poverty, chastity and obedience, and to fight in His holy army. Templars had been accused of hideous crimes: that they renounced God and worshipped Satan at their initiation ceremonies – accusations which were ludicrous! Baldwin's Order had demonstrated near-fanatical devotion to Christ. At Safed, two hundred Templars were captured and told they could live if they renounced Christ and accepted the true faith of Islam. Next morning they were forced to watch while their commander was hideously butchered: skinned alive in front of them. When he died at last, his men were ordered to abandon Christianity or die. To a man they affirmed their belief in Christ and one by one were beheaded.

Safed and other instances of martyrdom proved that the Templars were honourable. Their trial was a showpiece. There was no justice involved; it was simply persecution with the aim of stealing all their wealth. In the aftermath Baldwin was fired with a sense of disgust and hatred for absolute power. He was determined to ensure that the innocent were protected and unjust decisions were quashed. That was the spur for Sir Baldwin. He was filled with a passionate loathing of bigotry, injustice and politics – for it was politicians who had lied about, and seen to the ruin of, his Order.

That was why he was aware of a niggling unease. The hanged felon had been known: he had a 'common fame'. Baldwin shivered. Many men, he knew, had been wrongly executed on the basis of flimsy evidence and wrong assumptions.

'Something wrong, my love?' Jeanne asked quietly.

'No, nothing. A man walked over my grave.' The merchant had identified the felon, so had his clerk. 'No, I am fine,' he said, and carried on at a faster pace as if he could leave his unsettled feelings behind him.

By nightfall the Secondaries were asleep, like the Canons and others. They must all wake for the first Mass at midnight, so tended to get their heads down early.

Peter was no exception. He lay on his palliasse and grunted and snuffled in his sleep, but nearby Jolly lay with his hands clasped behind his head and stared upwards. He had to wait a little longer, to make sure that the porter and others would be well gone. Then he could nip off out to see Claricia. Beautiful Claricia. Just the memory of the smell of her hair and sweet-scented body was enough to make the blood course faster through his veins. At last he could wait no longer. He stood, pulled on a thicker cloak against the chill and moved towards the door.

But on the way he froze as Peter cried out, 'No!'

Jolinde turned and looked at his friend, and then realised Peter was still asleep. He was about to ease open the door when he heard Peter begin to talk in his sleep. Words, wild and frantic, tumbled out of him. Although he was not by nature nosy, as Peter spoke Jolly listened, at first with amusement, but then intently and with a close horror.

Talbot's Inn was a good-sized property, not significantly larger than the other houses in Paul Street, but then there was no reason why it should be. It had been a merchant's home until recently, when the merchant in question decided to profit from the excess of ale which he regularly brewed; however, the only sign that he had opened his parlour and hall to guests was the large blackthorn bush which he had tied over the front door. Baldwin entered and ushered in his wife, relieved to hear only a few voices murmuring in the hall and sniffing at the smell of roasting fowl and fresh bread.

He followed Jeanne into the hall, then stopped dead as he recognised the man coming towards him. 'Simon? God's blood! What are *you* doing here?'

'As I recall, Baldwin, you weren't much use during the investigation into the murders at Belstone,' Simon Puttock laughed, grasping Sir Baldwin's forearm. 'So, as I was the poor devil who had to do all the work, the good Bishop decided to reward me too.'

'And deservedly, too. The *good* Bailiff of Lydford should be rewarded,' Baldwin said heartily. 'Edgar, more wine from the landlord. Now,' he continued, helping his wife to a seat near the fire and drawing up a stool for himself, sitting upon it and studying Simon with a steady eye, 'tell us about Meg. How is she?'

Simon let his head fall back and roared with delight. 'She is well, Baldwin. Only a couple of weeks to go and she'll pod. And then I hope I shall have another son!'

Baldwin nodded without speaking. He prayed with all his heart that Simon should win this single desire. Simon had been the proud father of a boy, young Peterkin, who had died quite suddenly two years before. With that death Simon had felt that all his dreams and hopes were also dead, and the fresh-faced, middle-aged man had suddenly lost his square, rugged appearance. In his place was a grey-faced man, his brown hair shot with silver; deep gashes were slashed at either side of his mouth, wrinkles appeared at his brow, and all at once Simon had looked ready for the grave himself. It was only his work which had kept him on an even keel, Baldwin felt. Thank God the Bailiff had recovered some of his easygoing nature since then.

And it had not only affected Simon. His wife had been a pretty, contented young woman, with a tall, slender frame, long, blonde hair and an appealing face. As soon as Peterkin died her flesh fell away, leaving her ghostly thin, with a white complexion. Baldwin had always felt a strong affection for Margaret, and to see how she had faded was dreadful.

'How are you keeping, Jeanne?' Simon asked, turning to gauge her shape with an experienced, measuring gaze. 'You're just beginning to show.'

She reddened, but held her head high. 'Perhaps my waist is thickening a little.'

'Waist? Hah, more your belly, my dear! You wait, you'll be heavier than ever before in four or five months' time. Why, Meg puts on at least a third as much again as her usual weight.' He nudged Baldwin with a broad grin. 'More to cuddle up to at night!'

Baldwin almost laughed, but stifled the sound when he saw the expression on his wife's face. He cleared his throat. 'So we are to be presented with our rewards together?'

'I suppose so,' Simon agreed. 'I don't know what the exact procedure is, but the host of this inn says the clerics of the Cathedral will present them to us with the boy-Bishop on Holy Innocents' Day.'

Baldwin groaned. 'Another five days, Simon.'

'He has been bemoaning his duty since the good Bishop Walter invited him here,' Jeanne said caustically. 'Anyone would think he disliked the thought of the Bishop's generosity.'

'I don't reject the honour – indeed I am grateful for it – but five whole days, Jeanne! We could be enjoying our own quiet Christmas at home. Our first together at Furnshill.'

'Instead we shall be here,' Simon said happily, refilling his jug. 'Eating, drinking and relaxing, and for my part I am happy to be away from the freezing blast on the moors, away from the mires, the mists, the snow and driving rain. No need to worry about the miners arguing with the land-owners for a few blessed days. Ah, for me, I have to say I am content. Especially since we get to attend the Christmas Eve Mass at the Cathedral; I've never seen it here at Exeter before but I've heard it's special. And there's the mayhem of the Holy Innocents' Day celebrations. I look forward to them too.'

Baldwin was not to be soothed. 'Yes, but it's five days. What will we do until then?'

If he had but known, Peter Golloc would soon ensure that he had plenty to occupy him.

Early the next morning, while Baldwin and his wife lay asleep, the Cathedral began to wake to the new day. The Secondary stationed in the church looked at the clock and saw that it was time to call the Cathedral's congregation together for Matins. Yawning while he bowed to the altar, he instantly offered up an apology for his disrespect before shuffling through the dark chamber, scarcely lit by a few remaining candles, and began pulling upon the bellrope.

In his bed on a palliasse on a large bench by the fire in the hall of Talbot's Inn, Simon didn't stir beyond giving a short snore, smacking his lips, and mumbling in his sleep. Upstairs, behind a curtain in a large chamber, Baldwin heard the bell and snapped awake. He couldn't help it: the early call to Matins reminded him of his time in the Knights Templar when he would have risen at this hour to go and give praise to God. He heard the wakeful breath at the other side of the curtain: Edgar. He insisted upon sleeping on a bench near his master to protect him from any nocturnal attack. Edgar had also been a Templar; for many years he was Baldwin's own Sergeant, the man-at-arms who trained with Baldwin and was constantly at his right side whether on horse or on foot. Since they had left the Order Edgar had taken it upon himself to protect Baldwin. Clearly he too remembered their youth as warrior monks, for from the sound of his yawning Baldwin could tell he had also woken on hearing the bell.

Lying in the crook of his arm Jeanne twitched her nose, but then continued to sleep. Baldwin smiled gently. He wanted to touch her face, to feel the soft smoothness of her cheek, to stroke her naked belly and thighs – but he checked his hand. She was tired, especially after the long journey to get here. No, he would leave her to rest.

Baldwin closed his eyes resolutely and waited for sleep to overwhelm him once again.

Peter awoke with a shivering ague that started in his belly and griped, threatening him both with vomiting and soiling himself. He swallowed with an effort, shuddered at the acid bile, closed his eyes and prayed.

The bell tolled relentlessly but he couldn't rise. His belly was a source of heat and pain. He could only roll over and grip at it, sobbing out a plea to God to ease this terrible agony, and as if in answer to his fervent prayers, the sensation of rending and stabbing within his guts retreated a little. Gasping with relief, he gradually eased himself upwards and stood, swaying. He almost called out to Jolinde for help – but then he saw that his mattress lay empty. Jolly had gone to his woman again.

He must wipe his face. That might help soothe him. There was a pot on a chest near his window, and he stumbled to it, dashing cold water over his face and standing still while the dampness dripped down his cheeks and onto his chest. There was a kind of relief, as if the purity of the water helped to drive away his suffering – but not for long.

A wave of relentless pain rocked him. He had to grasp the chest's top to steady himself, head hanging, while his belly clenched. There was a burning in his throat and he choked, spitting out a little bile onto the floor. The bell rang once more and he whimpered quietly. This was his terror, the pitiable horror that he had not dared confess to Jolinde: that he was possessed by a devil.

It was the only explanation. A foul spirit had him in its grasp; his sins had allowed the creature to win him over, his weakness had let the evil into his soul. Now the demon was forcing him away from the path of righteous praise of God, so that he could be more easily bent to the will of the Devil. 'Oh Holy Mother Mary, please save me,' he pleaded as he felt the liquid movement in his bowels again, and he wept as he lurched to his chamber pot.

Afterwards he felt much improved. He rinsed himself and his hands, pulled his cloak on, slipped his feet into his shoes and prayed quietly. The action of calming his breath and thinking of God soothed him, and while the effect lasted, he dipped his spoon in the broth he had made the night before out of the joint Jolinde had brought him. It appeared to sit easily on his belly, but made him feel hungry again. Well, he reflected, after throwing up half my food and having the rest pass through me like water, it's no surprise. He broke off a portion of bread from Jolinde's loaf and popped it into his mouth, chewing it dry as he prepared to leave the hall for the Cathedral. After vomiting earlier he was aware of a curious taste to it, but shrugged it aside.

Jolinde wasn't downstairs in the hall, but there was nothing new in that. These days, he was rarely at home. He went out drinking until far too late, or stayed with Claricia Cornisshe at Sutton's Inn, but as Jolly's father was rich and a friend of the Dean, he felt he could get away with it. It seemed disgraceful to Peter, but he was in no position to condemn any man while he was racked with his devil-inspired malady.

He shut the door and crossed the grass to the western door. Jolinde would be inside, no doubt. Probably darted there as soon as he returned to the Cathedral precinct – although how he managed to scale the walls was beyond Peter. Having sated himself with his drinking and lusting, Jolly would beg personal forgiveness while his companion clerics prayed for other men's souls. Jolinde! Peter gave a dry smile.

Jolinde's girlfriend allowed him to stay with her overnight. That was why he was so often late back, usually rushing straight to the first service. 'First service?' he had laughed bawdily when Peter had asked him. 'This isn't *my* first service tonight!'

His behaviour had shocked Peter at first, but Jolinde was no hypocrite. 'I'm not going to be a priest, I don't want to be, but my father insists that I should learn to read and write. That way I can be more use to him in his work.'

To Peter, whoring about the city was a disgrace to the cloth, but there was no sin if a man confessed and Jolinde had sworn that he would. And since Peter had no rich parents to help support him, Jolinde's occasional gifts of extra bread, meat or poultry were welcome. There was a twinge of near guilt each time Peter accepted the presents, as if he was taking a bribe again, as he had from Karvinel when the merchant begged him to confirm the identity of the felon, but Peter had persuaded himself that there was little point in starving himself. He might as well take advantage of Jolinde's patronage as another's. If not, he'd be no better off than a cripple or leper begging at the Fissand Gate.

Not that it was easy to imagine someone being worse off than him. He was the unwilling participant in the killing of the innocent Hamond and the unwilling accomplice in a theft. A wave of self-pity washed over him. Perhaps if it weren't for them, he wouldn't be prey to this horrible punishment: possession. He had reached the great western door now, and took a deep breath before entering. The Punctators spotted him as soon as he slipped inside, one of them shaking his head at the sight of the Secondary arriving late once more. Jolinde was already in his place. The singing had begun and Peter stood in dumb confusion for a moment before coming to himself and tottering forwards to his stall, trying to disturb as few other clerics as possible on his way.

The church felt hot, but a moment later it was freezing. A fine sweat broke out upon his back, then chilled him to the core as all warmth fled. The candlelight flickered while the choir's voices rose in song, praising God. Peter settled upon the *misericorde* and attempted to focus his attention on God.

He survived the first half hour, but then the changes in temperature began to accelerate, and he suddenly felt much worse. The choir appeared to move about him. Perspiration dewed his forehead and then he felt the surging rush in his belly and bowels. There was a final, terrible, clutching agony in his belly, squeezing again and again, while he closed his eyes trying to hold back his screams. The room began to spin faster; the fumes of the censer filled his lungs and made him retch.

No! He mustn't be sick, not here in church. It would be obscene, an insult to God. Swallowing, he tried to keep the urge to vomit at bay, but then a spasm made him spew up a thin dribble. He felt it drip down his chin and he desperately tried again to swallow, but then the sharp pain ripped at his stomach. He bent over, vomit projecting from his mouth. While his fellow-clerics stared in shock, he fell to his knees, sobbing, coughing up bile which was bright with his blood.

He managed to croak out a single cry, a heartfelt plea to Holy Mother Mary for Her forgiveness, before collapsing in his stall, his body convulsing for a minute or two after the poison had stopped his heart.

CHAPTER SEVEN

The urgent summons reached Simon and Baldwin before they had risen from their beds. Baldwin's eyes snapped open at the first sharp rap, and he listened as the landlord of Talbot's Inn shuffled along the screens passage to the door. It sounded, from his grumbling, as if mine host didn't like to be pulled so early from his bed.

A second loud knock echoed through the almost empty building to be answered with the host's testy, 'I'm on my way, you bastard, cool your bollocks! What's the hurry?' Confident it could be nothing to do with him, Baldwin swung around gently, so as not to wake his wife, and sat on the edge of his bed stretching. He was here as a guest of the Cathedral, not in any official capacity. It was probably an early customer wanting his morning whet.

Rising and pulling on a shirt to cover his nakedness and combat the cold. Baldwin went to the window. The shutter was held up by a thong looped over a nail, and overnight the string had become stiff and frozen. He had to struggle to unhook it and push the warped shutter down in its runners. Once it had fallen away, Baldwin found himself gazing upon a dark and grey view. Although it was not raining, the gloomy black clouds overhead were threatening. Baldwin snuffed the air. It was too early for most citizens to have lighted their fires, and he could taste a metallic tang in the air. It was too cold to rain; if anything, there would be snow and lots of it. The prospect made him give a fleeting frown at the thought of his manor, so many miles away, but then he shrugged. There was nothing he could do from here and in any case, his staff knew their jobs well enough. The cattleman would have his beasts in the byre, the shepherd would be out in his hut, his fire lit. All the hay was stored, all the grain in the chests ready to be ground as it was needed. All the same, he would prefer to be there if the weather was going to deteriorate.

As the thought passed through his mind, he heard the door open and the angry voice of the host was cut off by the curt tones of another. Baldwin listened carefully. He could hear Edgar walking across the floor towards the door, and knew that his servant would have grabbed his sword and gone to listen, as always thinking of his master's protection before anything else.

Christmas Eve, Baldwin thought to himself sourly. Thursday twenty-fourth December, and here he was, miles from home, not knowing what was happening at his manor and now he couldn't even be granted a decent rest in his bed.

'Sir Baldwin,' Edgar called quietly after a short while, 'there has been a death in the Cathedral and the Dean has sent his Bailiff to ask you and Master Puttock to see him.'

'But we've only been here one night!' came a small plaintive voice from Baldwin's bed.

He smiled at his wife, snuggled well under a pile of blankets and cloaks. 'Tell the good Bailiff that we shall attend the Dean as soon as we are dressed,' he said.

The Bailiff of the City had hurried off as soon as he had delivered his message, so Baldwin and Simon had to make their own way to the Dean. At the great gate they were pointed to his small house and were soon hurried upstairs to his hall.

Simon was unimpressed by the Dean. It took only a few minutes to classify the fellow as a foolish old dolt. Dean Alfred stood before his table, rubbing his hands together as if he was washing them, and surveyed his guests with an anxious face that reminded Simon uncharitably of Baldwin's old mastiff.

'My friends, I am grateful that you should have come so speedily to our aid,' he said. 'Hmm. Um, this matter is so serious that I fear I must ask for help from whichever quarter I . . .'

'There was no need,' came an uncompromising voice from behind them, and Simon spun to meet the stern gaze of another man.

'This is Roger de Gidleigh, Coroner of Exeter,' said Dean Alfred unhappily. 'Ahmm, he claims the right to perform the inquest.'

'It is my duty under the King's laws,' the man stated.

'But not Canon law,' the Dean said miserably. 'Um, I have to ensure that the Cathedral itself is represented within the Cathedral's walls.'

'You could as easily send a cleric as your representative.'

The Dean ignored his loud, rasping voice. 'Sir Baldwin, Bailiff Puttock, hmm, would you please help the Coroner in his enquiries? Poor Peter is dead.'

'It would be a pleasure,' Simon lied, wondering who 'Poor Peter' could be. It didn't take long for the Dean to tell them, explaining how the boy had died during the service.

Baldwin was puzzled. 'So this fellow went into convulsions and collapsed?'

'Just like a man who had been poisoned,' said Coroner Roger grimly. 'And he had been showing symptoms of illness for some days, so I am told.'

'As if he was being slowly poisoned?' Baldwin asked. No one answered.

'Why should someone wish to kill a cleric?' Simon asked.

The Dean looked at him with an infinity of sadness in his eyes. 'Some men would do anything for revenge, Bailiff.'

'Revenge? What makes you mention that?' Simon pressed sharply.

'This cleric helped identify a robber and felon in the city recently. I wonder whether the outlaw's leader might have wanted to avenge his hanged associate.'

Coroner Roger had been listening with growing impatience. 'Rubbish. It was because the dead boy had been supposed to take jewels and money to a glover in the city . . .'

'The glover who was killed by his apprentice?' Baldwin demanded. First there was the fact that the cleric had been with the merchant Karvinel, now he was connected to the dead glover as well.

'The same, yes. Only since his death, the money and some of the jewels have disappeared.'

'And the gloves, too, were gone?' Baldwin asked.

'No, they were found and have gone to another glover to be finished. Most of the jewels were already on them, and they only need a little work to be completed,' the Dean sighed. 'Ummm, it means the Cathedral must buy even more gems and pay more money to finish the work on time. It is terrible, especially since we only recently lost money to the hanged outlaw. You er probably saw him hanging?'

Baldwin wanted to concentrate on the central point. 'How many jewels are missing?' he asked. 'You have a receipt, I suppose, to check against the gloves as they stand?'

'Of course. Ahm . . .' the Dean produced a roll of vellum. 'Here is the account held in the Cathedral, and er here,' he set a sheet on top, 'is the ah receipt. As you can ah see, it is dated on sixth December, the Feast of St Nicholas.'

Baldwin read aloud, '"Four rubies, fifty assorted gemstones and fifty small pearls with two pounds five shillings and sixpence for the trouble, etc, etc." Yes. This is signed by two men – Golloc and Bolle . . .'

'Peter Golloc is the dead Secondary.'

'I see. And it is marked with a cross and a seal for the glover himself.' He looked up. 'So you know that the gems and everything tie up; you have proof that the glover received his delivery. What could they have to do with this dead fellow?'

'If the Secondary decided they would be pleasant to have,' Coroner Roger said with an unpleasant leer, 'he could have gone back and stolen them. Even perhaps killed the glover, if he was discovered in the act.'

'That is a most ahm unreasonable and er unwarranted suggestion,' cried the Dean, his face flushing with anger.

'Anyone could have taken them,' Baldwin said reasonably. 'There is nothing in what you have said to suggest that this poor fellow might have robbed and killed his victim. Could Peter have committed suicide?'

'What reason would he have to do a thing like that?' the Dean protested in a squeak.

'A woman, a debt, a guilty secret . . . the reasons for murder are varied – and self-murder is no different from ordinary homicide. People can hate themselves as much as they can detest others,' Baldwin mused.

Coroner Roger responded slowly. 'Certainly I have seen another cleric wandering the streets at night. Whether this one did as well . . . I'd have to speak to the Bailiff and the Constable.'

'That might be worthwhile. Then again, you said immediately that it could be poison. It could as easily be a severe illness.'

'One that causes a man to shit his hose and puke blood?' Coroner Roger said.

'There are such diseases,' Baldwin said. In his mind's eye he could see the foul, beleaguered city of Acre in 1291. The city had been under siege for ages when he arrived, and there were many pale, skinny folks there who suffered from a bloody flux and vomiting. Honesty made him add, 'Although I have only seen them in battlefields and in camps. When they occur, God sends them to afflict many at the same time.' He gave an enquiring glance to the Dean, who shook his head.

'Nobody else has exhibited the same symptoms as far as I know.'

'Did he live alone?'

'No, he was in a hall with a friend. Jolinde Bolle.'

Baldwin saw the Coroner peer at the Dean through narrowed eyes. 'Bolle?'

'Who is he?' Baldwin asked.

'Another Secondary,' the Dean answered. 'Men here at the Cathedral are all of different ranks, Sir Baldwin. Ahm, when the voices of the Choristers break, they often remain here to study and learn all they can, hoping to be promoted later if they can win the patronage of a Canon, er, but sometimes they cannot and stay on as Secondaries, mere assistants to the priests and clergy. Jolinde is one such.'

'He also spends much of his time in alehouses and taverns in the city,' Coroner Roger said sternly. 'I've seen him about the place often enough.'

'Jolinde was never going to be a priest,' the Dean said. He was washing his hands more vigorously now as his anxiety grew. 'Oh, may God forgive me if I am wrong! Hmm, Sir Baldwin, um, I fear that Peter was murdered by someone who wanted to avenge the dead felon. Only a man who wasn't a priest could behave like that, poisoning a clerk in the Cathedral.'

'A man like Jolinde, you mean?' Coroner Roger enquired dryly.

'It's always the same with the blasted Dean and his Chapter,' Roger said as he walked with Simon and Baldwin over to the cemetery at the northernmost point of the Cathedral. He stopped and gestured at the Cathedral. 'They keep everything hidden that they can. If they'd been able to, they'd never have told me about the lad's death. Tchah! What can a man do?' He turned and stalked off, but Baldwin and Simon followed more slowly.

'What do you think?' Baldwin asked his friend.

'I don't know what to make of it. We need more facts.'

'Yes. It is intriguing, however. A robbery and this Secondary recognised the felon; a glover is killed and this lad was the one whom the Coroner suspects took the money – although the apprentice has been charged with the same crime – and now he himself dies. I find this all fascinating,' Baldwin observed. He called after the Coroner, forcing him to slow his furious pace. 'Coroner, were you serious when you implied that this lad Bolle could have killed Peter?'

The other man was still seething with frustration over the secretiveness of the Cathedral staff.

'I'd suspect myself for that amount of jewels and cash!' he snapped.

There was something about him that Baldwin rather liked. The Coroner was a thickset man, with a slightly flabby belly that showed his practice with his sword was not so regular as it should be, but whose solid posture revealed his strength. He had a square, kindly face, with warm, slightly bulging brown eyes, and a short, cropped hairstyle. His gaze was frank and honest, unlike so many corrupt officials Baldwin had met, and his brow was strangely unwrinkled for a man who must surely be no younger than Simon. His hair was frosted about the temples, but that was the only proof of his increasing years.

He was appraising Baldwin in his turn, saying, 'They guard their privacy jealously, do the staff here, but from what the Dean told me, they were preparing gifts of gloves for some of the more senior citizens for the Holy Innocents' Day feast. You among them.'

'Yes,' Baldwin agreed. Simon remained silent, looking over the rebuilding work which continued around the Cathedral even today in this cold and miserable weather.

'Well,' the Coroner said, pulling his cloak closer about his shoulders, 'the dead man, this Peter, was working in the Treasury – that is the building over at the north side of the Cathedral itself – and was tasked, along with his friend Jolinde Bolle, with delivering money and jewels to the glover who was to make your gifts. Except the glover himself is dead, murdered by his apprentice, and the apprentice denies taking the money. He denies killing his master, come to that, but they always do, don't they? You asked me about the young man living with Peter, this Jolinde Bolle. If Peter *had* taken the stuff, Bolle could have been an accomplice. Maybe he got greedy – killed Peter and took what they had thieved rather than share it.'

'Would Peter have known where the glover kept his strongbox?' Simon interrupted.

'I don't know. Perhaps the glover took them to it.'

'And then he killed the glover to conceal his theft . . .'

'It's possible.'

'. . . Only to be robbed, and killed in his turn,' Baldwin murmured. 'It sounds complicated. Is it feasible that two murders could happen in so short a space of time?'

'This is speculation, but two murders within a few days in a city this size is not unheard of. And what if Peter's death was by his own hand? After all the Dean hinted at it: he seemed to suggest that if the lad *had* stolen the jewels and cash, he might have felt so remorseful that he could only see the one way out.'

'Do you believe that?'

Roger stopped dead and placed his hands on his hips. He gazed up at the sky, then around at the Cathedral's grounds. 'Do I think he killed himself? No. If he did, where are the jewels now? It's not too far-fetched to suppose that there were two murders, but that there were two unconnected robberies as well does stretch my imagination.'

Baldwin gave a dry smile. 'Good. I would also add that I find it unlikely that a fellow would take a lethal dose of poison and then walk into his church to expire during a service.'

'You say you've seen this Bolle about the city at night,' Simon noted. 'Couldn't *he* have killed the glover and stolen the money? Perhaps Peter saw the jewels and recognised them – threatened to tell someone?'

'So Jolinde Bolle placated him, said he would replace them or whatever, and then slowly poisoned his friend?' The Coroner grinned cynically.

'Yes, it does seem a little unlikely,' Baldwin admitted. 'What of the other people who live here?'

'There are more than I can count: twenty-four Canons in the Chapter; the Dean and his four dignitaries . . .'

'Go on,' said Simon. 'These places all have different groups of men. Who serves the Cathedral?'

'There are the Precentor, the Sub-Dean, the Chancellor and the Treasurer. Then there are four Archdeacons, for Totnes, Barnstaple, Cornwall and . . . oh, for Exeter, of course. I think each Canon has his own Vicar; there are some twelve or so Secondaries like this Peter; fourteen Choristers; at least twenty Annuellars, the chantry priests. And there are all the other members of the clergy, too: clerks and sub-clerks to the Exchequer, clerks to the Lady Chapel, clerks of works, clerks of God knows what . . . There's probably two hundred folk living here within these walls.'

'They live within the grounds permanently?' Simon asked. He had been educated by the Canons of Crediton Church and had a better understanding of the canonical life than Baldwin, whose Order had been divorced from other religious groups.

'They all do, these choir members,' Roger sniffed. 'Keep themselves to themselves. Apart from a few of the youngsters they hardly ever mix with the likes of us, Sir Baldwin. We're too far beneath them. Even the lowliest of the Choristers is probably looked upon as more important than you or me. *They* are all religious.'

Baldwin nodded. The whole of the Cathedral grounds had been encircled by great walls some twenty years before, while he was still abroad. It had been a surprise for him when he had first seen the precinct on returning. They made the Cathedral feel divorced somehow from the city itself. 'I presume that the gates are all locked at night?'

In answer the Coroner pointed towards the city's south gate. 'Down there is the Palace Gate, called that because it's opposite the Bishop's Palace. There, in Bear Lane is the Bear Gate.' He turned and pointed to their right. 'Up there is Little Stile, for pedestrians only. Next is St Petrock's Gate, which leads through the church itself. Then there's the Fissand Gate, although many call it Broadgate now. And last,' he said, turning and pointing back the way they had come, 'there is St Martin's up there, and the Bicklegh Gate. It's called that because the Bicklegh family owns the house alongside. All of the gates are locked and barred from inside, every night, and only when the porter rises at dawn are they opened again.'

109

'So this Peter would have found it hard to get out after they were locked?'

Coroner Roger gave a twisted grin. 'Now, then, Sir Baldwin. What were you like when you were a horny young buck and you knew that women were over a wall waiting for a rutting? Jolinde Bolle has often been out in the alleys and streets; I've seen him myself.'

'How would he get out when the gates were locked?'

'Come on, Sir Knight! If the fellow is randy enough, he'll find a way. And if Bolle knows how to get out, you can bet that his friend did too. And if they knew how to get out, they must have known how to get back inside again.'

'It follows, then, that if this Peter was murdered with poison administered at night, then the killer is someone within the Cathedral, unless that person secreted himself in the grounds after the gates were locked last night or knew how to clamber over the wall,' Baldwin continued musingly. 'Anyone who knew Bolle or the dead clerk could have followed them and learned their route.'

The Coroner shot him a quick look. 'In other words, anyone in the city could have done it.'

'Let's just see whether this poor devil was truly murdered before we leap to conclusions, eh?'

'It's the Dean who's doing that. He hardly needs my help.'

Simon was unimpressed. 'The Dean can invent what he wants. I've often seen priestly men like him. Their imagination is given too free a rein. Surely he has little understanding of the real world.'

'Yes, Bailiff. Men like the Dean read books and learn more than is good for them, looking at odd stuff about all the temptations devils can throw in their paths to tease them.

Think what it must be like! Temptations of the flesh torment-ing them all the time and never allowed to touch . . .'

'If they don't they'll be among the only clerics in the country who manage to keep from sheathing their daggers where they shouldn't,' Simon grunted. Although he had himself been brought up by Canons, he had grown more sceptical about the behaviour of religious men and women after his experiences in Belstone earlier in the year.

The Coroner gave him a contemplative look. 'You won't be surprised to hear that the younger clerks here are no different from the ones you've come into contact with, Bailiff. It's not only Bolle and the dead lad. Any of them will leave the precinct and run about the town when they get a chance, whoring and drinking just like ordinary lads. And why shouldn't they? I doubt whether God would concern Himself with a boy who enjoyed natural pleasures.'

Baldwin was stung into objecting. 'The Bible tells us that fornicating and wallowing in gluttonous behaviour is as obnoxious to God as it is to other men,' he began, but Roger gave a short snort.

'You think so, Sir Baldwin? If God cares so much, why doesn't He send a thunderbolt every so often, hey? No, for my part I'll believe my own priest, who tells me that so long as I apologise and confess before I die, I'll be all right. Not that I admit to any wrongdoing, of course,' he added with a twinkle.

CHAPTER EIGHT

Hawisia le Berwe was in the Cathedral as the Bratton Chantry priest began the Mass. Her husband had left the house before she was dressed, muttering something about a meeting he must attend, but it was no surprise to her. Staring at the altar, she closed her eyes with patient suffering and prayed for him.

She knew all about the rumours. Others saw him about the city; no doubt her own servants had told others that he rarely visited her bed any more. Her mother had heard a tale from some gossip or other, had written warning Hawisia that older men lost their urges, became phlegmatic and corpulent, and for a woman to find that her husband had deserted her was dreadful. Had he lost interest in her?

The recollection of that message made Hawisia smile now. No, Vincent still showed her plenty of affection. When a man left his wife, he showed little concern for her feelings; that was what she had heard from other women who tried to broach the subject with her. Some were women who had lost their husbands to the warmer, more acrobatic beds of younger courtesans. Thinking Hawisia was a new recruit to their ranks, they had spoken candidly of their search for their own new bedfellows, seeking out younger men who would appreciate their wealth and patronage. Hawisia was appalled by their behaviour. It convinced her that they were dishonourable and it was hard for her to maintain her calm and courteous demeanour with them.

For Hawisia was a polished hostess. She knew that in order for her to be accepted she must befriend all the women who visited. Especially the wives of the more influential men in the area. That was why she had been so meek and deferential to Jeanne when she had visited with her husband Sir Baldwin. Hawisia knew that she must not shine compared with the wife of so important a man.

Not that he had looked particularly impressive, she reflected, listening with half an ear as the priest began to preach his sermon – badly as always, she sighed. Rumour had it that he had only won his post owing to the size of his father's pocket, and listening to him Hawisia could easily believe it.

Her husband was often not with her because he was very busy with his work. Hawisia knew that. She could trust him; he was a good husband to her. And she was immensely proud of him. He kept her well, and now he had his senior post in the hierarchy of the city there was every possibility of greater rewards. It wasn't as if he didn't love her any more. It was all down to business.

First, she knew, he had been fretful because he feared that Nick Karvinel would persuade enough of the members of the city's Freedom to support his bid to become Receiver. The post was important. Of course it restricted other business because the holder couldn't leave the city without a special licence from the Mayor, but even so, the potential for making a small fortune was there.

If Karvinel had got it, poor Vincent would have been dreadfully damaged. His career would have suffered – or so he told Hawisia. And *he* would have suffered from the loss of face before his peers. Not that she was terribly concerned by what impact that might have upon her; to her the most important aspect would have been the hurt and disappointment felt by her husband. She didn't want to see him shamed.

But then Karvinel had suffered disaster after disaster, one after another, in an unending sequence. It had been quite strange really to see how the strutting, arrogant little man who had begun his campaign to win the Receiver's job the previous year had gradually gone downhill. Then he had been Vincent's leading competitor in the city, someone to be reckoned with. No more. Now Karvinel was no sort of a threat whatever. And Hawisia had a shrewd idea why: because Vincent had ruined the man.

He was too bright to risk his own neck, of course. When Karvinel lost his ship and entire cargo, it wasn't because Vincent had stolen it, but Vincent le Berwe still had family who lived in the Breton lands on the northern coast of France. It wouldn't have taken much to send a message to them about his enemy's ship, and although that was five years ago, he had never fully recovered from that blow.

The beauty of Vincent's efforts after that lay in their subtlety. The robbery from Karvinel's house that left him so anxious about even his own home – especially when the second robbery occurred. Both times Karvinel was away with friends of his and Vincent's; Vincent himself was with them. The perfect alibi! Nobody could connect Vincent with the thefts or the arson attack on Karvinel's house.

But Hawisia knew that there were plenty of men who would consider anything – maybe even murder – if the money was good. And Vincent could afford to pay well at that time.

The priest finished; the service was over, and Hawisia left by the great door. She saw Adam as he hurried about his duties and smiled at him.

'Adam, how are you?'

'Well enough, my Lady. Too much work as always.'

They exchanged a few words and then she continued home. Once there, she asked her servant where Vincent was, but he replied that the master was in meetings at a tavern with other merchants, so Hawisia walked through to the hall and asked for some thin ale and bread to break her fast.

Her routine had been like this much of the time recently. Vincent was rarely about when she came home from church. He was so worried about his work.

So far they had managed to keep news of the disaster from their friends – once those foxes got to hear about it, they'd all want their debts returned – but the truth was bound to slip out soon. It was ironic, really, after Karvinel's problems, since it was Vincent's ship which had caused their financial troubles, only in his case it wasn't pirates, it was the normal maritime risks. It had struck a rock. Only two sailors survived to tell the story and the cargo was lost.

That was why Vincent was so engrossed in his work. He was desperately trying to cover himself, carefully investing what little money he had left into a variety of new ventures.

It was money that was stolen from Karvinel, she recalled. With a shock she wondered whether her husband had helped to waylay Karvinel on his trek back from the coast – but then Hawisia relaxed. He had been with her that day: she recalled it clearly. And if Karvinel had any thought that his worst enemy could have had a hand in his destruction, he would have shouted it from the rooftops. No, it must have been as Karvinel had said: a band of outlaws.

When a fluttering, as of a tiny butterfly, tickled her belly she rested a gentle hand upon it and smiled contentedly. No matter what other people said or thought, she knew that Vincent was still hers. And that he would be pleased when he heard of their child. She had kept her pregnancy secret until she was quite certain that she wouldn't miscarry, but now she was sure. And it would be a boy, she felt.

An heir; a boy to help her husband. It was terrible to see him working himself to the bone all because he was so worried about their livelihood. Not that he would ever tell *her* that directly! Hawisia felt her heart swell. It was wonderful to be married to such a strong man. He never confessed to any weakness, never moaned or whined, only got on with whatever he needed to do. In comparison Karvinel was a weedy little man; Hawisia had married a titan.

She was so proud of him.

Adam was also considering weaker men as he refilled his box with candles and made his way back to the Cathedral. At the door he bowed to the altar and the Virgin's statue, before quietly moving across the paved floor to the candelabra. He began to remove the used lumps, cleaning the thick gobbets of wax from the metal sockets as he went, and only when all was clean did he insert the replacements.

This was a neverending job – a life's work, he sometimes felt. As soon as he had completed his rounds, changing all the candles which were burned down, it was time to go to a service, and once the service was done, he must replenish another group.

If it wasn't mentally stimulating, at least it left him time to consider, reflect and contemplate. He could allow his mind to wander while he moved among the flickering lights.

He would have to order some more wicks, he thought as he slotted the last in place and moved to the next candelabra. One month ago he had ordered 150 pounds of candlewax from Vincent le Berwe, but he was already running short of wicks sufficient for the remainder. After Christmas he would need to make many more for the Candlemas service at which the local population would come to buy candles to keep them through the coming year. If someone fell ill, if someone died, the candle flame, blessed by the Cathedral, would offer some solace.

It was pathetic, though, that he should be out here slaving away while others relaxed, taking their ease. There were plenty in this Cathedral who could benefit from a little hard work, he thought. The Dean himself, for one. Stupid old prat! Just because he'd been able to read and write well, he'd been given power over all the other Canons. Stronger, brighter men like Adam were left to do all the menial tasks.

This was no life. Other Secondaries, Jolinde for instance, had something to aim for, something they hoped to achieve. It was easy for them – they had help. Peter Golloc, for instance had been friendly with people in the city. He had been close to Karvinel, clerking for him every so often. He could have got a job with him, maybe, until Peter took that poison. As for Jolinde, he could make something of himself yet. With his father being Vincent le Berwe, there was bound to be a position for someone with Jolinde's skills.

Adam, like the other two, had once been a Chorister, but when his voice broke he discovered that it had been his only asset. Without it, he was unwanted. True, the Bishop had made sure he had a roof over his head with this responsibility for candles and a home with Canon Stephen, but that was nothing. Both Jolinde and Peter, before he died, had jobs in the Treasury, because they could read and write and add: three skills which Adam had signally failed to acquire.

He thrust a candle roughly into its holder. To his surprise, the arm of the sconce snapped off at the base where it had been welded to the stand and he stood staring dumbly down at the wreckage. He would have to report it to the smith to be mended, he told himself, moving on to the next stand.

It wouldn't have troubled him except he knew he had a good head on his shoulders; he had more up top than most of the others. Yet they had a chance, while he had none. He'd have to make his own way. That was why he'd formed his plan. All he needed was a little money. He had it all mapped out: he'd go to the coast, take a ship and travel to the Cinque Ports. With the money he had saved, he'd invest in a little fur-trading, and as soon as that took off, he'd move into wines as well. There were huge profits to be made on wine. He'd learned that from le Berwe. Now he had some cash, he could soon go. Get away from this dump.

The older lads like Jolinde could stick their days scribbling and scratching at their vellum in the Treasury; he'd be enjoying the high life, drinking and whoring in London or Bordeaux. Jolinde could slave away: Adam would be having fun. He shoved another candle into a holder – more gently this time. It was the last. He returned to his store, set the used stubs to one side, then replenished his box with fresh ones.

Work, work, work. Adam sometimes felt that if it wasn't for his own personal efforts the place would fall apart. His candles kept it all going. Without the light he provided, the services couldn't continue. It was a source of pride to him that his post was so crucial. Not like some, who simply idled their time away.

This thought came to him as he caught sight of Jolinde standing in a private vigil at the feet of his dead friend. When he left, perhaps Jolinde could take over the candles, Adam thought with a chuckle. Do him good!

It was sad Peter had died. And strange, too, Adam considered, collapsing like that in the middle of the choir.

Rumours already abounded in the Chapter that he must have been poisoned. Adam had heard two Canons discussing the matter. They had nodded to him as they passed by while he was fitting candles into wall brackets, but no one appeared to have any idea *why* someone could want to hurt Peter. It wasn't as if the fellow was a pest or caused anger with other members of the Chapter. He was reasonably well liked. Adam had quite liked Peter and only knew of one man who could have had a reason to wish to harm him: Jolinde.

Jolinde had his little secrets. If they were ever exposed, he would probably be evicted from the Cathedral. And Peter had known all his faults. So who else would have wanted Peter silenced?

Knowing that, it was strange to see how Jolinde stood there for hour after hour, his hands clenched. Adam paused in his continual passage up and down the church, watching him for a while.

'Pathetic!' he sneered under his breath.

Karvinel had heard of the death of the boy while he was still in John Renebaud's tavern, a short while after Vincent left him there.

Left him there? If he'd stayed any bloody longer, his guts would be on the floor! The bastard, the God's-body whore-son *shit*! If Vincent had been in similar trouble, he, Nick Karvinel, would have helped him, but oh no! Not our new high-and-mighty Receiver, not the Seneschal of the Common Goods of the City, not Master le Berwe.

There had been many times in the last few years when Karvinel could have paid Vincent a bad turn, but he'd never tried to. Karvinel had always believed that a Christian Freeman of the City would consider any other Freeman to be honourable. It was only now that he realised his error. Le Berwe was *not* a decent, gentle man. He was a thieving, grasping usurer.

Snapping his fingers, he attracted the attention of a serving-girl and ordered another flagon of wine, gazing sombrely into the distance while he waited. When it arrived, he sank a quarter in one long draught. He was a long way from being maudlin drunk, but anger was overcoming him again and he needed the strong wine to counteract it.

One thing was clear. He'd get little help from Vincent, unless he paid the bastard up front in hard cash. Vincent thought he had him over a barrel – and that was no position to be in with a man as powerful as the Receiver. Greedy *shit*!

Karvinel took another long pull at his wine. It was starting to warm him, easing his blood and making him feel stronger, more vital. Earlier he'd wanted to punch Vincent. Now he was ready to kill him. If le Berwe were here now, he'd stab the bastard: shove his dagger up to the hilt in the fat man's gut, twisting it slowly to let the bastard feel the pain. Yes, that'd be good: watching le Berwe's features screw up in agony, his eyes pop out in horror as he realised he was about to die.

For Vincent le Berwe wanted all his money back. The lot. And although Nick had enough to repay all the debts he owed him, if Nick paid the lot he'd have nothing to live on. He wouldn't be able to buy stock, food or booze. A man couldn't live like that. This year had cleaned him out completely, until his gamble made him a little money. It was still dangerous, though. He daren't show off his new wealth by paying Vincent. Better that everyone still thought he was finished, washed up.

His eyes narrowed as he suddenly made a connection. His poor clerk Peter was dead, and it was Peter who had told him about the day that Ralph had died. He had been in Correstrete and had seen Vincent outside Ralph's shop, collecting leathers and hurrying away with them.

Maybe he could use that, Karvinel thought. After all, a Receiver could hardly afford to be accused of robbing the dead. And then he had another thought, one which made him stop and stare into the distance. One witness, and he was now dead.

What *had* Vincent been doing in Ralph's road the day the glover was murdered?

*   *   *

Simon and Baldwin entered the Cathedral with Roger de Gidleigh, the Coroner, all three bowing and genuflecting at the cross. They asked the candle-bearing Secondary where they would find Peter's body, and were directed forward to the small Lady chapel near the choir in which Peter lay. Jolinde still stood at the dead man's feet.

'He was brought here because one of the clerics said he heard Peter speak the name of the Blessed Virgin,' Jolinde told them in a hushed, reverent voice. 'Poor Peter.'

'Did you know him well?' Simon enquired.

'I shared a house with him, sir.'

'This is Jolinde Bolle,' Coroner Roger said shortly, glowering disapprovingly at the clerk.

'Ah. Then we shall wish to speak to you soon,' Baldwin said. 'Leave us, but don't wander far.'

Jolinde nodded tearfully and left them.

As soon as he had gone Baldwin motioned to Roger. 'As Coroner, you should inspect the body.'

'As Coroner, yes I should,' the man agreed. 'But I should do so before witnesses, before the whole jury.'

'Why don't I call the cleric back in?' Simon suggested, eyeing the corpse unhappily. He had never come to terms with this manhandling of dead men. He loathed the indignities of death, the smells and sights of violence and suffering. Any escape was to be seized upon. 'I could go and ask him to return to witness your enquiry . . .'

His hopes were dashed. 'Leave him out of it!' Roger snapped. 'There's nothing he can do to help. Especially if he is implicated in this crime.'

Simon nodded and subsided and the Coroner resolutely began to undress Peter. The Brothers had cleaned the poor emaciated body and rolled him in a plain winding sheet. When the corpse was naked, he inspected it, first studying the lad's hands and feet. 'No sign of his struggling with an attacker,' he noted. The hands were soft and unmarked by slashes or cuts.

Simon glanced at Baldwin. 'Attacker? I thought he keeled over in the choir here.'

'Even if he died here, if, as the good Dean tells us, this lad was poisoned,' Roger said heavily, 'I would want to confirm that he wasn't forced to swallow it against his will. No, there's no sign that he had his hands bound, nor his ankles.' Nor were there any scratches on his body. The lad's body was remarkably flawless. That, Roger thought to himself, was what happened when you were fortunate enough to spend your whole time living in a pleasant, secluded environment like the Cathedral grounds. This lazy devil probably never even had to mount a horse or journey outside the walls of Exeter. The Coroner felt an uncharacteristic wave of jealousy wash over him. There were attractions to the religious life. Even chastity could appeal, he thought, although he'd never dare say *that* to his wife, the shrewish bitch.

'What of his mouth?' Baldwin asked. 'Any loosened teeth? Scraped gums? A bruised or enlarged tongue?'

The Coroner's voice was muffled as he bent and peered in and around the dead man's mouth. 'Ugh! Still stinks of vomit.'

'Let me see,' Baldwin said, and peered in his turn, holding the man's jaw and cheeks. He sniffed. 'He was certainly sick. I should not be surprised if he inhaled his own vomit and drowned – but let us continue to assume the poison ended his life. His tongue has been bitten, look, but I should imagine that would be from his death throes. A man dying from a poisoning will sometimes go into spasmodic convulsions. At such times, he might well bite his tongue. There is no indication that he was forced to eat poison, though.'

'Which means he either took it willingly or by accident ... Or wasn't poisoned at all and we're chasing a will-o'-the-wisp.'

'Yes. Let us speak again to that admirable cleric who was here just now.'

'Good idea,' said Simon fervently. Anything, he thought, to get away from that hideous stench of death.

CHAPTER NINE

Jolinde paced anxiously up and down outside the Cathedral, wondering who the visitors were. The Coroner he recognised, of course, but the other two were strangers to him.

He was sad Peter was dead, for they had been good companions. It was never easy to share rooms with another male adolescent, but Peter and he had tolerated each other's company since they had met seven years ago, when both were Choristers. Almost at once they had recognised a similar set of interests: the same abilities with numbers; the same fascination with the writings of Bacon and other clerical dabblers in nature; the same urge to advance.

Both should have been able to anticipate some kind of progress in their careers. As Jolinde knew, you only had to be eighteen to become a sub-Deacon, or twenty-five to be a full Deacon. And he was almost twenty himself now. He should have been given some sort of senior responsibility by now. But no, he had no patronage in the Church hierarchy.

That was something his Succentor had told him when he was much younger, that there was no point being the best priest in the world if he never told anyone about it. Those who won promotion within the Church's hierarchy were either those who had money and friends and didn't need help, or those who were careful to make sure that they grabbed every opportunity for self-promotion. The best priest could remain a lowly countrified yokel seeing to the cure of souls within a tiny parish without friends to exercise their influence on his behalf: those who advanced were the men who were prepared to tell their superiors how they had succeeded in their posts and all the good work they had achieved. Only then would their patrons have ammunition to see to their advancement. And then the friends they had won in higher places could assist their progression upwards, easing their path for them. All benefited, since the recipient of the patronage would win greater financial rewards with his increased power, while the patron himself could expect to receive gifts – both early on in anticipation of his help and, later, in gratitude for it.

The Succentor's advice was welcome, because until then Jolinde had not realised how Byzantine were the politics of the Church. Not that it mattered now. He accepted that his own prospects of elevation were remote in the extreme. His father was friendly with the Dean, but Jolinde knew that the Bishop himself, and the Precentor beneath him, both had little time for Jolinde. There were others with greater abilities in writing and arithmetic, and many with better contacts at a higher level than the Dean. The Precentor himself had a young nephew who was intended for the next sub-Deacon's post.

He had no chance compared with the likes of that boy. Jolinde was nothing more than the illegitimate son of a local merchant. Hardly the sort to be made a Bishop – although he had once hoped to become a Deacon in his own right, or even a Vicar, or perhaps be fortunate enough to win the seat of an Annuellar. That would be a good life – up to £4 a year in stipends and little responsibility apart from ensuring that the daily service was conducted.

Illegitimacy was no barrier, of course. It could be viewed with disdain or contempt in a small village if the bastard concerned was born to a poor family, but that was natural. The vill itself would have to see to the child's feeding, his education, and if the place had little money, the peasants could be bound to a useless mouth in a time of famine. Conversely, if the father was rich, he would usually see to the feeding of the child and help the family and their friends by small gifts of money, perhaps even taking the child's education in hand.

As Jolinde's father had. Jolly would hardly have been brought here to the Cathedral if he hadn't been pointed out to the Succentor by his father. Sir Vincent had wanted him to be helped as far as possible and educated, for after all Jolinde was his first child, his only child in those days, before Vincent was married.

Jolinde knew that his father was a lusty man, always happy to go wenching, but that didn't colour Jolinde's view of him. If it wasn't that Vincent's first wife had been very jealous, Jolly might have gone to live with them in the house in the city. But the young girl *had* been jealous, and God knew what sort of a fuss she'd have kicked up if Jolly had been invited to live there. Her death had been very . . . convenient.

By then Jolinde was already living as a Secondary. He, like Vincent, thought that a career in the Church would be most congenial, but if that failed, he could easily learn law, which would make him still more useful to the merchant his father. That remained a possibility, but he would have to travel to University to learn more about the Common Law and that idea held little appeal for Jolinde now – since meeting Claricia at Sutton's Inn.

Peter had been thinking along the same lines. They had often spoken about their hopes for the future, and although Peter was inclined to remain in the Church, he knew that without a patron or relations who could assist him to a sub-Deacon's post, he too would have to consider the law.

Wincing, Jolinde recalled the scene of his death. It had been dreadful seeing his friend collapse like that, vomiting and crouching on all fours, then toppling sideways and going into convulsions, his face contorted with agony. It brought home to Jolinde just how fragile life was. They were much the same age. It could so easily have been him instead. He shuddered at the thought. Horrible!

It was a relief to glance once more at the Cathedral's doors and see the trio leaving. He walked to join them. 'Sirs? Can I return to him now?'

'No, you can wait here a while with us,' Coroner Roger snapped. 'We have some questions for you.'

Baldwin shivered. Roger appeared quite oblivious to the cold that was sinking into the knight's bones; when Baldwin looked at Simon, he saw the same indifference to the chill.

Neither man would mind remaining out here, Baldwin realised, and with the realisation came the solution. 'Rather than
question him here,' he intervened, 'I think we should go and
talk in the place where the two lived. I want to see all the
dead man's belongings.'

Jolinde nodded effusively. It would be better than staying
out here in this frost with the clouds preparing to smother
them with snow, he thought. 'Follow me, gentlemen.' He led
the way at a sharp pace, hurrying down the shallow incline
towards the southern wall and following around the new
Bishop's Palace. 'It's not far.'

'This is where you and your friend lived?' Baldwin asked
when they arrived at a small house near the city wall east of
the Cathedral.

'Yes, sir. We have been here in this chamber for several
years. Both of us left the Choristers at much the same time,
but we neither of us won advancement. I think poor Peter felt
it very strongly. It was like a failure to him.'

'You lived here? Ate here, slept here?'

'Um, well most of the time, yes. Peter lived here, although
he and I tended to eat with our Canons when they were here.
It is their responsibility to feed us, you see, but both of our
Canons are away from the city at present. Mine, Mark, is in
London with Bishop Walter, while Peter's, Geoffrey, has
gone on pilgrimage to Santiago, so we have been feeding
ourselves . . .'

Baldwin didn't comment and after a moment Jolinde
opened the door and thrust it wide. Beyond was a small hall
with the embers of the previous night's fire.

'Oh, it's out.' He felt suddenly tearful, realising that
from now on he would never again have company in this

place, not now Peter was dead. 'Forgive me,' he said shakily, 'I'll relight it. It won't take a moment . . .' The simple task was enough to drive away some of the sadness. He gathered up tinder and set it atop the few glowing chips, then added dried sticks and small pieces of kindling about and above it, crouching down low to blow steadily. Within a few minutes there was a faint crackling, and soon afterwards the kindling caught. He balanced a handful of thicker twigs, then a pair of small logs over the flames and rested back on his heels.

It was enough. The fire should be fine now. He smiled up at the three men. 'Please, gentlemen, sit if you wish,' he said, waving a hand at the two stools which were all the house possessed. 'I am happy to kneel. It is one thing we become accustomed to.'

'Were you there when he died today?' Baldwin asked.

Jolinde couldn't help the grimace of horror from passing over his features. 'It was terrible. He was late to the service, but he often has been recently and I didn't think much of it until I saw his face. Oh, poor Peter! He was yellow and green, as if he'd been up till late drinking and was about to spew, right there in his stall. I could see he wasn't really concentrating. He was so ill-looking, I felt sick myself just to look at him. And then he started spluttering, just frothed at the mouth and fell to the floor, as though his legs had been fighting to keep him upright and then couldn't do it any longer. He went down like an axed hog, and his limbs all wriggled and jerked . . . My God, it was awful!' he blurted, and covered his face with his hands.

'What sort of person was Peter?' asked Sir Baldwin after a moment or two.

'He was kind and good, sir.' Jolinde drew his hands away regretfully. 'I loved him like a brother. He was with me from the age of – oh, nine, I think. From then on we were insepa-rable. But when we both failed to proceed to become Deacons, we took on this place. It was an ideal base for us to continue our studies, and – well, it is a sociable Cathedral. We could study if we wished but if not, we could walk about the city.'

'We have heard that your friend may have stolen from Ralph the Glover – maybe even murdered the poor devil. What do you think?' Roger demanded brutally.

'Peter? Oh, that's rubbish,' said Jolinde, but he didn't meet the Coroner's eyes.

Baldwin spoke. 'We've also heard he might have been killed by felons because he pointed out one of their number.'

The young man shrugged. 'Who can say how outlaws will behave?'

'Was he wealthy?' Baldwin asked.

'Well, no. He had no patron here in the Cathedral.'

'Poverty is a common cause of theft,' Baldwin noted.

'Peter earned enough. He clerked for merchants who couldn't read; he helped Nick Karvinel occasionally. Anyway, if he had robbed Ralph, where is the proof? Where is the money he's supposed to have taken? There's nowhere to hide it in this hovel.'

Baldwin asked, 'How long do Secondaries remain here usually?'

'Oh, not terribly long . . . perhaps until they are twenty-one or so.'

'How old are you?'

'Twenty.'

131

'Where do Secondaries go when they get to twenty-one?'

'They would become Vicars or Annuellars, sir. Perhaps a few would leave to become Chaplains to a minor lord, and some might remain here as clerks.'

'What was Peter going to do?' Baldwin said.

'He was happy working for the Exchequer, sir. He was ever good with numbers: they held no mystery for him. He was considering learning the law but had not the money to go to University. I think Peter . . .' He hesitated.

'Yes?' Roger rasped. 'Spit it out, man!'

'Peter was not a worldly man. He liked the peace of the cloister. Outside that he was shy, confused. Anxious.'

'He is dead and some think he might have been murdered, others that he might have killed himself,' said Baldwin. 'What do you think?'

'He wouldn't have murdered himself willingly, but . . . He has not been well for some time, since the Feast of St Nicholas, sixth of December, when we took the money and jewels for the gloves.'

'In what way?' Baldwin was suddenly alert.

'He was anxious and fretful at first, sir,' Jolinde said. The words burst from him in a rush. It was a relief to be able to tell the story at last. 'He'd been upset since the glover died, and I thought it might be some sort of imbalance in his humours. I was concerned about him, especially since he wasn't being fed with his master, so I brought food to him.'

'Why should you do that?' Baldwin asked.

'He was pale, withdrawn . . . I thought he might have food poisoning. But he wouldn't go to the infirmarer. I think he was scared that he might find out he was more ill than he thought. Or maybe that he would find he was as ill as he feared.'

'And how ill was that, do you think?' Baldwin murmured.

Jolinde looked up, his face blanched. 'I heard him in his dreams – he thought he was possessed. He was convinced that he had been taken over by a demon and was gradually being driven away from the Church. It terrified him.'

Baldwin interrupted the sudden silence. 'He told you this?'

'No, sir. He wouldn't. He was too fearful of the way he was being pulled apart; yet I heard him crying out in his sleep, and then pleading with the devil he thought was inside him. Oh sir, it was *awful!* But there was nothing I could do.'

'You could have told one of the Canons or a Vicar. Sought assistance for him,' Coroner Roger pointed out with a frown.

'With him denying it? What could I have done to help him? I made sure he was fed, saw to it he had wine . . .' He broke off, miserable.

Baldwin took pity on him. 'You say that his Canon was away and that was why he wasn't being fed, and yet you seemingly had food for yourself. Was this from your Canon's table? He must be generous with his victuals if he provided so much you could fill a friend's mouth as well.'

Jolinde couldn't meet the grim, dark eyes. He had to look away. Still kneeling, he spoke quietly. 'Sir, I am not so honourable as Peter. I didn't notice how he was before last night because after we delivered the box to Ralph Glover, I met a girl and stayed in town. Since then I have remained in town most nights, only returning here for services.'

'You have been staying with this girl?' Baldwin confirmed. When the lad nodded, he asked for her name.

'Claricia Cornisshe, sir. She lives out near the Shambles, working in Sutton's Inn.'

'And she can confirm you have been with her?'

'Oh, yes. I've been with her each night.'

'Where did the food come from?'

'I bought it, sir. I have a good allowance.'

Simon was intrigued by this. 'You know that people say Peter was murdered, that he ate or drank poison and that is what killed him? This food you provided, where did you get it from?'

'The wine was from my barrel out in the storage room,' Jolinde said, pointing to the small door at the back of the hall. 'The bread came straight from the Cathedral's baker – it's delivered to us by Adam, another Secondary – while the meat came from butchers in the Shambles near the Fleshfold.'

'And how often did you purchase this food?' Simon pressed him.

'Regularly. I would bring him something every two or three days,' Jolinde said. Then he gaped. 'You don't suppose *I* could have killed Peter, do you?'

The Coroner sniffed. 'Who else would *you* suspect? You admit you brought him food. It would have been easy for you to have put poison into it, wouldn't it? And you brought it straight here to give to your room-mate, so no one else could succumb to it. It was a well-conceived plan, I'll give you that.'

'But I wouldn't have killed him – *why* should I kill him? What possible reason could I have had?'

'Maybe he'd already stolen the jewels from Ralph Glover and you wanted them for yourself?' Coroner Roger hazarded, squinting pensively. 'Or maybe it's simpler than that. You say you went with him to deliver the money and stuff early in the month?'

'Yes, the Feast of St Nicholas. We got a receipt for it all. Check with Canon Stephen, the Treasurer. He'll confirm that Peter and I brought the receipt back. He should have it now. Ralph the Glover signed it himself.'

'But what if you thought you could rob him, eh?' Roger asked shrewdly. 'What if you went back there on the twenty-first, killed the glover and took his money? What if your friend saw the jewels and money here in this hall after he heard about Glover's death? You might feel the need to silence him for ever, mightn't you?'

Jolinde felt as if his world was toppling about him. 'Me, kill Peter – kill the glover? Why, when I have enough money already? And where could I have hidden it?'

'Show us the rooms where you and your friend slept.'

Still ashen-faced with shock, Jolinde took them to the ladder and clambered upstairs. 'This was Peter's. That is mine,' he said, pointing to palliasses separated by a hanging cloth.

Baldwin studied the place. As Jolinde had said, there was nowhere to conceal even a small amount of money. Jolinde's area was as messy as Peter's, with blankets over the floor and a spare dirty shirt bundled up and hurled into a corner of the room. No chest, no box, not even a small sack was visible. No vial of poison – but that would have been discarded long ago in case of suspicion. Baldwin tentatively prodded at the bedclothes, but there was nothing beneath them.

Returning to Peter's side of the chamber, he crouched with the Coroner at the side of the messed bedclothes. Roger sniffed and looked at Baldwin, who nodded, saying, 'Yes, it smells as though his bowels were loose. I don't wish to put my hands into the filth there.'

'Poor fellow,' Jolinde said. He was close to tears. The sight of the scruffy bed, merely a leaking palliasse of straw with cheap blankets lain atop, brought home to him once more that Peter would never return. 'Poor Peter.'

Baldwin lifted the blankets gingerly and shook them. There was nothing here. The palliasse beneath was of thin material stuffed with a cheap filling of straw and hair. Baldwin took his dagger and slitted it from top to bottom, pulling out the stuffing, but there was nothing hidden inside.

He rose and went to Jolinde's own bed. He glanced at the lad, who nodded. 'If it'll prove my innocence,' he said.

Baldwin pulled his bed apart, but there was no money hidden among the straw. There was a chest with a water jug on top. Baldwin moved the jug and opened the chest, revealing robes, cloaks, shirts, the detritus of a young man. 'Did he have any other places in which he could have secreted things?'

'No. All our belongings are kept here.'

Simon could see that his friend was confused. A thought came to him. 'What of other friends? Could Peter have given the money to someone else? Someone who could hide it for him?'

'His only friends were among the Cathedral staff, sir,' Jolinde said dismissively. 'To whom could he have given such a treasure without being denounced? No one here would help him steal from the Cathedral.'

'Perhaps his friend wouldn't have known what he was being asked to look after,' Baldwin mused aloud.

'We are forgetting another person,' Coroner Roger said nastily. 'If *you* had stolen the stuff, Jolinde, you'd have given it to one of your friends to protect, wouldn't you?'

'Like who?' the young man scoffed, but then his expression took on a nervous look when the Coroner continued:

'*What about your woman?*'

137

CHAPTER TEN

When they left the glum Jolinde, Coroner Roger led the way to the gate and out to the High Street. They were walking along in the direction of Sutton's Inn where Jolinde's woman worked, when the Coroner suddenly saw a man he recognised. He called out and waved, and the man crossed the road to join them.

'Bailiff, Sir Baldwin – this is the city Bailiff, William de Lappeford. It was he who found the dead glover's body.'

'Oh?' Baldwin said, turning to the man with interest.

'That's right, sir. I found him when his apprentice Elias had murdered him.'

De Lappeford was a large, slow man with a heavy forehead and a fixed frown of concentration. He looked the sort of person whom Baldwin would trust to obey an order entirely honestly, but who should never be put in a position of authority where independent thought was needed.

Sir Baldwin asked mildly, 'What do you think of the apprentice?'

'Elias? A fool, if he thought he could get away with killing his master.'

'Did you find any money in Elias's belongings?'

'No, nor jewels. He must have hidden them somewhere already.'

'How old was the corpse?' Simon wanted to know.

'Oh, it was fresh. Still quite warm to the touch, and the blood hadn't congealed.'

'So it's not likely the lad had much time to run away and hide things, is it?' Simon pointed out.

'Perhaps not. But Ralph was up early.'

'Ah, Bailiff Puttock,' the Coroner smiled, 'you don't know the people of this city that well, obviously. It happens that Ralph was up well before dawn each day, when it was his habit to leave his home for a walk. The apprentice could easily have waited until his master had left the house, before going to the strongbox, taking the jewels and money, then dashing off to hide them somewhere. His master must have returned, realised what had happened, so his apprentice killed him.'

'Would the glover have gone to his parish church each morning?' Baldwin enquired.

'He went to the Cathedral for the Lady Mass at first light every day. He always used to say it was the most pleasant of all the services, standing there before the statue of the Virgin. He said She reminded him of his own wife.'

'The lady is dead, I assume?' Baldwin asked gravely.

William nodded. 'Yes, sir. Mistress Glover and their daughter died when a wagon overturned in the street. They were smothered with barrels of stores.'

'An accident?'

'Oh yes, Sir Baldwin,' the Coroner confirmed. 'A wheel came off and it rolled over. Nothing suspicious in it.'

Baldwin continued, 'So Ralph was out of the house that morning and Elias meantime could have taken his money and hidden it elsewhere. Is there anywhere that seems likely?'

'I wondered about his woman, young Mary at the baker's, but she denies it,' William said. 'She admitted that Elias had been there that morning, but as for giving her anything, she just said no. Said that he had seen her almost every day for the last few months, but that morning he arrived and they stood chatting for a long time. Nothing more. They were in her father's shop, and he was there. He confirmed her story, and in fact he said that Elias ran out, realising he was late.'

'Was his master cruel to him?' Simon interrupted. 'I've seen plenty of cases where a man was so scared of being beaten that he took action first to protect himself. Could this Elias have attacked his master in self-defence?'

'No, I don't think so,' Roger answered. 'The bread was still quite warm in Elias's hands, so he *had* hurried back from the baker. And Ralph Glover was the kindest of men.'

Baldwin asked, 'Has he confessed?'

'No, murderers rarely do,' William said off-handedly. 'But Ralph himself had asked me to call on him, saying he'd discovered a theft. I daresay the apprentice was the culprit.'

'Ralph spoke to you that morning?' Simon asked.

'No, the day before, but it was in the street and he said it was a matter to be discussed in private. Obviously because it was embarrassing that his own apprentice was robbing him.'

'So it was a theft that had already happened – yet you say the boy took the stuff and killed his master *before* going to hide it!' Baldwin smiled. 'This sounds inconsistent.'

'Look, the main point is, the apprentice is a fool. He stabbed the glover with his own dagger then admitted it was his own.'

Baldwin studied de Lappeford a moment. 'You are telling me that the boy left his knife in the body?'

'No, he had dropped it.'

Simon and Baldwin exchanged a glance. Simon said doubtfully, 'Was he drunk?'

'No.'

'But you're saying he was stupid enough to kill his master and steal his money, intelligent enough to conceal the money where you can't find it, but thick enough to drop his own incriminating dagger there on the floor by his master?'

'Felons often make mistakes.'

Baldwin tilted his head to one side. Addressing the Coroner, he asked, 'Did the boy's blade match the stab wound?'

'The wounds were about half an inch wide, while his blade was an inch at the base.'

'Is the body . . .?'

'It's buried, Sir Baldwin,' Coroner Roger admitted apologetically.

'Well, at least tell me how many wounds there were.'

'Seven at the front of his torso, all about the heart; another four in his back.'

'So it was a frantic attack,' Simon mused.

Baldwin was trying to calm himself but the excitement was almost overwhelming him. 'Coroner, if a man is stabbed

141

so many times, I've always found it was a berserk attack, not one committed by a rational person. And the dagger is always thrust in up to the hilt – bang, bang, bang. That would mean the wounds should be at least an inch wide. How long was the blade? Would it have gone from one side through to the other if forced hard?'

'The glover was a big man, Sir Baldwin. No, the blade couldn't have gone all the way through.'

'Nonetheless, the lad's blade was surely not the murder weapon. Did the apprentice show any sign of being wild? Did he appear ferocious? Enraged or mad?'

William de Lappeford cleared his throat. 'There was no one else to arrest. Who would kill a happy-go-lucky fellow like Ralph for no reason? It makes no sense. At least we know that the apprentice was aware of the money. He must have wanted to steal it, that's what we . . .' He threw a glance at his Coroner. 'It's what *I* think, anyway.'

'And you think,' Simon pressed him, 'that the death of the Secondary in the Cathedral ties up with Ralph's murder?'

'I don't know.'

He was saved from further interrogation by the Coroner's dry chuckle. 'Enough! William, you may leave us now.' While the sulking man stomped off, Coroner Roger said nothing, clearly amused by the discomfiture of the city's Bailiff. Then: 'I think that shows the standard of the local investigation. You heard, Sir Baldwin, how that fool of a Bailiff – saving your presence, Master Simon! – said the glover was stabbed? Well, his body was in the shop. If Elias was acting on a sudden whim or killing his master out of fear, having already robbed him, why should he have stabbed Ralph there, when the money box was in the house? Did

Ralph tell Elias to go to his shop, then, when the robbery was discovered, did he accuse his apprentice, who was by then so petrified with terror that he stabbed his master?'

'It is feasible,' Baldwin commented doubtfully. 'Yet I think the apprentice may well be innocent.'

The Coroner answered briskly: 'Let me just say that I would appreciate a second opinion of the matter. I find it difficult to imagine that a weakly looking twerp like Elias could attempt to murder his master. Most people were fond of our Ralph, Elias among them. And there is another thing.'

'I rather thought there might be,' Baldwin smiled.

'Put simply, Sir Baldwin, I have to wonder whether there is a connection between the death of the glover and the Secondary. And, if the two deaths *are* connected, how should I explain the fact that Elias was in gaol at the time of the second death? *That* is my difficulty.'

'And you would like our assistance in investigating it?'

The Coroner smiled innocently. 'If the Dean can ask for help with his dead Secondary, why shouldn't I request your advice on Ralph Glover's demise?'

A short while later the three men were seated at a table in Sutton's Inn near the Shambles. Simon caught the eye of a girl and beckoned but she carefully turned from him to serve another man, presumably a local. It took the Coroner's hoarse bellow to persuade the girl to deign to acknowledge them.

'Sirs? Ale or wine?'

'Wine for me,' said Roger. Baldwin asked for a thin ale, while Simon ordered a strong winter brew and a meat pie.

143

When she returned, Roger took his wine and eyed her contemplatively. 'So you've taken to young clerics now, have you, Claricia?'

'Who told you that?' she demanded, a flush rising in a steady tide from her neck upwards.

While Roger questioned her, Baldwin studied her dispassionately. Claricia Cornisshe was pretty, in a very simple way: her pale-featured, oval face had high cheekbones and slanted, almond-coloured eyes under delicately curving brows. Her nose was slender and slightly tip-tilted, and her lips were full with a faint upward lift, as though she was considering sharing a joke.

But her humour was apparently in short supply as Roger spoke.

'Your lover boy: Jolinde. His friend Peter, did you know him at all?'

'Peter? He wasn't the sort to come to an Inn. I wouldn't want to entertain him anyway.'

'But you're happy to entertain this other one, this Jolinde?' Simon asked. He had sunk a good half of his ale and suddenly the world was looking and feeling better as he took up his pie and bit into it.

She looked at him without interest. 'Jolly's different. He's not all holier-than-thou. I doubt whether he'd manage to stay on at the Cathedral until he gets anywhere – not that he cares. He's too grand to remain a cleric.'

'Too grand?' scoffed Roger. 'What's so grand about a pissy priest?'

'He's the son of Vincent de Berwe, didn't you know? Jolly'll be worth more than you when his father dies, Coroner,' she stated tartly.

Claricia instinctively liked the look of both strangers with the Coroner. The older one, the one with the beard, had interesting features, with a jagged scar that reached from his jaw almost up to his temple, giving him a slightly rakish appearance. Apart from that, when his attention was on her she could feel his utter concentration, as if everyone else in the place could hang; he had ears only for what she herself had to say. It was immensely flattering.

The other, the Bailiff, had a vulnerability about him. His face had a rugged, lived-in look. Grey eyes returned her frank study with a hint of amusement, as if he was challenging her, but there was a lot of sadness in his face, too.

It was the bearded one who spoke first, while the Coroner sat back, grumbling.

'Claricia, I wanted to ask you just a few more questions. Would you mind helping us?'

'Don't see why not. Depends. Are you trying to hurt Jolinde? I won't see Jolly stuffed just to find a scapegoat for the Dean.'

'There's no risk of that. No, I just wanted to hear what you thought of the two boys.'

'Jolly's fun. That's all. We've been seeing each other for a few weeks.'

'You say he will inherit Vincent's money?' Simon asked.

She glanced at him, nodding slowly. 'Vincent's promised him. Jolly couldn't make it as a priest. He hasn't got the learning – or the willpower, to judge by what he's been doing with me! And le Berwe hasn't got any other children, so who else would inherit?' There was a pride in the way she lifted her chin, as if daring them to condemn her. All trace of her flush was gone, and in its place she wore a knowing smile

145

that made Simon grin and Baldwin cough with faint embarrassment.

'And he was friendly with this Peter?'

'They had lived together for many years. They were comfortable with each other.'

'Sometimes even the closest friends can kill when tempers flare,' Simon murmured.

'Not Jolly. He's not the sort to turn to a blade. He wouldn't want to risk someone hurting *him*,' she chuckled, then saw their expressions. 'What?'

'This Peter,' Baldwin said slowly, 'was killed with poison – *if* he was murdered. A man who fears attacking another might well use such a weapon.'

'Not Jolly,' she repeated with conviction. 'He wouldn't kill a man. Why'd he want to?'

'Why would anyone want to?' Simon shrugged. 'Do you know of someone who might have had a grudge against Peter?'

'No. Why should someone want to harm a man who lived in the Cathedral and only came to the city to help merchants? How could he offend people? He was hardly ever here.'

'Peter and Jolinde delivered money and gems to the glover who died,' Baldwin told her. 'And when the glover was killed, the gems not already stitched to gloves were missing. It has been suggested that Jolinde or Peter killed the glover, that Jolinde wanted the money and took it, killing his friend in the process . . .'

'Oh, rubbish! Don't you think that if Jolly was going to rob Peter, he'd do something faster than poison? If Peter had suspected something or seen Jolly doing the deed, he could have spoken out – said that Jolly had poisoned him to steal the money. *Did* Peter tell anyone?'

'No. Peter died in the Cathedral, but he didn't accuse anyone,' Baldwin said slowly.

'I'd think it pretty unlikely that he was poisoned by Jolly, then. If he was, he'd have accused Jolly in front of witnesses. And if he *was* the accomplice of a murderer and thief, wouldn't he have wanted to confess his sins? Surely he'd admit to having killed a man so that he could win absolution before he died?'

'You met Jolinde on sixth December?' Baldwin asked, abruptly changing the subject. 'The Feast of St Nicholas?'

'Jolly came in here to the tavern on his way back to the Cathedral after delivering the money to Ralph. Dragged Peter in after him, not that Peter really wanted to be here. He was quiet-looking – anxious, I suppose, but Jolly persuaded him to have just one cup of wine with him.'

'And you liked the look of Jolinde.'

She pushed out her lips in a *moue*. 'Well, he was polite, and interested in what I said. It's not as if many men will listen to a wench from a tavern, but he did. It was nice. And the next night he came back, and the night after that.'

'Yet he manages to get back into the Cathedral when the gates are locked in order to attend his services on time.' Baldwin mused.

'He has his own way in and out,' she agreed, her expression smug.

'Which is?'

'How should I know? I've never asked him.'

'When the two of them were in here, how did they seem together?' Simon asked.

MICHAEL JECKS

'Not very happy,' she admitted slowly. 'They'd been having words, I reckoned. Both looked a bit warm, you know? Maybe they'd had a disagreement. But Vicars and so on are more serious about things, aren't they?'

'Did Peter lose his temper, or Jolly?'

'Oh, neither really. I only saw Peter look angry the once.'

'When was that?'

'It was yesterday, early in the afternoon, when Nick Karvinel came in. I saw Peter deliberately turn his back on him. It looked really rude – a calculated insult. I've no idea why he did it. Jolly was left standing there gaping, with his pot halfway to his mouth. Peter wouldn't turn around again until Karvinel had gone. Mind you, Peter didn't stay long afterwards. He looked really ill . . . sick as well as furious.'

'But Karvinel was the merchant whom Peter helped, wasn't he?'

'Yes.'

'And you have no idea why Peter should have reacted like that on seeing his master?'

'I asked Jolly a bit later, but he didn't know. Said Peter always took things too seriously; said he had to learn that life was too brief not to be enjoyed to the full.'

'What did he mean by that?'

'Ask him. All I can say is, he's had his own troubles in his time.' Claricia eyed the two men with a hint of exasperation. 'Go on – talk to Jolly. He's no murderer. If he was upset with someone, he wouldn't kill them. Anyway, if Peter *had* thought he'd been poisoned, he'd have told someone, wouldn't he? He'd have called for help and accused his killer. I reckon he probably just ate a piece of bad meat or something.'

148

'You know Jolinde has been buying food for Peter?' Baldwin asked suddenly.

'Of course I know. He'd buy it on his way here. So what? It was kind of him. Maybe you ought to go to the butcher who sold him his meat and see if any other customers have fallen ill. A few times he brought bread, sometimes meat, sometimes sweetmeats. The bread was certainly all right because we ourselves ate it. He'd bring some of it up to my room and we'd eat there in peace. I've not become ill so it can't be that food.'

'Did you always take the food up with you? For example, last night?'

'Not always. Sometimes he'd leave the rest of it in the hall in his bag. He did so last night.'

'Where exactly did he leave it?' Simon asked.

Claricia looked at him. He was leaning forward and staring at her like a hawk fixed upon a mouse. A swift shudder of fear went through her. 'Just there,' she gulped, pointing to a rough table near the door to the screens passage.

'Then anyone could get to it,' Baldwin noted.

Simon nodded. 'Tell us, girl. Was there anyone you recognised in here last night?'

She shrugged off-handedly. 'Only Nick Karvinel. It was a quiet night. Nick actually asked about Peter – but only because he said he had some business coming up soon and Peter always clerked for him, taking notes and so on.'

'So he could have tampered with your boyfriend's parcel?' Simon said shortly.

Claricia looked from him to Baldwin, who now sat gazing into the middle distance with a faint puckering at his brow. 'What do you mean?'

149

'He could have put poison on it,' Simon explained.

Her face paled. 'But I ate some last night.'

'While you ate, someone may have sprinkled poison on the rest,' Simon grunted.

'Only the meat then. We ate all of the bread,' she said.

'Ah!' Simon exclaimed. 'That narrows it down.' He glanced at Baldwin, but the knight merely shrugged, his expression thoughtful.

CHAPTER ELEVEN

The gaol was in the castle, at the northernmost tip of the city – a large, red-stone block which dominated the city from its perch on the hill.

Elias was in a squalid cell, along with many other men. All were forced to make use of a single leathern bucket for their toilet. A man had apparently become ill overnight, calling out and then going into convulsions; he had kicked the pail over, adding the noisome reek of its contents to the already foul interior.

The suffering man lay on his side near a wall, his face gaunt and grey with a faintly green tinge.

'He won't last the day,' Baldwin murmured compassionately.

'I fear not,' the Coroner agreed. The fellow had evidently rolled over in his fever, and now his clothing was bespattered with the bucket's contents.

Elias turned out to be a tall, gangling youth in his early twenties, pale-faced with terror. 'There are rats in here, sir,' he said pathetically to Roger as they called him out of the cell and studied him in the corridor outside.

'Sod the cell and sod the rats,' Roger said unsympathetically. 'You're here to answer any questions these gentlemen wish to ask you.'

'I didn't do it, sirs,' Elias stated. Although he mumbled the words they were clear enough, as was his bitterness at being incarcerated. 'I've never been in a place like this before, and I didn't ought to be here now.'

'What didn't you do?' Simon asked.

'Murder my master. I couldn't have!' he cried. 'He was like my father, was Master Ralph.'

'Is that why you robbed him?' demanded Roger harshly.

While he professed his innocence and denied any involvement in either the theft or the murder, Baldwin studied the apprentice carefully. His long slender fingers twitched and moved as he spoke, pointing at his breast in devout rejection of guilt, clasping together as he fervently implored their belief, washing over and over as he proclaimed his innocence. There was helplessness and despair in his eyes but not, so far as Baldwin could detect, any hint of guilt.

'Tell us exactly what happened that morning,' Baldwin said at last when Roger had run out of accusations.

Elias licked his lips, then went through the whole sorry story once more. He had told it so often now that the tale was beginning to sound artificial even to himself. Could he have remembered things wrongly? Might he have invented something by mistake? He had heard of such things. It was growing difficult to know what was true and what wasn't.

Baldwin listened attentively. 'So you tried to get in by the door at the front of the hall, then went to the back. You didn't at any time go into the shop?'

'No, sir. I tried the shop's handle, but it was locked.'

'Yet when Bailiff William tried it, the shop was open,' the Coroner grunted.

Elias held out his hands helplessly. 'It was locked when *I* tried it.'

Baldwin nodded. 'With regard to the money and jewels your master had been given – had you ever seen them?'

'Yes, I saw them when the two clerks brought them, early in the month.'

'Who were they?'

'Master Peter and Jolinde Bolle.'

'Did they bring them to the shop?'

'Yes. My master and I were working when they arrived, so they had to.'

'And your master's shop has how many rooms?'

'Only the one.'

'So you were in the same room with your master? You saw everything as the two clerics handed over the jewels?'

'Yes, sir. I saw it all. The clerics had brought money and gems with them and they passed over the money and counted it with my master, getting him to sign their receipt with his mark and seal, then they tipped out all the jewels and pearls that he was to use to decorate the gloves and got him to mark their receipt again.'

'Do you remember the amounts?' Simon asked.

'There was two pounds, one shilling and one farthing in cash; in stones there were two rubies, forty-four gems and a small number of pearls. My master was not happy because the

MICHAEL JECKS

money was less than he had agreed with the Dean and he wasn't
sure how to split up the quantities of gems between gloves, for
he had been asked to make ten pairs and the gems and rubies
wouldn't divide easily between them. He was grumpy about it
and said that he'd speak to the Dean, but one of the clerks,
Jolinde Bolle, said that the Treasurer had decided they couldn't
afford so much, not with the building work continuing.'

'I see,' Baldwin said musingly, then he looked up as a
sudden thought struck him. 'You say your master put *his
mark* to the receipts?'

'Yes, sir.'

'Could he read?'

'No, sir.'

Baldwin's face cleared. 'Good. I begin to see a way
through part of this mystery. Perhaps, anyway. Where did
your master put the money and jewels?'

'Sir, he had a strongbox in his chamber. When he was in
his shop, he would take it there with him so that he had
money to give in change to buyers, but also so he knew
where it was. He didn't want to be robbed like poor Master
Karvinel. He has . . .'

'Yes, yes, we know of Karvinel,' Baldwin interrupted
testily. 'Tell us about the money.'

'When the clerics and my master had counted it all, he put
it into his strongbox. That was that.'

'To return to the day he died: the money was all gone?'

'Yes, sir.'

'So someone could have broken in, taken the money from
the box and fled with it,' Baldwin considered. 'Maybe that
was happening when the glover arrived and he confronted
the thief. The thief struck him down, then made his escape?'

154

Baldwin turned to the Coroner. 'You told us that there were some seven wounds in the front of his chest and four in his back. Simon said at the time that it sounded frenzied, but all the lunatic killers I have known lose all sense of restraint when they stab. They thrust with main force, and that drives the blade up to the hilt. Yet Elias's knife was an inch broad at the hilt. The wounds were all half-an-inch wide, so it couldn't have been Elias thrusting home his own knife.'

'It's a thought,' Coroner Roger said.

'Let's take it as a proposition. Perhaps someone went to the glover's door and asked to see something in the shop? They entered, and as soon as the killer could, he whipped out a dagger and stabbed him four times in the back. The glover fell to the floor, and the killer made sure he was dead by stabbing him again in the chest. Then he made his way back into the hall, up to the chest, took what he needed, and departed.'

'But, sir,' Elias protested weakly, 'if he'd done that, I'd have been able to get in. As it happened, the door was locked, and so was the back door. Yet when I returned to the front, the door was ajar.'

'Right.' Baldwin started again. 'The murderer went to the glover's door and asked to see something in the shop. He followed Ralph inside, murdered him, took his keys and locked the shop door. Then he returned to Ralph's house, locked the doors after him, and ransacked the place looking for the chest. When he . . .'

Simon growled, 'Baldwin, what about the apprentice? He'd have known that Elias would soon be back with bread in the normal routine.'

'Ah yes,' Baldwin said, turning to Elias. 'You were away a while, talking to Mary, you said?'

'Yes, sir.'

'Would you say you were away for longer than usual?'

Elias recalled his hasty rush back to the house. 'Oh, yes, sir. I was very late, I knew that.'

'The thief obviously knew he had plenty of time,' Baldwin said. 'He knew Ralph was alone, and that must mean he knew that the apprentice was out.'

'You are assuming someone planned this?' Coroner Roger demanded. 'What if it was a mere spur-of-moment attack?'

'There are too many coincidences,' Baldwin told him. 'A man decides to rob the glover just at the time that the glover has all that wealth; he stabs the glover without knowing whether someone else is there. How often does someone do that? And just by chance, this is the day that Elias is particularly late home . . . No, it does not sound likely to me.'

'You mean it was all premeditated?' the Coroner asked sceptically.

'The murderer knew what the household routines were; he had either been watching it, or had someone tell him,' Baldwin said. 'The man who killed Ralph must have been confident that Elias would be late back. Yes, he knew he had plenty of time.'

'And yet Elias was back before he had finished,' Roger pointed out.

'Yes, but maybe the man couldn't find the chest as quickly as he had hoped. Maybe he hadn't expected Elias to be back so quickly.'

Roger stood and motioned Elias back into the gaol. 'Sorry about this, lad, but you'll have to stay in there a while longer.'

'Just one last question or two, please,' Baldwin said. 'Elias, your girlfriend – has she been able to visit you?'

'No, sir. I wish she could, but Mary is very busy and I doubt her father would want her to come to a place like this.'

'Quite understandable!' Baldwin said, glancing about him. 'Now: is there anything else you can tell us about that day, Elias?'

The apprentice licked his lips and peered at the Coroner. 'There is one thing, sir,' he said hesitantly. When Baldwin nodded, he spoke slowly. 'That morning, not long after Ralph had left for church, I stayed a while in my bed, but I was woken by the cleric Peter. He wanted to put some more jewels and money in my master's strongbox. He said that he and his friend had made a mistake when they had delivered the payment and the jewels before. There wasn't enough, just as Ralph had said. I let Peter upstairs and opened the chest, and added the extra coins and jewels in the purse he gave me.'

Baldwin and the other men were frowning uncomprehendingly.

'He brought extra treasure for Ralph?' Baldwin muttered, baffled.

'He asked me not to tell anyone, said it would get him into trouble,' Elias nodded wretchedly. 'That was why I didn't mention it before. But it can't hurt him now, can it?'

Coroner Roger glanced at Baldwin. 'That's enough,' he said. 'I have other cases to look into. Is there anything else you want to know?'

Baldwin shook his head. 'No. Godspeed, Elias.'

'Merry Christmas!' Elias said, mournfully, as he turned and trudged back to his cell.

*　　　*　　　*

157

The nervous, smiling boy capered into the woods when he returned from the city. He was worried, because his master was sometimes in a bad mood when he came back, but today Hob was relieved to see that Sir Thomas was laughing as he sat back on a tree trunk, one arm around Jen, the other gripping a wineskin, from which he poured wine into his mouth. He stopped, grinned wolfishly, then tipped wine over Jen's breasts, making her squeak. Sir Thomas dropped the skin and thrust her backwards, grasping her torso and slobbering over the wet tunic, sucking the juice from it, then, pulling her tunic apart to free her breasts, he began to lick more slowly at her flesh while she smiled down at him, cradling his head with an elbow like a mother with her child.

Seeing Hob approach, she frowned and shook her head, signing to him with her eyes not to interrupt, and Hob slipped back into the trees again.

He left them there. There was no point in trying to speak to Sir Thomas if he was busy with Jen. When he started squirming on top of her like a dog on a bitch, neither would listen. Worse, Sir Thomas would get angry. Aye, he'd throw something at Hob, scare Hob. Make him run. Hob didn't like Sir Thomas to be angry; Hob had to please Sir Thomas, because Sir Thomas was his protector. That was what Jen had told him. She said Sir Thomas was their guard. He looked after them. That was why she had to keep him happy, and Hob had to as well.

Hob wandered disconsolately along the pathway through the trees. All the branches were empty now. Hob didn't like seeing them bare like that. It took away all the places to hide. The beech trees, they tried to keep their leaves: there were still a few clinging to the bough overhead. Hob liked beech trees.

It was a long time since he and Jen had met Sir Thomas. Beforehand, Hob and Jen had lived alone, ever since the dreadful famine when the crops all spoiled on the ground and their parents died. They had been allowed to remain in their little cottage after they were orphaned, living on whatever Jen could bring in. She knew Hob would never be able to earn enough to keep them. It hadn't been easy for her, not at a time when grain rose in price daily.

Their mum had brought eight kids into the world, but only three survived the hungry years. Or so Jen said: their oldest brother had been taken away by the Bishop's men when their parents were still alive and she fondly assumed he had lived. Hob was only young when he'd gone. That was before his mother had died. It was years ago now. Ages. Jen said it was better to forget, but Hob couldn't. Not after finding her body.

Hob's eyes filled with tears at the memory of the wretched, emaciated corpse sprawled in her feeble agony. Hob had found her lying over the fire when he came back from his work scaring crows from the fields. It looked as if she had just toppled over and died on the smouldering logs. She must have felt the flames scorching her flesh, but was too weak to get away. Hob had stood in the doorway staring. He couldn't even cry out for help. Not that anyone could do anything for her. Her body came away in halves when they dragged at her, burned through in the middle.

That was when their father arrived, called by one of the other men in the vill. Strong, good-looking, he was, but all Hob could remember was his face cracking with horror when he saw what had happened.

So many others had died, there was scarcely anyone to offer sympathy. All had lost family or friends; the vill itself was falling apart. Rain fell in torrents and the plants that took root withered where they straggled upwards. Those which produced grain were so sodden that it must be dried in special ovens first, and when bread was baked, it was un-nutritious and unwholesome. Not that the villagers would have refused it. There was nothing else, not after that hideous summer. All the winter food was gone, the pigs and sheep eaten long before.

It was midwinter when their father gave up. He had kept Jen and Hob in scraps of food as and when he could, but with the loss of his wife, he had lost his desire to live. One morning Hob woke in the family bed knowing that something was wrong. Jen wasn't there, but she often wasn't. She had her own friends and more and more often stayed away from the home. Father was past caring. But this morning Hob jerked awake to find that his father was dead. His face was slack, the jaw hanging. Hob hadn't even been able to cry that time. Lost in the depths of despair, he rocked back and forth, cradling himself, until Jen came.

That was 1316, so Jen said. He had been almost thirteen if the priest could be believed. And not long afterwards Jen and Hob left the village for ever.

Jen was clever: Hob knew she was. When she realised that their father had abandoned hope, she had made up her mind to find someone who could protect them both. Another man in the vill had already suggested that she should give herself to him and live under his roof. He had promised to feed her and look after her – but Hob, he said, would have to find somewhere else to live.

That was no bargain as far as Jen was concerned. She told Hob later that she wouldn't take a mate who wouldn't look after Hob as well. Hob wasn't sure what she meant, but he was glad that she wasn't going to leave him. That much registered.

She had known Sir Thomas already; confessed to Hob that she had been as good as married to the nobleman since the summer. He had ridden past the vill and she caught his eye. The knight had offered her food and she had accepted. When their father was gone and buried, Jen and Hob left the vill and went to live at Sir Thomas's manor. Jen was welcomed, although Hob was abused, being little use for anything but the most menial work; at a time of famine no one wants a useless mouth to feed. Sir Thomas's men made their feelings plain. They kicked Hob, hurled stones and spat at him, and beat him with sticks, just as they might ill-treat a cat or a stray dog. Hob didn't know why, but everyone hated him. Only Jen loved him.

He sniffed again, wiping at his eye with a grubby sleeve. Hob wouldn't whine; Hob wouldn't complain. Hob was strong.

He'd never been popular in the vill. He was used to being made fun of, being thrashed. It hurt, but everyone treated him like that because he was different. One day, Jen saw him being kicked and she told Sir Thomas, who saved Hob. Rushing out into his yard with a cudgel, he smashed the hardened knob over one man's head, then another's, and hauled the squirming boy to his feet. That was when Sir Thomas had bellowed at them, 'You leave him alone – he's under my protection. He has no father, no brother, so *I* am his defender. If you want to beat him you'll answer to me!'

Hob had not been hit by Sir Thomas's men since then. Only by Sir Thomas himself – occasionally. But it was his own fault. Hob knew he must deserve it if his own defender clobbered him.

'Hob? Where are you?'

'H-here,' he stammered, standing.

Jen stood in the track a few yards away. Her breast was covered again, her hair decorously tied up, but her face was flushed. She saw his tear-streaked face and held out a hand. 'You been thinking about Mum again?' He nodded. 'Come on, Hob, let's get back. I hope you have good news for him.'

'Yes, sister,' he said hesitantly, trying to get the words out before the stammer strangled him. 'The m-merchant's clerk is dead.'

CHAPTER TWELVE

'What do you think, Sir Baldwin?' Roger asked. The three men walked from the gaol, across the castle's court, and stood in the road outside.

'It is hard to know what to think,' Baldwin admitted. 'I cannot see that poor creature as a murderer and I am confused by Peter's visit to the glovemaker on the day Ralph died. Why should he go there? And where did the additional gems and money come from?'

'And how did Peter die?' the Coroner grunted.

'And why did the Dean want us to investigate?' Baldwin mused.

'I think he himself is certain Peter was murdered,' the Coroner grumbled.

'If so, he must believe the man responsible is from the city, not the Cathedral,' said Baldwin.

'Why?' Roger asked.

'Because a religious man would hardly expect to find a murderer among his flock,' Baldwin said dismissively.

'Well, he may think as he wishes; I have a duty to seek out murderers,' the Coroner growled. 'Wherever he lives, my duty is to see the person responsible captured. If he is answerable to Canon Law I may pass him back to the Church authorities, but only if he is so answerable. Until such time as he can prove that to me, I have every right to investigate and keep him in my gaol.'

'And when he's found guilty, you have the right to be in the Bishop's Court to officially witness the sentencing,' Baldwin said.

'Yes,' came the uncompromising reply. '*And* witness the hanging.'

'But if the murderer wasn't from the city, what then?' Simon continued.

'Then we have little authority to do anything,' said the Coroner. 'Sir Baldwin, Bailiff, I have much other work to occupy me, but this affair troubles me – especially the idea that the dead man might have stolen from the Cathedral.'

'What will you do?' Baldwin asked him.

'Frankly, I have no idea. There's nothing much to go on. With no witness seeing the theft, with no witness seeing Peter hiding his stolen goods, with no witness seeing poison being administered, I don't see how I can do very much.'

'If Peter *was* murdered, it would be a great shame to let his murderer go free,' Baldwin said slowly.

'Undoubtedly. But what would you recommend? I am a busy man. Even now I expect there are calls for me to go and view corpses between here and the Cornish border. I haven't the time or inclination to search for killers when they may be as insubstantial as marsh gas.'

'I quite understand,' Baldwin said. He sighed. 'And you are probably right. But I am struck by the fact that so many things seem to have happened: Karvinel's robbery, the murder of Ralph, and now this fellow Peter dying. It seems odd, especially now we have heard from Elias about Peter's curious second visit. What lay behind that?'

Coroner Roger stretched. 'God knows. Since he's dead, we may never find out. Anyway, as far as I am concerned, with Christmas Day tomorrow, I won't be able to do more for a while.'

Baldwin looked at him, his features serious. 'What do you think, Roger? Was Peter murdered?'

The Coroner met his gaze without blinking. 'My report will note the facts. There is no evidence to suggest he was murdered.'

'Which means Elias is still in danger.'

'If Peter was murdered, it'd make me more inclined to consider Elias innocent.'

Simon interrupted them. 'Now we know what will go in your report, what do you *think*, Coroner?'

Roger glanced away. 'I don't think Elias is a murderer, but if he didn't kill Ralph, who did? And why would someone poison Peter?'

Henry mockingly held out his hand for the other Choristers to kiss, just as they would usually bow and kiss the ring of the Bishop. He held his head superciliously, nose in the air, peeping at his peers as they filed past, some giggling, most trying desperately to hold their faces in a solemn mask – and failing.

'You shouldn't be doing that,' Luke cried. His voice was petulant, he knew, but he couldn't help it. It was horrible seeing Henry making fun of the most important aspects of the Feast Day. Henry was a cheat: a liar and a cheat. He'd taken the election when Luke knew *he* should have won. It wasn't fair that Henry had got all the others to vote for him. Not that there was anything he could do about it now. The cheat had won unfairly, bribing other Choristers to give him their votes, and Luke had fallen by the wayside. As soon as the hands went up for Henry, those who were wavering saw how the rest were going and supported Henry too. And when the boys who had promised themselves to Luke saw that their leader was lost, they instantly conformed. It was a unanimous vote.

In his heart of hearts Luke might have been able to sympathise with them. If he had been one of them, he would probably have voted along with them. After all, the boy-Bishop would be unlikely to forget who had failed to support him. It might only be for one day that the boy-Bishop reigned, but that was long enough to make the life of an intransigent elector painful. There were summary punishments to be given, like the refusal to allow him to sit at the same table and perhaps make him go hungry for the day, or even the extreme of embarrassment, making a fool of him on Holy Innocents' Day when all the Choristers were enjoying themselves. It would be easy to make a boy feel a complete dottypoll on such a day. Especially when all the other Choristers were determined not to stand out by defending someone else in case they might be picked on next.

Luke turned away in disgust. It was stupid, and insulting to God. And He only knew what the Succentor would say if he caught them all at it. It was tempting to go and find Brother Gervase to tell him, but Luke resisted the impulse.

He knew that Henry would simply tell the other boys to disappear and keep quiet. Then it would be Luke's word, Luke, the boy who had wanted to be the boy-Bishop, against that of Henry, the boy who had won it. There was no skill in guessing which of them would be believed. Henry would put on his sad, innocent, forgiving face and kindly tell Luke that he mustn't invent such stories, that telling lies was displeasing to God. And Luke would be looked upon as a vindictive liar.

He left the sniggering clan grouped about their leader and walked through into the hall where they all studied. Only a small room, it had a series of trestle tables set about it. Luke went to his desk. Although he wasn't supposed to keep food here, he had concealed his half loaf on the shelf beneath. If he became hungry during his work, he could take a lump of the drying crust and chew it. Not that he would want to, because the coarse loaf was growing hard. Luke hadn't had a chance to pick at it, for the Choristers had been spending almost all their time in the Cathedral practising their singing for the Christmas celebrations and the Feast of Holy Innocents. He wasn't hungry now anyway, he thought, putting the loaf back; he was too angry to think of food.

At least Henry hadn't attacked him out in the Cathedral grounds since that last time when he hurled horseshit at him. Luke still hadn't found Henry's hiding place. Yet another failure. The common, nasty boy had a hideaway, somewhere that Luke couldn't even find, let alone use himself. It wasn't *fair*.

Rising, he wandered disconsolately along the desks, glancing at the work being done by each of the boys. At Henry's was a rough picture in fine charcoal with the words

167

of a prayer alongside it and Luke peered forward to read it. It was a text from the Bible, the piece from the Book of Revelation which told how the boys were all murdered at Herod's command. Henry had worked hard, using the most expensive materials to colour it in vivid yellows, reds and greens.

'*Centum quadraginta quatuor milia qui erupti . . .*' he read, translating easily as he did so: 'The hundred and forty-four thousand which were raised from the earth reign in Heaven and the Lamb of God is with them.'

He recognised the text. It was the reading which would be given on Holy Innocents' Day, one of those spoken by the boy-Bishop. The sight made his bowels twist with impotent rage. From his outer appearance it would have been impossible to detect, but he was filled with a loathing of Henry so strong that it almost choked him.

Slumping down into Henry's seat, he stared at the badly executed picture. He could have done it better. And the text was hardly clear. If Luke had drawn the characters, they would have been greatly improved. It was tempting to smudge the page, to eradicate the hard but essentially ill-conceived effort. But he couldn't. No, it would be an affront to God. God had decided that Henry should become the boy-Bishop, and he had decided to draw and colour this page in praise of God. To damage it would be to insult God Himself. The only means Luke had of revenge was by doing a similar picture and doing it better.

That was what he would do, he decided. Another picture, working on the same text, but this one with the careful attention to detail that only Luke could achieve. He smiled unpleasantly. That would show them – *all* of them. He should have been the boy-Bishop, and he'd show them how wrong they were.

There was a pot of orpiment on Henry's desk, the naturally occurring arsenic that all the students used for the richer gold colours. Luke picked it up with a smile. He would use Henry's own colours.

Vincent le Berwe thrust his hands into his belt, whistling. He had to stop a while and watch outside a tavern where some apprentices and maidens had commandeered the roadway, dancing and singing in celebration of Christmas. One girl spun round so fast, she grew dizzy and fell on her rump with a scream of delight, hiccuping and burping, her head moving still, forwards and backwards, as she attempted to focus on her friends. They laughed and grabbed pots from a table nearby, moving out of the way of the people waiting patiently in the roadway, and Vincent could walk on again.

Peter's death was already common knowledge. A boy dropping dead in the middle of a service was hardly the kind of news which could be hushed up, especially since several churchmen had been heard to allege that it was poison. Vincent smirked to himself. This was turning into a much better end-of-year than he could have hoped for: Karvinel emasculated, Ralph dead and buried – and now Peter too had died, the only witness Vincent had needed to fear after Ralph's death.

There was something troubling him, however. He was not at all happy that Jolinde might be implicated in Peter's death. It was one thing to see his enemies ruined or destroyed, and quite another to see his sole heir at risk because of it. He had heard a pair of men in the road discussing the affair and deciding that Jolinde must have had a hand in it.

That was something he would have to see to. He didn't want Jolly to suffer in any way while he triumphed. Still, if Jolly was accused of anything, Vincent would arrange the best protection for him. He would bribe the Sheriff, if he could – or the Justice sent to try the case, if it came to that.

It would cost a great deal of money, though, he reflected. And that, ironically enough, was one thing he didn't have a lot of at present. But provided that his other competitors didn't hear about his little reverse, there was no reason why he shouldn't survive this crisis. By the time the Justice arrived, Vincent was sure he'd have enough to protect his son.

Glancing up he realised that it was already past noon and strode off towards his home once more, beaming as he passed more revellers in the streets, laughing as he joined in an impromptu dance.

He was so proud of his boy. Vincent knew what his son had done for him.

Baldwin looked over at Simon as they walked the quiet streets towards Talbot's Inn where Jeanne awaited them. He knew that the Bailiff's brain was not so logical as his own, but he also knew that Simon had a stronger intuition when it came to offences or to the behaviour of people. 'What do you think?' he asked.

'Me? God knows!' the Bailiff answered with a shrug. 'I don't think we'll get anywhere with an investigation. Peter's dead, but he was poisoned without being forced, if he *was* poisoned, which means his food was poisoned without his knowing, or he willingly took the stuff, whatever it was. And although Karvinel was there just at the right time to poison Jolinde's food, why would Karvinel have wanted to harm his own clerk? More to the point, how would he know that the food was destined for Peter Golloc's belly?'

'Could he have been hoping to kill Jolinde instead?' Baldwin mused. 'And what of the dead glovemaker? There must surely be something that makes sense of all this mayhem.'

'God knows!' Simon laughed weakly. 'I thought we were here to enjoy ourselves.'

'But think of the glovemaker a moment,' Baldwin persisted. 'Elias said that the doors to the shop and house were locked, so he went round to the back door. Then he hurried back to the front and found the door ajar. Why should the murderer leave it open?'

Simon considered. 'If the killer was there, he'd have locked the doors while he was inside.'

'Yes. And as soon as he was done, he would have unlocked the front door and left the scene as quickly as possible. Bolted from the place.'

'Why leave the shop unlocked?'

'Through sheer cunning. Think about it, Simon. What happened? The Bailiff arrives and finds the apprentice's knife and keys at the dead man's side. What inference can he make, but that Elias is the guilty party. It's the perfect set-up. The killer knew Elias was there. He'd been banging on the door. So the killer waits inside the house until Elias has gone round the back, then he unlocks the front door, leaves it, runs to the shop, unlocks it, throws in the keys, stabs the corpse of Ralph with *Elias's own knife*, and then dashes off. It was a very clever, bold crime.'

171

'Committed by a vicious murderer,' Simon commented coldly. 'And where does Peter come into all of this?'

'A good question, but very hard to answer.'

'We don't actually know Peter's death was a crime, do we?' Baldwin said. 'But I think you are correct to emphasise that there may be a link. After all, he was there that morning. If he was the chance victim of food poisoning, we could expect someone else to have succumbed. If he bought a pie in the street, he would not be alone – others would have eaten the same foul meat. The same does not go for the food Jolinde brought him.'

'Jolly, you mean?' Simon enquired dryly.

'God give me strength!' Baldwin winced. Every time Claricia had used the name it had grated. Baldwin did not like names to be shortened.

Simon laughed. 'This place is the same as Crediton Canonical Church: each Canon eats with his own Vicar, Secondary and Chorister, except Peter's Canon wasn't here so the lad ate food given to him by Jolinde. The trouble is, since Jolinde himself told us he bought it, I find it hard to believe that he tried to poison Peter. If a man uses a weapon like poison, it's in order to keep things quiet. There was no need for him to tell us about the food, so I'm inclined to think he didn't tamper with it.'

'That is a fair summary. There might have been something else he had poisoned.'

'In which case we're even less likely to discover it. Which brings us to the second likely possibility: self-murder.'

'A fellow like him? It is possible. Certainly we cannot afford to exclude it as a potential solution.'

Simon nodded. He and Baldwin both knew of men who had committed that sin while their minds were unbalanced.

Simon himself could almost comprehend the despair which could lead a man to do so. When his little son Peterkin had died, he had thought he would never recover from the hideous black depression which engulfed him. But the pain had eased eventually, as all such miseries do. 'A fellow of his age – what could lead him to commit suicide? A girl?'

'Not, perhaps, the most likely possibility,' Baldwin grinned.

'You may not think so, but priests are always being caught with women. Look at Jolinde. He's been sleeping with Claricia – they both admit it.'

'Yes,' Baldwin agreed thoughtfully. 'Which means that anyone else could have visited Peter in that little hall and given him food. A sweetmeat or pie – it wouldn't have to be much to hold enough poison to kill a man.'

'Wait! Jolinde said that Peter had been unwell for a few days. Would a poison kill him so slowly?'

Baldwin considered. 'There are poisons which would do that, yes. The Saracens know more about poisons than you would wish to have commonly understood, Simon. But there are other poisons that a man could consume which would slowly weaken him until a large dose finished him off. And don't forget that he might have *looked* as if he was being poisoned because he was so worried about being inhabited by a demon.'

Simon shivered. He had never lost his superstitions. 'Don't,' he said.

Baldwin smiled. 'Very well. But what if someone had taken to poisoning the bread each evening, slowly increasing the dosage?'

173

MICHAEL JECKS

'Why should someone wish to kill him? Because of the glovemaker's robbery?'

'The motive is still unclear but the two murders must be connected. And that, I think, means it is likely that someone in the city was responsible, not someone from the Cathedral.'

'Why?'

'Because most of the men from the Cathedral would be locked up behind their walls at night. We know that Jolinde went to the tavern, but surely most of the Cathedral staff were in the precinct when poison was put in the food . . .'

'*If* it was put in the food while it lay in the tavern.'

'If it was,' Baldwin agreed. 'Also, Ralph died first thing in the morning. All the Cathedral staff should have been within the choir.'

Simon nodded. Both knew that all the clerics would be expected to attend every service. 'All I wonder is, whether someone wanted to kill Peter but make his death look natural, or perhaps it was someone who was squeamish about using a knife and preferred to kill in this foul manner. And either way, did he decide to murder Peter purely in order to get his fists on the money?'

'Yes. The money.'

Simon threw his friend a quick look. 'What is it? The difference between the receipt and what Ralph was given?'

Baldwin laughed. 'I long for the day when I can surprise you. Yes. The good Dean told us that the receipt showed four rubies, fifty small gems and fifty small pearls, as well as two pounds five and sixpence. Yet Elias told us he counted two pounds one shilling and a farthing and there were only two rubies and forty-four gems. And then Peter went back on the

174

day Ralph died and delivered the shortfall.' He stared into the distance, trying to make sense of it all.

He raised both hands in a gesture of despair. 'Ah! Look at the sun! It must be well past noon. Jeanne will be wondering where we have got to. Let us return and see her. It is Christmas Eve and here we are dawdling like two old peasants.'

The quiet streets had become bustling and raucous. Youths chased each other or girls; hawkers bellowed their wares from the street corners while shopowners leaned against their doorframes watching the passers-by with measuring expressions.

They had almost arrived at Paul Street when Baldwin stopped and glanced at the shop they were passing. It was an apothecary's, and on the trestle before the window were displayed many different herbs and powders.

'Look – *orpiment*,' Baldwin said, 'and *realgar*. Yellow and ruby arsenic. I wonder . . .'

Simon followed him inside.

'Godspeed, sir,' said the keeper. He was a tall, hunched man in his late twenties, with a significant pot-belly, but pale and slender in his build apart from that. He had acid scars on his hands and a livid burn above one eyebrow that made Simon wince at the sight. It could so easily have taken out his eye, had it been one inch lower. 'Can I help you? My name is Gilbert of Lyme. What can I do for you?'

'Good day,' Baldwin said. He had drawn himself up to his full height, and with his hand arrogantly set atop his sword-hilt, he looked very much the elegant, courtly knight, even with his unfashionable beard. 'I see you sell orpiment.'

'Ah, yes sir. It's quite local, from a mine not far from here.'

175

'Can you refine it?'

'It is not difficult, my Lord. I can produce some for you,' the man said, but now there was a hooded wariness in his eyes. 'However, I should have to warn you – it is a very potent poison.'

'I am glad to hear your warning. Is there anywhere else to buy it in the city?'

The shopkeeper glanced from Baldwin to Simon. 'Sir, I do not understand why you are asking me so many questions, but yes, you could buy it from the rat-catcher, I expect. He likes it for poisoning vermin. Others use it to kill wasps and flies in the summer. And then again there are many uses for orpiment. It's a most practical and adaptable substance. It is used for colourings – the yellow for golds, the ruby orpiment for good, strong reds . . .'

'Such as the Canons would use!' Simon breathed.

'Why, yes, sir. Only last week I supplied a pound of the yellow to the Cathedral.'

'Who bought it?' Baldwin said.

'It was a young Secondary from the Treasury, sir – a fellow named Jolinde.'

CHAPTER THIRTEEN

Jolinde had no idea that his name was being linked to the death of his friend in this way. As Baldwin and Simon exchanged a meaningful stare, he walked from the small house back towards the Cathedral.

It had taken him some little time to wrap up his friend's clothing and the palliasse, now sadly leaking all its stuffing, and take the lot to the hall downstairs, where he set it against a wall, wondering what to do with it. Perhaps, he thought, the laundrymen would take the robes and wash them ready for some other new Secondary. With that thought he returned upstairs and stitched together his own palliasse where Baldwin had slashed it.

There was no point in going through his friend's things, since he had already checked everything as soon as he was released from the services that morning. While the congregation sat dumbfounded, staring at the figure shaking and quivering as his life fled, he had gone to Peter's side, listening for the last prayer. Not that he had heard anything. Peter's eye had met his own accusingly, but only for a second, and Jolinde could well have mistaken it. But as soon as Peter was dead, the thought of the money waiting to be collected was like a cattle prod in his arse. At the first possible moment after the body had been carried away and the services had been completed, Jolinde scurried off to their rooms.

'You fooled me again, didn't you, you hypocrite?' he said sadly, perusing the paltry belongings of the lad he had lived with for so many years. 'You thought I was going to try to take it all back from you, didn't you? But I wouldn't, I never wanted it for myself.'

That was the thought that nagged at him as he walked towards the chapel: Peter hadn't trusted him. He'd taken the stolen jewels and hidden them somewhere Jolinde couldn't find them. Or maybe he'd sold them? Tried to make his own profit?

The theft itself had been remarkably easy. They had collected the jewels and money for delivery to Ralph on sixth December as instructed, but while they were still walking to the glover's place, Jolly had casually mentioned how easy it was to make fun of people. Peter hadn't understood, perhaps intentionally, but then Jolly explained how simple it would be to remove some jewels and make off with the proceeds. He hadn't introduced the concept as a suggestion that they should rob either the Cathedral or Ralph, but merely as an idea, a conversational twist, and it had worked. Peter had scoffed when he took Jolly's drift.

'You think so? They would notice if we took some of the jewels!'

'Not necessarily,' Jolly had answered, and the two of them made a wager. And of course Jolly was right. They left the glover's shop with a handful of money and the precious and semi-precious stones. Ralph was a trusting man, pious and honourable. It had been all too easy to pull the wool over his eyes.

Almost immediately, Peter had begun to fret. 'We have to take it back to him – this is theft,' he whimpered. 'We're no better than felons if we keep it!'

'We can't,' Jolly responded shortly. 'If we try to take it back, we'll have to explain how we made the mistake, and as soon as we do that he'll realise we robbed him.'

'But if we don't we shall be felons!' Peter stated despairingly. 'We have to take them back or how can Ralph make the gloves? And we shall have to confess what we've done in Chapter too, before the Canons and the Dean.'

'Now listen to me, Peter!' Jolly said, and he gripped his companion forcefully. 'Look, we can't go back to the glover's now or he will accuse us of theft – right? If we confess in Chapter we'll probably be thrown out of the Cathedral. You want that? To be evicted under a cloud, with no prospects?'

Peter's eyes slid away and Jolly knew he had hit the mark there. Peter would have liked to have become a Canon if he could; to be a Vicar would be enough to keep him content – but he knew that he would only ever remain at best a clerk while he had no patron. He was like Jolly; he had to find a new career away from the Cathedral if he wanted to advance. If he was to become a lawyer he would need money to travel to University, but even more than that, he would need the support of the Bishop. The thought that he could lose his

179

place in the Cathedral was terrible. That would mean the end of his dreams.

Two or three weeks ago, that was, and Jolly could recall it perfectly. How Peter had argued and whined until Jolly pulled him into the alehouse, and there he had ordered drinks from the beautiful Claricia. He was smitten at once. And Peter's continual whispered hissing in his ear was a distraction from his pursuit of her. Perhaps his desire for her was a means of forgetting what he had just done to Ralph, but it felt good.

When Peter said again that he couldn't keep the jewels, that he was no thief, Jolly responded that his attitude was fine, but how was he going to get them back to Ralph with no one noticing? As proof of his own disinterest, he placed his small purse, which contained the money and gemstones, in Peter's hand, telling him to give them back however he wished. Peter gripped the purse like a man holding a death sentence.

But Jolly could feel the guilt and shame fall from him as he gave the purse to Peter, and immediately he set about battering at Claricia's defences. His assault had been successful: he had taken her by storm, and since then he had shared her bed regularly, in the small room over Sutton's Inn. And because Jolly knew the secret of the tunnels, he could stay with her until late, making his way back to the Cathedral when he wanted, with no one any the wiser.

He had found the tunnels because of the building work. It was one day while he walked near the cloister that he saw it. He was idly watching builders working on the foundations for the new eastern section when a builder slipped into a hole. Laughing, he had called over the architect. Interested, Jolly wandered over.

'Nearly fell in, sir,' the workman was saying.

Peering over his shoulder, Jolly saw a cavity lined with stones. It was arched, and beneath was a gaping hole. The architect dropped a stone in and there was a rattle. 'It's an old sewer, that's all. Not used now, I suppose. Nothing exciting, anyway.'

But Jolly knew he was wrong. To him it looked very exciting indeed. The men filled in the hole, but Jolly thought to himself that an old tunnel would be straight; there was no need for it to curve. He looked forward and mentally noted where the tunnel might meet the Cathedral wall. Later he found the entrance: it was the ideal means for him to get into and out of the Cathedral when the gates were locked, useful too for meetings which required a certain secrecy. That was why he had met his father there when Vincent had that special favour to ask him – the favour that led to the conning of Ralph. Which in turn had led to that session in the tavern with Peter, who had been so upset about the way Jolly had used him.

Although now Jolinde thought about it, Peter had looked even more angry and upset yesterday on seeing Karvinel, than he had while talking about the theft.

Baldwin was quiet, meditating as he walked back to the inn. Simon knew him far too well to interrupt his thought processes, and refrained from conversation until they reached the inn yard and Baldwin threatened to walk straight past.

'Hey! In here, Baldwin.'

'Hmm? Oh, sorry. Yes, of course.'

They entered to find Jeanne sitting in the parlour with Edgar.

'Well, Baldwin? Was the murder not to your liking, that you should return so early?'

He smiled grimly. 'I have not yet eaten lunch, so if you wish to hurl verbal barbs at me, at least let me sample some bread beforehand. Otherwise I may well expire.'

'Not tonight, Sir Baldwin,' the imperturbable Edgar remarked.

'What is that supposed to mean?' Baldwin demanded, sinking into a seat.

Jeanne was frigid as ice. 'Perhaps you have forgotten that today we feast with Vincent le Berwe. He wishes us to share his evening meal before going with him and his family to attend the Mass in the Cathedral.'

'Wonderful,' said Baldwin with such hollow sarcasm that his wife rose and rested her hand on his shoulder.

'It's only a few more days, husband.'

'It will feel like an eternity – except that with you at my side the time will fly past,' he said gallantly.

But even as she smiled down at him in return, she saw his eyes lose their focus as his mind returned to the dead Secondary.

The Christmas Eve feast was an important event at Vincent's house. There were eleven messes, Baldwin saw as he walked into the hall, so there were places for at least forty people, allowing four to each mess.

A twinge of guilt snagged at his consciousness as he sat down. He ought to be at his manor. It was his duty to provide seasonal hospitality for his villeins. They would bring their own faggots and he would provide the cooks, the food and the ale. Many lords, he knew, would expect the villeins to bring their own food and drink as well as the wood, but Baldwin felt strongly that his men had provided the food that would fill his belly for the year, so it was only right that he should feed them, just as he did at Michaelmas and Candlemas.

It was always a pleasant affair, Christmas at Furnshill. Baldwin would provide a loaf of heavy bread for his shepherd's best dogs, and a variety of foods for all the men and women of the vill. There was usually a good strong chicken soup, bacon with beef and mustard, cheese and as much ale as the villeins could drink in the day. Usually the devils took that on as a challenge and there was little enough remaining when Baldwin's steward went over the accounts at the end of the day.

Today would be very different, of course, because it was a fast day. Although Friday was an official fast day during an ordinary week, the fact that tomorrow was Friday twenty-fifth December meant that it would have to be a Feast Day, which logically meant that today, Thursday, Christmas Eve, would be one without red meats.

On the sideboard, glistening under the yellow candle-flames, Baldwin could see herrings, eels, codlings and a variety of jellies. Pies were piled high on platters, and from the look of them they were probably Norwegian pasties, filled with cod's liver and fish flesh; there were fried rissoles made from chestnuts, hardboiled eggs and cheese next to fresh codfish, trout and a salmon. And on one side were the fish that disgusted Baldwin: lampreys.

He loathed and detested lampreys. Any man who had ever seen a villein stumbling home from collecting these weird-looking fish, his sack over his back, and blood dribbling

183

down his tunic where the foul fish had squirmed and sunk their fangs into him would also hate them. Baldwin had seen his cook prepare them once, splitting the mouth from the chin upwards, then tugging the tongue out and bleeding the horrible creatures into a dish so that their blood could thicken the gravy. The thought still made him shudder now.

But he would enjoy the other dishes. For once, the food was not overspiced and unrecognisable. Many of the dishes could be discerned – or, at least, their main constituents could be.

Vincent had placed Baldwin and Jeanne at his own right hand, a position which gave Baldwin some amusement. He scarcely knew Vincent and was sure he didn't merit so privileged a position, but clearly Vincent wanted to ally himself with the knight in the eyes of his other guests. That thought made him glance along the tables.

When he and Jeanne had come to the hall the day before, only one table had been set up; now Vincent had a further four long trestle tables installed. Trestles were so much easier to rent and put up; they only needed long sections of cloth spread carefully over them to make them decent. The guests had benches.

Vincent had spent a small fortune on this feast, Baldwin thought. There were four large silver salts, one in the shape of an eagle, rather well executed, which remained before Vincent himself, while the others were simple lidded bowls for the guests. As soon as Vincent had washed his hands the bottler signalled to a waiting valet. The valet disappeared and while the bottler was pouring wine for his lord, the valet returned leading a train of servants, all with white napkins draped over their shoulders and with which they held the dishes.

Those on the main table were first to receive their trenchers. Vincent's carver arrived before the main table with a small retinue of assistants. He took a round, heavy brown loaf of maybe eight inches diameter, and faster than Baldwin would have thought possible, he removed the crusts and converted the bread into four perfect square trenchers. On top of each he placed three hunks of good, white pieces of bread for eating, handling all only with his knife or napkin, before moving away to begin serving the other guests.

The initial courses were arriving now, and Baldwin was pleased to see that the dishes were simple and relatively plain.

From his own seat a little further along the table – since he wasn't a knight, he could hardly expect the place of honour at Vincent's side – Simon munched happily. He was fortunate in that his palate tolerated any and every mixture of dishes. He was some distance from Baldwin and Jeanne, but had struck up a conversation with the woman at his side, a pleasant lady called Juliana, whose husband, Simon discovered, had been raised not very far from his own birthplace near Crediton.

'But you aren't from Crediton yourself, surely?' he said, trying not to spit crumbs from his tasty fish pasty.

She was chubby and happy, clearly enjoying her food and drink. Roguish dark eyes glinted with amusement, as if she was better born than anyone in the room and found a certain satisfaction and pleasure in observing the quaint, old-fashioned ways of people so far from civilisation. 'No, I came from east of here. My husband and I met when he was visiting Winchester Market.'

He glanced at her man, who was talking loudly to his other neighbour. He was a large fellow, with broad hands and stumpy fingers, a thick, heavy body, jowled, with small eyes but a cavernous mouth when he roared with laughter. Simon felt sure that Juliana could not be happy in her marriage. 'So you have travelled a long way?' he said pleasantly.

She should have annoyed him, with her up-country attitudes, but he felt a degree of sympathy for her, and she seemed happier with his company than she would have been with any other man in the room. He found the fixed concentration of her green eyes very flattering.

'Yes, a very long way. I miss my home.' A shadow passed over her brow, but it was only there a moment and she said brightly, 'But it is good to see new areas. You know, my mother never saw more than the lands maybe two leagues from her home.'

'Really?' Simon considered, slurping a mouthful of wine to wash down the fish. 'Exeter's a good city to live in, too, isn't it?'

'Well, it is pleasant. But Winchester is rather better.'

Deciding to change the subject, he emptied his mazer and held it aloft for the bottler to refill. Then he selected a piece of salted fish. 'Here – try some of this,' he said politely. 'It's excellent.'

She took a morsel, touching his finger for longer than was really necessary, and to his faint disquiet, she held his gaze while she slowly placed it in her mouth.

'I think I should be careful,' Simon told himself. 'This woman could eat me up and spit out the remains.'

*   *   *

186

Hawisia rested her hand lightly on her husband's. She could see that he was still worried, no matter how he attempted to conceal it, his eyes blinking quickly in that nervous manner she recognised so well, the little nerve twitching in his left cheek where the candlelight caught it. Patting his forearm reassuringly, she gave him a smile and was warmed to see him return it – slowly, to be sure, but with genuine affection.

She returned to observing her guests. All were important people in their own way; she had been careful about whom she should invite. It was quite a coup to have succeeded in getting Sir Baldwin to attend. The way people spoke of him, he was respected highly in the city. His was just the sort of friendship her husband must foster. Friends of influence and power were necessary to a man.

The Bailiff, Puttock, she was less sure of. He was important over on Dartmoor, but Vincent had no interests so far to the west. It was such wild, dangerous land out there, not the sort of place that Hawisia had any desire to visit. But it was said that Simon Puttock was a rising star, well looked upon by the Abbot of Tavistock. She would have to be careful to listen out for any comments which passed down to her about the Bailiff. If he was soon to be in the ascendant, she wanted her husband to make his further acquaintance.

He was talking to that foolish wench Juliana. Hawisia maintained her smile but couldn't help it becoming more than a little brittle. Juliana Karvinel was still an important woman in the city, someone with whom she, Hawisia, must deal, but that didn't mean Hawisia had to like her. Vincent's henchman had overheard women in the city whispering about Juliana, saying that she was tempting all the men

MICHAEL JECKS

hereabouts. Perhaps the stupid woman thought she could tempt Puttock with her doltish wit, or more likely with her heaving breast, Hawisia sniffed. The way the woman was thrusting her tits at the Bailiff was outrageous.

Not that Nick Karvinel, right at her side, seemed to care much, she thought. Nicholas was roaring loudly with laughter, his nasty little piggy eyes narrowed with amusement, his mouth wide to bellow his pleasure, pounding the table with his fist. Yet it was not genuine. His face never quite lost its haunted aspect. While he laughed, his eyes flitted over the other people in the room. Assessing who would and who wouldn't be a threat to him. He knew that his future was uncertain. If his luck didn't change, he would be ruined before long. It was bad enough that he had been robbed, his house burgled, his status within the city reduced, but Hawisia knew that Karvinel had more concerns. Men to whom he owed money were asking for it back, including her own Vincent. If he couldn't find enough to cover his debts, he would be utterly destroyed.

It was an important consideration, Hawisia acknowledged. If everyone went to Karvinel and simultaneously demanded that their loans be repaid, the money he owed to her husband might never be recovered.

She suddenly caught a glimpse of Juliana's hand patting Simon Puttock's thigh before lifting his cup and pressing it into his hand. It was no accident, Hawisia was convinced of that. And of course she knew full well that Juliana was as aware as any other of the serious nature of her husband's finances. How could she not be, with such a series of terrible disasters? Juliana almost looked as if she was practising her flirting, reminding herself how to win a man, preparing to find a lover to run away with.

188

The concept was an idle one, not a rational thought at all, but it snagged on a barb in Hawisia's mind and made her catch her breath with delight. It would be the final embarrassment for Karvinel. If his wife were to run away with a different man – especially a younger man like the Bailiff here – he would be distraught. He might even decide to throw himself upon the adulterer.

What would be in it for Juliana? Hawisia recalled the shame heaped upon Earl Thomas of Lancaster when his wife Alice left him. He had been the butt of jokes up and down the kingdom. Surely if he had been a mere gentleman like Karvinel, he would have been shattered by the discovery of his wife's unfaithfulness.

Karvinel was almost wrecked as a threat to Vincent now, but Hawisia could not forget that he had until recently been Vincent's leading competitor for all positions of importance in the city, and he could return to take up that rôle once more. But if his wife should leave him, he would be finished. It could be desirable, even if it meant Vincent didn't recover the money he was owed. Perhaps Hawisia should warn him, advise him to collect Nick Karvinel's debt sooner rather than later?

There was a speculative look in Hawisia's eye when she next glanced in the direction of Simon and Juliana and it was with an almost absent-minded gentleness that she rested her hand once more upon her husband's and softly stroked it.

CHAPTER FOURTEEN

Gervase the Succentor closed the door behind him and crossed the grassed pathway to the cobbled street that led up to the western door. He had need of peace and an opportunity for thought, now that poor Peter was dead. The lad's horrific demise in the Cathedral had appalled all the Canons and Chapter. It was as if a demon had intruded upon their devotions and mocked them all – and God. It was deeply unsettling. Some had murmured that the place should be reconsecrated, although others pointed out that it would be, since the Cathedral was being rebuilt. It was good to find some peace and quiet where he could think without the pall of gloom sinking into his bones.

Peter had been a good fellow, a companionable sort, but that wasn't the reason why Gervase had valued him. Peter was no great scholar, and his memory was poor – the two main reasons why he had not progressed beyond his position as a Secondary. He had a great skill with numbers, which was always useful, but for Gervase Peter had an infinitely more important rôle. Peter was one of his Rulers, or Rectors, a special clerk who knew the music and orders of service for all special events. While his memory regularly failed him when he tried to recall Biblical events or the correct services to hold on specific Feast Days, he could be entirely relied upon to carry a full sequence of songs and prayers, leading the choir in all the more fiddly ones. Gervase wasn't sure how he could fill the place left by Peter. He had wondered about using young Jolinde, but it wouldn't do. He had no interest in the music or services.

Peter had been a capable singer, if no better than that, but in terms of arranging the services, he was more talented than Gervase himself. He would have been an ideal replacement for Gervase – in fact the Succentor had been going to suggest that he should be allowed to go to University. It might have helped him develop. Everyone needed education.

Gervase himself had been to Oxford. Some years ago Bishop Walter had generously sent him away to study, and he had not only enjoyed his theological and astronomical studies, he had also been fortunate enough to meet and later be tutored by a man who had known the great 'Doctor Mirabilis', Roger Bacon. From this teacher Gervase had acquired some Arabic, and he had looked over many of the same Saracen documents which Bacon himself had read.

There he had learned about poisons which could be used to kill a man. Some were rare, curious mixtures of strange roots and leaves, which could gradually make a man fade without his knowing why. Others were more simple and crude. Putrefying flesh from a long-dead animal smeared upon a knife or arrow could be effective, but as Gervase knew, the more common a powder or liquid, the better for a poisoner.

Gervase shook his head and frowned. Peter's death had affected the whole Cathedral. It was a dreadful thing to happen at Christmas. But there was no need for people to assume that Peter had been poisoned. So many died from food poisoning of one form or another – surely the young man's death was the same: a tragic accident.

In years to come, Gervase might have a suitable replacement in Luke, he thought, not that he honestly believed he would be able to claim Luke for the next Succentor.

Luke and Henry were very different from Jolinde and Peter. Neither was so capable with music yet, and both were competent enough at their studies, a great deal more so than Peter had been. Gervase occasionally risked a small wager, and he would gamble a tenth of his annual £2 stipend in support of his view that both Luke *and* Henry would be Deacons before they were twenty years old. Both spoke and wrote Latin clearly and intelligibly, both sang well, and both had a good feel for the ritual of their jobs, although Luke was undoubtedly the better at each accomplishment.

Their rivalry was an irritation, certainly, but boys would be boys. As far as Gervase could recall, Jolinde and Peter had fought in much the same way when they were young Choristers. Fortunately they had patched up their differences.

Entering the Cathedral, he bowed to the altar. Rising, he saw Adam lighting candles near the Bishop's throne. Poor Adam, he thought. The boy would never be allowed to rise through the ranks, no matter what his friends wished. It was odd that the Dean should have so taken to Adam, giving him his post as a Secondary and supporting him at every turn.

Most others couldn't stand the boy. Too uncouth and bullying. Still, Gervase reflected, walking to Adam's side, there
was hope even for the roughest boy.

'Adam, could I have a word, please?'

'I am very busy, Brother.'

'Not too busy to hear that if I see you tipping wax down
the necks of the Choristers again, I shall personally report
you to the Bishop myself. You understand me?'

Abashed, Adam ducked his head sulkily. 'Yes, Brother.'

'Good. Now, may I help with these candles?'

The lad stood aside and allowed the Succentor to take a
handful of candles. With them he set off to the nearest sconce
and removed the old ones, replacing all with new. It was the
way on Christmas Eve.

Gervase allowed thoughts of the dead Secondary to fall
from his mind like rain dripping from a damp cloak. This
was no time to be filling his mind with such macabre things.
Infinitely more important was the service tonight, preparing
the church, ensuring that the choir was ready and understood
the order of songs and prayers. It was essential to perform
the *Opus Dei* to the very best of their mediocre abilities.

The Cathedral had been decorated suitably and the candles
reflected the bright green holly which adorned the window-
ledges and filled any convenient gaps. Berries gleamed
among the leaves like rubies. Ivy had been carefully twined
about pillars as if it had grown there. The floor was well
swept, displaying the old tiles and slabs, all the metalwork
was polished, reflecting the light in sharp, clean bursts,
making the woodwork glow as though it were illuminated
from within. The whole church was as perfect as human
hands could make it, Gervase sighed happily. That was, after

all, the point, as the Dean had reminded them all that morning immediately after Chapter.

It was more gloomy than previous Chapter meetings. The Canons and Vicars walked in after Prime, taking the doorway in the southern wall of the Cathedral which led out to the Chapter House on the eastern side of the cloisters. Here the Dean gave a short prayer before sitting down, and Luke read out the calendar information for the services to celebrate Christmas while the Canons listened carefully, sitting on the stone seats that were fitted into the walls.

The calendar laid down the rules for every day: first the date, as if anyone wasn't already aware of it; the age of the moon; the name of the man to be celebrated. Usually the name to be revered was that of a saint, but today, knowing that they were to honour Jesus Christ Himself, the Chapter was strangely quiet and thoughtful. Normally a Canon would be bound to be thinking of something else and there would be occasional bursts of humour, but on the eve of Christ's birth no one felt the urge for levity. Especially after the horror of Peter's death.

And Jolinde had felt it keenly, Gervase reckoned from the look of him. When Jolinde stood to read the rota of the duties, his face was pale and strained, but that was only to be expected after witnessing the death of his friend. Again a nagging doubt reminded Gervase that Jolinde and Peter had *not* been the closest of friends when they were younger, but he thrust the uncharitable idea from him. Such thoughts were not to be borne, not on Christmas Eve.

Once Jolinde had finished and had sat down again, the Dean stood and began the prayers. But today he had additional prayers for Peter.

'Let us ahm, begin as usual with our prayers for our King,
King Edward the Second, God bless him and keep him and
send him good advisers . . . and for the Queen and her father
the King of France hmm and for our own Bishop, Walter
hmm and his family, especially his brother, Sir Richard
Stapledon, buried here in our Cathedral hmm and we remember our own parents . . . And last, we should all think of poor
Peter, who died so tragically this morning. It is a sad duty to
remember one of our own who has passed away, but we can
reflect on the joy his soul no doubt hmm feels, sitting now in
the presence of God. Please, Lord, hear our prayers.'

On a normal morning, that would have been an end to it,
but today there was much more, all to do with the Mass.
Holding a Mass at night was complex, and tonight's, the
Christmas Eve Mass, was the only one of the year which was
conducted by candlelight.

All in all, Gervase was convinced that the Angel's Mass
on Christmas Eve was the most beautiful and touching of
any. But it did involve a lot more work, and what with the
early beginning of the Mass, the early rising for the daily
prayers and rituals afterwards, at which all Canons, Vicars,
and their Secondaries were supposed to be present, every
man in the Cathedral would be exhausted by the end of
Christmas Day.

That was why at the end of Chapter the Dean had admon-
ished all of them to, 'Perform your service with absolute
devotion and edifying recollection. This is the most important service in our year, and we must all do honour to the
miracle and mystery of Our Saviour's Nativity. Ahm I expect
to see all of you in the choir for the service.'

*   *   *

Baldwin and the guests remained seated while the chaplain stood and said Grace after the meal, but when he was done and the bread for the poor had been collected in one large bowl, at least one quarter of all that which had been served, as well as the remains of the other dishes, the party rose and left space for the servants to clear the room. With the steward standing over them all and watching, the place was cleared in short order, the dishes all carried out to the scullery to be washed, the tablecloths folded and removed, the trestle tables taken apart, the benches moved against the wall.

The host and his wife stood and chatted to their guests and several times Baldwin felt Vincent or Hawisia's eyes upon him, but he declined their unspoken offers to introduce him to still more citizens. He was convinced that his presence at this feast was less for Vincent le Berwe to honour him, more to reflect a little of his own honour upon Vincent, and Baldwin was happy to repay a good meal by being polite to the man, but saw no need to be ingratiating.

It was quite some little while before they all heard the Cathedral bells tolling. Luckily the miserable weather which had threatened had held off and they only had to contend with mud-filled streets and the malodorous contents of the gutters. One man stepped into something so foul that he had to seek a patch of grass to wipe off the worst of the offending muck, but for the most part they reached the Fissand Gate none the worse for wear.

Jeanne was relieved to have arrived without besmirching her clean dress and tunic with horse manure or dog's turds, and she was congratulating herself when she caught the eye of a man at the gate's hinge.

He squatted with a stout staff at his side, which he used as a crutch. There was a dreadful scar that clove his jawbone and had left a large dint in his face. But for all that he smiled when he saw her watching him, and his eyes were kind and gentle as he ducked his head in an admiring half-bow. She smiled in her turn, feeling an urge to curtsey. A man who had suffered as he clearly had deserved the honour more than many she gave it to, she thought rebelliously as she was swept along by the flow of the crowd.

The grounds before the Cathedral demonstrated the popularity of the service. Above them, the bells were still sounding out their command to all Christians to come and perform their duty and honour their Saviour. All the folk of the city would be here or in the parish churches which were dotted all about: some from pure devotion, some from compulsion because the Cathedral could refuse to buy goods from merchants who didn't attend their services, and some from insurance, making certain of their places in the life to come.

Inside the great church Baldwin could feel the power and majesty of the building. It soared high overhead, the ceiling a dim pattern almost out of sight, supported by the magnificent stone columns. At his side he heard Jeanne gasp. She gripped his arm. 'This is wonderful, isn't it? What a fabulous building!' she exclaimed.

'It shall be even longer when they have finished the eastern end.'

'But it's already vast!' She was awed. This place was daunting in its size. How it could remain standing, she did not understand, but although it was staggering in its dimensions, she was soothed by the familiar scent of incense and the sight of the small portable altar which stood before the

197

screen. Obviously the choir itself was concealed from the general population. The Cathedral was here for the congregation of Canons to honour God, not only for the edification of the general public.

Yet it was good to see that the Cathedral allowed even the poorer folk to enter. From the corner of her eye she saw a squatting figure being helped inside. It was the beggar she had noticed at the Fissand Gate. He grinned widely at her, but in an instant he was bowing his head in a prayer. At his side she saw a black-clad man, while in the shadows next to him a lad was grinning foolishly. This gave Jeanne a pang. She always felt sorry for the witless, and now, knowing she bore a child in her womb, she was struck by a quick anxiety, worried that she could give birth to a fool, but then she forced her mind to empty.

This was no time to be entertaining morbid thoughts.

CHAPTER FIFTEEN

As the Canons assembled in their stalls, Brother Stephen looked about him beaming with pleasure. This service was, he felt, the most meaningful of all through the year. For some reason the simple fact that it was the only full Mass celebrated during the night made it more symbolic, more important – and certainly more beautiful.

The candle-flames fluttered gently in the sconces and candelabra, making the whole place alive with warm light and dancing shadows. There were more candles than at any other service: seven on the high altar, three before the Cross, hundreds in the ambulatories. Occasional gusts of wind from the works at the eastern end of the crossing, where the new choir was being constructed, twitched the flames, making them dance in unison, bringing the stench of burning tallow with it.

He felt a shudder of delightful expectation shiver up his spine and he whispered a prayer of thanks that he should have lived to have participated in yet another Christmas Eve. It was a distinct honour, he thought, to have been allowed to witness the celebration in this, the most beautiful of all Christian churches.

Finishing with a short 'Amen,' he took in the faces of the other Canons, all glowing in the light.

The men stood in their stalls in rows at either side of the path to the altar; three at either side of a narrow corridor in which sat the two Rulers. The two inner rows were filled with Choristers; behind them were the Annuellars and Secondaries; last, furthest from the corridor, were the Canons and Vicars, with the four Archdeacons, the Dean and his four dignitaries. The Bishop, when he was in attendance, sat on his throne near the altar.

Stephen's own post lay at the south-western side of the choir, from where he had a good view of all the other members of the congregation. He could see that all the men had excited expressions, although some of the oldest displayed signs of apprehension. They knew how long it would be before they could seek their beds and rest their weary legs.

The younger folk showed no anticipation of pain or exhaustion. Stephen smiled to see the bright expectation on their boyish faces, for this service was the beginning of *their* season, when they would begin to take all power from the Church's authorities. The boy-Bishop would soon come into his own, and then the Choristers would rule the Cathedral for twenty-four hours. Lunacy, of course, Stephen reminded himself, but a necessary madness. And it made up for the rest of the year's solemnity, making routines bearable for boys of eleven or twelve years old.

There was a sudden hush which broke into his thoughts, and he settled back against his *misericorde* as the service began.

Gervase watched his two Rectors like a snake studying two mice, his attention constantly moving from one to the other, preparing to leap at any moment should either fail in his duty, but his anxiety appeared unnecessary.

One Rector stood and the nave fell silent as he prayed with his eyes closed, one hand gripping his staff of office, and then called loudly the invitatory to Matins.

Too loud, Gervase considered critically. But well spoken, and at least each word was clear. The Rector sat once more on his revolving white-leather seat; at the opposite side of the aisle was the second, facing him. Both clasped their wooden staffs ornamented with silver; they held each other's gaze a moment, then gave a slight nod as they began.

It was the job of the two Rectors to regulate the singing and prayers. This service, the Angel's Mass, was Christmas Day's Matins, but it was held before midnight on Christmas Eve and required more complicated sequences of praise. It was too much to expect the Canons and Secondaries to remember the details of every service through the year, so the Rectors were carefully briefed by Gervase on the precise order for each special service. This one was perhaps the most important of the year and one of the most confusing.

But also the most breathtaking, Gervase added to himself as the first lesson was chanted and a Chorister appeared in the doorway of the screens next to the high altar.

It was Luke. He stood there on the highest step, dressed in plain white *alb* and *amice*, a lighted torch gripped in his left hand, facing the altar. As the lesson was completed, he turned to the choir and sang out in his clear, sweet voice.

'*Ho die nobis celorum . . .*'

Gervase nodded, translating to himself as the child went through the beautiful little ceremony.

'*On this day the King of Heaven consented to be born for us of a virgin.*'

The lad did well, Gervase told himself. He had thought he would. It was the best he could do to compensate Luke for being passed over for boy-Bishop, giving him this rôle.

Luke remembered all the instructions. He raised his right hand upwards as he mentioned Heaven; he turned and reached out to the statue of the Virgin Mary as he spoke of Her, and finished by falling to his knees before the altar. This was the signal for the rest of the choir to respond, and Gervase began to sing, but all the time half his mind was on the next sequence, and it was with a sense of mild relief that he saw the three Choristers from each side of the aisle, all similarly dressed, proceed to the lowest step of the altar. Luke descended, his head bowed, and when he reached the bottom with the others, all seven sang '*Gloria in excelsis Deo, et in terra pax, hominibus bonae voluntatis.*'

At the exquisite sound Gervase felt tears spring into his eyes once more. He smiled blissfully with the sheer loveliness of the ceremony as the children passed in procession through the midst of the choir and disappeared.

The Dean stood to celebrate Mass. This was the first of the Masses for Christmas Day, and the secular congregation, many of whom had feasted before arriving here, began to jostle and shift weight from one foot to another long before the end. Too many men and women had drunk quarts of ale or pints of wine for them to be entirely comfortable.

Baldwin felt fine, but he had restricted his own consumption. At his side, Simon grunted to himself every so often, standing with his hands clasped behind his back with his weight squarely balanced upon both feet. Vincent le Berwe was not so fortunate. From the corner of his eye Baldwin noticed him fidgeting uncomfortably, then chewing at his lip, before finally making his way through the crowds to the door.

It made Baldwin shake his head a little. Men should concentrate more on the importance of the ceremony of Christmas, rather than feasting to excess in celebration of it. There would be many painful heads on the morrow, he thought uncharitably.

It was as the Dean lifted the golden chalice high overhead that Gervase felt the first flicker of concern.

Initially it was only a wry observation that Luke had not returned from changing out of his silk robes, but his cynical assumption that the little devil had decided to return to his bed for a snooze, or maybe was even now raiding the buttery for a pottle of strong wine, began to turn to slight concern – even anxiety – as the lad didn't return. It made him begin to wonder whether Luke could have fallen and hit his head, or tripped into a hole. The workings here were quite dangerous at night.

It was a relief when he saw the Chorister walk back and sit down – but when he saw Luke's features he saw with a shock that the boy's face was as pale as a corpse. The face of someone who had seen a ghost – or someone who had been terrified beyond belief.

Simon was standing next to Hawisia near a pillar when Vincent reappeared. The congregation had returned to their places after the Communion, and Simon eyed the folk about him idly. Suddenly he found his gaze falling upon Juliana Karvinel and her husband. Juliana smiled, and Simon was sure her eyebrows rose momentarily, as if she was giving him an invitation. In his alcoholically bemused state, Simon felt a vague libidinous attraction to her, but then the crowds moved and the sight of her was lost.

She was an attractive woman, he thought, thinking of her breasts and that special, lazy way she had of smiling. And she clearly thought him a good-looking man, too, from the way she had flirted with him. Simon had a feeling that if he asked her to warm his bed, she'd agree with alacrity. It was something to think that a married woman would behave in so flagrant a manner.

For his part Simon was like any other man. In the past he had made use of whores when he was taken by the urge, but since marrying Meg he had rarely felt the need. He didn't stay away from home that often, but now, here in this strange, unfamiliar city, Simon felt that the comfort of a woman would be pleasant. He could almost feel Juliana's flesh in his hands.

As soon as he had the thought, a picture of his wife's face appeared in his mind, his laughing Meg with their daughter Emily in her arms. Meg was tall, fair-haired, gentle in manner, for ever calm. Simon adored her, and his daughter.

The thought made him smile to himself. In any case, he was probably confusing a woman's polite chatter and unintentional flirting with the professional eroticism of a slut. It was lucky he had realised his error in time.

Returning to watching the priest at the altar, he began to pray. Meg would be giving birth soon. Simon asked God to give them another boy, an heir to replace poor Peterkin, the son he had buried two years before. The priest moved with a slow deliberation, and Simon wished he would hurry and finish the service so that the Bailiff could leave and find a private spot in which to empty his bladder, but his train of thought was broken as Vincent pushed his way back through the crowd.

Clumsily, Vincent bumped into a cleric who was fitting fresh candles into a candelabra, knocking the box of replacements from his hand. The wooden box fell with a loud crack and the expensive white cylinders rolled hither and thither while the young Secondary scampered after them.

Vincent scarcely seemed to notice the mayhem he had caused. He merely snorted with amusement before peering ahead, trying to see where Baldwin and Simon were; when he saw Simon, he shoved his way over to the Bailiff's side. Simon could not help but notice the relief and satisfaction on the merchant's face. It made his own discomfort all the worse, and he was mightily glad when, only a short while later, the service ended. The priest at the altar finished his last sung prayer, holding up his hand and making the Sign of the Cross over all those present while they bowed their heads and crossed themselves or held their hands together in prayer. Then the crowds began to move away from the screen and towards the door.

'Sir Baldwin, Lady Jeanne, you must come back to my house and celebrate the new Christmas Day,' Vincent said. 'It will only be ourselves. No one else has been asked back.'

Seeing the expression on Jeanne's face, Baldwin refused the offer with as much politeness as he could muster. 'I would like to, but we have been up since a very early hour, sir. Please excuse us, but with my wife pregnant, I think she should be allowed to find her bed as soon as possible.'

'Oh, of course. My apologies, Lady Jeanne. I wasn't thinking. Please forgive me.'

'There's nothing to forgive,' she smiled, grateful that Baldwin had seen her mood.

'I must ask the Bailiff, though,' Vincent said, gazing about him as they walked out of the western gates. 'Where is he?'

Baldwin laughed. 'Where there is a dark alley and no prying eyes.'

'Oh, he was desperate for a piss as well, was he? In that case, Hawisia, would you like to return home?'

Jeanne watched the merchant stroll away and pushed her hand through the crook of her husband's elbow. 'Try as I might, I cannot like that man,' she whispered confidentially.

Luke and the other Choristers filed from the Cathedral and made their way to the door, then out to the grassed area.

In the clear night air Luke shivered and felt a heavy lump weighting his belly. From here in the doorway, he was facing the graveyard and charnel chapel. Never before had he given credence to the foolish rumours and silly stories of ghosts and dead Canons who walked the precinct, but now he felt less sure.

He could have jumped out of his skin when the man had taken his arm. It was just after he had left the Cathedral and had removed his silk clothing ready to return to the choir. The other boys had already gone, but Luke had more to remove, and he was a conscientious boy. He wouldn't throw good silks onto the floor. No, he carefully shook out and folded his robes, installing them in the chest before leaving the room. And it was then, as he shut the door silently behind him, that the man had loomed out of the shadows, grabbing his elbow.

'Luke?'

He couldn't answer. There in the gloomy shadow of the Cathedral wall, he was overcome by fear. It was as if a long-dead Canon had risen from the grave to terrorise him.

'Are you Luke, boy?'

'Who are you?'

'Me, boy?' Sir Thomas smiled with the brittleness of melancholy. 'I'm your father.'

Luke had instinctively known he was telling the truth, yet Stephen had told him for so long that his father was dead, that accepting Sir Thomas who had appeared as if from nowhere, was difficult to swallow. Easier by far to believe him a ghost.

And his reason for turning up seemed equally odd. He wanted to talk to Luke, he said, but he appeared more interested in learning as much as he could about the dead cleric, Peter.

Janekyn yawned and shut the great doors that comprised the Fissand Gate, nodding to the two clerics. They dragged the massive wooden bars from their sockets in the left-hand wall and hauled them across to fit into the shallower seats in the wall opposite. Janekyn shrugged himself further into his robe and tried to protect his throat from the biting wind that threatened to flay the skin from his neck.

He had the one remaining duty, and that was to walk around the gates and make sure all were locked for the night. After so many years of performing this nightly service, he had a set routine. He had already seen to the Palace Gate, the Bear Gate, St Mary's and St Petrock's. All were locked. Now he had two remaining: the Bicklegh and St Martin's Lane. One of the two Secondaries helping him was slapping his arms together in an attempt to warm them and Janekyn said kindly, 'Come, the faster we walk the sooner you'll be able to stand before a fire.'

The pair nodded enthusiastically, thinking of the jugs of steaming wine set before Janekyn's fire.

As soon as they had gone, a figure drew away from the charnel chapel and stood listening for a moment. Hob of Whyteslegh shivered and it was only partly from the cold. He was petrified of being discovered.

The grounds of the Cathedral precinct were deserted. Above him the moon showed bright and clear in a starry sky, while the chill breeze from the south sent clouds scudding across at speed; each looked like a silken feather, billowing and changing shape in the silver light.

For Hob, the moon's stark brightness was terrifying. He felt that, if he were to step another yard towards the gate, he must be seen by someone. Even now, there might be a Canon or clerk watching him, probably calling for armed guards to cut him down for desecrating the Cathedral's grounds. The idea made him want to sidle back into the shadows of the charnel chapel and hide there, but fear of all the old bones interred within made him dread returning even more than he dreaded leaving.

At last he heard the faint whistle. It stirred him into action, and he scampered across the grass, slipping once and almost falling as his foot caught a loose cobble, but then he was at the corner of the Cathedral. The whistle came again and Hob gurgled with happiness to know he wasn't alone out here with all the dead bodies in the cemetery. It was a moment or two before he could compose himself enough to whistle back in return, and a few moments later Sir Thomas walked around the wall. He nodded curtly to Hob, then peered cautiously about the precinct.

Sir Thomas was not in a contented mood. After searching through all Peter and Jolinde's belongings in their room and finding nothing, since Jolinde had already removed his dead friend's effects, he was bitter at the waste of time. Every moment he spent here, in the Cathedral's grounds, he was in danger. If he should be found, many would recognise him, and there was only one punishment for an outlaw: the rope.

Sir Thomas was not sanguine about his prospects. Outlaws tended to die young. One day, if it was possible, he might give himself up and find a new, legitimate life, but not yet. Not while the murderer of Hamond lived. Hamond deserved to be avenged. That was why Sir Thomas had run the dreadful risk of joining the congregation in the Cathedral to hear the Mass, to seek out his son and learn all he could about the dead cleric Peter – the man who had born false witness against Hamond.

Unfortunately, Luke had been no use at all, apart from pointing to Peter's and Jolinde's house. And now he must escape from the Cathedral grounds before he could be discovered. In the past, Sir Thomas had made use of the Church's wealth, robbing well-endowed parish chapels of their silver and pewter, selling their goods for cash. If he were found, the Bishop would be delighted to see him hang.

At first Sir Thomas had been forced into his outlawry when his lands had been overrun. It was impossible for him to compete when his neighbour, who was a friend of Hugh Despenser the Younger – at the time not a well-known man, but still related to the King by marriage – had launched first a legal attack, and then an armed sortie against Sir Thomas.

If Sir Thomas had been wealthy and renowned, he could have beaten off both. But he wasn't. He was only a knight by birth and his poor little manor was scarcely able to support itself in peace, let alone raise funds to fight a small army. Perhaps if his wife, Luke's mother, had lived he could have used her diplomatic skills to effect some kind of peace, but she was dead. Thrown from her mare only a year or so after Luke had left to join the Cathedral.

Without her he had no chance. All he knew was how to fight, but against this overwhelming force he was powerless. His neighbour's men moved in and beat up all his servants in the fields until some were killed and the others feared going to their work, his crops rotted on the ground and he was forced to leave the place. There was nothing there – no income, no food, nothing.

In revenge Sir Thomas gathered up the men whom he could trust and launched a swift *chevauchée* against his tormentor. It had been successful, but the result had been the declaration some weeks later from the King's own courts that he, Sir Thomas, was an outlaw. 'If that is their decision, so be it,' he had declared, and his men had cheered him. They slept that night in a tavern, then rode to his neighbour's land. There he and his men executed their vengeance. The granaries were put to the torch; the barns, the outhouses, the cattle sheds, all were razed to the ground after Sir Thomas and his men had taken the best horseflesh, and then they had ridden off to the forests.

The first months had been tough, the succeeding ones infinitely worse as famine continued to scour the land. There was little to buy, let alone steal, and the only advantage to Sir Thomas was that his ranks were swelled by adventurers who were prepared to risk their lives to win a meal rather than die of starvation. Churches yielded their wealth to him and his men; rich travellers gave up their purses.

Up and down the county of Devonshire men and women paled at the news that Sir Thomas and his band were nearby. His face was described by those whom he had caught and released and since Karvinel's accusation that he and his band had robbed him, Sir Thomas knew that if he were recognised in the city, he would be bound to be caught. That was why he now could come out only at night when he could walk in shadows. It wasn't safe, but it was safer than daytime.

At least he had learned something. After talking to Luke, he had gone to Peter's small home, had spotted Jolinde coming out of there and had followed the youth round the side of the cloister, observing him as he surreptitiously ducked below a beam and disappeared into a small space near the Cathedral's wall. When Sir Thomas investigated, he learned how Jolinde had left and re-entered the Cathedral at night. The discovery pleased the grizzled knight. It could prove useful to him too, at some time in the future. If he didn't have other men to meet now, he'd take the tunnels as a shortcut into the city. Only then did he return to search Jolinde's house, but without success.

Hob was whimpering with trepidation; the moon was shining down upon them. Sir Thomas nodded and walked to the wall. There Hob untied his leather jack and unwound a thin rope from about his belly and chest. Sir Thomas wrapped a stone in linen and tied it to the rope, then hefted it in his hand. They were at Little Stile now, a small gate without a tower above, and Sir Thomas waited a moment, then whistled. There was nothing at first, so he tried again. This time there was a low, cautious whistle on the other side of the gate. Sir Thomas stepped back, whirled the stone at the end of the rope a few times over his head, then hurled it up and over the gate.

The cloth bindings silenced its fall. A moment or two later Sir Thomas felt the line being pulled. He let it pay out, and then it was stationary. There was another whistle to show that it was securely anchored, and Sir Thomas immediately began to climb.

At the top of the gate he swung a leg over and surveyed the ground. Soon, he promised himself, soon he would have his revenge. And with that thought engraved on his mind, he dropped over to the ground.

CHAPTER SIXTEEN

Christmas Day was clear and bright, with the sun shining unhindered. Occasionally, solitary clouds drifted past at speed. The wind was strong, rattling the shutters of the inn, and it was their repetitive hammering which woke Baldwin before the dawn itself.

He lay on his back staring up at the ceiling. A cresset, a small wick floating in a reservoir of oil, had been left alight all night, and now it threw strange shadows upon the rafters above.

Jeanne grunted and moaned beside him, snuggling closer and throwing a leg over his, but today he felt no erotic surge beyond a mild affectionate stirring. He rested a hand on her thigh and slipped the other under her neck to cuddle her to him, kissing her hair. It still smelled of incense from the Cathedral the night before.

The two deaths, Peter's and Ralph's, intrigued him, yet he could see no link between them. Baldwin didn't believe

Peter's death was suicide, nor yet that it could have been caused by food poisoning but he could not see who could wish to murder the fellow.

Baldwin had enough experience of enquiring into murders to know that men rarely, if ever, killed without a good reason: even if that reason later appeared to be ridiculous. At the time that the murder was committed, the killer had a clear, understandable motive.

There was another aspect to this killing, Baldwin reminded himself. Poison was a peculiarly coldblooded and cowardly method of murder. Someone had decided to kill with poison – and *Jolinde had bought orpiment from the apothecary.*

Had Peter been the target? It was quite possible that Jolinde had argued with his friend and decided to murder him – but if so, why? There was no hint that the two had suffered a break in their friendship. Someone else could have put the poison onto or inside the food while it was left unguarded in the tavern. Jolinde certainly wasn't going to notice while he was upstairs with the delightful Claricia; could the deadly food have been intended for him? And if it wasn't, if it *was* meant for Peter – who, then, had known that Jolinde was supplying him with food? That would give Baldwin a starting point.

Jeanne mumbled, half asleep, and Baldwin felt her hand stroking his chest, slowly moving down his body. He grinned and caught it, ignoring her murmurs of disappointment. There was little time if they were to get to the Cathedral for the second Mass of the day. He smiled down at her sleepy face, but then stood, wincing at the cold air on his naked body. He quickly pulled on his clothes: it was far too chill to linger. When he was dressed, he woke his wife with kisses and gentle entreaties, and only left her when her eyes opened and she gave him an ungracious snort as welcome. Jeanne was not at her best at this hour.

Downstairs he found Edgar already kneeling by the fire stirring a pot filled with spiced wine while Simon sat on a stool nearby scratching at his head. The pleasant aroma filled the hall: cinnamon, ginger, nutmeg. All good, warming spices for a man who was about to go out into the cold. Baldwin took the proffered cup and sipped at the drink. The heat travelled straight down to his toes and he gave his servant a smile of gratitude. 'Thank you, Edgar, but today of all days . . .' He took the pot from Edgar and poured out a large cup for his loyal Sergeant.

'Thank you, Sir Baldwin.'

'What about me?' demanded Simon.

Soon they heard footsteps in their host's small chamber. Outside, the Cathedral bell was ringing loudly and from the noise in the streets, many citizens were moving towards the churches and Cathedral for the next Mass, the Shepherd's Mass, which was always celebrated at dawn. Baldwin refilled his cup and took it to his wife.

Jeanne was reluctant to rise from her bed. The freezing air made her wish to remain beneath the covers. It was too cold, and too early as well. Her head felt light from lack of sleep. She was used to getting to bed much earlier, and her attendance at the Mass last night had left her quite dozy and unaware. She could feel her eyelids dragging like leaden weights, forcing her to close them. When her husband laughed, it was no consolation.

'Laugh now, *hus*band, but remember that I shall visit all your humour upon you when you are suffering from too much wine. And my vengeance shall be not swift, but longer-lasting, and entirely painful for you,' she growled as she squinted at him in the meagre light of the cresset.

Her temper had greatly improved when they came to the great Fissand Gate. There in the gloomy arch, she once more saw the crippled figure sprawled at the edge of the gateway. Today he looked so meagre, so destroyed, that the sight tugged at Jeanne's heart. She quickly left Baldwin's side and fumbled with her purse.

'Lady, thank you,' John Coppe said, taking the coins and ducking his head in gratitude. He smiled, his mouth twisted up as he watched her give him a gracious little gesture of her hand, then turn and walk back to her waiting husband; she pushed her hand through Baldwin's elbow, matching her pace to his as they walked in through the great open gates to the Cathedral.

Coppe sighed faintly as another coin was casually tossed towards him. 'Thank you, Master,' he called automatically, stashing it away with the other coins he had collected already. That, he knew, was the good aspect of Christmas. The priests would all look after him anyway, but on this one day of the year, people wouldn't begrudge him a few pennies. With any luck he could get enough to keep him in drinks through the next week.

The man who had thrown him the coin stalked off towards the Cathedral, and Coppe watched him go, his eyes narrowed. Coppe wouldn't turn down any man's generosity, but there was something odd in the way the fellow threw his coin and marched off. He was dressed in a thick woollen cloak, with a hood over his head. Even his face was concealed, giving

Coppe the impression of glittering eyes, but little else. Not that there weren't any number of others dressed in a similarly defensive manner against the icy air.

Coppe saw him make for the western door, but then slow down and dawdle, as if waiting for someone. Last night, when that idiot boy came and offered to help him into the Cathedral to attend the Mass, there had been a man like this one standing nearby. It hadn't been easy to see his face, for it was hidden beneath a large hat, but from the build and height it could have been this same fellow.

'Do you, um, want to go in again?'

Coppe looked up to see that his friend of the night before had returned, suddenly appearing at his side; a malnourished and dim-looking idiot. Coppe gave an inward groan. He hadn't intended going into the morning's Mass. He'd been to Mass the night before, and one Mass a day was enough for him. 'You back, then, eh? I don't know why you want to drag me about, lad. You go in, I'll be all right here.'

'No, you must come! Please, let me help you, yes?'

'You go on in. It was kind of you to help me in last night, but you don't have to today.'

To his astonishment, the fellow looked as if he was on the verge of tears. He wrung his hands, his mouth working uselessly, alternately gaping at Coppe, then at the Cathedral doors. The crush in the Fissand Gate was dwindling now, and it was obvious that the service must soon begin. 'You must come with me.'

'Bugger off, lad,' Coppe said curtly. 'I don't have to go nowheres I don't want. You carry on, just do as you want.'

The lad had the brains of a fool. Probably he'd been told to help cripples; perhaps his village priest had told him to

give any service he could to a beggar – knowing what hypo-
critical bastards some village priests could be. Half the time
the village idiot was born to one of the priests' own mounts.
Never mind that they were supposed to be chaste; Coppe had
seen them, out in the streets, small dogs on leads to tempt the
women. As soon as a woman expressed delight in the priest's
toy dog, he knew he had her halfway to his bed. Coppe
understood much. That was how he spent his life: observing.
He was no fool, he could make connections, could pursue
ideas until he explained things to himself.

He wasn't unique. It was how all the beggars with brains
spent their lives. Not that there weren't plenty of cretins
amongst the alms-takers at the Cathedral gates, but Coppe
knew several who had brains beyond the brute intelligence
of an animal. They saw and noted much, and for the most
part were ignored by the rest of humanity because they were
no one. They were nothing. As important as a gatepost.

The idiot's hand-wringing grew more pronounced and his
brow wrinkled as if he was tortured by the thought that
Coppe might be left behind. He glanced fretfully towards the
Cathedral doors.

Coppe followed his gaze. There, to the side of the door,
was the hooded man. When he glanced back at the boy's face
he saw the fear on it, and gave an inward sigh. The lad was
touched, but Coppe was convinced that his present anxiety
was due more to the cloaked man at the door.

The cloaked man had been there the night before. He had
joined Coppe and the idiot as they entered the Cathedral,
although he had slipped out during the service. Others had
too. Many needed to piss halfway through the Mass. But
now he thought about it, Coppe couldn't remember the man

returning. Perhaps he, like others, had been bored by the length of the celebration. Now he stood like a man trying to sink into the walls, as if he would crawl under a shadow if he could. Coppe had a feeling that he was trying to remain concealed from someone – but that was madness! Even if he was a felon, he was safe within the sanctuary of the Cathedral grounds. Perhaps he was as daft as the boy at Coppe's side.

All the beggar knew was that this poor idiot child was suffering the torments of the damned purely because Coppe wouldn't let him pull him into the Cathedral with him.

'Oh, damn me! All right, I'll go with you. But afterwards you'll have to let me get out and buy a pot of strong ale,' he grumbled. Only later did he wonder whether the two wanted him with them because two men helping a cripple were almost invisible. People's eyes went to the cripple and then away; if a cripple was of no note, of how much less importance were his attendants?

Jolinde was detailed to assist Adam with replenishing the candles, and he was in the main nave of the Cathedral as people began to arrive. He saw Sir Baldwin and Lady Jeanne in the crush, the Bailiff at their side. It would be a relief when the building work was complete, he thought. Everyone was so cramped up in the nave, pressed together like sheep in a pen. When the new eastern half was opened, the choir could move into their stalls beyond the towers, leaving all the nave to the congregation.

He saw the City Bailiff and the Coroner arrive together. They were talking in low voices, both frowning seriously as if their conversation was not pleasing to either. The Coroner's gaze passed over Jolinde, and with a shudder of guilt Jolinde saw Roger de Gidleigh's eyes return to him, studying him unblinkingly.

The knowledge of his crime made Jolinde stumble as he hurried to keep up with young Adam. The Secondary tutted irritably as Jolinde almost tripped, and took the box from him. 'Watch your step!' he growled. 'And mind out for clumsy bastards knocking you over. Last night it was the merchant, le Berwe, and half the folks today have already been at the wine.'

Jolinde nodded, but his mind was elsewhere. If anyone here had seen him abroad on the night that Peter died, or worse, if they knew he had been about in the city on the morning that Ralph had died, they would have many questions for him. Especially if someone had guessed at his theft as well.

He was relieved when the bells stopped ringing, and he and Adam could collect their boxes and tapers and make their way to the other side of the screen and into the choir.

When he felt the man shove at his back Nick Karvinel snapped his head round ready to curse whoever it might be, but he held his tongue when he recognised the clerical garb. A candle cleric, he thought to himself with a sneer. Pathetic fool! The best he can manage is to fill empty candle-holders for a living.

His wife was at his side, glancing openly about the nave, eyeing up the men present, the bitch. Juliana had been happy enough with him when he'd been a success, delighted when he made his big deals, getting a name for himself, making it into the Freedom of the City with all the big merchants. If things had gone right for him this year, she'd still be content.

He kept a surreptitious eye on her as the crowd moved forward, jockeying for the best position to hear what was going on beyond the screen, or perhaps find a point from which they could peer through a section to where the Canons were singing their praises to God.

She wasn't watching the priest up at the altar, she was still ogling the men, he saw. Especially that Bailiff, Puttock, who'd been at her side the night before at le Berwe's feast. Karvinel peered over the heads of the people nearest. The Bailiff was up to the right side of the nave, following the service attentively. At his side was his friend the knight, whose lips moved in time with the singing as if he knew the words. His wife Jeanne made a show of her piety, keeping her eyes downcast like a bloody virgin.

People like that made him sick. As he returned his gaze to the altar, occasionally glancing at his wife, Karvinel couldn't help a sneer distorting his features. Knights and their ladies had no idea what life was all about – just like the merchants in Vincent's league. They hadn't a clue what a man had to do to survive, to succeed. It was hard enough when times were good, when competition undercut your prices and forced you to find cheaper suppliers, but when times were bad and you couldn't persuade anyone to buy what you had, that was really tough. And then you got troubles like Karvinel's, when some bastard broke into your house and nicked everything. And later torched it.

Sometimes the only way a man could survive was by betraying his own soul. Occasionally a man must steal and risk damnation just to be able to live. Karvinel knew that now. Had known it two days ago when he went down to shout at his bottler for not waking him, and had found the man's bed unslept in. The last of his servants, bar the cretinous urchin who swept the hall, had left.

Juliana had shrugged carelessly, saying it was lucky. It would be a relief to be rid of so expensive a mouth to feed, and he wasn't really necessary now.

'What do you mean, not necessary?' he had shouted.

'You don't have that much business to conduct, do you, my dear?' she had returned coldly

'There are the gloves to finish for the Cathedral, the wine for—'

'Precisely. There really is very little for you to do, husband. Perhaps there will be more soon, for if your creditors all appear and ask for your money, I suppose we shall be forced to sell the house and all our belongings. But until then, there is little to be done that you can't do alone, is there?'

Her spiteful manner had made him see red. He could have hit her, punched her, and the release would have given him immense satisfaction . . . except he knew what the end result would be. She would simply look at him contemptuously and go quiet, perhaps silently walk away from him – and from that moment she would be entirely lost to him.

That was the trouble, he knew, watching his wife as she studied other men. Everything he had done was intended to keep her as his own. He couldn't risk losing her. The loss of prestige should she leave him was too appalling even to contemplate. But he couldn't tolerate her flirting with other men, not even if that was the price he must pay for her continued company. Swallowing painfully, he viewed the future. Unless he could soon reveal his renewed financial status, she would leave him.

Then a new resolve stiffened his spine. There was no need for him to go on suffering this intolerable situation. Juliana's stupid behaviour must improve soon. She would hardly go looking for another man to support her if she learned that her own husband was immensely wealthy again. That was the reason for her coldness recently – the belief that he was a failure. Well, soon he'd be able to show her – point to the large sums of money he'd acquired – and then she'd warm up towards him, she'd love him again as she had before.

Right now she was drooling over every available male in the area. It looked as though she was determined to find anyone who had money so that she could desert him. Any fellow with a well-filled purse would do, Nick thought cynically; she'd leap into his bed without compunction. There was nothing to hold her to Nick. Not while he was bankrupt. In Juliana's mind, her marriage to Nick Karvinel was a financial transaction: he could possess her, provided that he gave her access to his money. While his finances were healthy, she was happy.

And, at this minute she was far from happy. His recent difficulties had turned her frigid, impervious to his needs. He could prove to her that he was strong, but there were risks: if she boasted about his money, others could get to hear. It was far too dangerous. No, he'd have to keep his secret hidden, even from her.

Especially from her.

CHAPTER SEVENTEEN

In his thick cloak, Sir Thomas stood trying to keep out of the view of the general public. He couldn't keep his hood up, for that would have appeared disrespectful in God's house, so he partially concealed himself in shadows wherever he could away from the brightest candles. Then he caught sight of a figure he recognised: the Bailiff of the City, William de Lappeford. Sir Thomas retreated slightly. He knew de Lappeford only too well, and de Lappeford knew his description. All the officers involved in the law knew of Sir Thomas.

It was then that Hob gasped and pulled at his sleeve. 'That's them, Sir Thomas! Karvinel and his Lady.'

Following his pointing finger, Sir Thomas caught a fleeting glimpse of the couple. Although he had been responsible for stealing from the man, and even setting his house on fire, the outlaw had never actually seen his victim in the flesh. Fearing he might lose sight of them, Sir Thomas slipped away from his place of concealment and went up the side of the nave, his eye fixed upon the pair. The candles lit up his face a couple of times, but he didn't care. He kept on going, resting at a pillar from where he had a good view of them.

And as he waited there, he saw Juliana's gaze pass along the men at this side of the Cathedral, saw her notice him, look him over appraisingly. With a thrill of amusement Sir Thomas realised that her look was as blatant as a whore's. Her husband didn't look up: he was praying, Sir Thomas saw as he returned her smile. Karvinel was bending his head and murmuring quietly, crossing himself regularly.

'As you should,' Sir Thomas whispered to himself. 'After you murdered Hamond.'

Brother Stephen watched the two Secondaries return to their places in the stalls. Adam stood facing him, while Jolinde was in the row immediately before him, and Stephen could look down upon his tonsured head.

The service was not as beautiful as that of the night before. The midnight ceremony, the Angel's Mass of Christmas Eve, was intended to reinforce the notion that the light of salvation appeared at the darkest moment in the depths of winter, and because it was held by candlelight many people came to witness it, but fewer attended this, the Shepherd's Mass. It was difficult to persuade people to go to any service at dawn, but today only the most determined and committed would come – especially if they had been up late the night before to attend the Angel's Mass.

He sensed that the choir was lightening and glanced up, past the altar. Although there was a massive wooden partition to separate the nave from the new choir and high altar which were still being built, there were slats in the screen to allow the light to enter. In years to come he would be able to look up from his stall and behold the sunlight streaming in through the coloured glass panels of the new eastern window. He longed for that day. It would be a wonderful sight. Once he had seen it, he could die happily, for then he would know that his most important work, that of ensuring that the Cathedral could afford to pay for this rebuilding, would be almost done.

So many years of effort. Stephen sighed inwardly as he thought about it. The man with the vision had been the first Bishop Walter – Bishop Bronescombe. It was said that he had had the idea while attending the consecration of Salisbury Cathedral. That was in 1258, more than sixty years ago, and so far only the new choir's external works had been finished. There was still at least another five or six years' work in fittings: the *reredos*, the new Bishop's throne, the *pulpitum* and the *sedilia*. Until they were all completed, the choir would remain out here in the ancient Norman nave, often singing in the dark, all waiting for the time when they could migrate beyond the wooden fence that kept them from the new building. And then all the services could be held in there, while this, the oldest remaining part of the church itself, could be razed to the ground – well, to the window sills, anyway – before being built up, layer on layer, in the new style. It would be at least another sixty years before the project was complete.

But Stephen would have succeeded in completing his task if the works could progress during and after his life. It was his duty to ensure that the funds were there.

Of course, Bishop Walter Stapledon was a good financial bulwark against the problems which invariably occurred. He took as much interest in the rebuilding as Stephen himself, walking about under the gantries and scaffoldings with the eye of a man used to overseeing such works. Stapledon had already contributed much of his own money to building a school in Exeter and a college in Oxford, for he was firmly convinced of the importance of education. He believed that all his priests should receive constant training, and he was committed to finding the best scholars from all over Devon and giving them the benefit of a true education. To Stephen's knowledge, Walter Stapledon was the most widely travelled Bishop the Chapter had ever possessed, constantly on the move and dropping in on all the parishes within his See. He took such matters seriously, for how could a Bishop be sure that the poor souls within that See were being properly guided if he didn't know the strengths of his priests?

And while travelling over his See, he found boys who could be of benefit to the Cathedral or used in churches. If they had the ability to learn, they could be moulded to be useful. Bishop Stapledon had found many like that. Adam was one such, as were Luke and Henry. All of them had been found and saved from lives of irredeemable poverty, educated to the limits of their abilities and trained to sing and praise God.

Luke, of course, had to be recommended to the Bishop, but Stephen couldn't regret his actions. At the time he was convinced it was best for the boy and for the Cathedral; but he was less convinced of Adam. The boy helped about the place, it was true, but he had an unpleasant streak in his nature. Not really suitable material for the Cathedral. He was capable of making and distributing candles, delivering loaves within the Close, sweeping floors or cleaning metalwork, but he was a sad failure when it came to Latin, to writing or counting. The best that could be said of him was that he had found his niche. He would certainly never advance, whatever the Dean wished.

The Dean stood. Stephen idly considered the importance of Mass. In a normal day a priest was allowed to say only one Mass. All others were given by different priests. There were few exceptions to this rule. On Good Friday no Masses were permitted, because of the Agony of the Crucifixion, so on Easter Day two Masses were allowed, as they were on special occasions such as marriages or funerals. On Christmas Day three Masses were needed.

Funerals. Stephen thought again about the death of the Secondary. It was a shame that a man so young should have his life ended, but the fellow shouldn't have tried to commit theft. Stephen would have to consider raising the matter in Chapter. The Secondary had committed the heinous crime of theft from the Cathedral; he couldn't be given a funeral within these sacred grounds. Although many would argue that he deserved kindness, that he should be buried like any other cleric, that there was no proof of his guilt, Stephen had no such qualms.

Peter Golloc had deserved to die, the liar!

Nicholas Karvinel went home with his wife as soon as the service was over. They must prepare for the feast at Vincent le Berwe's, making themselves look presentable, clean and *grateful*, Nick thought savagely.

Gratitude was to be his lot in future, so far as Vincent was concerned. The latter obviously thought that Nick would be thankful for whatever morsels fell from his plate. If there was something that he could give to his poor friend, Vincent's smug attitude seemed to imply, then he would be glad to help. It was like receiving charity, and all the more frustrating and humiliating because Nicholas couldn't complain to anyone about it.

At his door he handed Juliana inside, but then a spirit of rebellion rose in his breast and he walked out to John Renebaud's tavern. It was near his house, a haven to which he often repaired. Vincent patronised it too, but he would be busy at home. He needed a few moments' peace, a quart of ale or a pint of good strong wine to set him up so that he could tolerate the graciousness of the good Receiver of the City, Vincent le Berwe. For although Karvinel was out of the woods now, thanks to his little windfall, courtesy of the Cathedral, he couldn't let anyone know. The theft was too recent. Were they to hear of his sudden wealth, they might guess at the source of it – and that would be catastrophic. No, better keep his mouth shut. He would continue paying cash from his meagre supply of coins, waiting until he saw a suitable opportunity to declare his wealth. A ship with goods for him, something that would explain the appearance of his new money. After all, any man could speculate; a glover could double his income with a lucky gamble on a shipload of spices.

If Vincent became insistent, Karvinel thought, he would definitely ask what the other man had been doing outside Ralph's house on the day he died. That would shut the bugger up! So taken up was he with his thoughts, Nick never saw the cloaked man pausing at his door, glancing up at the sign and picture of gloves which hung above it, then smiling coldly, following Karvinel to the inn.

*   *   *

Hob waited after the service, confused when his master didn't return. He left Coppe to make his own way back to his seat by the gate, then walked outside to look for Sir Thomas, but there was no sign of him. The cold began to eat into Hob's bones.

Eventually he gave up and left for the camp, walking carefully along the road to the South Gate in the city wall, then out past the terraced fields which led down to the Shittebrook and on to Bull Meadow. He skirted past the Maudlin, where the lepers congregated, watching the gates of the colony with a superstitious dread, recalling the stories of how they could grab passers-by to rape them or eat them, but he was lucky: no one was keen on taking him and he could continue unmolested.

The trees here were much thinner. Many had been cleared for the use of the citizens, whether for building or for firewood, and there was more coppicing than old woodland.

He soon heard the sharp whistle as he hurried along the rough track. The weather wasn't cold enough for the ruts and hoofprints to solidify, and the mud was awful. His feet were sodden as he stepped into deeper puddles which filled his boots and made him grimace with revulsion as the chilly water slopped about, squelching with every step he took.

The band was waiting near a large oak, one of only a very few which had survived the demands of construction in Exeter. About it tents had been erected, enough for the fourteen men who followed Sir Thomas. A charcoal fire was smoking in the middle, over which were spitted two ducks, a goose and a small pig.

'So, Hob, you came back when the hunger got to you, did you?' Jen called lightly. 'Where's Sir Thomas?'

'I thought h-he'd be back already. Isn't he here?'

Jen had been stirring at a pot but now she stopped and stood upright. 'You lost him?'

'He was in the crowd, but he went off to see the . . .'

'He saw the merchant?' Jen asked.

Hob was worried by her expression. Jen looked angry with him, very angry. 'He asked me to take him there, to the big Church.'

'That was so he could see his other son.'

'That was last night. Today he said he wanted me to point out the merchant.'

'You idiot! Are you mad?'

'He told me, he told me!' Hob asserted, his head retreating into his shoulder, gazing down at his feet. He hated upsetting his sister; she was all he had in the world, but he couldn't help it. Sir Thomas scared him, and Sir Thomas had told him to point out the merchant if he saw the man. He couldn't disobey Sir Thomas. He scuffed his boot in the dirt, doodling with a toe.

'Stop that! Don't you realise anything? Jesus! You're so thick on occasion,' Jen said scathingly. She threw the wooden spoon into the pot and went into the tent she shared with Sir Thomas, returning with a bonnet and thick coat. 'You'll have to stay here, Hob. Look after that food and don't let it burn!'

One of the lookouts had witnessed Hob's discomfiture from his vantage point. Now he called down, 'Where are you going, Jen?'

'You heard. Your leader has gone to seek the man who says he was robbed.'

'The one that got Hamond killed?'

231

She looked up as she shrugged into her coat. 'Yes. The one who had Hamond hanged.'

Luke the Chorister sat sedately as he should, waiting until the cup of wine arrived before him. He sipped slowly, holding it carefully with both hands, and even when Adam, at his side, nudged him viciously in the ribs with an elbow, Luke didn't spill a drop.

The food was good, but not too rich. Stephen didn't enjoy overly spiced foodstuffs, and refused to spend large sums to obtain them. Thriftiness was his watchword, as it should be for a Treasurer. He looked upon all the money spent within the Cathedral as his own, and when he spent his own, he measured his expenditure against what it could acquire for the Cathedral itself.

It was an irritation, but Luke ate politely and with silent determination. Stephen did not like disruption at his table, and Choristers who chattered were as obtrusive and annoying as a guest who rudely denounced the quality of his wine. Neither were to be borne.

Not that Luke wanted to talk. Since the shock of the night before, he had wandered about feeling quite dazed, as if someone had struck the back of his head with a club.

For years he had been told that his father was dead. His father, a knight from the Soth family, the last to live in the small manor at Exmouth, had been killed when a neighbour had attacked him, or so Stephen had told him. Why should the Canon have deceived him? His father had become an outlaw, a felon, and Luke had not even been told.

Luke moved in time to prevent another nudge from Adam forcing him to knock over the salt. He had to bite back the angry words which rose to his lips. It wasn't fair that Adam should keep pushing him, forever trying to make him look a fool, when Luke had never done anything to upset him. It wasn't his fault Adam was a failure.

That was the problem, though. Luke knew it well enough. He'd even been warned about such things when he first showed promise. It was Stephen himself who drew him aside and told him that other Choristers might pick on him because of his abilities. In fact, at the time Luke was quite sure the Treasurer was letting him know that Henry would probably make his life difficult, but now Luke knew the Treasurer had meant people like Adam.

Adam wasn't the only one. There were quite a few like him in the Cathedral precinct: fellows who had expected to move up the church's hierarchy until they themselves ran their own See as Bishop, or perhaps became a Precentor or a Dean. So few ever seemed to appreciate that for every Precentor there were some hundred or more who were of a lower level even within his own church. No, few realised that there was every likelihood that, if there were fourteen Choristers, none of them would become a dignitary within that church. Luke himself had already seen how many boys fell by the wayside.

He broke off another piece of bread and popped it into his mouth. It wasn't only because of bad behaviour or manners that the boys were thrown out of the choir. There had been two in Luke's first year who simply couldn't make head nor tail of Latin, spoken or written. Another fellow had taken to weeping each night before sleep. Lonely and miserable, he had come from a lord's household, and suddenly being dropped into Exeter had been too much for the eight-year-old. He had been sent home before six months had passed.

But when the Choristers' voices broke, their troubles multiplied. Then they had little genuine reason for remaining within the cloister, apart from trying to better themselves, learning as much about writing and reading as they could so that they might prove their value as clerics. If they were successful, they would be able to continue in this manner, as Secondaries, before they gradually received enough attention to be promoted. Some would then remain at the lowest levels, perhaps after many years of striving achieving the status of a Chaplain, while those who were lucky might progress from Deacon to the exalted heights of Vicar or Annuellar.

Being a Vicar was probably best, Luke judged reflectively. A Vicar had all his food and lodging provided by the Canon he served, and when there was a gap in the number of Canons, there was the possibility of promotion. There was also much to be said for being an Annuellar, a chantry priest. These men were appointed by the Dean and Chapter and lived in rented chambers in the Close, but were free for much of their lives. They did not have to go to their Canon to obtain food or lodging, they were given an annual stipend, and from that they could buy what they needed. Nor were they forced to turn up at all services in the way that Secondaries and Vicars were. The only people free of compulsion to attend were the Canons, who could ignore the bells' summons if they wished, and the Annuellars. The latter had the one duty, performing a Mass every day at a specific time and at a specific altar.

Luke rather liked the idea of becoming an Annuellar. It might not offer so much potential for advancement, but with his ability to read and write, it would be an easy life.

Many Secondaries failed; usually because of laziness on their part, Luke reminded himself. He had heard that sage comment passed by another Secondary talking about Jolinde, and was privately convinced that the same applied to Adam. He was not suited to the Canonical life, anyway. He was a bully and a cheat.

With a wash of cold anguish, Luke recalled his father's face from the night before. Now he had his own notoriety: he was the son of a felon, related to an outlaw. Perhaps Stephen's deliberate concealment of his father's survival had been intended as a kindness, Luke realised. The Canon might have considered it preferable that other Choristers couldn't discover what had truly happened to Sir Thomas. If so, perhaps he was right. Luke shuddered as he thought how Henry would torment him, should he learn that Luke's father had become an outlaw. It would reverse all the insults Luke had hurled at him for being lower-born. Henry could at least assert that *his* parents had never broken the King's Peace.

It was a relief when Adam kicked his shin beneath the table. The cruel pain took Luke's mind off his father.

If the stories were true, Adam had been a good Chorister, with a fine voice, but when his voice shattered during a long Psalm one Easter Day, it had destroyed his confidence. His whole existence up until that point had been built upon the solid foundation of his ability to sing, and as soon as that was taken from him, he appeared to lose all motivation. He failed in his studies and proved himself incompetent at figures. Now the strong rumour in the Close asserted that he would be lucky if he was permitted to remain in the Cathedral as an acolyte.

Some did. They stayed, hanging about the place like sad and mournful hounds who had lost their master, getting in the way of the choir as they hurried from cloister to choir to Chapter to dormitory. Many simply left while in their early twenties. There was no point haunting a place where you weren't wanted, Luke thought, but Adam seemed to have no idea where else he could go. Pathetic.

Luke reached down to pick up his bread, but there was nothing there. Staring at the table where it had been, he was astonished to see it had disappeared. Then he saw Adam smiling derisively as he crammed the last piece into his mouth and chewed slowly, with evident relish.

The meal was finished. Arthur, Stephen's Vicar, stood and said the Grace, and the small group left the table to go and watch the plays in the Cathedral. Luke couldn't help but cast a regretful eye back at the table as he rose. There had not been enough food. His stomach was calling for more. Perhaps if Peter's half-loaf hadn't hardened to a rock-like consistency, he could eat a little of that later. He could toast it beside a fire – make it more edible.

With that decided, he was about to head for the door when he felt a foot lash out around his leg, making him stumble. He tripped, felt himself falling and grabbed at the first thing he could. It was the tablecloth. Pulling it with him, he fell to the ground, ducking as trenchers and the salt showered down on top of him.

'Luke!' he heard Stephen gasp.

'I'm sorry, but I—'

'You clumsy *cretin*! What in God's name . . . Go! And do not return for food today. You will get nothing more from here!'

Luke turned away and averted his head as tears threatened to flood his face. He ignored the grinning face of his tormentor and left.

Simon smiled broadly as the boar's head was carried in. This was more to his taste than a whole mix of fish dishes. Vincent le Berwe had done his best yesterday, but no matter how you arranged the dishes, fish didn't appeal to a man with a strong carnivorous appetite like Simon. He preferred red meat every time.

And this was the way to feast, he thought. Plenty of good venison: a haunch or two of doe, one fresh, one salted, two hares and a boar that Vincent said a grateful friend had provided as the result of a little favour he had been able to perform. Simon felt his mouth water as he stared at the dishes piling up in front of them. He only wished he could do someone a similar 'little favour'.

He grabbed at his drinking horn and drank deeply. It was a pleasant cup, with a small face moulded into the end, the whole thing glazed in green. Far better than being down on one of the other tables, where the drinkers had to share a pitcher and wipe it before passing it to their neighbour.

By the time the servants had arrived to clear the tables of their debris, Simon was feeling very relaxed. He belched quietly behind a hand, smiling apologetically to Juliana at his side.

Soon the tables were away, secreted out into the buttery or in the small yard behind, and all the guests had been moved so that their benches ringed the room; now they could rest their backs comfortably against the walls. It was at this point that the musicians entered and started singing.

Not bad, Simon thought, although by this stage he would have thought a dog's howling contained a certain merit. There were three men playing, one with a fiddle, one with a citole and the last with a drum, which he tried to beat in time. From the glazed look in his eyes, his failure was down to Vincent's over-lavish hospitality. The trio sang several carols, and then were joined by a dark-haired young woman who gave a demonstration of her tumbling and dancing skills.

Simon waved his drinking horn in time to the music as she sprang onto her hands and walked the length of the room, then somersaulted, landing with her legs outspread before and behind, waiting for the applause to finish.

'By God's Cods,' Simon cried. 'She's damn good!'

She rose and continued, this time with a slower, more contemplative dance. The drummer had been persuaded to return to the buttery, and now the music was more sedate; soon the girl stopped her dancing and stood before Vincent to sing a carol. It was a popular one, and several of the other guests joined in. Simon himself did with gusto, singing the chorus enthusiastically, if not entirely accurately.

Looking about the group ranged on benches at the walls, Simon saw only delight on all faces, except when he looked to his left and caught Nicholas Karvinel watching him. As soon as Simon met his gaze, Karvinel turned away, but Simon had seen his face and recognised the self-loathing of the cuckold.

CHAPTER EIGHTEEN

Baldwin too had enjoyed the meal, although he was careful to eat and drink less than he could. His system had been used to a sparse diet for so long now that if he consumed too much it caused a reaction and his whole body was upset for days afterwards. So instead of having his mazer of wine topped up continually, he insisted upon waiting until he had emptied it before allowing the bottler to refill it.

He saw that Simon was fascinated by the dancer. She was light on her feet when whirling to the music, elegant and deceptively subtle, just like a Saracen woman would have been, although she walked with the heavy precision of a professional dancer.

Baldwin could remember Eastern women from his time in Acre and Cyprus, before he joined the Templars. This one had the same smoothly flowing movements, the same confidence in her body and ability, and he wondered for an instant whether she was perhaps the daughter of one of the soldiers who had gone out to the Holy Land to defend it – but then he realised how ridiculous such a thought was. Although she was darkly beautiful, her complexion was of soft English peach and she was in her early twenties, no more. The daughter of a soldier in Acre would be at least thirty by now.

'An excellent dancer,' he complimented Vincent.

'Yes. She is the daughter of a baker of ours. He pulls his hair out, as you'd expect. A girl like her flaunting herself before the eager eyes of so many men,' Vincent grinned. 'There are enough to be jealous of Elias.'

'She's Mary?'

'Yes, I thought you knew,' Vincent said off-handedly.

It was intriguing to watch her. Baldwin, his eyes on her feet in an attempt to keep up with the rapid movements, could easily imagine how a young lad could become infatuated by her: a boy brought up in the secluded, bachelor environment of the glover's household. Meeting this splendid creature each morning to collect his daily loaf of bread, was it any surprise that he should be knocked sideways?

'Sir Baldwin,' Vincent had risen and was standing before him. 'You haven't met my friend, have you? This is Nicholas Karvinel – the man who has helped to make your gloves.'

'Master Karvinel, it is a pleasure,' Baldwin said, with a faint hint of remoteness in his tone. 'Tell me, aren't you the poor fellow that was robbed on the road south of the city? And you later found one of the outlaws in a tavern?'

Unaccountably the man looked wary, glancing at Vincent. 'Um, yes,' he said after a pause, 'and I'm glad to say the bastard swung, God rot him!'

'Well, at least you caught the villain,' Baldwin said politely.

'Yes, that at least was good.'

Vincent excused himself and went to speak to another guest, and Baldwin was left smiling blankly at a man about whom he knew nothing except for his reputation for miserably bad luck.

At his side, Jeanne rescued him. 'It must have been dreadful to hear that the other glover was murdered. Such a terrible thing to happen to anyone, that kind of *petit treason*. The thought that your own servant should kill you . . .'

'It is a horrible thing to dwell upon, my Lady,' Nicholas Karvinel agreed. 'But there is murder and madness upon all the streets. All we can do is hang those who would break the laws. It's the only rule they understand. And the apprentice who kills his master is very certainly deserving of his end. What sort of world would we live in if we allowed that kind of lunacy?'

'Ugh, yes! Horrid,' Jeanne said, with affected revulsion. Baldwin restrained the grin that threatened to crack his serious features. His wife was already bored with the man and disliked his opinions, although she was too well-bred to contradict him. 'Tell me,' she continued, 'how magnificent are these gloves to be?'

'Ah, my Lady, you wouldn't expect me to give away the secrets of my work? My commission was to produce splendid gloves so that the Dean and Chapter could show their appreciation to the city and the friends of the Cathedral. I couldn't possibly tell you what they would be like.'

'Oh, I see. But you got all you needed from the poor dead glover?'

'The gloves were almost finished. I only had to add some gems – ah! You have made me confess that much already!'

241

'But I understood that jewels and the money for the commission were already paid to poor Master Ralph. Has the Cathedral had to pay twice?'

'I couldn't afford to do the work for free,' Karvinel smiled, 'but the Cathedral needed only to pay me for finishing Ralph's work.'

Baldwin was listening to him with interest. 'I suppose you have had to help many other people who would have made use of Ralph the glover's services?'

'A few people have come to me, Sir Knight,' the man conceded, then added: 'but I hope you don't think I might have arranged poor Ralph's death just to win over some of his clients!'

'My Heavens! What a thought,' Baldwin said, as if shocked. Then: 'What happened to the rest of the attacking outlaws?'

'Eh? What, the men who waylaid me and my man?'

Baldwin didn't bother to nod. He merely remained staring unblinking.

Karvinel was more heavily set than Vincent, but was sluggish; he lacked the drive which seemed a major part of le Berwe's make-up. Baldwin reflected that it was probably due to the fact that he was financially in dire straits. Vincent was a success, Nicholas Karvinel a failure.

Vincent was suave and confident in his manner, no matter what he was talking about or to whom; Karvinel was, in comparison, wary and aggressive. The latter now stood with every sign of being cowed by Fate. His eyes moved about the room constantly; his hands were clasped with an outward show of humility and meekness, but there was something about him which Baldwin distrusted.

At his side, Jeanne felt the same. It was hardly a surprise that Karvinel's business should fail, she thought, when the proprietor was so oily and unpleasant. She would never buy gloves from so unsavoury a character. He reminded her of a snake preparing to strike.

After a moment or two Karvinel replied, 'They all turned and ran down the road beyond the Maudlin. Like the cowards they are!'

'Does anyone know who they are?' Jeanne asked.

'Oh, their leader styles himself a knight; he has some fifteen or so men with him. All sorts, all ages, all characterised by their willingness to flout the law. It's a disgrace.'

'You called the Hue and Cry when you returned to the city, of course?'

'Well, of course I did! What else would a man do when he has been robbed?'

'I was merely wondering. Vincent told us that you saw one of the men in a tavern or somewhere, and had him arrested immediately.'

'Yes, I caught the devil myself. Hamond. God's blood, but the cheeky sod said he hadn't been down that way at all. It didn't do him any good; he was known to be a man of manifest guilt. He was indicted for going about at night-time with a weapon some years ago.'

'Ah!' Baldwin said. He recalled his first thoughts on hearing of the hanged man's background. This Hamond had been so well-known for his nefarious behaviour that when a crime was committed, he was the first to be arrested. Men in his position were often found guilty because the jury who presented them to court thought they were the most likely culprits. So long as someone in the Hundred was convicted of a crime, the King's Judge would be content, and any jury would prefer to see a useless or dangerous man removed rather than risk a prolonged investigation which would invariably prove still more expensive.

By now, Baldwin was growing to actively dislike this Karvinel. The man had a face rather like a toad's, with small narrow eyes placed rather widely apart; his nose was thick at the base, broken before the nostrils and badly set. He had not been shaved well, and his stubble was thicker on the left than the right, which made him look sloppy. Normally Baldwin would not think to condemn a man for his dress or toilet, but today was Christ's, celebrating the infant's birth and although Baldwin himself was very ambivalent in his attitude to the Church since the destruction of the Temple, that did not affect his adoration of Christ.

When he studied Karvinel, the merchant looked away, a trait which Baldwin had learned to mistrust in any man, but Karvinel added to the knight's feeling of unease in his presence by staring at Baldwin's shoes. It was not Karvinel's fault that Baldwin's shoes proved how wet and muddy the roads were, but irrationally it made Baldwin feel that an intentional slight was being offered.

'I assume this man's family stood up for him?' he asked stiffly.

'I don't know where he came from,' Karvinel said dismissively. 'I shouldn't think anyone else did either.'

'Vincent told me he was a local,' Baldwin remembered.

'I am surprised Vincent knew of him,' Karvinel said, and his expression confirmed his words. He frowned after their host doubtfully. 'The lad had every opportunity to defend himself, but he couldn't get away from the fact that my clerk and I saw him there. We actually saw him with the gang.'

Baldwin set his head to one side in exaggerated surprise. 'You mean his face was not masked or covered? He must have been the veriest fool in Christendom to attack travellers and not try to hide his identity.'

'Perhaps, but such is how it was.'

'What of the rest of the gang?'

'They *were* masked.'

There was a lightness to his voice which could have indicated boredom, as if he found the repetition of his attack infinitely dull – or maybe the man was simply ashamed of the attack. But that was foolish. How could a man be embarrassed about being set upon by fifteen or so men? 'They were all armed, I suppose?'

'All with sticks or axes. Some had billhooks. It was terrifying, I assure you.'

A whole band armed with such weapons would be a fearsome sight. 'I wonder why this one had no face covering.'

'He was a fool.'

'It is merely odd. In my experience, outlaws would happily kill a traveller to prevent their being recognised later – especially if they are local and could be seen by another local man.'

Karvinel shrugged but said nothing.

'And your clerk has died too, hasn't he?' Baldwin continued after a moment. 'The young Secondary, Peter?'

'Yes.'

'You saw him in a tavern a few days ago – the twenty-third, I think. He turned from you as if angry – why should he do that?'

'He never avoided me.'

'But I heard . . .'

Karvinel had been surveying the other guests but now he turned to face Baldwin, and the latter could see the naked rage that simmered under the polite exterior. 'Are you suggesting that I am not telling the truth, Master Knight? Do you call me a liar?'

'No, Master Nicholas,' said Baldwin with a suave smile. 'Of course not.'

He had no need to when Karvinel's manner convinced him of the fact.

The Bailiff was enjoying himself immensely as his drinking horn was topped up once more. He stood, a beatific grin spread over his features, the horn gripped tightly in his right hand.

Some of the guests were sitting at low tables and playing merrills or backgammon, while servants brought in harps and other instruments ready for more singing. Simon was all in favour of gambling and singing, especially after a good meal, and now he leaned against a table, eyeing the throng with a benevolent expression on his face.

Baldwin saw Simon swaying gently and smiled to himself. Walking over, he nodded at the drinking horn. 'It is my fervent wish that you should regret your consumption tomorrow, Simon.'

'Me? Hardly had more than a few. No, I can handle my drink.'

Baldwin curled his lip. More than a pint or two of wine and his head was unbearable the next day, not to mention the acid in his belly.

'The dancer was talented, wasn't she?' Simon continued

pensively. 'She could tempt a man, that one.' In his mind he recalled the tall, slim woman springing up onto her hands, then backwards onto her feet again. The thought of such suppleness brought a happy smile to his face. 'Yes, she could tempt a monk, that girl. God's balls, but she can move!'

'Sad, considering her man is in gaol,' Baldwin said, explaining that Mary was, in fact, the baker's daughter: Elias's girlfriend. 'You should consider yourself lucky she hasn't looked at you, anyway,' he chuckled. 'After all you've had to drink, you would hardly manage a smile even if you found her tucked up in your bed!'

Simon blinked slowly as he considered this. 'That,' he slurred carefully, 'is an entirely unwarranted comment. I can father children with my great sword.'

Baldwin's bellow of laughter made others in the room turn. 'Great sword? I should think after all that drink it would be more like a bent knife that has been used too often for cutting leather. Old, weak and blunted.'

'Hurtful,' Simon said sadly, shaking his head. 'Anyway, whatever you think of it, and since I doubt that I will be able to prove my virility with that girl, I shall go out and use it for its secondary purpose.'

'Walk cautiously, then,' Baldwin smiled as his friend took a slightly indirect path for the doorway.

Outside, Simon immediately felt more clear-headed. The plot was long and narrow, with vegetables growing near the house and a small enclosed arbour concealing a farther garden. He walked to this and lifted his tunic, peeing content-edly against a fruit tree. When he was done he was loath to return immediately and instead strolled a little further, enjoy-ing the quiet.

It was then that he heard the short gasp. He stilled, listening intently. Slowly he stepped forward with extreme caution.

All too often thieves had been known to break into parties and rob all the guests. Simon intended to see whether outlaws had clambered over Vincent's wall. He advanced past a small fence with apple-trees trained against it, along the line of a small hedge, but then he was close enough to see that there was no risk from either of the two who so enthusiastically grappled and strove together.

Grinning, Simon tiptoed away. There was no point in disturbing them. He returned to the house.

Baldwin was in the doorway. 'You took your time. I was wondering whether you had blundered into a hole.'

'No,' said Simon. 'I thought there was an intruder, but then I realised it was a welcome intrusion I heard.'

Baldwin eyed him. 'Are you feeling all right?'

Simon said nothing, but nodded back towards the garden. There, walking towards them was the dancing girl and one of the musicians, both strolling with all the arrogance of youth and satisfied lust.

'Ah, I see,' Baldwin grinned once the two had pushed their way back indoors. Then Simon wiped the smile off his face with his next remark.

'I should think she has anticipated her marriage. In fact, even though the nuptial bed was green and damp, I'd say young Mary Skinner had just performed the most important of the marital duties.'

'My God! She scarcely seems overly concerned by Elias's incarceration, does she?'

* * *

While Simon fetched them fresh drinks, despite Baldwin's protestations, Baldwin noticed that Vincent was talking to Karvinel again, quietly in a corner. The Receiver appeared calm, but Karvinel seemed to be restraining his anger with great difficulty. Baldwin only wished he could get a little nearer, but before he could approach, Lady Hawisia was bearing down on him. Baldwin steeled himself.

'Ah, there you are, Sir Baldwin. There are so many men here who wish to meet you. Couldn't you come with me for a moment?'

Despite Jeanne's opinion, voiced to Baldwin, that Hawisia was 'vacuous – really empty-headed', she exhibited little foolishness in her dealings with the men in the room. She courteously introduced Baldwin, explained a little about the man whom he was meeting, allowed a short conversation and then apologetically withdrew, taking Baldwin with her, to show him off to another person of influence.

It was only after she had circled the room that he could persuade her to allow him to rest. 'It is tiring to meet so many people,' he protested.

She smiled up at him. 'I am sorry, Sir Baldwin. It is so vital that I don't insult anyone by not introducing you, that I forget my duty to you as our honoured guest.'

'I am not that honourable, so I should not worry unduly,' he said kindly.

She grinned nervously. 'It is difficult for me. I am not used to dealing with knights and nobles, Sir Baldwin.'

'There is nothing to fear about people. They are all much the same.'

'It is very important that I make a good impression for Vincent's sake,' she said. Looking over to her husband, she added, 'And I can be so foolish on occasion. I must be a terrible burden on him.'

'Nonsense! You are too loyal and thoughtful to be anything other than a source of pride.'

She gave him a dazzling smile. 'That is most kind of you, Sir Knight, but it isn't true. I can be very impetuous and silly sometimes, and I know that when my poor husband is desperately trying to keep his business alive in these difficult times, my silliness can be very frustrating. Still, I try to improve myself and make myself useful to him as a good hostess. Is there anything else you need?'

'Just out of interest, Hawisia, yes. The glover who died, did you know him?'

'Ralph?' She looked surprised. 'A little, but not much. I didn't buy my gloves from him.'

'You use Karvinel?'

'*Him?*' Unexpectedly she giggled. 'Oh, no. I get mine made in London. I couldn't use Nick. His work is . . . well, a little shoddy. I suppose it's his troubles. His wife was telling me that she's concerned that his business may collapse. He owes a lot of money.'

'And he has been robbed so often.'

'Yes.'

Baldwin nodded. 'Tell me: when that poor glover died, where was your husband?'

'You suspect Vincent of killing that man?' she shot back seriously. All trace of humour had fallen from her face and she stared up at him with disquieting intensity.

'No, but I would like to know where he was.'

'Let me see . . . It was early in the morning on the Feast of St Thomas the Apostle when he died; I was in the Cathedral for Mass but later I went to see Vincent in his counting house. He is normally there during the early morning. He attends a later Mass.'

'Where is his counting house? Is it near the dead glover's house?'

'So, you *do* ask whether my husband killed him,' she said quietly. 'Well, no. His counting house is down near the Guildhall. When I got there he had been within for a while, so he couldn't have been to the glover's house.'

'Who can confirm that?'

'I could grow quite alarmed, Sir Baldwin,' she protested. 'You are our guest and yet you ask where my husband was as if you think he could be a murderer. But if you must check, his clerk was there and will happily confirm the time my husband arrived. Or you may ask the Coroner. He was there with us. He can confirm my statement.'

'Thank you. I didn't mean to trouble you,' Baldwin said, smiling down at her anxious expression. 'But it is always best to make sure of these details.'

'Why? The apprentice has been arrested already.'

He said nothing, but bowed, preparing to leave her. She remained staring up at him with a severe frown. 'Sir Baldwin, I can assure you that my husband is no murderer. He would not be able to commit such an act.'

'Many wives have thought that of their husbands, Lady,' Baldwin said as he left her to go to his own wife once more.

CHAPTER NINETEEN

Henry finished his meal, thanked his Canon with the signs of respect he knew would be expected, and made his way across the precinct to the dormitory where the Choristers all slept. On the way he twirled his sling around his finger meditatively, looking for a cat or dog to fire at, but no target came into view and disappointedly he shoved the sling back in his belt as he entered the cold hall. There was no fire at this time of day and he shivered, walking to his desk and bench.

The work he had been engaged on was boring. The colours were daubed in the same way as the older clerics who spent all their time with their noses almost on the sheets of vellum they painted, watching so closely to see that not one droplet of ink or colouring went where it was not wanted. Not that Henry took quite so much care about his own work. There seemed little point. He got the right effect without having to struggle, so why bother spending the extra time to make something 'perfect' as the Canons would say? There were better things to be doing.

Henry wasn't related to an important family like Luke. Henry's father was dead. He'd been a soldier in an army that went up to the north, his mother said, to a place where rebels had tried to wrest the King's lands from him. Scotland or somewhere, something like that. It was right up at the farthest extent of the King's lands. Way up beyond Bristol, she said.

It was a long time ago, and it happened a long way away, so Henry couldn't get upset about it, but he did miss having a father. It made him stand out a little from the other Choristers. Especially since his competitor, Luke, was so different, even if his father was dead, too.

That was why they were enemies, really. Henry was happy that Luke was there, because it gave him someone to fight against. Someone to pick on when he had a chance. Life without Luke would be odd. Empty.

But he was glad he'd got one over on Luke this time. It would be Henry who stood up on the twenty-seventh and began the celebration of the boy-Bishop; it would be Henry who presided over the festivities for the whole of the next day when the Cathedral was turned upside down.

He was so looking forward to his episcopacy! The boy-Bishop was an old institution; Henry was the latest in a long line, and he intended enjoying his day to the full, inviting all his friends at breakfast, then going down to St Nicholas's Priory, nearer the river, where they would be entertained and given gifts which he could keep.

Later he would return to the city, and it was then that the gloves would be presented to the honoured guests, while more gifts would be collected for Henry. At noon the main feast would take place, followed by celebrations in the city's streets. Actors would set up their stages on wagons and play out their pieces in the High Street and even in the Cathedral grounds, for although Stephen and some other Canons disliked seeing the public desporting themselves on the cemetery and other sanctified areas, Bishop Walter II had stated that he preferred to know that the people were receiving some form of religious education, and if they only took in what the actors showed them, that was better than nothing. But this was where the real fun started, as Henry knew all too well.

All the Choristers and Secondaries, even a few of the Vicars and Annuellars, could for one day in the year throw off their sombre, clerical demeanour with their regular garb, for this was a celebration of life. The twenty-eighth was the Feast of the Holy Innocents, a feast in remembrance of the appalling day when Herod exterminated tens of thousands of young boys in his attempt to kill Jesus after His birth.

As a result, for that one day, all usual rules were forgotten: the elected Chorister became Bishop, and the whole hierarchy was reversed. For one glorious day the men and boys who slaved in religious and holy seriousness for the rest of the year were allowed to relax. They could enjoy the excessive pleasures of their topsy-turvy world without fearing reproach.

Henry stood and walked idly around the other desks. It was because the other Choristers knew he would ensure that all had a good time that he had won the election, back at the Feast of St Thomas the Apostle, on twenty-first December. It wasn't because the other lads disliked Luke, nor because they thought Henry was the better Chorister. He wasn't, and they all knew it. He was much worse than Luke at singing, at his addition and at drawing and writing. Of course he was worse; Henry knew it was all silly. He wasn't going to be a priest – he didn't want to be. But he did want to be boy-Bishop, because with the money he was given he could help his mother.

She was still up at the manor in Thorverton, working herself to a shadow while trying to grow enough food to keep herself going. The Feast Day gifts would ensure that she could eat well for a few days, if nothing else. Henry saw it as his responsibility to feed his mother and brother. The family had lost his father, but Henry had been given this position in the Cathedral and it offered potential for providing food. That was what he intended to do. Feed them.

It was good to beat Luke, though. They were enemies, and that was all there was to it. Luke and he had early on decided that they were rivals, and their enmity had been cemented when Luke had superciliously laughed at one of Henry's pages of writing. Henry's early attempts at writing had been more than a little inept, but that was no reason for the snotty bastard to laugh, although now he looked back on that moment with pleasure. Because he hadn't been raised in the same strict manner as Luke, the moment he realised the other boy was making fun of his efforts, Henry had taken prompt action and swung his fists.

Luke had responded with gusto, seeing this as nothing more than a direct challenge to his position as undisputed leader of the Choristers. Both soon had bloody faces, Luke with a nastily bitten shoulder, bruised shins, and a nosebleed, while Henry had bruises all over his chest and upper legs. Their shirts and robes were badly ripped and an enraged

Gervase called them in to explain their sudden ferocious battle. However, neither would account for it. It was too demeaning to confess. Luke had no intention of admitting that he had caused the fight by his sneering, and Henry refused to lose the moral high ground by sneaking on his peer, so both were held down and slapped across the backside by the Succentor with a stiffened leather strap.

In some cases Henry had known beatings to create a sense of mutual trust, but with Luke this didn't happen. Luke knew himself to be superior, with the same fixed, ineffable certainty that told him that his father was in every way the moral, mental and social superior to Henry's father, and that his mother was better in comparison to Henry's. No discussion was needed. Luke *knew* himself to be the more worthy person in every way.

Such confidence niggled constantly at Henry. He felt it was his duty to break through the exterior of Luke's pride and show him that he was wrong, that Henry was as important a boy. At first his sole means of doing so, in order to avoid a second thorough flogging, was to excel at all the tasks given to him.

He had enjoyed a measure of success. Somewhat to his own surprise, he found that he had a certain ability at reading, and the Latin he was given to learn soon held little mystery for him; in a little under a year he was better at reading and speaking Latin than Luke. Yet no matter how hard he worked, he could not make much headway with his writing or painting. His fingers failed him when he picked up a reed and tried to form perfect, precise circles and straight lines. The effort involved seemed too great. It was pointless: it wasn't as if Henry really needed to know how to write. When he was no longer a Chorister, he would go back to Thorverton to help his mother look after their property. Writing wouldn't be much use then.

At Luke's desk he gazed down critically. His rival had drawn some pictures of peasants working in a field. It wasn't bad, either, Henry thought privately. Women threshed grain from their long stems, a shepherd with his dog drove a flock towards a pen, young boys pulled on a string to trip a fine net trap, catching a pair of songbirds. All as it should be.

Henry leaned closer. The colours were very good, the reds and blues of the tunics looking just like real cloth. Luke had coloured the lettering all in gold, and it fairly glowed on the page. It was entrancing. Henry wished he could draw and paint like that. But he couldn't.

Walking back to his own desk, he looked down without interest. There was something missing, he could tell, but he couldn't be bothered to see what it was. He'd already got what he wanted, the boy-Bishopric: both for his mother, and to slight Luke.

As the thought struck him, the door opened and Luke himself walked in. He cast a contemptuous look at Henry, then crossed to his desk, pulling a bundle concealed beneath it. Henry tried not to look interested, but he couldn't help squinting sideways to see what it could be. Luke obviously knew he was intrigued, but shoved the thing under his coat and gazed at Henry as if daring him to make a comment; it was unnecessary because Henry refused to look up. He sat doodling idly until he heard the door slam behind Luke.

He couldn't go and look at the other boy's desk, since Luke might return at any moment. So instead, Henry reached for his little pot of yellow colouring to touch up some of his lettering, only to see that it was gone.

'Oi, who's swiped that?'

Jen hurried along the streets with her coat gripped tightly about her to protect her from the cold. At the Fissand Gate she entered the Cathedral precinct and stared about her. There were still some people milling around, but what with the freezing weather and temptations available in taverns and alehouses all over the city, most had gone. Even the clerics were mostly indoors.

She chewed at her lip. The only consolation was that if he had been found here, there would be bound to be more men, all chattering and laughing at the capture of the famed outlaw. Even if they hadn't caught him, people would be standing around discussing how they had just missed him.

Turning, she fled through the gates and sought out his favourite taverns. There was a hot, stinging sensation at her eyes as she ran. The fear that Sir Thomas might be in danger was enough to set a panicky urgency thrilling through her veins. Since Hamond's death he seemed to have lost his fear of capture.

She had got to know him so long ago, soon after her mother had died so horribly, fainting over her fire and burning to death. Father was wasting away to nothing, as were all the other people in the vill. Afterwards Jen promised herself she would never again suffer from a lack of food. To be without money was one thing, but to die the lingering death of starvation was hideous. Jen could feel herself fading away, sinking into a lassitude like her mother, with bleeding gums and loose teeth as scurvy attacked her undernourished body.

It was Sir Thomas who had fed her. He had come across her one day before her father died, when she was desperately looking for bird's eggs in the soggy hedge just as another downpour drenched her. Past caring, she scarcely noticed that a rider was approaching, but when she heard the hooves, she glanced over her shoulder at him.

It was enough. Within a day she was sleeping in his bed, a fifteen-year-old girl with a knight who had been entranced by her. When her father died, she had begged room for herself and her brother, and Sir Thomas had agreed. He didn't need to. She owed him a large debt for that reason. When he lost his manor he offered her freedom, but she refused it. Where else could she go? She had remained his lover and he had repaid her by feeding and protecting her and Hob.

She had to protect him now, in her turn.

It would not be easy. He had a great sense of debt to the men who had remained with him after he lost his manor, and Hamond was one of his longest-serving men. The dead clerk and Karvinel had confirmed that Hamond had been in the gang that attacked them south of Exeter on their way back from Topsham. The knowledge that Hamond had been killed on the man's word had sent Sir Thomas into a cold rage at first, swearing that he would avenge his man, but then, later, he had taken Jen to his bed filled with a languishing sadness.

'He's gone; my lad is dead, hanging from a gibbet, for all the citizens of Exeter to point and laugh while he swings. It's terrible. And he was nowhere near the robbery.'

She had soothed him, rocking him as he lay upon her breast, gentling him as she might their child one day if she ever conceived, and at last he succumbed to sleep, but he wouldn't be able to forget that his man had died in that demeaning manner. He could never forgive the city, and especially not the merchant who had condemned Hamond. He wanted his vengeance, and he would have it.

That was Jen's greatest fear as she hurried along the streets. She was convinced that she would hear that the merchant had been struck down in the streets, stabbed and left dying, but fully able to point his finger at his assassin, the leader of the gang he said had attacked him and robbed him.

But her anxiety was misplaced. In the fifth tavern she entered, the Cock, she found Sir Thomas sitting at the back of a gloomy hall filled with smoke from the damp logs that the host had optimistically set in the central hearth.

He sat on a stool, a slumped, rather sad figure huddled in his cloak and gulping wine from a pint pot. Seeing her shadow, he started, then gave her a lopsided grin. 'So, little lark. You've come to fetch me home, have you?'

'I thought you had been killed. I thought you had stuck your dagger in him and been caught. Why didn't you come straight back with Hob? You could have sent a message with him to stop me worrying.'

He took her hand and gently tugged her towards him, then pulled her onto his lap and rested his head upon her breast. 'Because I saw this Karvinel in the crowd. Your brother pointed him out to me and I followed him home. I know where he lives. Then he went to an alehouse and I followed him again. I could have killed him there, Jen, if I'd wanted to. I could have slipped my blade between his shoulders and left him dead in the gutter. Easy. But before I kill him, I want to know *why* he did it.'

'You left him and came here?' she asked sarcastically.

'No. After the tavern, he returned to his house where he collected his wife, and they went off to another house where there was a Christmas feast; I ate from the alms dish at the door to find out whose house it was. It is owned by Vincent le Berwe, the steward told me. He's the City's Receiver.'

'Does that tell you something about Karvinel?'

'No, nothing. I still don't know why he had Hamond killed,' Sir Thomas said. 'But I will!'

Why *had* the bastard sent his fellow to the gallows? All that day, Sir Thomas had been with Hamond in the city. Hamond had walked with Sir Thomas to the city gate and waved him off only a half hour or so before Karvinel ran up to the city's gate and pointed out Hamond as being a felon.

Not knowing was dreadful, but Sir Thomas *would* find out. A firm resolution filled him with the warm satisfaction of revenge to come. Yes. Sir Thomas would not let Karvinel get away with his crime. Sir Thomas was a knight and he demanded satisfaction from the mere merchant who had murdered his servant. That was what it was: murder by proxy. Karvinel was too cowardly to kill Hamond in a fair fight, so he sought Hamond's death by deceit, telling people Hamond had robbed him. And then had Hamond executed by the city.

'You could have been seen – been captured,' Jen said fearfully.

'Not today,' he said. 'No one is looking today.' But his attention had already returned to Karvinel. As soon as he could, he would catch the *shit* and beat the truth out of him. Before killing him.

* * *

Adam saw Luke at the corner of the chorister's block as he left the Cathedral, his box of candles in his hand.

It was chilly out in the open air again, and now, with the dusk giving way to full night, Adam was tired and cold. He gripped his box of candles to his chest as he hurried over the grass towards his chamber.

But the boy walking ahead of him was too tempting.

Adam had never liked Luke. Truth to tell, he hated the cocky little shite. He hated the way Luke always contrived to be smart and clean, the way he was always being commended for his efforts, the way the little brat accepted the compliments of Canons and clerks for the purity of his singing, like a little male whore with that smug, smarmy smile on his fat face.

It wasn't so easy for the men about the place, Adam knew. He'd done everything in his power to learn the lessons he'd been given from the first day he entered the Choristers, but he'd failed. The letters moved on the page before his eyes, he couldn't make head nor tail of them, and the pictures were as bad. What was a man supposed to do when the reed in his hand just didn't work? He couldn't help the fact that his sketches and drawings were smudged and out of proportion. And try as he might, he couldn't make the scenes he drew look neat. Where others formed pretty little pictures with balance and elegance, his ended up as the worst of cartoons, with men and women looking sharp-faced, bestial.

His time here must be drawing to an end soon. He couldn't remain with any likelihood of preferment. The Canons would grumble, asking that someone else be brought in to take the spare place, someone who would be of more direct and immediate use to the Cathedral. Perhaps he'd be lucky, get offered a post as an acolyte. He could stay in the Cathedral provided he agreed to continue looking after the candles, delivering loaves to the older members of the choir, and a few other duties.

It almost made him throw down his candles in rage and disgust. Why should he be cast off, when these little bastards were allowed to stay? They had other places they could go to, they had homes: in Luke's case, a wealthy home. Everyone knew how well off his people were. He came from the Soth family. It was *unfair*!

Luke was still walking slowly ahead of him. As Adam watched, Luke pulled out a lump of bread. He broke off a piece just as Adam saw an object that would allow him to take out his revenge in a mean and cruel manner on one of his most hated rivals.

The first Luke knew was when he heard the slap of sandalled feet behind him.

After seeing Henry in the hall, Luke had been musing over the celebrations for Holy Innocents' Day and wondering whether he could somehow escape the humiliation of waiting upon the new boy-Bishop. Sadly he came to the conclusion that there was no escape: any attempt would show Henry that he had won, that he had succeeded in destroying Luke's equilibrium.

Luke's appetite had wakened. It felt like days since the feast in Stephen's house; Luke sometimes thought that the whole of his life was spent in hunger. The amounts of food given to him and the other choirboys were never enough.

He was about to slip the first piece of bread into his mouth when he heard the feet. There was a hollow, empty-sounding rattle as Adam dropped his candle-box, and Luke was suddenly convinced that a ghost was coming to grab him, maybe to pull him down under the ground with him. Squeaking in terror, he felt strong arms grip him, felt himself swung up and over, upside-down, and his face was heading towards the ground.

Henry frowned at all the other desks, but before he could make a search, he heard the muffled cry from outside. Forgetting his pot of orpiment, he rose and went to the door. There, in the dim light that streamed from behind him in the doorway, he saw a figure lying on the ground. He felt the flesh of his scalp creep as he wondered whether it was a dead man, but then he realised that the body was lifting itself up.

He heard the sobs and frowned. It was weak to cry; but he would help if he could. Only when he arrived at Luke's side did he recognise who it was, and the hand he had put out in sympathy stayed in mid-air as he realised that his sympathy might not be agreeable to this victim.

'What in God's name is going on?' roared Gervase. He had been in his hall when he heard the first hiccupping cry, and now he peered from the door to see, as he thought, Henry leaning over Luke, having pushed him or thumped him.

Henry's face turned to him, almost white in the cold moonlight, and Gervase instantly marked him down as guilty. He stormed out and went to Luke's side, picking him up and then wincing. 'Are you all right?'

The boy had been pushed headfirst into a gutter, which was filled with horse manure and dung from the animals which had passed through there today. Luke's face was a grimace of revulsion and hatred as he tried to keep the tears at bay. 'Someone picked me up and threw me into that,' he declared with a sob.

'Was it Henry?'

'I haven't done anything, I was in the hall!' Henry stated emphatically.

Gervase's anger burst. 'You and Luke have always had this silly dispute, haven't you? And now you've made him suffer like this, you little heathen. Your behaviour is a disgrace to the Cathedral and to the robes you wear, you devil. My God, I am tempted to rip the robe from you and throw you from the precinct at once!'

'I didn't do anything! I came out to help him when I heard him cry out!'

'I saw you there, pushing at him, you devil! Get back inside and go to your room. I'll not have you trying any more tricks on this poor child. Go on! Go!'

Henry turned and shuffled away, snivelling. Luke was still weeping as he was wiped and cleaned as best he could be by the Succentor before being led away to have his face washed.

When they had all gone, Adam slipped out from his hiding-place, collected his empty candle box, and then, after a moment's thought, picked up the loaf, which had fallen on the grass and had missed following Luke into the sewer. With a skip to his steps, Adam made his way back to his own little chamber in the Close, chortling as he remembered Luke's panicked squeak. He wouldn't forget that for many a long month.

CHAPTER TWENTY

On the day after Christmas, Simon woke in the early hours to find Baldwin in the hall with him. The knight was squatting by the side of the fire, ruminatively prodding at the coals with a stick, sipping every now and again from a pot of ale at his side.

'Baldwin! Are you all right?'

'Oh, Simon, I am sorry to have woken you. I thought I was being quiet. Ah well, I shall leave you. My apologies.' He stood and collected up his pot.

'No, sit down again. What's the matter?'

Nothing loath, the knight dropped onto a stool beside the fire again. 'I cannot help but feel that something bad is going on here, Simon, and the feeling is growing stronger. Someone is going to suffer unnecessarily and unfairly, I think, unless we do something to help him.'

'Obviously you mean the poor devil in gaol.'

'Yes,' Baldwin sighed. 'That poor apprentice. I can see no reason why he should be confined, and if we do nothing he may well be executed for something he didn't do. The only motive we have been given is that the lad might have robbed his master – and yet there is no money or jewels to prove that he did. They say he could have run away and hidden them – but no one can show where he might have put them. No, it is more likely that he had nothing to do with the murder or the theft. They came as a complete surprise to him.'

'Then who did have a reason to kill the glover?'

'That is the all-important question,' Baldwin said heavily. 'Jolinde had bought the arsenic, but what would be *his* motive? Although I am intrigued by Jolinde and Peter delivering the money and gemstones to Ralph. It is significant, too, that Peter also contributed to the death of the felon.'

'You think one of the outlaws might have decided to kill him?'

'It is possible. Unlikely but possible.'

'And the Dean asked us to look into the Secondary's death as well,' Simon pointed out, yawning.

'Yes. That in itself is odd. Why should he ask us to enquire into that when he had the Coroner there to investigate?' He scowled at the fire, trying to make sense of it all.

Simon leaned across to take Baldwin's pot from him. Sipping from it he said, 'There is one obvious conclusion: the Dean and Chapter don't trust the Coroner.'

'Possibly – and yet I find it hard to believe. Coroner Roger is transparently innocent, especially now he has suggested other courses for us to look into. He didn't need to introduce us to the City Bailiff.'

'Fine, so if we assume he is straight, perhaps there was another motive behind the Dean's suggestion that we should help. Maybe he feared that the Coroner himself could get into deep water.'

'Or was it something to do with the suspects?' Baldwin mused.

Simon took another gulp and considered. 'It's feasible. What if he was concerned like you that the wrong man could be accused? You are worried about the apprentice, and maybe he's worried about someone else?'

'Who?' Baldwin scoffed.

'Don't be stupid! There's only one real suspect in Peter's death, and you know it as well as I do: Jolinde. He's the only man who had the chance. God's bollocks! He even told us about his delivery of food. How easy it would have been for him to have slipped poison into Peter's food. And he told us that he didn't eat it.'

'But what could lead Jolinde to kill Peter *now* when he had had opportunities for the last few years?' Baldwin demanded. 'There's nothing to suggest that they had a row about anything.'

'Jolinde's girl said that they were a bit odd in the tavern.'

'I think Claricia was more struck with the way that Peter snubbed Karvinel later on.'

Simon said slowly, 'If the Dean realised that the evidence pointed to Jolinde, wouldn't that be reason enough to get another pair of heads in to help the Coroner?'

'I don't see why.'

'Baldwin, you've left your brains in bed with Jeanne. Think! The Cathedral survives on the money it wins from the city and the people living here. There are a number of wealthy men, but one in particular stands out in terms of potential income.'

'The Receiver!'

'Vincent le Berwe,' Simon nodded. 'The father of Jolinde, if our informer was correct. I think we have the Dean's motive right there. He didn't want to upset one of his major financiers by being responsible for having his son arrested, not unless there was absolutely no alternative.'

'Vincent would be upset if his son was taken, presumably, although I've seen nothing to suggest that he is particularly fond of the boy.'

'Just because he doesn't have the boy in his house with him and with his wife, don't hold that against him,' Simon warned. 'Just imagine that you had an illegitimate son twenty-odd years ago – then imagine that your only child with Jeanne had died. Would you inflict upon Jeanne the presence of your child out of marriage? It would be a dreadful reminder to her that she herself hadn't provided you with your heir when a village slut could manage it perfectly happily. If Jolinde is his son, he *must* have some feelings for the lad.'

Baldwin nodded. 'True, but there is the other aspect, which is that if Vincent was concerned, surely he'd have paid the Sheriff to see to it that the matter never reached the court with his boy. In the best courts in the land there is normally someone who can be persuaded by cash.'

'Maybe Vincent would try that if his boy was actually arrested. But the Dean would still have the embarrassment of being involved with that arrest – and I doubt he wants that to happen to the man with possibly the biggest purse in the parish.'

'The trouble is, we have no idea why Peter Golloc should have been killed. Unless he killed himself, as we said. And Jolinde had every opportunity.'

'He had several with the very fair Claricia,' Simon added with a leer.

'Yes, yes. Vincent le Berwe surely fits into all this somehow, but I cannot see how. And there was something about Karvinel: he appeared very jittery when I asked him about the robbery. I suppose the attack could have unsettled him, but he didn't seem to want to discuss the affair at all. That seems odd. Most people want to talk about their misfortune. He had all his money taken, but was reticent on the details. And I have to say that so much bad luck itself looks suspicious, when you add it all together.'

'What, you think he conspired to have his goods stolen from him?' Simon laughed.

Baldwin looked at him seriously. 'There are other possibilities. He could have made a powerful enemy, for instance. You recall this man they all talk about as a vicious outlaw leading a large band of men – Sir Thomas of Exmouth? Perhaps he has a specific grudge against Karvinel.'

'What?' Simon grunted, tugging the cloak and blanket which served as his bedclothes more closely about him. 'What are you saying, that this poor fool Karvinel has upset someone who can hire an entire outlaw band to give him a kicking? Does it sound reasonable?'

'Remember what we were told about Karvinel's legendary bad luck,' Baldwin said, looking at his friend with a serious, worried expression on his face. 'Karvinel lost his ship years ago, his house was burgled, then put to the torch, and finally this outrageous attack was sprung on him as he was approaching the city. Does that sound normal to you? How often have you known evil luck of that nature dog a man's footsteps?'

'That's not the point. The point is, you have no rational explanation as to why someone should be, as you say, dogging Karvinel with such foul luck.'

'No,' Baldwin admitted.

'It could as easily be someone else who could afford to pay for this Sir Thomas's services. Until you know who is wealthy enough to pay him, you'll never find out anything.'

'We have to find out more, yes,' Baldwin said slowly, and then he sat upright with a beatific smile on his face. 'Thank you, my friend.'

'Eh? What for?' Simon demanded suspiciously.

'Why, for showing me what I should do, of course,' Baldwin said innocently and walked from the room.

Simon swore under his breath, then swore again when he saw his breath hanging on the air in front of him. Reaching forward he threw more logs onto the fire, and shivered glumly. He knew he'd never get back to sleep again now.

Jolinde walked from the inn to the cookshops, scratching at his head and yawning luxuriously. It astonished him how Claricia could work until late, bed him until he must run to the Cathedral for the early-morning services, and then welcome him back to her bed later in the morning without showing any apparent signs of exhaustion.

For his part, he was utterly tired out. Even when Claricia left him alone, he found it hard to sleep. He kept seeing poor Peter's face in his last agonies, puking and fouling himself in his stall. And then there was the thought of the stuff. Where could it have gone? Not that Jolinde truly cared. He would never have thought of making off with it. It was tainted money, stolen from Ralph, the rightful owner.

271

'So you are up early, Jolinde?'

'Canon Stephen,' Jolinde said. 'You startled me.'

'Most of the Secondaries are back in their beds trying to catch up with the sleep they missed during Matins and Prime. I am pleased to see that you need less sleep.'

'I couldn't sleep,' Jolinde said. It was nothing more than the truth.

'You mustn't concern yourself with your friend's death, Jolinde.'

There was a kindness and gentleness in Stephen's voice that made Jolly look up at him. 'Canon?'

'Your friend was a bad sort,' Stephen explained. 'I saw him on the day he died, late in the afternoon. He was a sinner, Jolinde, and quite undeserving of his position here. He committed a dreadful act, a truly awful crime, and I would not have you worrying yourself over his death. If he was deserving of forgiveness, God will recognise His own, but having learned what I did from him, I would scarcely think Peter could achieve a place at God's side.'

Shaking his head sadly, he walked on a short way.

Jolinde could not speak. It was all too clear what Stephen meant: he had learned that Peter had stolen the money; even now he was blaming Peter for the theft of Ralph's cash. It was terrible! Jolinde must do what he could to defend Peter's name, but how?

Then the means came to him. He would admit to being responsible for the theft. It would destroy his position in the Cathedral, but he didn't think he had any future there anyway, so that was no loss. No, he would confess to his own part in the matter and that would clear Peter's name.

Except it might not, he realised. Men demanded tangible

proofs, otherwise they might simply assume that a loyal friend was taking all the responsibility upon himself. And there was another point: they might decide that if he *was* truly guilty, he should not benefit from his theft.

He must find the money. That little purse with the filched cash could be produced to show that Peter was innocent, and could prove that he, Jolinde, had no intention of profiting from the theft.

Where the Hell could Peter have hidden it?

Justice was much on Henry's mind. He had woken with a backside still smarting from the lashing Gervase had given him the night before. The Canon had laid into him in front of all the other Choristers, taking a stiffened strip of bull's leather and whipping Henry for all he was worth.

The memory made Henry's eyes fill with tears of frustration. He had been made to look a fool and thrashed in front of all his friends and enemies when he was completely innocent! He'd not pushed Luke – he'd not even known the other boy was out there. No, he'd been working, keeping his head down, the sort of thing that Gervase kept telling him he should do, and look how he'd been repaid!

He wouldn't be surprised if Luke had shoved his own face in the muck just so he could put the blame onto Henry. Henry was a fair-minded boy, and he accepted that there would be a certain justice in Luke getting his revenge like that, because after all Henry had made his life difficult often enough.

Henry cast a glance to his right where the cloisters lay. A naughty smile crossed his features as he recalled putting that beetle down the back of Luke's neck. And then when he'd hit him with dung; it had been deeply satisfying, hearing that damp slapping noise. Brilliant! He had fled Luke's justifiable rage, hurrying into the cloisters and out the other side, to the works where he had his refuge.

It was a small gap in a wall in a cellar, near where the new workings met the old Cathedral tower. He had found it the previous summer in an idle moment, wondering what lay behind, and when he squeezed his way inside, he discovered that a wall had been knocked down, and beyond was a shaft going down. A ladder was propped, and he descended into a large, airy tunnel. He had no idea what it was for, but as soon as he discovered it he knew it was a perfect place to conceal himself. After any attack on Luke he would scurry down the shaft, dragging the ladder after him, and stay there, listening with beating heart and eager ears, feeling the thrill of the chase, even if from the prey's perspective, mingled with the delight of the battle he had instigated.

Yes, he decided, if Luke wanted revenge, the easy approach would be to mess himself up, then pass the blame on to Henry. But hang on! That couldn't be right. Luke wouldn't even have known Henry was there. And his cry sounded genuine – really terrified. Henry shook his head doubtfully. It was very confusing.

He shuffled idly along the path that led around the Cathedral up towards the Choristers' hall where he intended doing a little more work before attending his next service. That reminded him of his yellow orpiment. Someone had taken it. He'd known something was missing. The thought made him glower. He hadn't finished with it.

He soon found the bottle on Luke's desk. Henry picked it up and noticed how low the level had sunk. Huh! Typical of Luke to splash the stuff all over his pages. He was just lucky that his daubings always seemed to turn out to look so good. He put the orpiment back on Luke's desk. There was no point in keeping it.

Even if he couldn't draw and paint as well as Luke, he could at least take pleasure in the fact that he was going to be the boy-Bishop – and he could enjoy running about the streets with other boys.

Going to the door, he glanced out. The weather looked cold, but bright. There were several clouds, but at this moment the sun was beaming down on the city. Henry smiled. His arse was still bruised from the lash, but that happened yesterday, and Henry was nothing if not sanguine. Today was a new day, with new opportunities for fun. He stepped out.

He had only gone five paces when he heard a noise behind him. Henry was not so slow as Luke. In a split second he had darted to one side and ducked behind a tree.

There was a chuckle, and when he peered around the trunk, he saw Adam standing and rocking with mirth. 'You should have seen the way you hurried off! Like a startled rabbit, you were, with a slingshot up the backside.'

Henry kept his mouth shut. There were loads of Secondaries and other clerks who enjoyed beating or bullying the Choristers. They largely got away with it, because they held out the threat of even more punishment if their victims told a Canon or Gervase. And even if Gervase was told, that was no guarantee that the perpetrator would be punished.

'You're lucky. I thought you were Luke. If it had been him, I'd have ducked his face in the shit again,' Adam said comfortably. 'Obnoxious little bastard that he is.'

Henry watched him with narrowed eyes as Adam walked to the Choristers' hall, looking in through the doorway. 'More candles here,' he said, and walked inside.

Chewing his lip, Henry stood scowling at the shut door reflectively. He could go and tell Gervase, but the Succentor probably wouldn't believe him. He'd think Henry had invented the story to make Gervase feel guilty, or perhaps to work off a grudge against Adam. No, Henry couldn't go to Gervase. But there must be someone he could tell.

Yes, if no one else, at least Luke would be interested. He might not believe Henry at first, but Henry was prepared to forgive that. All he wanted was to make sure Luke realised Henry himself was innocent.

Anyhow, he couldn't have picked up Luke and thrown him into the crap.

Luke was far too fat and heavy.

CHAPTER TWENTY-ONE

Coppe grunted as he eased his position. The cold was affecting his big toe. The toe of the leg he had left in the sea near France.

It was the same with the scar that so transfigured his face. The scar could predict with unerring accuracy when the weather was about to change. Now, looking up and snuffing the air, he could distinguish, over the scent of the woodsmoke, horse dung, dogs' urine and mud, the metallic tang of the cold. There would be snow soon, he told himself with a grimace.

Snow was an additional burden to him. Not only would he freeze his arse off, sitting on the ground as he must, but he'd not see many folks either. They'd prefer to stay inside rather than pass by his station here.

A shadow passed over him and he looked up to see Janekyn. The old man was cupping a drink in his hands. 'Want some?'

'Thanks,' Coppe said, taking the steaming wooden mazer from him and sipping. 'You won't believe this,' he said, sadly contemplating his legless stump, 'but I can feel the heat going all the way down to my toes.'

The older man chuckled. 'We're a pair of wrecks, you and me, John. You're all cut to pieces, and me, I'm so old I've got little time left to me.'

'You'll probably see me out, Jan. In fact, I'd be glad if God would take me right away. I've had enough of this. It's no way for a man to live, begging for alms all the time.'

Janekyn looked down at Coppe. He'd known the cripple for most of his time as porter, for he had only taken on the role three years ago. The thought of standing here without the cripple huddled by the wall was strangely upsetting. It would leave a horrible gap in Janekyn's life. He enjoyed his occasional arguments with the old sailor. Abruptly he turned and walked back inside, calling for a clerk.

Jolinde was hurrying past the entrance as Janekyn disappeared, and Coppe looked up brightly. 'Come, Master, a coin or two for wine to warm my veins?'

'I have nothing.'

Coppe was surprised at the snarl in Jolinde's voice. 'There's no shame in that, Master. No need to be angry. At least you haven't run into anyone like your friend did with Ralph that morning.'

'What do you mean? What friend? What morning?' Jolinde cast a baffled look at the cripple.

'Why, the morning poor Ralph Glover was killed. Your friend pelted back to the gate and ran slap into him, wasn't looking where he was going was he? All agitated, he seemed.'

'He ran into Ralph?'

'Yes. The glover was with Stephen. I saw your friend run into him down near St Petrock's and then he came haring up here to the Fissand, nearly tripped over me there, and nipped straight inside.'

Jolinde was frowning now. 'Are you sure? What on earth would he have been doing out of the Cathedral at that time of day?'

'I don't know, sir,' Coppe said, automatically waving his bowl under Jolinde's nose. 'He was back in time for the service, though only just, I'd guess. He ran past me here just as the bells stopped.'

Jolinde dropped a farthing into his bowl and walked on slowly and musingly. Only a few feet from Coppe, he suddenly stopped and cried, 'Shit! He can't have taken them back! He *can't*! What can I do if he took them all back?'

He burst into a shambling run, and Coppe stared after him as he hurried over to the lane that led to his house. As he disappeared from view Janekyn appeared dragging a lighted brazier by a rope which he had lashed to one of the legs. 'What was that about?'

'I only wish I knew,' Coppe said with transparent honesty.

'Never mind. Here you are, one brazier, and more wine to warm your veins. Merry Christmas! And if it gets colder . . .' He dropped a few pennies into Coppe's hand. 'You can go and find yourself a warm tavern where you can sit before a fire.'

Sutton's Inn was blessedly quiet. In the hearth a fire was burning strongly, with three faggots throwing out a delicious scent of applewood and oak as they flamed and sputtered. Smoke rose up to the rafters high overhead – a fine, thin smoke that provided the room with a pleasant, incense-like odour. Occasionally there was a minor explosion as a log split in the heat, but then the wood settled again and was quiet.

Simon and Baldwin had arranged to meet the Coroner to discuss progress.

'Do you really think that poor fellow in the gaol could have murdered his master?' Baldwin began.

'No. That was one reason for taking you there, to meet him in the flesh. The Bailiff, William, always was too keen to pick the easiest victim. Personally I think I have as much of a duty not to imprison the innocent as I have to capture the guilty.'

'I should like you to tell us about some of the other people in the city. For example, this girl Mary with whom Elias fancies himself in love. What do *you* know of *her*?'

The host appeared and the three men ordered two quarts of spiced wine to be set by the fire to warm. When the man had brought a large pot of strong Bordeaux flavoured with cinnamon and nutmeg he left them and Roger leaned forward thoughtfully.

'She's a bright little thing, very comely. Daughter of a baker called Rob near the Shambles, and often works with him, since her brother Martin died. But she's flighty, that one. I doubt whether she was ever all that serious about Elias.'

'Is she vain? Greedy? Deceitful?'

'Ho, Sir Baldwin,' Roger smiled, leaning back. 'She's a woman, but she's no worse than many, I swear. No, I don't think she's overly greedy or vain. No more than any woman.'

Baldwin fleetingly reflected that it was fortunate that his wife was not present to hear the Coroner's views, but then he was considering the issue again. 'This is too serious for us to worry about upsetting her or her friends. I only wonder whether she herself may have been persuaded to keep Elias with her.'

'What, you think someone tried to keep him back?' Roger exclaimed, watching Simon pour their wine.

Simon had heated his dagger's blade in the fire. Now he used it to stir his wine. It sizzled as it touched the liquor and he watched the steam rising. 'It's an interesting thought. The one day that Elias happens to be really late is the same day that a random thief happens to find his way clear. Too much of a coincidence. It's more rational to assume that the boy was delayed intentionally – which means that Mary was involved in it somehow. She was bribed or blackmailed into chatting to Elias and keeping him back for longer than usual, so that the assassin had plenty of time.'

'No. I can't swallow that. Mary is many things, I don't doubt, but this is implicating her in two deaths: that of poor Ralph Glover, and the possible execution of Elias, an inno-cent man.'

'Last night she danced for Vincent le Berwe,' Simon said. 'And in the evening I saw her rutting enthusiastically with one of the musicians. She didn't seem very concerned about Elias then.'

The Coroner looked appalled. His brows came down and he glowered into his pot of wine. 'The young bitch!'

Baldwin sighed. 'Let us consider the two clerks who visited the glover early in December. They were together for that delivery, as they were in their rooms, and yet one is now dead.'

'Yes?'

'Does it not seem suspicious to you? One specific fact leaps out at me.'

Roger shook his head in bafflement.

Baldwin continued patiently, 'Coroner, if someone knew that the money was there, it is reasonable to assume he might have known where it came *from*: he knew it was Cathedral money. If somebody heard about it, did he hear about it before it was delivered, or did he only hear about it *after* it had been delivered?'

'Do you believe in dissecting every enquiry in the same manner?' Coroner Roger asked dryly.

Simon shrugged. 'Two clerks could be robbed easily enough. A couple of taps with a stick and they would be unconscious. Then the thief could help himself to the money. Why wait until they had delivered the stuff?'

'He probably thought it would be easier to break into a place where there was only one man, rather than knocking over two youngsters. So would I,' Roger added with emphasis, knocking back his wine and smacking his lips appreciatively.

'Perhaps. But most felons would prefer to take their chances in the open. Except,' Simon added musingly, 'we don't know how he could have known what the two carried.'

'There you are. He saw two clerical types walking about the city. So? Not much new in that. Then Ralph shot his mouth off in a tavern and people got to hear about his fortune in winning so lucrative a contract. A short while after, someone decides to take a little of it for himself. He breaks in and steals it all, killing poor Ralph at the same time. Problem solved.'

'Nearly. But not quite. Did Ralph often frequent taverns?'

'Not very often, but so what? A man can decide to visit one if he wants.'

'True,' Baldwin breathed. 'Very well. What of others? For example, how much do you know about Nicholas Karvinel and his wife?'

'Karvinel? He's a lousy businessman from what I've heard. Can't make money to save his life. And he has managed to amass huge debts. You heard about the attack on him? Set upon by a gang of thieves in broad daylight, for God's sake? It's getting so you can hardly leave your front door nowadays. Crime is increasing all the time.'

'What exactly happened?' Simon asked.

'I was in the Guildhall when a messenger arrived saying that there'd been a robbery. Apparently that fool Karvinel had been down to the port to check on a cargo. He had a load of wine and iron arriving, and he went there with the Cathedral's steward to check it all . . .'

'Why with the Cathedral's steward?' Simon interjected.

'The wine was for the Dean and the iron was for the Cathedral works. Karvinel went down there, and as soon as the goods were checked out of the port, straight onto the Cathedral wagons, Karvinel took his payment and set off back. He was also carrying money back to the Dean, but when—'

Baldwin interrupted him with a sharp gesture. 'You say he was carrying *other* money, not only his own?'

'Yes. Is it important?'

'It might be nothing,' Baldwin said, but with a smile of calm satisfaction. 'But if I am right, this could be the explanation of much.'

'I see . . . you mean that someone within the Cathedral could have advised the thieves and arranged for the robberies?'

'All I will say is, consider the curious similarities between the two events. One robbery was out in the open, some distance from the city; the thieves must have been ready warned. At Ralph's place likewise there was clearly a lot of planning, making sure of the household's routine, speaking to Mary, perhaps, and ensuring that the scapegoat would be delayed.'

'If Karvinel *was* robbed on his way back to Exeter,' said Simon. 'How many others were robbed that day?'

'Nobody I know of.'

'So,' Baldwin summed up, 'we have one man who was robbed of his money and the Cathedral's when his goods had been sold – and another who was murdered and robbed in his own house when there was Cathedral money in his strong box.'

'You seriously think that is relevant? Sir Baldwin, if you spoke to any man in the city, you would find that the Cathedral held some place in their lives. It reaches into every aspect of the city. Everyone here has something to do with it.'

'All the Freeman of the City, you mean?' Baldwin asked.

'Certainly all the merchants. And many of the others too. We all profit from the presence of the Cathedral.'

'Let us return to the day of the robbery. You heard about it in the Guildhall, you say?'

'Yes,' Roger grunted, pouring himself more wine. 'I was there with Vincent le Berwe and Ralph to witness some documents when a messenger from Karvinel came and hammered on the doors. He told us about the robbery and wanted me to join Karvinel at an alehouse near the South Gate. Said Karvinel had recognised one of his attackers sitting drinking.

'Obviously I went with him immediately. The fellow was beaten, but what do you expect when an angry crowd grabs hold of a wrong-doer? He was lucky that most men had joined the posse to catch the other members of the gang. Then Peter arrived and . . .'

'Where had he been? Surely he should have arrived at the same time as Karvinel,' Simon frowned.

'Yes. Well, he said he'd been so shocked he'd had to go and get some wine down his neck,' the Coroner said dismissively.

'Someone told me that the leader of this band goes under a knightly title,' Baldwin recalled. Who had told him that, he wondered. Was it Karvinel again?

'That's right. Sir Thomas of Exmouth. Miserable sinner that he is! The man we caught wouldn't tell us anything, sadly. He denied having anything to do with the robbery, but he was known as a disreputable character. He'd been found out of doors at night a couple of times when people had been knocked on the head, so his guilt seemed pretty obvious. Anyway, they decided he was guilty on the proof of Karvinel's evidence and that of his clerk. Who would disprove a cleric?'

'Did the posse catch any other members of the gang?' Baldwin enquired.

'No. Not a sight or sound. In fact we heard afterwards that a band attacked some people up towards Silverton, so maybe they've moved on. The posse must have missed them. Then again, who knows how long it was from Karvinel being thumped to when he got back to town?'

'This wasn't his only bad piece of luck this year, was it?' Simon said.

'Oh, the poor bugger's been robbed at home, had his place burgled again, and fired. He won't want to remember the year 1321: it's been foul for him.'

'And yet Karvinel and Vincent le Berwe get on well?'

'I don't know about "well". They know each other, certainly. I believe they have some mutual business interests.'

'Tell me, what was the document that Ralph Glover and le Berwe wanted you to sign?'

'That? It was a sales agreement. Le Berwe had imported several bundles of basan and cordwain, and Ralph was buying it. He passed over the money after both had signed the document and the wagon was loaded at once. I saw it as I left to see Karvinel.'

'You read the document yourself?'

'Of course,' he said patiently. 'Vincent called me into the room just as Ralph left it to find a privy, and Vincent told me what they were proposing, which was for him to sell twenty dozens of basan and twelve of cordwain. I read it, and then Ralph came back, and he made his mark and stamped his seal upon the document, as did Vincent, and then me. Ralph was all frowns, though, and hardly looked at the document when he put on his mark.'

'Why was Ralph like that? Because of Vincent's business methods?'

'No, it was a box of candles out in the screens. He told me later that he thought they were the Bishop's – only the Bishop had his personal candles coloured that way or somesuch nonsense – and wanted me to find out where they had come from. I refused – I have little enough time to seek out all the bodies in Exeter and parts of Devon without searching for more mysteries. I told him, "No one from the Cathedral has asked me to investigate the Bishop's candles," but he was quite insistent. In the end I told him a few stolen candles were not my concern. If he was truly troubled, he should see the Constable or Bailiff.'

'What did he say to that?'

'Oh, he muttered something about duties and responsibilities, but then he shut up. I was right, you know. I have a hard enough job without finding myself more work.'

Baldwin paused, sipping. 'What is the difference between cordwain and basan, I wonder?'

Roger drained his cup. 'Cordwain is the finest goatskin from Cordova, carefully tanned and dressed; basan is good sheepskin tanned in oak or larch bark.'

'How do you know that?' Simon asked in surprise.

'Bailiff, when you live in a town like this where there are many leather tanners, dyers, furriers and leatherworkers of all sorts, but which also happens to be a major port with hundreds of ships offloading cargoes of fine foreign leathers in our estuary at Topsham, you learn quickly.' His face became thoughtful. 'Perhaps that's why Karvinel got robbed. His ship was unloaded down there at Topsham. Maybe someone there warned this gang of robbers and that's how they got to know about him and his money.'

'Coroner, how long would someone have had to watch the money being handed over before sending a message to his friends in the robber band? No, someone knew *before* Karvinel left the city that he was going to be bringing back a goodly haul in cash. The question is, how could a wandering band have learned such a thing?'

'We'll probably never know. At least one man involved was caught and dealt with swiftly. Maybe that was his job? Listening in taverns and alehouses for hint of such transactions.'

Baldwin looked doubtful. 'Perhaps. But in the meantime, we clearly have three problems to resolve. The robbery from Karvinel, the murder of Ralph and the death of the clerk Peter. And I am intrigued by the fact of the purchase of the basan and cordwain – especially since it was a little while before the delivery of the jewels and money for the gloves.'

'What has that to do with anything?' cried the Coroner.

'Perhaps nothing . . . but perhaps it has as much to do with it as the strange disappearance of Karvinel's clerk after the robbery until Hamond was accused, or Peter's anger in the tavern a short while later when he saw his master.'

And the frowning Baldwin would say no more.

CHAPTER TWENTY-TWO

Stephen sat at his table and waited patiently while his servant brought in a large platter with the pies and dishes. Another man bowed and placed the salt at his side, and then the trencher was before him, a small loaf at his side, which he methodically broke into four precise pieces. One quarter went straight into his alms dish for the poor, the rest was for himself.

He began to eat, his eyes on his guests. Adam looked as scruffy as usual. Stephen watched him fixedly until he took his own loaf of bread and dropped an offering into the alms dish. Gervase had told Stephen about the attack on Luke, so he was not surprised to see that Luke looked tired and pale. Stephen wondered whether he was feeling unwell. 'Luke?'

In answer to his Canon's kindly enquiry Luke assured him that he was fine, thanking him for his concern while, from the corner of his eye, he saw Adam smugly grinning to himself.

'Thanks for the bread,' Adam muttered a short while later.

'What?'

'The bread you left for me yesterday. It was lovely . . . Mmm.'

Luke stared, then glanced down at Adam's plate. The bread didn't look the same as the one he had carried yesterday, not at all. Adam was surely only trying to upset him. It was Henry who had thrown him into the shit.

'Shame Henry came out a moment or two afterwards. I was going to roll your face in the crap and stuff it down your shirt. I think,' Adam considered judicially, 'I think I'll do that later.'

Adam pulled off another piece of bread and studied it with a satisfied grin, but Luke hardly noticed. It had never occurred to him that it could have been Adam all the time – Henry's presence had made his guilt so apparent. As he watched, Adam turned, shoved the bread into his mouth and chewed with a smile.

It wasn't the half-loaf he'd dropped, but that was probably too old and stale for him. Or he'd eaten it earlier. Maybe he had, just so he could gloatingly tell Luke that he'd eaten it. Adam didn't need it himself, not with his access to the bakery, for he often delivered loaves to Canons, and he could select his own, picking the largest when he wanted to. And now Adam was taunting him with the knowledge that he had stolen Luke's own dried-up bit of bread. Adam had attacked him last night, and Luke had seen to it that Henry was punished.

Luke felt a simmering anger beginning to rise in him. He felt his face flush, his belly tighten and the muscles of his throat contract. It was hard to swallow. Somehow, he didn't know how, he would have his revenge.

Stephen reached for the salt and glanced about the quiet table. Seeing Luke's expression, he hesitated. It looked as though Luke was remembering his attack, he thought. Children like Henry could be horrible little beasts if they weren't controlled. He hoped the matter hadn't upset Luke too much. The boy did look rather peaky, he thought.

As Stephen was considering asking Luke whether he had thought of visiting the infirmarer, Adam hiccuped. He went a little pale as he burped again and glanced apologetically at Stephen. He felt rather appalled that he might have offended his Canon. All knew how Stephen hated noise at his dining table. He was the precise opposite of a courtly noble: there was no place at his table for frivolity or merriment. Dancers and musicians were unwanted. It was like living with a saint, but a saint with a streak of cruelty, Adam thought. Stephen could be unkind when he wanted. Sometimes he would use his tongue to pull a man apart, reducing even a strong fellow to a quivering wreck in a short time. Adam looked up warily and saw that Stephen's gaze had moved on. That was a relief.

In reality Stephen's mind was hardly on Adam at all. He had scarcely registered his Secondary's lapse. Stephen's attention was fixed upon the problems with the Cathedral. Even today, which was theoretically one of rest, his mind whirled with numbers and expenses. There was so much to be done.

It was ridiculous that when the Dean and Chapter had a crucial task to perform, which was to finish the Cathedral that they had begun, they should relax for over a week. The workmen should be back now, creating the fittings for the new Lady Chapel, the new High Altar and the screens for the choir. Instead, they were probably rutting on their sluts, stuffing their faces with strong ales and rich foods, or lying moaning after the event.

Stephen felt very strongly about it, knowing that if there was a temptation, he could easily fall prey to it. It was many years since he had enjoyed an encounter with a woman, longer still since he had realised the danger that lurked in too much strong ale or wine, but he always had the fearsome example of his brother before him. If he should lapse, he could become a sinner. Better by far that he should divorce himself from all temptations. Only that way could he guarantee himself a place in Heaven.

The Cathedral would be a magnificent building, he considered. In his mind's eye he could see the place rising up. The two towers, each with its tall steeple, the massive western doorway with its profusion of carved figures, all painted to make them the more lifelike: Kings, Queens, Bishops, Saints; all honouring the great work that had gone on in the Cathedral. And inside the magnificence of the gold and scarlet paintwork and the long, sweeping ceiling. It made his heart beat faster just to think of it. And, inside, the multiple chapels. To the Virgin, to St John the Evangelist, to St Gabriel and St George among others. It would be a wonderful place for any man to enter. Tall, wide, with beautiful voices rising in the clean air while the sun streamed in through the marvellous, coloured eastern window at dawn, or the equally impressive western window at sunset, it was a dream to make a man's blood rush!

And Peter had threatened it all.

Stephen had seen him that last day before he died, the twenty-third. It was the first opportunity he had found to speak to Peter alone. He had gone to Jolinde and Peter's hovel and questioned Peter closely. He had to, for his brother's words had burned into him after he had visited Sir Thomas in the woods that morning.

Aye, he had watched and listened to Peter's answers, and the lad had lied to him. He knew it, for Peter was not a good liar, and his deceit rang discordantly in the Canon's ears. Eventually, worn down by Stephen's questions, Peter had confessed. He had told Stephen all, under the promise of secrecy. He had *not* been with Karvinel when Karvinel swore he had been attacked; he had not witnessed Hamond attacking anyone. He had been in his hall all that day until Karvinel came and claimed to him that he had been attacked, said that one of the outlaws was even now sitting in a tavern. Peter had urged him to call the Hue and Cry, but Karvinel protested with tears in his eyes that no one would believe him.

To Stephen, Peter had begged forgiveness, had declared that he would do anything to atone for his crime, but he had been urged to lie in order to support the law. It was only after Hamond had hanged that he had learned that Hamond had been innocent. And that knowledge tore at him.

It was no excuse. Stephen could give him no hope for absolution. Peter had sent an innocent man to his death by swearing a false oath. By his perjury, he was a murderer. He deserved his own end.

Stephen sighed, then glanced down to see that a fresh course was already before him. It was a steaming dish of mussels, the whole served with a piquant wine sauce. The steam rose, giving off a wonderful smell.

The steward passed along the table setting the bowls before each diner. Using his knife to take a little salt from the silver pot, the Canon sprinkled it over his bowl. His cook never used enough salt. With a little sigh of contentment he dipped his spoon into the dish and extracted the first of the succulent creatures.

There was a slight movement from the end of the table. Stephen made a point of not looking. It was important that the Choristers should learn to respect and admire their elders, and if Adam took to bullying his nephew Luke, Stephen felt strongly that he, as a Canon, should not interfere. It was for them to resolve the issue. Luke in particular, he thought grimly, should learn humility. Otherwise he could succumb to the family's weakness and sinfulness.

As he finished his bowl and began scraping up the last of the delicious liquor, there was a cough, and a stool scraped. Stephen looked up irritably.

It was Adam. His face had gone green. 'I . . . I . . . feel . . .' He clapped a hand over his mouth, but too late. To Stephen's disgust a stream of vomit issued, spattering the table. 'Good God!' Stephen cried. 'Go outside, you cretin, before you . . .'

He was too late. Adam fell to his knees, threw up once more, then collapsed retching.

Calling his steward, Stephen thundered: 'Take that repellent fool out and get someone in here to clean the table. Ugh! He has quite ruined my appetite. What is it, is he drunk? Eh? Have you been drinking, you sot?'

Adam stared back, his eyes red and streaming, his mouth besmeared with vomit. 'I've been poisoned, sir!'

After leaving the Coroner, Baldwin showed Simon Ralph's shop. It was a small, narrow-fronted place, and Baldwin tried to peer in through the closed shutters while Simon stood back at the opposite side of the street and looked it over.

The shop in Correstrete had lime-washed walls and carefully painted woodwork to show that the dead owner had valued his property. The roof was shingle, and the wooden slats still possessed the fresh almost orange tints of newness. There was no chimney, nor any louvres through which excess smoke could leave. Two doors gave access, one to the shop, the other to the hall behind, and both were well protected by the overhanging jetty from the upper chamber, whose oak timbers looked newer than the rest of the surrounding woodwork, making Simon think that the glover had only recently put in the second storey.

Not many of the other houses in this street were so well appointed or modern. Most looked little better than hovels, with a uniformly slatternly appearance; Ralph's stood out like a gentlewoman surrounded by drab sluts.

It was while he stood there that a beggar came limping along the road and Simon cast a scornful eye over him. From his threadbare fustian cloak to his scuffed and ruined shoe, the bowl hanging by a thong from his neck, the fellow looked every bit the professional beggar, and Simon had no wish to be bothered by his sort today. He and Baldwin were too busy.

Seeing how he curled his lip, John Coppe changed his mind about asking for money. Coppe was perfectly used to being ignored. He gave a mental shrug and considered the second man. Baldwin was at the door studying the shop, peering in through a gap, and Coppe began to wonder whether he had arrived just in time to prevent a theft. The cold had persuaded him to go and seek the warmth of a tavern, but now it looked as though his old friend's shop was about to be broken into. He should call the Bailiff – and yet why bother? Whatever Ralph had owned was no longer his. The poor fellow was dead. Perhaps it was as well to let someone rob the place rather than see all Ralph's goods fall under a tax or be legally stolen by the Receiver and others.

All these considerations flashed through Coppe's mind as he hobbled along, and by the time he was close to the knight he had made up his mind. He tentatively held out a hand. 'Master? A coin for some pottage?'

Baldwin gave the man a long, thoughtful stare, then nodded and reached into his purse. He drew out a coin. The beggar's face lit up with delight when he saw it, and he bowed. 'Thank you, Master, thank you.'

Coppe wanted to leave and invest the money in a refreshing pot of ale, but something made him remain standing there, watching the knight peering again through a shuttered window. 'He's dead, you know.'

Simon crossed the street casually as Baldwin nodded slowly. 'I had heard. I wanted to see where he had lived.'

'They ought to make him a saint,' Coppe said gruffly.

Simon glanced up at the house. 'Why? Was he good to you?'

'He was always giving us money. Not like some of the tightfisted bastards in this city. If you was on fire they wouldn't piss on you without charging for their time and trouble – aye, and for the ale they'd drunk, too.'

'But Ralph was generous?' Baldwin asked.

'Him? He used to give feasts to the poorest of the city. At Christmas and Candlemas, and if the weather stayed bad, he'd give another on Lady Day. Any of us who could get to his door was always welcome to a pot of wine and some bread. He didn't feel the need to wait for a feast day.'

Coppe was gazing up at the house with an expression of such sadness and longing that Simon found himself wishing he could have met Ralph. Certainly for a man to have earned the trust and loyalty of even a tatty beggar like this one spoke of his Christian spirit.

Baldwin interrupted his reverie. 'Have you often been inside his hall?'

'Often enough.'

'I should like to go inside to see whether anything is missing. Would you know if anyone would have a key to it?'

John Coppe cast an eye up and down the knight, his mind recalling his first assumption. Baldwin did not look like a thief, but sometimes the wealthiest men in the land could behave worse than the poorest. That was how they became rich. 'Why would you want to go inside?'

'I am Keeper of the King's Peace in Crediton and the Coroner has asked me to enquire about Ralph's death. I want to see whether he was robbed of anything other than his money when he died.'

'Oh! Well, in that case I'd try there,' Coppe said, pointing at the house next door but one. 'Ask for David. He used to see quite a lot of Ralph.'

It was a larger place, but not so well looked after, to Simon's mind. The paint was peeling from the woodwork and the limewash hadn't been renewed for many a long year. Strips had faded or been discoloured by the smoke and soot of the adjoining buildings and it had an air of shabbiness, like a woman who has lost interest in her looks and cares only for the essentials of life: no longer bothering about her physical appearance, only about being comfortable.

The owner was a cheerful enough fellow: stooped, peering through narrowed eyes under a thin greying thatch of curling hair. He wore a good quality shirt and tunic, although both had seen better days. He looked enquiringly at the three men when he came to his door, and when Baldwin told him who he was, he agreed to let them see the house and shop so long as he himself stayed with them.

'This is fair,' Baldwin said. 'I would prefer witnesses.'

The four entered the dead glover's hall first. The neighbour had a key and he threw open the front door, standing aside to let Baldwin lead the way inside, Simon behind him.

It was much like any other little hall. The corridor from the front door led along the length of the shop into the hall itself, behind which was a small pantry and parlour. Baldwin stood and contemplated the hall, then went upstairs with David while Simon went out and opened the door from the pantry. At the back was a little yard with a variety of plants growing in raised beds prettily laid out with wickerwork walls to keep the compost and manure in place. The back door was locked with a wooden peg that fitted into and securely held a latch.

Simon surveyed it, but it told him nothing about the death of the glover or the identity of his killer.

Walking back inside, he crouched at the fireside. Coppe had sat down on a stool at the wall and Simon saw that his foot had left ashy prints over the floor. When the door opened, a little of the fire's ashes were disturbed by the draught, blowing out of the hearth and onto the floor where people would step in it and, like Coppe, tread the ashes all over the place.

When Baldwin came down the ladder, he saw Simon at the doorway. 'Nothing up there, I'm afraid.'

In the shop itself Baldwin and Simon asked their companions to wait in the street doorway while they looked around. Simon in particular had hoped to find ashy footprints, but there were none. So many people had come in after finding the body that there was nothing more to be discovered. He leaned against a large counter-top with his arms crossed while Baldwin stood in the middle of the floor and gazed about.

The room was square, with skins and leathers tied together and hanging from strings looped over hooks on all the walls. Behind the counter were shelves, and here lay some of Ralph and Elias's finished products: soft pigskin gloves; delicate and dainty light gloves for ladies; heavier, working two-fingered gloves, into each finger of which the wearer pushed two of his own; fine soft gloves for a gentleman; even thick gauntlets for men-at-arms.

Simon found his attention wandering. He looked at the hanging furs and leathers, smelling the faintly sour odour of the smoke, barks and urine used in the tanning processes. Then he found himself contemplating the paintwork. On the wall at the front there was only good, clean whitewash. Only when he noticed some marks low on the side wall under some skins did he feel his interest waken. He crossed the room and bent, touching the marks and sniffing at his fingers. 'Aha! This is where he died, then.'

'Why are you so sure?' Baldwin asked.

'Men who've been stabbed will often thrash about and kick, won't they? The floor in the house there had ash on it.

299

Some had got onto Ralph's boots, I guess, and when he fell, his boot caught the wall. These smudges are wood ash. I imagine he opened the door to someone, turned to lead the way in here and that was then they threw the first blow, getting him in the back. Ralph fell, and his boots scuffed up the wall here.'

From the doorway, David spoke up. 'He wasn't there when they found him.'

'Where was he?'

'Here.'

Simon crouched again. There was blood in a dried and crusted pool where David pointed. 'Someone must have moved him.'

David shrugged. 'Does it matter?'

'Only in so far that he was moved away from the door. The killer couldn't get in and out with him lying in the way,' Simon said. 'Then again, perhaps someone wanted to avoid trouble.'

The 'First Finder' of a murdered man would be fined to ensure he appeared at the Coroner's court. Many chose to avoid that cost by pretending not to see a body.

Baldwin added, 'So many men prefer to deny seeing anything. It is cheaper.' He noticed a small frown on David's face as he absorbed all this. Baldwin's tone sharpened. 'Did you see anyone here the morning Ralph died.'

David looked as though he was about to shake his head, but then he grimaced unhappily. 'Masters, it's so hard to know what to do for the best, but yes, I saw someone with him that morning.'

Baldwin's eyebrows rose. 'Did you tell the Bailiff or anyone?'

'There was nothing to tell! I saw Ralph and another man entering here. That's all. I looked away, and when I looked back, they were gone.'

'Didn't it occur to you that the man with him might have killed Ralph?' Baldwin exclaimed disbelievingly. 'You saw Ralph with his murderer and did *nothing*?'

'I didn't see who was with him, so there was little I could tell anyone. And I didn't know Ralph was going to be killed. I just thought he'd opened up early for once and there was no reason to report that,' he said defensively.

Baldwin glared at him furiously. 'You mean you didn't want to get involved in the Coroner's inquest and risk getting amerced to turn up when the murder trial is held, preferring to hold your tongue to avoid paying anyone.'

The man flushed slightly but didn't speak.

John Coppe gripped his crutch as if readying himself to strike David with it. He rasped, 'You saw the man? You saw the bastard who killed the glover and didn't do anything about it? You'd rather see the apprentice hanged, is that it?'

The other three ignored him. 'So,' Baldwin said slowly, 'was the man with Ralph his apprentice – Elias?'

'I didn't see clearly . . .'

'Be damned to that!' Simon roared suddenly, his anger getting the better of him. He took a couple of quick paces towards the man. The neighbour would have bolted, but the beggar grabbed his arm, and before he could free himself, Simon had his shirtfront in both fists. He hauled the man closer until their noses almost touched. 'The knight asked you if it was Elias who was there with his master. Think carefully, you God-damned shit, because if you start lying to protect your own arse, I'll have you in gaol before you can fart.'

301

'You can't – you have no authority here. I'm a Freeman of the City, I . . .'

'Fetch Coroner Roger,' Simon spat at the beggar.

'*No!*' the man cried, wilting in Simon's grip. 'All right, I don't think it was Elias. I would have told the court, I wouldn't have let the pathetic wretch hang for it. I just didn't think it'd matter if I didn't tell people just yet.'

'You *bastard*!' Simon said. He maintained his grip. 'You saw that poor devil stuck in gaol for something he never did, and did nothing to protect him. Just to save you a few pennies.'

'Did you recognise the man?' Baldwin demanded.

'I told you, no! He was under the overhang in the shadow and wearing a cloak or something, with a wide-brimmed hat. I only had a fleeting glimpse, no more. I thought it was just a client.'

'That tells us nothing. Everyone will have a cloak and a broad-brimmed hat against the rain,' Baldwin said.

Simon studied the man in his grasp. 'Not necessarily, Baldwin. A cleric wouldn't, would he?'

'You consider this finally proves Peter's innocence?'

'Perhaps,' Simon said. He shook David, not ungently. 'It wasn't Elias?'

'No. Elias is taller, more gawky and clumsy. This one moved confidently, easily,' David muttered. 'I just thought it was someone after an urgent bit of work or something. How was I to know he'd kill poor old Ralph?'

'Was this fellow taller or shorter than Ralph?' Baldwin pressed him. At the same time Simon began to relax his grip a little.

'I don't know. Perhaps . . . no, he was shorter. I remember now. Ralph opened the door and thrust it open, allowing the client in first, and Ralph was taller.'

The beggar hawked and spat on David's shoulder. 'You make me want to puke. You were going to let the apprentice swing for something you knew he didn't do, just so you could keep away from paying money into the court.'

David pursed his lips while Simon hastily withdrew his hand from the spittle. 'Get inside,' he said. Then to the beggar: 'You stay out here and there'll be another penny for you. Yes?'

'Yes, Master,' Coppe said, his head hanging low.

Ignoring David, Simon addressed Baldwin. 'We know Ralph was murdered in this room. The killer didn't run much of a risk. All he had to do was stab Ralph and leave him, dart next door and take everything from the cash box. Easy.'

'Perhaps.'

Simon ran his hand over the gloves on sale. 'He was a good worker.'

'So was Elias,' David offered.

'*He* still bloody is,' Baldwin snapped.

David appeared fully cowed and like many who find themselves on the wrong side of the law, he was keen to show how total was his conversion. Taking a deep breath he cleared his throat. 'Sirs, there is another thing. A while before the two entered here, I saw another man.'

'How long before and who was it?'

'The bells were still ringing for the service, so I think it was before the first Mass, and it was a cleric of some sort – I think a lad of twenty or so years. He had a thin sort of face, long and anxious. I saw him quite clearly.'

'Was he a Vicar?'

'No, I don't think so. I think he was one of the Secondaries.' He hung his head. 'I think it was the one you mentioned. The lad called Peter.'

'Peter was out that morning,' Coppe agreed, and told them about seeing the cleric running smack into Ralph outside the gate. 'If it wasn't for the Treasurer, Ralph would have fallen,' he said. 'But I don't think Peter was well that day. Later I saw him leave the Cathedral again, walking as if he was in a daze. He left after Ralph and didn't return till much later.'

'You didn't see him come back here?' Baldwin asked David.

'I was working after that. Maybe he returned. There was someone outside with a wagon, I know. While I was out back I heard the wheels stop outside here.'

'I see,' said Baldwin. 'So now we know Stephen was outside the Cathedral that morning as well.'

David jerked his head at the door. 'I saw Peter go to the front door of the house and walk inside with a small bag in his hand. He didn't look guilty or furtive. If he was breaking in to commit a crime, he was begging to be caught.'

Baldwin gave a dry smile. 'I think that is the most observant comment you have given for a long time. Did you see him leave?'

'It was a short while later. He came out, looked up and down the road, and then hurried off back to the Cathedral grounds. I noticed that he didn't have anything in his hands then. It was quite some while later that I saw Ralph and his visitor, and then my wife called me and I went back to my own hall.'

'Well, I think you have cleared up much that was confusing,' Baldwin said. He was handling the hanging leathers, a small frown puckering his brow.

'What is it?' Simon asked.

'The Coroner told us Ralph paid Vincent le Berwe for basan and cordwain and took it away the same day, but there's none here.'

CHAPTER TWENTY-THREE

They watched while the subdued David locked the doors, then with the beggar directing them, they left him and sought a tavern.

Coppe led them to Will Row's alehouse down an alley off the High Street, run by a pleasant woman in her fifties, who smiled with toothless gums when she saw their companion. 'John, where have you been? I was beginning to think you'd got pissed, fallen down a well and drowned.'

'I wouldn't do that, Joan. Not while you were still around to tempt me back again.'

He grinned, his mouth likewise all but empty of teeth, when she playfully cuffed him over the head, cackling.

'Come on, wench, there's gentlemen here to be served.'

A young girl appeared, but Simon was more attracted to the wizened old woman. She shouted at the girl like a harridan, but her face was more composed of smiling wrinkles than frowns. What, he wondered, would he look like when he got to her age? Or his wife, Meg, come to that. This Joan had a calmness about her that was pleasant and motherly, while the beggar, for all his scruffiness, was clearly trusted by her.

As the two women disappeared to fetch drinks, Coppe told the others, 'She was the wife of my best mate. I was a sailor, see. I used to have a good life going off all over the place – oh, from here to Venice I've been. God, some of the seas you'd see there, it was amazing that the ships lasted the trip.'

'If you get the old sod talking about his sailing days, you'll never get away from him,' Joan said, returning with pots for all the men. The girl appeared a moment later with a massive jug from which she poured them spiced wine, hot and sweet.

'Oh, give me leave to speak a moment with friends,' John Coppe said aloofly and Joan roared with laughter before dropping into a seat nearer her fire and starting to knit.

'Joan's old man Will was a good sailor too. Him and me, we went all over. All along the Breton coast, and the Norman one, all the way down as far as Bordeaux. Often did that run, buying wines mainly. Then one day we were attacked by French pirates and had our cargo taken.'

'My Will was hit by an arrow,' Joan said, this time more quietly. She paused and let her knitting fall to her lap, sighing, then continued, her needles flying faster than before as if concentration was itself a cure for her sadness, 'So since then I've made shift as best I can.'

'And I never had a wife or a house; when I got back, I was forced to start begging to survive. At first I stayed a while with my brother, who lived over near the South Gate, but he died a while ago, and his wife had to sell the place, so since then I've not had a place of my own. There was no point when I was young, because I was always looking for the next ship. But if you're wrecked like me, the masters don't want you. Anyway, no one would have used me even if I wasn't ruined like this. I have a bad reputation.'

Baldwin stirred his wine with a finger and sucked it. 'Why do you say that?'

'Nicholas Karvinel. It was his ship, his cargo, that was taken by the pirates and he was sure that someone warned the French when our ship sailed, and that was how the pirates caught us. He thought a crew member gave away the ship for a bribe.'

'Is it possible?' Simon asked.

'Anything is possible, but is it likely? Pirates don't wait and ask who is their friend, they attack as soon as they can and kill everyone. Anyway, a ship saw us as we left Topsham that day to go to France, and it almost caught us a couple of times. We reached port and loaded with wine and set off for home, but then the pirate caught us out in the Channel and came at us with the wind behind him. It was quite a chase, sirs, because our master had a good head for the sea, and he could make good use of every little gust, but then our wind died, and the French paddled with oars to approach us. The wind picked up, but they caught it first, and with their ship being lighter, they catched us quick. And then it was all down to the axes and the bows.'

'Old John here was one of three men who survived. All the others died,' Joan said matter-of-factly. 'So of course a lot of the merchants thought that if someone had given away the ship to the French it would have been one of the men who lived afterwards.'

John Coppe snorted in disgust. 'How any man could have protected himself in a mêlée like that, I don't know. If there was a spy among us, he was as like to be knocked on the head as any other. And I lost my leg and had my face wrecked like this. It's just stupid rubbish!'

'But Karvinel wouldn't use any of the survivors again?' Simon asked.

'Oh, he did better than that,' Joan said with wry coldness, but Coppe held his hand up with impatience.

'Karvinel couldn't use me – look at this,' he said, tapping his stump. 'Anyway, he'd lost his ship and with it much of his wealth. Up until then he was a powerful man here in Exeter, but from that moment nothing he's touched has come good. No, I think he told his friends about his suspicions and now none of them will use me.'

'What happened to the other two?'

'They're dead. This is going back a few years, sir. I'm talking of five or maybe seven years ago. One died two years ago in a brawl in a tavern, the other froze to death in the winter during the famine, God bless them both.'

'Talking of famines,' Baldwin murmured, but just then the girl returned. She had run to the Cook's Row, and her pale features were pleasantly flushed. 'Thank you,' he said, taking a large pie from her apron and dropping coins onto the table.

Simon meditatively watched Coppe as he ate voraciously. 'It's some time since your last meal, I'd guess.'

'Other than Cathedral bread, aye,' came the response, with a few crumbs. 'But they bake a good loaf. Adam delivers some at the gate on his rounds.'

Baldwin sipped at his wine. 'What else do you know about Karvinel?'

309

'He's not far from being in the same position as me. He owns little now that isn't pawned. All his high hopes to recover his losses with the last shipment have been dashed, and I don't know if he'll be able to afford any of the city posts. His friend the Steward might try to help him, but I don't know if he'll succeed. I hope not!'

The last words came out with a cruel hopefulness, but the fire of hatred which had flared so briefly in his eyes, quickly subsided and Coppe finished his pie, picking at the crumbs on the table top before him.

'What of le Berwe?' Baldwin prodded. 'How is he looked upon in the city?'

'He is respected, I suppose. He's one of the stewards . . . more than that, he's the Receiver: in charge of all records, seeing that justice is upheld, visiting all the markets and fairs within the city to make sure the victuals are wholesome as well as collecting all the city's rents and money due.'

Joan sniffed. 'He would be well looked upon. He has the money to buy influence and friends.'

'You think he doesn't deserve such treatment, Mother?' Simon said with a grin.

'No, he doesn't. He's a sharp, calculating devil that one, and some day the Devil will come and take his own.'

'Why do you say so?' Baldwin in some surprise. He didn't much like the Receiver himself, but the old woman's loathing went further than mere dislike.

'Because he uses people and breaks them when he has no more use for them, that's why. Like his first wife. There's enough people in the city reckon he killed her, poor little chit. I wouldn't trust him further than I could spit!'

*   *   *

Hawisia rose from her needlework when she heard her husband return.

Their marriage was undergoing some strain, it was true. She had expected that the expressions of love which Vincent le Berwe had used to woo her were proof of undying devotion, and yet now she rarely saw him except to entertain others. He spent so much time with his business, especially now he was the Receiver.

Hawisia wondered sometimes whether he had been the same with his first wife. She had died very young, just before giving birth to her first baby, and Hawisia asked herself whether Vincent had been always so busy while she was alive. Certainly his business had suffered after her death. Vincent had been forced to try to rebuild it, or so he had told Hawisia.

The muttering against him was caused because his dead bride was so young. At only fourteen, many people thought his interests in wedding her were suspicious. In some areas that sort of age was considered all right for a wife, but here in Exeter people were more conservative. And when she died, rumours began to circulate about him. It had taken some little while for him to rebuild his business interests afterwards, for many customers faded away and sought new suppliers.

It had taken all of Hawisia's diplomatic skills to help him build up his business interests again.

'My love?' she called.

Vincent appeared in the doorway. 'I have to go out for a while. Amuse yourself, dear. I shouldn't be very long,' he said, and was gone.

'But you've been away all . . .'

311

She stopped herself. He was already out of the door and in any case there was no point in making a fuss. He had business to attend to, didn't he? Of course he would have to go out every so often. She only wished she could be of more use to him. Rather than sitting back in this insipid manner she should try to help him more . . . except she had no idea how.

Hawisia was the daughter of a happily married couple whose lives had been filled with joy. She herself was the fourth daughter, and her father, a furrier, would have liked to have had a son, but he never showed disappointment in his children. Each was to him a wonder and perpetual source of entertainment. And his love for his wife, Hawisia's mother, was no less obvious. He and she hugged each other and could often be caught kissing in the street like young children but they never displayed any shame, only laughed, and her mother smoothed her skirts and tried to look solemn while he coughed and then grappled with her when he thought she least expected it.

That was how a marriage should be, to Hawisia's mind, but she knew that her man was so worried about his work that he had lost interest in the marital bed and in her. That was the simple explanation.

She only wished she could help him more.

Brother Gervase was in his room working on a heavy, leather-bound tome of music when the banging came at his door. The interruption was welcome: the piece he was working on should in theory have worked well during an interval while a priest was holding up the offerings for the miracle of transubstantiation, but somehow he couldn't get the music to work in the way he had hoped. Perhaps if he came back to it later . . . he thought, and set the book down as he went to his door.

It was cold, but that wasn't the reason for the greyness on the messenger's face. 'Brother Adam has been poisoned.'

Gervase gaped, then grabbed a heavy cloak which he threw over his shoulders as they hurried together down the row of Canons' houses.

Entering Stephen's house, Gervase was immediately greeted by the retching figure of Adam on the floor. 'My God!'

The boy was past caring about what he looked like. As his body attempted to eject the poison from his system, he writhed, his tongue protruding with each spasm, his arms wrapped about his torso, his legs drawn up to his chest in the foetal position.

Nearby was Stephen, who shook his head in rejection of this hideous sight, counting his rosary and muttering a low prayer. Feeling a shudder of revulsion pass down his back as another shaking-fit caught the frail-looking youth's body, Gervase came to a decision. He pointed to Stephen's Vicar. 'You! Fetch Gilbert from the apothecary in Waterbeer. Tell him a man has been poisoned, and he should bring all that is needful. *Don't delay, man, run!*'

The startled Vicar's mouth fell open, and then he was off, haring up the road towards the middle of town like a deer which has seen the hounds behind him.

Gervase slapped the beads from Stephen's hands. 'Have you helped him, Stephen? Canon! Have you heard his confession?'

The only response he was given was a blank, horrified stare. Then Stephen looked down at his beads and picked

313

them up again, his lips moving once more as the wooden spheres passed through his hands.

'God's blood!' Gervase swore, and crouched at the side of the injured man. 'Adam? Adam, listen. You may be about to die. If you are, you must confess to me. Understand? You have to confess to me in case you die. And you must give me the seven responses to the seven interrogations. Can you hear me?'

Adam opened his eyes and gazed up, but another jabbing pain in his bowels made him clench his jaw and snap his eyes shut, the lids compressing as he tried to hide from the pain. And from his mouth broke a high, keening sound, like a rabbit caught in a trap.

The apothecary arrived at a cracking pace, rushing into the room with a small cloth sack which he dropped to the floor as he entered the hall. 'Christ Jesus!'

'Do not blaspheme,' Stephen said severely. He had begun to come to his senses in the time since Gervase had knocked away his rosary. Now he could watch as Gervase held Adam's hand, the Succentor weeping as he tried to comfort the groaning lad.

Stephen was transfixed; petrified. Never had he expected to act as host to a man who expired at his table. It was revolting – incomprehensible. Adam was no scholar, was not, if truth be told, of great use to the Cathedral, but to see him suddenly collapse like this was an atrocious shock.

He walked shakily to his chair and waved to his servant. 'Wine,' he commanded. Watching while the apothecary shook his head, studying the youth, he was suddenly convinced that Adam would die and the only thing that he,

Stephen, would be remembered for from now on was that he had served a meal that poisoned a Secondary. It would over-shadow all his achievements, smothering reports of his financial probity, hiding his successes behind a veil of rumour and vicious slanders.

'How could this have happened?' he moaned.

Gervase moved to allow the apothecary to approach with his knife and a bowl. When he stepped out of the way, his foot touched something. Bending, he picked up a small flask of orpiment. He studied it with a frown, but then the apoth-ecary was asking for help. On a whim, Gervase put the flask in his scrip. Both men gripped Adam's arm firmly enough to let a little blood flow. The apothecary dipped a finger in it, holding his reddened forefinger up to the light, smelling at the bowl, then tasting a little on his tongue thoughtfully, stir-ring the blood as it thickened in the bowl and shaking his head.

'I think that should be enough,' he said and bound the arm, tightening a tourniquet and applying a styptic. He placed the bloody bowl on the table and reached into his bag again. 'Fetch me salt and water, please.'

Gervase watched while the apothecary withdrew a long clyster tube and a pig's bladder from his bag. 'Right, first we have to force the salted water into his throat, to make sure he's brought up all the poison, and then we need to empty his bowels as well,' he said, in the bright tone of one who had never yet performed such an operation.

Jeanne and Edgar were in the High Street, passing down the long line of trestles upon which were laid all manner of choice goods.

They had not yet lunched, and as they walked along the road Jeanne became aware of a faint light-headedness. Looking up at the sun she realised how long it had been since she heard the Cathedral bells toll for the midday service. Her hand went to her belly and the growing child. She must try to remember to eat more regularly. That was one thing that Simon's wife had told her, because the dizziness of hunger could attack at any time. 'I need some food, Edgar,' she said.

He grinned and led them back the way they had come to Carfoix, the meeting of the four main roads, then right along the street of cooks. The smells were enough to tempt the most jaded palates. Roasted honeyed larks and pigeons, pies of good beef and lamb, hot pies, cold pies, pies filled with vegetables, pies with strong spices, pies with sweetened custards filling them. Jeanne picked a roasted pigeon and a pie filled with sweetened almond custard while Edgar, who didn't have a sweet tooth, selected a strong-smelling beef and onion pasty which had much garlic added, from the odour.

The smell made Jeanne wince. She had taken a dislike to garlic recently. Usually, like most people, she loved the flavour for, after all, it was one of the most common herbs used to strengthen a pottage or soup, but since becoming pregnant, she had found the stink of it turned her stomach. Accordingly she stood upwind of Edgar while he ate his pie with every appearance of relish.

While standing there, they were jostled by two clerks who erupted from St Petrock's and ran past laughing. Shortly afterwards a red-faced porter came out of the church and glared up and down the streets before throwing up his hands as if in despair and returning.

'I think the revels are beginning early this year,' Edgar noted laconically.

Jeanne agreed and they made their way to a tavern. Jeanne was feeling a little chilled so she had a mulled cider, sweetened with honey and scented with cinnamon, ginger and galingale. It sent its heat shooting straight to her toes and fingertips, scalding as it passed down her throat, but filling her with glowing delight when it reached her belly.

Outside they strolled idly along the Northgate Street, and soon saw the two youths who had run from St Petrock's. They were walking up behind two men, obviously important fellows, for they swaggered as they walked, their feet in step but at a pace too slow to be dignified as a 'march'. Giggling, the two boys darted up to the two older men, there was a burst of angry shouting, and the youths pelted back past Edgar and Jeanne, laughing like idiots, one gripping a bowl, the other a handful of what looked like rags.

The two men looked at each other, shrugged, and continued on their way. And Jeanne saw that both had a large patch of coloured material stuck to their back. The boys were glueing patches of cloth on unsuspecting citizens as a joke.

Jeanne giggled to herself and glanced at Edgar. He too was smiling, but he wasn't looking at the men. His attention was on a large copper pot hanging above a nearby trestle. Edgar had recently married, much to Baldwin's oft-stated astonishment, for Edgar had been a noted philanderer ever since he and Baldwin had left the Knights Templar, but there it was: Edgar the bachelor was now Edgar the married man. He had given his vows before everyone. Jeanne saw his peering study of the pot and was touched that he should be thinking of his new wife even now, miles from home. Not that he or she had need of a pot that size. If he ever wanted something to cook in, there were plenty of large coppers in Baldwin's kitchen.

Jeanne was about to suggest that he should borrow one of theirs, when Edgar whirled. Jeanne squealed with alarm as a boy in clerical garb fell in front of her, and when she turned to look, the second was wearing his bowl of glue, sitting unhappily in a large puddle.

'Should we return now, do you think, my Lady?' Edgar said imperturbably.

CHAPTER TWENTY-FOUR

Once Gervase saw how professionally the apothecary was treating his charge, his mind flew to the question of how the lad could have been poisoned. He was no trained inquisitioner, but he was no fool either, and with his University training he felt sure he could learn something. In the kitchen he asked a fearful and defensive cook about the food.

'There was nothing in that to hurt anyone. It was fine. All he had was a dish of thin pottage. I made it last week, and there wasn't nothing wrong with it. Good lettuce, dried peas, some cabbage and onion, garlic, barley and a marrowbone to give it some body. I swear that pottage would do any man good.'

'Where is it?'

'Here,' the cook said. He scooped up a ladleful and held it out. 'Want to taste it?'

Gingerly, Gervase sipped a tiny amount. It certainly tasted all right. A little insipid, perhaps, but there was no bitterness or sourness such as he recalled the Arabic tracts warning of.

The cook was offended by his caution. He drank the whole ladleful and then a second. 'See? It's fine. If there was something wrong with my soup, it was done outside of my kitchen. The idea!'

He was still muttering as Gervase hurried back across the yard to Stephen's door. Inside, the apothecary was kneeling by Adam. He had removed his clyster from the unfortunate clerk's mouth, and was in the process of inserting it in Adam's . . . Gervase delicately termed it Adam's posterior orifice. The sight made Gervase wince.

Stephen had left the room, and now only the apothecary and Gervase remained to administer to the unfortunate invalid. Adam shuddered and winced as the tube was pushed deeper and deeper, and then Gilbert filled the bladder with salted water and began the process of pumping it into Adam.

To distract him, Gervase spoke, trying to ignore what was going on at the youth's nether regions.

'Do you have any idea what happened here?'

'It was Luke, Succentor. He poisoned me.'

'Why should a lad like him wish to poison you?'

Adam looked away. He felt considerably better after his belly had been purged and he didn't want to admit to his behaviour in front of the apothecary. 'I don't know, Succentor. Maybe he just doesn't like me.'

Gervase patted his shoulder meditatively. He didn't believe Adam, but he shrewdly guessed that Adam had been guilty of bullying Luke, just as he had other boys.

Gilbert finished his operation and withdrew rapidly as Adam's bowels voided themselves.

Adam burst into tears of frustration and shame. 'Why should he try to murder me, Succentor? Why?'

Baldwin and Simon responded instantly to the Dean's urgent summons. They were almost back at their inn when the pale-faced and anxious Arthur, Stephen's Vicar, ran towards them, calling for Sir Baldwin, and as soon as he had caught his breath and blurted his news, the two men turned and ran at full tilt to the Cathedral.

It was in a state of near uproar. The whole precinct was filled with confused and worried voices. Arthur led the way past the milling throng and up to the Dean's hall, where they found him standing and biting his lower lip in consternation, talking to the Succentor.

'You have ahm heard the facts?' the Dean asked anxiously as soon as they had entered.

'Yes, although I find it extremely difficult to believe,' Baldwin answered.

'Sir Baldwin, you must question whomever you wish, whenever you wish, but hmm you have to find the killer. The thought that a man with murderous intentions is here within the precinct is ah unbearable.'

'Or murderous *boy*,' Gervase commented quietly. In his scrip was the small flask, which felt as if it was burning a hole in the leather. 'It is true, Sir Baldwin. The victim has accused one of the Choristers of being responsible.'

'Before anything else, Dean, could you answer a few more questions? First, I am not so convinced that the killer of Peter is from within the cloister. Are any of your Canons or Secondary clerics allowed out at night?'

'Good God, no! They all must sleep in their rooms.'

'Are any permitted to avoid services?'

'No ahm they should all attend every service. Even the Annuellars. Only the Choristers are um occasionally exempt. We only require four or five to each service and the rest of the time they spend with the Succentor here learning their singing and writing.'

'Of the Secondaries, would Peter have had a chance of a future as a Deacon? He seemed old to still be wandering about the Cathedral.'

The Dean licked his lips considering. 'You are correct,' he said at last. 'Peter and Jolinde are both old. They failed to show the necessary skills to ahm progress to Holy Orders. Peter could have remained as an acolyte, and perhaps, if he had applied himself, he could have anticipated rising to become a Deacon in years to come. Not Jolinde, I fear. He will have to um find more suitable employment. He should go to er University.'

'There are other lads here who are also old for their posts.'

The Dean peered at him unhappily. 'Yes?'

'Adam himself, for example. What does he do here?'

Gervase answered. 'Adam is like Jolinde, a Secondary looking for something better, although he's hardly the sort to advance himself.'

'There is time!' the Dean said. 'He is young, still.'

Gervase shrugged.

'What does he do here?' Simon asked.

'Odd tasks,' Gervase said. 'He makes candles and keeps the sconces filled so that the Cathedral is always full of light. And he delivers bread in the mornings.'

'Interesting,' Baldwin murmured.

The Dean washed his hands with apparent anguish. 'You cannot suspect him of anything, surely? He is a victim, not the perpetrator.'

'True enough,' Baldwin said. Then something in the Dean's tone communicated itself to him. 'Is there something else you would like to tell us, Dean?'

'God forgive me, but I cannot live without telling you. Ahm. It is Jolinde . . . Only rumours, I have to say – no one dared to allege anything serious, but even so . . .'

'Something he has done?'

'Done. Ha! You see, Ralph's wife and child were both killed when a wagon overturned.'

'Yes, we heard about this. But it was an accident, I believe?'

'That is what we all wanted to believe. Yet, rumours ah abound in a city like this one,' the Dean said wretchedly. 'You see, Jolinde was driving the wagon and some have commented that the dead woman looked much like Vincent's first wife. Many umm thought that Jolinde tried to kill her, to destroy the baby which would steal his inheritance.'

'Oh, surely not!' Simon exclaimed.

Baldwin was thoughtful. 'As I understand it, Vincent's wife died while pregnant.'

'Yes. And although I never wanted to believe it, it ah remained at the back of my mind, the suspicion that he might have removed ah a competitor, as it were. Could he have umm done the same to Peter? I fear that when a competitor is removed, a man can feel more at ease. If Jolinde thought that Peter was in his way, could he not fear that poor Adam too was a threat?'

'I understand,' Baldwin sighed, shaking his head. 'But how could Jolinde consider Peter a threat? Or Adam? It makes no sense.' He nodded to Gervase. 'Could we be taken to the room where this boy was poisoned? I wish to see where it happened, and then I should like to talk to the boy accused – and the victim.'

Gervase stood and held the door for them. As they descended the stone steps to the ground floor, they could hear the Dean still talking to himself. 'Such a thing to happen. Terrible, terrible.'

Over at Stephen's house, Baldwin stood in the doorway while his dark eyes took in the scene. Before him was a table, now knocked askew. At the nearer end was a mess of food, vomit and excrement. 'My God,' he muttered disdainfully. He would have hoped that the servants might have cleaned up the worst of the muck. 'How, er, how is the victim?'

A voice behind him answered, 'As well as can be expected. Sore, exhausted, dreadfully weak. The poor fellow hardly knew what had hit him.' It was Stephen. He sat by the doorway staring at the ruins of his room. There was nothing he could do now. All was unravelling. The Cathedral would be blamed; pilgrims would avoid a place of so much disaster.

Baldwin asked him about the meal and Stephen answered dully. It was all rather irrelevant now. 'Who could have wanted to kill him?' he wondered aloud.

'Do you know anything about the other two deaths?' Simon asked.

'Ralph and Peter? I know nothing about Ralph, but I know enough about Peter. He deserved his death. He caused another man to die,' Stephen blurted, and then a hand flew to his mouth as if to snatch back the words or prevent more escaping.

'Who?' Baldwin asked, and when there was no answer, he squatted before Stephen, making the Canon look into his eyes. 'It wasn't Adam, and you say it wasn't Ralph. Does that mean you reckon it was the outlaw? The hanged man?'

'My brother wanted to avenge him. Hamond and my brother were nowhere near Karvinel when he was robbed, so I knew Peter lied when he identified Hamond. He deliberately saw a man turned off a ladder and hanged because he was paid. He must have been *evil*!'

Baldwin stood. 'Or a dupe.' Then Stephen's words hit him. 'You mean you are Sir Thomas's brother?'

'I have said enough,' Stephen said weakly. He rose. 'Peter deserved his death, but these others . . . There must be a curse on us all.'

Gervase fetched the household's steward, who stood before the three men with a wary expression on his features. All the servants knew their lives would be worth little if they were accused of trying to poison a clerk.

'You served the food today?' Baldwin began. The steward nodded. 'Good. Tell me exactly what happened.'

'Nothing was wrong, sir, until the middle of the second course. The Treasurer had a dish of mussels, as did Vicar Arthur and the Chorister. But Master Adam, he never liked mussels, so he had a pottage instead.'

'And halfway through it he vomited,' Gervase added.

'What was the first course?'

The steward blinked. 'Pies and fish dishes.'

'Was there anything that only Adam ate from that course?'

'No, sir. All partook of the dishes together. It was only the pottage that he alone tried.'

Gervase interrupted to tell Baldwin how the cook had proven the pottage to be safe.

'I see,' said Baldwin. 'And how was Adam today?'

The steward gave an offhand shrug. 'The same as usual. Perhaps . . .'

'Yes?'

'Well, I thought he was teasing Luke. He often does. And then he began hiccuping and burping, and went a bit green. But at this time of year, it's normal for a youth to overindulge himself. If he can't at Christmas, when would he be able to?'

'A good point. Now, Gervase,' Baldwin said, turning to the Succentor. 'You say you saw the cook eat a whole ladle of this pottage?'

'*Two* ladles. He insisted that his food was wholesome, and from the way he swallowed it with no ill-effects, I have to believe him.'

'Yes, except this fellow Adam vomited almost immediately.'

'As I heard Stephen say, he had almost finished his bowl of food,' Gervase said hesitantly.

His doubting tone made Baldwin give him an expectant look. 'Yes?'

'That is remarkably fast for a poison, not that my experience is particularly extensive, but I have a little knowledge about the subject.' Gervase explained about his time in Oxford.

'And that means?'

'I think it means he ate a very large dose of poison – so large that little was absorbed. It sometimes happens that too much poison will make a man sick, while less would kill.'

Simon had been silent, but now he interrupted their thoughts. 'The victim accused the boy Luke, you say. Did he say that he actually saw the boy putting poison in his food?'

'No.'

'The kitchen is out at the back of the house, but could someone have added some poison to his food between kitchen and hall? Someone other than this Chorister? A Chorister is hardly my idea of an ideal suspect for a poisoning.'

'It is good of you to try to find another possibility, but I fear the worst. After all, is a cleric of another sort any more likely as a killer?'

Simon nodded to the steward. 'Was anyone out in the garden when you were bringing the food in from the kitchen?'

'One of the Secondaries, sir, yes.'

'Who?'

'It was the youth who lived near Peter. The one called Jolinde.'

At the door to their inn, Jeanne paused a moment and pointed up the road. 'Isn't that Mistress le Berwe?'

Edgar squinted. 'I believe so, Lady, with a servant. I think she has seen us.'

'Ah, good,' said Jeanne, smothering the curse that rose to her lips. She forced a pleasant and welcoming smile to her face. 'Hawisia, how pleasant to see you. How are you?'

'Fine, my Lady, very well. I only . . . Have you seen my husband?'

'Vincent? No, why? Has he disappeared?'

'He left the house to go and see to a little business and returned for his breakfast, but a short while ago he said he must leave once more. I did wonder whether he might have come here to share a pot of wine with you and your husband.'

She looked so worried that Jeanne waved her inside with only a pang of regret. 'I have only just returned myself as you can see, but let us go in and see if they are all inside.'

The hall was filled with men and women talking loudly, their faces red and merry from work and drink, but there was no sign of either Vincent or Baldwin, and when they called the host over and asked him, he said: 'Master Baldwin left first thing this morning with Bailiff Puttock and I've seen nothing of either of them since.'

Jeanne smiled gratefully, but when she turned she could see that Hawisia was close to tears. Jeanne waved to Edgar, who correctly interpreted this as a demand for wine and disappeared. Seeing that Jeanne and Hawisia might wish for privacy, he took Hawisia's servant with him.

'Come, dear, tell me what's the matter,' Jeanne said soothingly.

Hawisia put a hand on Jeanne's forearm as the two sat on a bench. 'I am pregnant again.'

'Then I will pray for a healthy child,' Jeanne suggested with a smile.

'My husband already has a child.'

'Men are not so abstinent as their wives,' Jeanne said warily. She wasn't sure where this was leading.

'But I fear his son Jolinde will be the cause of sore distress to him,' Hawisia said, and she began to sniff as the tears started to run.

Jeanne had listened to enough of Baldwin's and Simon's conversations to know of whom Hawisia spoke. Now she sat silently while Hawisia wept, letting the silence draw the younger woman out.

At last Hawisia blinked to clear her eyes and wiped her face on her sleeve. 'I am sorry. I must seem the veriest fool to behave like this, but I have been worrying for an age now.'

Jeanne nodded sympathetically, but she could not like Hawisia and she inwardly cringed at the thought that this young woman should have sought her out as a confidante. 'What do you fear?' she asked.

'That my husband's son should be found to be the murderer. You must know that Nick Karvinel and Vincent have no affection for each other. They are not friends, they are competitors. And Peter was his clerk. If Jolinde thought that Peter had done anything for Karvinel that could have hurt my husband, I fear . . . I truly fear—'

'That your stepson could have killed Peter?'

Hawisia sniffed and nodded wretchedly.

CHAPTER TWENTY-FIVE

Simon and Baldwin strode over the precinct alone. Gervase had left them at the door to the infirmary, saying that he must visit Adam and try to comfort him. When he opened the door, Simon saw the miserable Secondary gripping his belly and spitting a slimy dribble into a pot. Simon had seen the effects of such treatment before and had no desire to witness the inevitable result. It was with immense relief that he left the scene and followed his friend to the rooms where Jolinde had lived with Peter.

As they approached the house, Simon saw the large figure of the Coroner appear at the Fissand Gate. He was accompanied by the City Bailiff, to whom he bade farewell at the gate before coming over to join Simon and Baldwin. 'The City Bailiff told me,' he said simply. 'You think it was Jolinde too?'

'Possibly he can help us,' Baldwin said. 'He was out near the Canon's house when the food was brought in.'

'Let's see what the bastard has to say this time.'

The door was opened almost immediately when Coroner Roger beat upon it, and Jolinde looked from one to the other with surprise. 'What is it?'

Coroner Roger shoved the door wide. 'We're hoping you can help us—'

He stopped and Simon soon saw what had caused his astonishment.

The room was a mess. The plaster had been hacked from the walls in long sweeps following irregular lines; the floor had been dug up in places, and the perpetrator of the destruction was the shamefaced Secondary before them. That much was obvious from his feeble attempt at a grin as the three men took in the state of the place.

Baldwin walked quietly over to a stool and sat as if unaware of the devastation about him. 'Jolinde, you have been accused of putting poison in Adam's food. He has collapsed.'

'Me?' Jolinde stared uncomprehendingly 'What on earth . . .'

'What happened to the orpiment you bought from the apothecary?'

'Orpiment? I was asked to fetch some by the Succentor for his students, but I gave it all to him.'

'I see. You were driving the wagon which killed Ralph the glover's wife and child, weren't you?'

Jolinde covered his face in his hands. 'It was a long time ago. Surely I can be permitted to forget an accident so long ago?'

'Did she remind you of Vincent le Berwe's first wife?'

'Mistress Glover? No, not really. Why?' Jolinde's expression was too surprised for him to be acting.

Baldwin returned to Adam's poisoning. 'You were seen out between Stephen's house and the kitchen.'

'Yes, I was there, but I never approached any of the staff. I was walking, thinking.'

Baldwin glanced about him. 'Yes, so I see. And you didn't find it?'

'Find what?' Jolinde asked, but he shuddered as if from fatigue and fear.

Baldwin walked to the wall and studied a long gash in the plasterwork. Shaking his head, he smiled sympathetically. 'It's not here, Jolinde.'

'I don't know what you mean.'

'The money that you stole from Ralph the Glover. It isn't here.'

There was a short gasp and Jolinde staggered as if about to collapse, but then he recovered and took a deep breath. 'Me? Steal?'

'Coroner, it was an almost embarrassingly easy crime. For the two Secondaries it was simplicity itself,' Baldwin explained. 'Two youngsters, one of whom I daresay was led on by the other. Jolinde here had no need of money, but neither he nor his friend were likely to progress far here. They both had need of new careers and hit upon a daring means of winning the initial purse to set them on their way. They were asked to deliver jewels and money to Ralph, and both dutifully went to his shop and gave them to him. Except they cheated the man, counting upon his trust in two men of the cloth. They had already taken some of the choicest jewels from the container and when they counted the pieces with Ralph, they counted the remaining ones and asked him to sign the receipt. He was trusting and did so, putting his mark and seal on the receipt. The original numbers were there in front of him, upon the paper, but because Ralph couldn't read or write, the simple fraud went unnoticed.'

'You mean he signed for more than he'd received?' the Coroner rasped. He scowled at the Secondary. It was hardly a new crime, but the Coroner found it disgusting. Relying on the trust of other men to deceive them was the lowest behaviour. At least a robber dared his own safety when he attacked to steal a man's money.

Baldwin continued quietly, still holding the Secondary with his stern gaze. 'Yes – and they pocketed the difference. Most merchants would not have been so trusting, but Ralph? He was pious, was he not? He believed in the integrity of other men, especially those who came from the Cathedral Close.'

Jolinde fell upon his knees. 'Sir, do not blame Peter. It was none of it his idea. It was all mine. Peter wanted to earn enough to be able to go and learn what he could at University, but he didn't want to do that at the expense of anyone else. I wanted to prove I was clever enough to steal and make my own way. I don't know. I know it was foolish, but I . . .'

'You intentionally stole the jewels and money from Ralph, didn't you?' Baldwin said.

Simon shot him a look. He was used to Baldwin being confrontational, occasionally brutal, but rarely so gentle, so calm and soothing.

Jolinde covered his face again. 'I did. Peter was unhappy about the scheme except I dared him and offered a gamble to tease him. I have money from my father every so often and Peter had none. It was easy to get him to agree.'

'Tell us what happened, Jolly,' Baldwin said.

Coroner Roger opened his mouth to tell the Secondary what he thought of him, but as he drew breath he saw Baldwin give him a sharp look and shake of his head. The Coroner was at first irritated to be commanded, but he decided to give the knight the benefit of the doubt. Clearly Sir Baldwin thought there was something more to be learned. Roger haughtily pulled his cloak about him and sank onto a small three-legged stool.

Jolinde hung his head and stared at the ground. 'You are right. I didn't need the money. I will be all right because my father is Vincent le Berwe and as his only heir I am secure, but poor Peter wasn't. He had nothing – no money and no patron, only the pittance he earned from clerking. Still, he would never have thought of stealing from anyone. Peter was always decent. He would no more have thought of stealing than he would of murdering. Yet he wanted desperately to go to University.'

Jolinde broke off and stared at his hands, shaking his head. 'The morning that we were to deliver the jewels and money to Ralph back in the first week of December, I teased Peter all the way to the Treasury to collect them, pointing out that he was too honest for his own good. If he didn't learn to relax in front of other people, he'd end up without any possibility of a patron. No one liked a dullard.'

'Then you pushed him into a challenge that you could fool Ralph?' Baldwin asked gently.

'More or less, yes. I bet him that I could take money from Ralph without the glover noticing. Peter refused to accept the bet at first so I told him he was a coward and he would never get himself a patron.'

'I kept on at him all the way, and then as we waited at Ralph's door, I said he'd never be able to become a Vicar or Deacon unless he was prepared to take risks. And if he wasn't even prepared to try this for a laugh, what chance was there for him?' Jolinde blinked hard as if to keep the tears at bay, and looked up to meet Baldwin's eye. 'It was all my fault, Sir Baldwin. I cannot allow Peter to take the blame just because he is dead.

'We entered and Ralph welcomed us gladly, as he always did. I felt bad, but I wanted the money. We counted out the jewels and money in front of him and then wrote the numbers on a receipt as if they were the same – but they weren't. We wrote down the quantities which the Treasury had given us. Ralph trusted us and put his mark alongside.

'Afterwards we went to a tavern. Peter had been silent in Ralph's shop but in the tavern he asked how I was going to get the money back to Ralph. I . . . I laughed.'

'You never intended giving the money back?' Baldwin asked.

Jolinde had flushed and now he shivered. 'No. Once we had it, it seemed stupid to think of going back to return it.'

'I see,' Baldwin said slowly. He was staring up at the ceiling now, but he gave a gesture indicating Jolinde should continue.

Behind Baldwin, Simon watched Jolinde with interest. It was rare to be given so detailed a confession. Naturally it was due to the fact that Jolinde felt safe – he was protected by Canon Law and would not be hanged for his theft as a common man would. Yet something rang false about his narrative. Simon moved so that he could see Jolinde's face more clearly.

Jolinde continued, 'Peter was quite furious. He called me all sorts of names, saying I'd persuaded him to be my accomplice and swore that he'd never touch a penny piece taken from the glover. I passed him my purse, into which I had put all the money and jewels, and told him to take them back. I was confident he wouldn't, though.'

'Why?' Simon snapped.

Jolinde faced him with an expression of faint surprise. 'Because that would be confessing to theft. How could Peter ever hope to persuade the Bishop to support him in University if he admitted to stealing? As soon as the Dean and Chapter got to hear he'd be out. Even if he wasn't thrown from the Cathedral, he would hardly be looked at for promotion. No, his only chance lay in keeping his mouth shut. And trusting me to do the same.'

'So what did you think he would do with the money?' Baldwin said.

'Hide it.' Jolinde's mouth twisted slightly as he waved a hand, encompassing the ruined walls and holed floor. 'I thought it must be here somewhere.'

'It's not,' Baldwin said quietly. 'He took it back, but not immediately. By an evil chance, he took it back later. On the day Ralph was killed. He rewarded Ralph's murderer.'

'We have heard,' Simon said, 'that you saw Karvinel in the tavern too. Peter turned from him – snubbed him. Do you remember that?'

'Yes,' Jolinde said, a faraway look on his face as he recalled the evening. 'It was the twenty-second, I think. The afternoon of the day the felon was hanged.'

Coroner Roger nodded. 'I remember. We had been going

to hang the bastard as soon as the court had concluded his guilt but we decided to wait. We had no scaffold,' he added apologetically, as if ashamed that they had taken so long. 'Peter was there when Hamond swung; he was all right with Karvinel then.'

'He and Karvinel were talking that morning?' Simon asked with frank surprise. 'What happened to change their attitude by the same evening?'

'You'd have to ask Karvinel,' said Jolinde. 'All I know is, he was depressed. And I think he was fearful already that he was possessed. He probably thought the theft proved it,' he blurted, close to tears.

'What we do need to ask you is this, though,' Baldwin said. 'Bearing in mind you don't need the money because, as you point out, your father is very wealthy, why did you need to rob a man like Ralph?'

'I wanted the money!' Jolinde asserted, but Simon saw that he did not meet any of his three interrogators' eyes as he spoke.

'That's rubbish,' Simon said. 'You knew you could have whatever you needed. You had enough to be able to feed not only yourself but your friend as well.'

'But I couldn't know how long that would last.'

It was Baldwin who now coldly dissected his motives. 'But you did, didn't you, Jolinde? I think you knew only too well. You had enough money. There was no need for you to rob Ralph. In fact, I think you were yourself disgusted by what you did, which is why you gave away the tainted money. It was thirty pieces of silver that Judas took, wasn't it? How much were you paid to ruin Ralph?'

Jolinde was silent, but his eyes closed and tears sprang from beneath his lids as Coroner Roger frowned with incomprehension. 'What do you mean, Sir Baldwin?'

'Just this: Jolinde didn't want the money – he gave it away as soon as he could! No, but he was so desperate to take it that he persuaded his own friend to help him. Why? First, there's the receipt. It showed Ralph had accepted the Cathedral's money and gems. In a few days, Ralph would have to present the gloves to the Cathedral so that they could be given to Simon and me, among other people, and as soon as that happened, the Dean or Treasurer would be sure to notice the missing jewels and they would accuse Ralph of stealing them. And how could he defend himself?'

'You whoreson bastard!' the Coroner breathed. 'You'd rob a man and then get him accused of the theft himself?'

'Ah – no, Coroner, not quite,' Baldwin murmured. 'I think this lad had little choice in the matter. Isn't that correct, Jolinde? No comments? Well, let me say what I guess and you can correct me as you wish.

'You see, I think this fellow was forced into an impossible position. He had no wish to lie or see Ralph accused. But someone did. Someone who hates competitors in the city. Someone who would be glad to see his last significant competitor for political power in the place removed.'

'Christ's blood! You mean Vincent.'

'Of course. Le Berwe told his son that he would be given enough money to seek a place at University or to win over a patron if he carried out this single task . . .'

'No, sir. My father said he would take away all my money if I didn't.'

'I see.' Baldwin glanced at Jolinde's miserable expression. 'So your whole future depended upon whether or not you were prepared to rob a man and leave him to suffer punishment for your crime.'

'A man who incites crime is more guilty than the weak weapon of his malice,' Coroner Roger grated.

'My father has suffered bad luck,' Jolinde protested. 'I don't think he would have hit upon this idea had he not been terribly scared for himself.'

'What should he fear from Ralph?' Coroner Roger scoffed, but then his expression hardened. 'Or was there something else he feared?'

'I don't know.'

'Well, as I said, the booty isn't here,' Baldwin said. 'Your friend decided he couldn't live with the guilt of his crime and took it back. As Elias will testify, Peter returned later that morning and gave him the missing gold and jewels. Ironic.'

Simon nodded understandingly. 'Yes. Poor Peter returned the stolen jewels and money just in time for the murderer to steal it all.' He frowned. 'Yet Coppe the cripple said he left the Cathedral later. Did he return?'

'He may well have done. To apologise in person, and explain what had happened,' Baldwin said. 'Jolinde, you should reflect upon this: you agreed to obey your father's commands and you would have caused the ruin of an innocent man as well as forcing a friend to be your accomplice against his will. Your father may have compelled you to obey him, but you repeated his crime in forcing Peter to take part. If Ralph had lived, he would have been wrongly accused of theft. Instead, the ruin has fallen upon your shoulders . . . and it will bring shame upon your father too.'

Jeanne poured a fresh pot of wine for Hawisia as the woman's tears began to well once more.

'Drink this, my dear. It will help.'

'I . . . thank you, Lady Jeanne. I needed something.'

'There, is that better?'

Hawisia gave her a brittle smile, her eyes strangely pale now that her face had reddened. 'Yes, I feel much better, thank you.'

'You really should not concern yourself with such terrible fears,' Jeanne said calmingly. 'I am sure your husband's son is a perfectly good man.'

'Jolinde was always a jealous fellow,' Hawisia said, dabbing at her eyes with a sleeve.

'Do you mean he was jealous of you?' Jeanne asked.

'Oh, Lady Jeanne! I love my husband, I love him dearly,' Hawisia burst out. 'But I live in terror of his boy.'

'But *why*?'

'My husband's first wife died, you see. It was just as she was due to give birth to her first baby. It was a girl child, but how would Jolinde have guessed that?'

'I don't understand you.'

'Jolinde wants no other children. I think that's why he killed Vincent's first wife.'

'What?' Jeanne cried.

'As soon as she became pregnant, Jolinde refused to speak to her. He was always a greedy soul, but I think the thought of a legitimate son so revolted him that he decided to kill it and his father's wife. He poisoned them.'

'You know that for certain?'

'No,' Hawisia said wretchedly. 'I don't know anything for certain. All I know is what I have heard in the city: that the girl grew ill suddenly just before giving birth. I think that was why Jolinde killed her. And now I am terrified that he will do the same to me and *my* child!'

CHAPTER TWENTY-SIX

'The *shit*!' Coroner Roger swore as they left the Secondary slumped near his cold hearth. 'Miserable, canting *shite*! I knew Ralph – and to think of that decent man being set up by that pair of turds makes me want to throw up. How dare they!'

'You can do nothing about the boy,' Simon reminded him. 'Benefit of Clergy.'

'True, but I can speak to his father, and arrest the sod if I can find any evidence – and I bloody will! Are you coming along?'

Baldwin set his head to one side and considered, 'I should like to join you, but I have another investigation which has been given to me. Before you go, however, we should tell you something we learned this morning.' Baldwin told the Coroner all that they had heard from Coppe, finishing with the discovery that the basan and cordwain were missing.

'Thank you for that. Not that I see how it can help us,' the Coroner grunted.

'It may be easier than you imagine. Basan and cordwain could be used for glovemaking, bagmaking, or any number of other products – but Vincent trades in such things. He sold them to Ralph in the first place. Ask whether he has heard of any for sale. Ask Karvinel too. Someone would be likely to offer him that sort of stuff. And now I suppose I should seek Adam's poisoner. I cannot believe his wild allegation, but he gave us a suspect: the Chorister Luke.'

Luke sat numbly in the chamber before his desk and tried to make sense of Adam's sudden collapse. Gervase had left him in the care of the Clerk of the Lady Chapel while he ran to see how he could help Adam, but now he had returned and was standing behind the Chorister. It was a relief for both to see Baldwin and Simon.

They entered without knocking and Simon nodded his head reassuringly to Gervase, trying to convey a little of his conviction that the child was innocent. Baldwin walked straight to Luke, taking up a stool en route and seating himself before the boy.

Luke found himself gazing into the darkly intense eyes of the knight from Furnshill. It was disconcerting. The man appeared to be looking through Luke's own eyes and into his soul. 'Sir?'

'Luke, Adam has made a dreadful allegation against you,' Baldwin said slowly and distinctly. 'Do you know what it is?'

'He said I had poisoned him. Gervase told me.'

'That is quite right. Now you are too young to be accused in a court, and even if you were, you would be safe because you are within the Cathedral, so you fall under Canon Law. I want you to speak the truth to me. Have you ever tried to poison someone in the precinct?'

'No, sir,' Luke responded immediately. 'I wouldn't know how to.'

'Luke, this was on the floor in the room,' Gervase said and passed Baldwin the little flask of orpiment.

'Arsenic?' Baldwin asked. 'Luke, do you recognise this bottle?'

'Yes. It's like the ones we use here,' he said, looking up at Gervase for confirmation. 'I had been using some for a picture. Look!' Luke said and showed Baldwin his work. The golden-yellow tints gleamed even in the meagre light of the hall. 'But I didn't have it with me at the meal.'

'So you didn't put any of this upon Adam's food?'

'No,' said Luke, adding with simple honesty, 'although I would have if I had thought of it. He's always bullying me.'

Behind him, Gervase rolled his eyes heavenwards. The little devils always had to make some sort of lunatic comment. He saw the Bailiff cover his mouth with a hand, trying to smother the chuckle.

'Anyway, sir,' Luke said, 'wouldn't someone see if their food was covered in yellow stuff?'

Baldwin nodded. 'I rather think they would, Luke.'

Gervase heard a certain conviction in his voice that made him peer doubtfully, but before he could say anything there was a light knock at the door. He sighed and went to open it.

In the doorway stood young Henry. 'What is it?' Gervase demanded. 'We're busy.'

'Sir, it's about Adam.'

*   *   *

Sir Thomas waited in John Renebaud's tavern until Hob returned. The place suited Sir Thomas's mood. Dark, crowded and evil-smelling, it fed his bitter and vengeful spirit.

He knew that Hob and Jen had a touching faith in him. On Hob's part it was solely due to his simpleness, but Jen was a more complicated soul. She professed her love for him – but then she would. He was her protector. It was little more than the affection due to a lord and master from one of his serfs; it was the duty of a woman to her mate. No more. Probably when he, Sir Thomas, was dead, she would easily slip into another man's bed.

Early death held no fears for Sir Thomas. He was well into his middle age already at thirty-four; he had lived longer than many of the folks with whom he had grown up. The men had died of disease or fighting; the women from child-birth or starvation since when there were famines the men were favoured with food in order that they might produce more. Women and children must starve.

Sir Thomas had lost everything. The small wars about his manorial demesne had wasted his whole fortune. There was nothing left but a few people, none of whom stayed with him anticipating riches, but from a sense of loyalty and their duty. Hamond, who had been of the same age as Sir Thomas, had been his most devoted friend and servant. Hamond, his long-est-serving companion, had grown up with him, and yet he was dead now. Chivalry demanded payment. There was a responsibility lying upon Sir Thomas to honour the debt; Hamond had served him faithfully through his life, and now Sir Thomas must repay that death with blood. The blood of the man who had willed his execution.

He knocked back the last of his mazer of wine and wiped at his lips with the back of his hand. The merchants of any city were a corrupt set of pirates, out to steal whatever they could from anyone with less money and fewer opportunities to protect themselves, but the men here had surprised Sir Thomas with their avarice and brutality. It didn't matter to him particularly if another man should die in order that he should survive the richer, but he was amazed that merchants should decide whether a man should live or die purely upon the basis of a potential benefit to them. It was unpleasant, an inversion of legitimate behaviour. It was one thing to travel abroad and fight Frenchmen or Moors, taking their wealth, but doing the same with Englishmen seemed wrong.

As he sat mulling over the black thoughts that chased themselves around his head, he noticed a figure standing near the fire. It was him again: Vincent le Berwe. The two men caught each other's eye and Sir Thomas nodded slightly. His paymaster acknowledged him with a slow smile, nervous that someone else might witness it.

Before Sir Thomas could go over and speak to his client, he saw a cowering shadow slip through the doorway. 'Hob! Over here, lad!' he growled.

'Master, I have seen him,' Hob said expectantly. His face was like that of a dog, Sir Thomas thought, a dog whipped daily but still eager to be welcomed.

'Where?'

'At the Cathedral. He was going there alone, Master.'

'Good,' Sir Thomas muttered. He rose. At the door, while Hob waited patiently, a vacuous smile on his face, Sir Thomas considered his options. It was always dangerous to go to the Cathedral, but he must question Karvinel. A bell tolled and Sir Thomas glanced up. It was the signal for Mass – which meant Karvinel's woman would be alone. Smiling grimly, he set off to Karvinel's house, Hob scampering at his side like a hound out for a walk.

It was one of the reasons why Sir Thomas had been prepared to allow Hob to remain with him, this happy-go-lucky attitude. He never moaned, never tried to blame others for things, and provided he was occasionally praised he remained content. It took little to please him. If it hadn't been for Jen, Sir Thomas would not have considered keeping Hob at his side, but Jen made it clear that the price for her body was that her brother should also be looked after. Sir Thomas had thought to point out to her that she was already his, and should he decide to rid himself of her half-witted brother, there was little she could do to stop him, but he knew that the threat was empty. He enjoyed Jen as a willing bed-mate, and if her fee was board and lodging for Hob, Sir Thomas was happy to accept.

It was strange how some lads were born without the brain of a dormouse, he reflected. Perhaps it was the horror of seeing his mother's body which had addled the boy's brains. Sir Thomas had heard such things could happen. However, the idle thought drifted from him as he approached the house of Nicholas Karvinel.

'Wait here, Hob,' he said, and knocked loudly upon the door.

He had expected a stout doorkeeper, but to his faint surprise there was no answer for a long period and then a young urchin opened it. 'Yes?'

Sir Thomas blinked. 'Who are you?'

The boy glared. 'Servant to Master Karvinel.'

Sir Thomas smiled. 'In that case, is your lady in the house?'

'Who is it?' came Juliana's voice. She was in the hall and Sir Thomas walked past the boy along the screens passage. Entering the hall itself, he found himself in a smallish, slightly shabby room. A fire smouldered meanly on the hearth, two benches were ranged against the walls, a moth-eaten tapestry hung on one wall and a table was strewn with poor wooden bowls and plates.

On a chair by the table was Juliana Karvinel, drinking from a jug of wine. Seeing him, she stood and gave him a disconcerted smile. 'Sir?'

'My Lady,' he said gruffly, bowing low. 'I am Sir Thomas of Exmouth, Knight Bachelor. My apologies for following you here, but I saw you at the Christmas Mass and I was ravished. I had to find out where you lived.'

She gaped. It was easy to see that she was at once flattered and worried. 'You . . . you saw me?'

'And you saw me, my Lady.'

'No, no, I am sure I . . .'

'Why don't you send the boy away and we can talk?'

She met his suggestion with a simper and a half-duck of her head, then bawled for the boy and sent him off to the tavern until he should be called for.

Returning to meet Sir Thomas's smile she motioned with a hand towards the door at the back of the hall.

'Why not?' he said. He allowed her to lead the way. 'It is very quiet and that boy said he was your servant – are all your servants away?'

'If you mean "have they been sent away", I only wish they had been! No,' she said disdainfully. 'My husband has failed in business and this necessitates the loss of all our servants. Surely you have heard about his evil luck? He has lost almost everything in failed ventures and thefts, and now we must make ends meet as best we can. Although,' she added confidentially, 'I don't know that I can stand it much more. Not only has he taken away my maid and my small pleasures, now he seems to have gone mad. He tells me that he can renew our fortunes. I tell you, I begin to doubt whether he is sane.'

'A merchant can hardly succeed without his servants. Where would he be without his staff: his bottler, his gardener, his steward? Without them he would be a poor kind of a host or companion to other merchants. And what would he do without his clerk?' Sir Thomas paused as if studying the poor tapestry at the wall.

'It is shoddy, isn't it?' she said, standing at his side and sneering up at it. 'I am afraid it was the best we could afford after the last of the robberies here and the fire.'

'Yes,' he said, and smiled. 'It must have been terrible for you.'

'Oh, yes.' She smiled and stood very close at his side.

It took him only a moment to reach an arm out to her, and he felt her shiver deliciously as he pulled her towards him. But she froze when she felt his dagger's point beneath her chin.

Henry blinked with concern as he stood before the serious-faced knight and his friend, but his fear was not based upon the two men before him; his concern was focused on the figure whom he knew was standing behind him: the Succentor.

'I know that Adam has accused Luke of trying to poison him and it's not true,' he asserted.

Baldwin had an easy manner with children. Simon often found it annoying that, while he was careful to behave with suitable, as he saw it, distant authority to children, they often responded far better to his friend Baldwin's solemnly respectful manner. It appeared to be working yet again right now. While Gervase hovered in the background, scowling viciously at the back of Henry's head, and Simon tried to maintain a diffident aloofness, the child met Baldwin's gaze with a quiet conviction as he told what had happened the previous night, how Adam had assaulted Luke and left Henry to take the blame.

Luke was near to bursting with fury as he heard what Adam had done 'You mean *he* attacked me? I thought it might be him at our meal today but when he was poisoned I forgot it. If only the poison *had* killed him!'

Baldwin nodded. 'I can understand your thinking, although at present he may wish the same, after being forced to be sick and then having a bladder squirt something revolting up his arse. I don't know about you, but having all that happen in front of his Canon can hardly make him feel good.'

Luke and Henry exchanged a quick look. They were by no means allies, but there was a mutual satisfaction in knowing that Adam had suffered. It mitigated the bullying they had endured at the older youth's hands. Luke frowned briefly, glancing at Gervase, thinking of how Henry had been thrashed the previous evening. Henry saw his look and grinned. Both had been beaten worse by Canons and others.

Baldwin continued, 'We must still discover where the poison came from.'

Simon looked at Luke. 'The bread Adam ate was not the loaf which he stole from you?'

'No. It was a new one. The one I had was older – it had dried with age.' Luke hesitated, then said, 'I got that loaf from Peter, sir, the night that he collapsed.'

'Did you eat any of it?' Gervase asked.

'No, sir. I was going to last night, but Adam stole it before I—'

'So he wasn't poisoned by eating the same one which Peter ate,' Gervase said.

'We don't know that,' Simon pointed out. 'He may have eaten it before going into the meal.'

'But what then of the bottle?' Gervase asked.

Another thought had struck Simon. 'Tell me – when you eat, is the bread brought in later with the meats, or is it served on the table already when you arrive?'

'Oh, it's already there.'

'So anyone could have gone in and poisoned the bread, knowing who would eat it,' Simon said with a look at Baldwin.

Baldwin stood staring thoughtfully at the ground. 'And the killer left the pot behind to implicate someone else in the room.'

'One thing is certain, Adam was not poisoned by that orpiment. It is too bright. No, he was poisoned with something else.'

'Yes. Gervase, could you tell us when this pot would have gone missing?'

'I noticed it was missing last night,' Henry said. 'I thought Luke had taken it. He often takes different colours for his pictures.' He hesitated, realised that his words sounded

351

snide, and added, 'He is the best at drawing and painting among us all.'

Baldwin smiled gently. It was clear to him that there was a considerable amount of rivalry between the two boys, but he was also sure that Henry was offering an olive branch.

'Who has access to the Choristers' hall?' Baldwin asked the Succentor.

'Everyone. Adam to change the candles, another to sweep and clean, the Choristers, me . . . If you want the truth, I suppose anyone who came to the Cathedral could drop in here,' Gervase said.

'And the Canon's house – I suppose the same is true there?'

'Provided the poisoner went there when all was quiet, yes.'

CHAPTER TWENTY-SEVEN

Nicholas Karvinel had been about to go straight home, and
although he didn't know it, his death would certainly have
been hastened had he done so, for he would have walked in
upon Sir Thomas with his wife.

Instead, Karvinel was delayed as he left the Cathedral. In
the High Street he bumped into Coroner Roger and the City
Bailiff, both standing angrily glaring up and down the road.

'Coroner? Are you all right?'

'No, I'm damn well not!'

'What on earth is the trouble?'

'That bastard Vincent. Do you know where he is?'

'He usually attends an earlier Mass. He's in around the
middle of the day, so no, I fear I have no idea where he is –
unless he's in the Guildhall or his home.'

'No, I've checked both,' Roger spat. 'The bastard could
almost be deliberately avoiding me. And so he bloody
should!'

Karvinel's confused expression made the Coroner relent a little. 'Vincent apparently got his son to try to ruin Ralph.' He explained what Jolinde had told him. 'I want to talk to him.'

'Ralph's death seems to become more confusing by the day,' Karvinel said.

'Well, not for much longer. I intend clearing up the whole sorry mess.'

'Good.'

Roger was about to walk off when a thought struck him. 'Tell me – cordwain and basan: Ralph bought some a short while before he died – I witnessed the deal – but it has disappeared from Ralph's shop. Do you know anything about it?'

Karvinel felt his heart stop in his chest. 'Ralph's shop? Why no, no one has offered me anything like that,' he said. 'When was it taken?'

It was a short while later that he suddenly realised what had happened: Vincent's cart had been seen by Peter outside Ralph's shop only a short time before the discovery of the glover's body. Only with difficulty could he stop himself bursting into delighted laughter.

Simon was staring at the grass as he walked a short distance behind Baldwin towards the Fissand Gate. 'I don't understand what is going on here at all,' he said at last. 'I thought we had a case of Peter's poisoning, and that he died because of someone inside the Cathedral, yet now it seems it could have been anyone.'

'It is not so complicated as it may appear, I think. No, not by any means. You have to bear in mind the sort of people we are dealing with. There are the city folk and the Cathedral,

and the two don't mix very easily. The city respects the
Cathedral and is grateful for the money the Cathedral spends
in the city, but does not truly like the Dean and Chapter. They
are an alien race to the secular people who live outside the
Close.'

'But we have an appallingly tangled mess here.'

'Perhaps – yet the more tangled this knot appears now, the
more I am convinced that a small tug at the right point will
unravel the whole thing.'

'Two men dead; a third almost killed and two boys who
have cause to hate him; outlaws attacking merchants . . . I
don't see how matters could get much worse.'

Baldwin gave him a sideways look. 'Are you happy that
Jolinde was innocent of the murders?'

'I suppose so, since he admitted to buying the bread and
meat with which Peter was poisoned.'

'If he was. We have no proof that Peter *was* poisoned with
the bread or meat. In fact, we have a lot of evidence that he
wasn't. Jolinde and Claricia said that they ate the food
Jolinde had brought, which seems odd. And still more odd, if
someone wanted to kill Peter, why should they poison food
which Jolinde was buying?'

'Why someone should want to kill Peter at all is still a
mystery to me,' Simon grunted.

'What if the murderer intended killing another?'

'Like whom?'

'Jolinde, for instance.'

Simon stopped, frowning. 'It would make sense.'

'More than that, it would be logical. If you wish to poison
a man, you poison the food he is buying. You don't assume
he'll give it away to someone else.'

'True. Yet the poisoner might have known that the food was to be eaten by Peter.'

'It is possible, but what if that wasn't known? Then we are left with the opposite perspective.'

Simon waited but his friend remained silent and the Bailiff was reluctant to break into his thoughts as they returned to the house where Adam lay recovering.

'Has he confessed?' Stephen asked.

Simon shook his head as he entered. He wasn't even certain whom Stephen was asking about: Luke or Jolinde.

Adam lay on a palliasse on the floor, a rolled robe was his pillow and he was covered with a pair of thick blankets, although his shivering seemed to show they were doing him little good. Stephen had taken on himself the responsibility of nursing the boy and sat on a stool near his head. To aid Adam's recovery, he had set a large crucifix on a table nearby, so that Adam could see it by turning his head.

Stephen had recovered greatly and now he could look upon the two law officials with a certain asperity. 'What is it? This poor fellow needs to rest. He was almost killed.'

Baldwin took in the room with a glance. 'We wish to ask him some questions,' he said. 'First, we understand you took a loaf from Luke last night. Is that correct?'

Adam glanced up at Stephen, but the Canon was telling his beads through his fingers and didn't meet his look. 'Yes, sir. I took it, but I didn't touch it. He dropped it in some muck, and I threw it away.'

'You didn't eat any of it?'

'No. Why should I? It had shit on it.'

'What does this matter?' Stephen asked.

'Jolinde gave food to Peter. The bread was given to Luke by Peter. It is possible that the bread was poisoned.'

Adam blenched. 'But I could have eaten it!'

'Perhaps it would have been justice if you had,' Baldwin stated unsympathetically. 'Did you have a bottle of orpiment with you today?'

'No.'

'A bottle was found on the floor afterwards. It wasn't yours?'

'No.'

Stephen stirred. 'It could have been Luke's.'

Baldwin looked at him kindly. 'No. I am convinced that he had nothing to do with this. I believe that while you and the Chapter were in the Cathedral someone went to your house and put poison on Adam's bread, leaving the orpiment behind to make it appear that Luke or someone else in the room had tried to kill him. Anyone could have got in.'

Stephen sighed. 'Oh, thank God!'

'What is it?'

'I had been convinced that my nephew had done this.'

Baldwin's eyebrows rose. 'Nephew? Earlier you told us about your brother . . .?'

'I was the second son of Sir Ranulf Soth of Exmouth. My brother Thomas took the manor and I came here. When my brother's wife died and he became an outlaw, I agreed to look after his son. That boy is Luke.'

'And you thought that his father's evil disposition could have led to his trying to poison Adam?'

'I had heard that Adam had waylaid him last evening, yes, and thought my brother's violent nature had been repeated in

Luke. It wouldn't have been the first time such things have happened.'

'Well you may relax in the knowledge that Luke is most certainly innocent.'

'And Jolinde took food to Peter?' Stephen said. 'I saw him once with something under his robe in the Cathedral. That must have been what it was. Bread and meat for his friend.'

'You mean Luke is really Sir Thomas's son?' Adam cried suddenly.

'Be quiet and try to rest,' Stephen said.

'Then it must have been Sir Thomas who tried to kill me! He wanted revenge for what I'd done to his son!'

'Was he here today?' Simon shot out.

Stephen wouldn't meet his eyes. 'I refuse to believe that my brother would have poisoned someone in my house. He is many things, but he would not risk harming me. And he would be more likely to use a dagger or sword – an honourable weapon. Not poison.'

'I know little about him,' Baldwin admitted, 'but I do not think any knight would resort to poison.' He looked at Adam. 'Tell me: I hear you are responsible for the candles and chandlery in the Cathedral. Is that right?'

Adam nodded.

'Is it true that Cathedral candles are being sold to a city merchant? Stolen from the Cathedral and Chapter and sold for your profit?'

Stephen gasped. 'Adam, you wouldn't!'

'I had to get away! I can't stay here and grow old as a candle-maker! What sort of life is that? I was only selling enough to make a little cash so—'

'You evil little devil! You're no better than that damned fool Peter!'

Baldwin smiled. 'Adam, to whom did you sell these candles?'

After his brush with death, Adam was past caring. His belly and bowels felt as though they were on fire, his throat was sore from vomiting and he only wanted peace: he wanted Baldwin and Simon to leave him alone. But if he was to get rid of them by confessing, he wasn't going to take the blame all for himself and leave his accomplice to escape.

'Vincent. He sells the tallow, wax and wicks to the Cathedral and I make the candles. I asked him if I could clerk for him because I want some ready money, but he refused me, saying that if I wanted money he'd help me get it. All I had to do was write up the accounts logging how much wax he had supplied and understate the full weight. Then I could make more candles than the Cathedral needed, and sell the excess back to him. He split the profits with me.'

'But *why*, boy? You were safe here for as long as you wanted! Why steal from your home?' Stephen asked.

'You've seen what happens to Secondaries. We never last long. We're either made into sub-Deacons or we're out. Well, I'll never get to be a sub-Deacon, that's obvious.'

'You were safe here for as long as you could have wanted!'

'I think that clears up Ralph the glover's suggestion that there was a theft going on,' Baldwin noted.

'Does this have to be bruited abroad?' Stephen asked. 'News of this would break the Dean's heart.'

'Come outside with us a moment,' Baldwin said.

'What do you want?' Stephen said when they were out in the chill sunlight.

'The truth. If you tell me the truth on two points, I shall swear to keep your secrets but I must know, just so that I can be certain that the killer is not escaping justice.'

Stephen drew in a breath. 'Very well.'

'First, Peter.'

'His crime was foul. My brother told me categorically that he and Hamond had nothing to do with the robbery of Karvinel, yet Peter's evidence helped condemn the man. I think Karvinel most cruelly and dishonestly forced Peter to lie for him. Perhaps – I cannot tell, but maybe Peter committed suicide realising his mortal sin. He had caused another man to be killed.'

'I understand. And the other: Adam's father. Who is he?'

Stephen gave him a hunted look. 'Why do you need to know? That is not my secret.'

The Cathedral doors opened and people began to flood out onto the grassed precinct. Simon watched the folk pass by and heard Baldwin murmuring into Stephen's ear.

The Canon nodded resignedly, then shook his head. 'Yes. I fear you are quite right.'

Vincent le Berwe shook hands heartily with the thickset Breton and then sat back in his chair as his client left. It was hard to contain his glee. He had confirmed orders for wine, for lead and for dyes. All in all, a good day's work. If he could keep up the momentum he would soon be able to cover his losses.

It had been a jolt to see Sir Thomas in the tavern, but the fellow had cleared off smartish, taking his half-wit with him, thank God. The dribbling weak-minded wretch repelled

Vincent; how Sir Thomas could bear the creature's proximity was beyond him. Still, the two had gone, and that was a relief. Vincent had no desire to be seen anywhere near his leading business associate, as he liked to think of Sir Thomas, in case he decided to talk to Vincent. Someone might have seen them together, which would have been disastrous. It was too risky. The man was a known outlaw, for God's sake!

Vincent jerked his head at a serving girl for more wine.

That was the pleasantest aspect of the position of Receiver – the fact that he could expect respect from everyone in the city. Not least because he would become one of the richest men in the place. It would depend upon how the revenues went during his term of office, naturally, but provided that he could keep afloat for a few more months, he should be all right. And that meant pulling in every debt he owned.

As if on cue he saw Nick Karvinel appear in the doorway. Vincent motioned to the other merchant to join him. Karvinel hesitated, but then he pulled a wry face and crossed the room, sitting where the Breton had been only a few minutes before. 'What are you after, Vincent?'

'Come on, Nick. There shouldn't be any hard feelings. All I want is the money you owe me. Do you have it yet?'

Karvinel took a mazer from the next table, glanced into it, then filled it with Vincent's wine. He drank deeply, then met Vincent's gaze with a firm eye. 'I don't think I care to pay.'

Vincent felt hot blood rush into his face. Karvinel's tone was insolent, intentionally rude. It was not the voice of a man who owed respect, it was that of a man who owed nothing. 'What do you mean, you "don't care to"? I don't give a shit what you do or don't wish, Nick. You owe me money and I want it back – all right?'

'Shut up, Vincent. I don't like the tone of your voice.'

'You don't like *my* voice? I don't—'

'Where did all Ralph's basan and Cordova leather go?'

'What?'

Karvinel leaned back and cast a contemplative eye over the people in the room. None had so far noticed their altercation, and Karvinel was happy that it should remain that way. He smiled coldly at Vincent. 'The fact is, I hear that you sold Ralph a load of basan and cordwain. It was witnessed by the Coroner, wasn't it? Yet there's none in Ralph's shop.'

'He must have sold it.'

'I don't think so.'

Vincent pulled his lips back over his teeth in what could have been a smile or a snarl. 'Prove it! Do you realise I can have you arrested for such an allegation?'

'I wonder what the City Freemen would think of a Receiver who took leathers from a dead man's shop. And if he did that,' Nick continued, now eyeing Vincent with a more serious expression as the Receiver went very still, '*when* did he do it? Did he take the stuff after his friend had been dead a matter of hours – or a matter of moments?'

'What are you saying?' le Berwe whispered.

'Did you kill him, Vincent?'

'I should stab your God-cursed body for that!'

'I know you were there that day. So did my clerk; he saw your cart outside.'

'Bollocks! Bring him here!' Then Vincent's face went white.

'Yes, Vincent. That's what I wondered too. How convenient that the only witness to your act was a man who is now also dead. My poor clerk Peter,' said Karvinel pointedly. He rose. 'I have to go now, but I think there's no hurry in paying you. You may be in prison soon.'

Outside, Nicholas Karvinel felt justifiably pleased with himself. He had effectively called a halt to the threat of a demand for money while at the same time putting the fear of God into Vincent.

Of course he had no proof that Vincent was actually responsible for the murder of Ralph, but it would make sense, bearing in mind that Ralph was a possible competitor for honours; honours meant money, and Karvinel was sure that Vincent would not turn down any opportunity for increasing his wealth. Ignorant of the foundering of Vincent's ship, Karvinel thought le Berwe's demand for his debt to be repaid was motivated by pure greed. This unreasonable demand from one whom Karvinel thought to be rich was an insult.

Reaching his door, he paused a moment. Farther along the street he could see Coroner Roger. On an impulse he waved and shouted to him to let him know where he could find Vincent. Then, with a feeling of satisfaction, he watched as the Coroner hurried away, calling to the City Bailiff as he went.

He could remember his clear, alcoholically-enhanced fantasy of killing Vincent while in the tavern on Christmas Eve, and the vision rose before him again of Vincent le Berwe's face as Nick shoved his dagger into the greedy bastard's guts. It would be good to see the bastard squirm while spitted like a capon on a stick. But if he couldn't do that, at least he could put the Coroner onto him. That might be even more enjoyable in its way.

The smoke above the city swirled, blown by a freezing blast from the south, and Karvinel saw the clouds scudding past at speed. It was getting dark now, and the weather looked as if it would break soon. It would be good to get inside and sit beside the fire.

Then a spirit of rebellion rose in his breast. What was the point of going home? His wife would be sitting sulking because of the loss of her maid and their bottler, and because of their financial problems. She would be waspish about any conversation he instigated, scathing about any new ventures he mentioned. Her companionship was the last thing he needed tonight.

He sniffed disdainfully and set off to an alehouse further up the street.

Coroner Roger saw Vincent le Berwe as soon as he entered the tavern. Nodding towards their quarry, the Coroner marched up to Vincent's table and pulled up a stool without offering a greeting.

Vincent gave him a welcoming smile, but the Coroner's face twisted into a mask of revulsion.

'I wanted,' he said in a low voice, 'to see you to ask what sort of a man could do it.'

'What?' asked the baffled Vincent.

'Pay his own son to perjure himself,' the Coroner spat.

Vincent felt his face go chill, as if all the blood had drained in a moment. 'Perjure? I . . . I don't . . .'

'Balls, you lying *bastard*! Your boy has confessed to his part in the fraud and theft from Ralph, and he's told us how you bribed him to make sure that Ralph was conned. Were you proud to have perverted your own son?'

'It wasn't a perversion, it was the only way to protect him!' Vincent snapped, stung into retaliation.

'How?'

'Ralph stood in my way: he was the only man who could have prevented my being re-elected as Receiver. I *had* to make sure that he was removed. Otherwise, how could I have built up my position in the City? If Jolly is to win my inheritance, I have to protect it. I couldn't allow Ralph to get in the way.'

'So you tried to ruin him?'

Vincent looked away. 'It seemed the best thing to do,' he muttered.

'And when you failed, you had him murdered.'

'No! I didn't do that. I've never tried to have a man killed.'

'Then who did? Everyone liked Ralph . . .'

'What about Karvinel? He couldn't stand Ralph, and Ralph was even more of a competitor to him, seeing both were glovemakers.' Vincent's brow cleared. 'That must be it! Nick Karvinel knew that the Cathedral always ordered gloves from Ralph to be made for the Holy Innocents' Day celebrations. If he could get rid of him, he thought he'd be able to win the contract to finish the job and earn himself some much-needed cash. So he murdered Ralph and took over that business, but he also stole all Ralph's money.'

The Coroner eyed him with distaste. 'So now you'll put the blame onto another unfortunate? Karvinel is no kind of a threat to anyone, not in his present state.' He frowned as he considered his words. Often in the past he had found that the most meek and humble people could turn to violence when they felt they had no alternative. Karvinel was moderately courteous and mild-mannered, it was true, but he also wore a dagger. He could have become so bitter that he had decided to take matters into his own hands.

'Why should I have killed Ralph?' Vincent said, holding both hands out, palms upwards. 'He was no threat to me once I had put my little plan into operation. There was no point in my killing him.'

'Maybe he realised what had happened,' the Coroner said speculatively.

'Not so far as I know. If I had to bet, I'd say Karvinel did it.'

Simon and Baldwin returned to their inn as dusk was giving way to full night. Jeanne met them in the crowded and smoke-filled hall, Edgar standing at her side to keep unwanted visitors at bay, glowering at any stranger who approached too close. Both appeared relieved to see the two men return.

Baldwin took his seat and motioned to the host to serve them. While waiting, he looked enquiringly at his wife. 'Are you well? Did you enjoy your tour of the city?'

'Yes, it was interesting enough, but not so fascinating as your enquiries. I heard another man was poisoned – is it true?'

'I am afraid so. It was one of the Secondaries called Adam, although, thank God, he should recover. So long as the apothecary's intervention does not put an end to him first!'

'Who did it?'

'There we have the difficulty,' Simon grunted, throwing a leg over a bench and surveying the crowd in the bar. 'Two folks have been suspected, but neither seem probable. One is only a child, while the other is le Berwe's illegitimate son, who has no reason to want to harm Adam.'

'I think I have news for you, then,' Jeanne declared, and told them of Hawisia's terrified appearance and her assertions about Jolinde.

'She suggests that he poisoned them?' Baldwin breathed. 'My God. That would follow on from what the Dean told us.'

Simon nodded. 'He said rumours suggested Jolinde had tried to kill his father's wife and got the wrong woman – Ralph's wife. Now Hawisia says she thinks he succeeded with poison. God's bollocks!'

Baldwin agreed. 'I loathe and detest poison. It is so cowardly. There is no courage in attacking someone with such an indiscriminate weapon. It is a tool used by the weak and feebleminded.'

Simon looked at him. 'I have never heard you so scathing, Baldwin.'

'The older I become, the more appalled I grow to see such foul behaviour. It is obnoxious to consider putting orpiment or somesuch in a man's food or drink. A man should be able to trust that his food is safe no matter what.'

Jeanne put her hand on his arm. 'Calm yourself, husband. Try to think of happier things.'

'How can I, Jeanne?' he snapped. 'The murderer is in the city somewhere and could well strike again at any time. Perhaps it is Jolinde, perhaps it was truly the child Luke! How on earth can I relax when anyone picking up a lump of bread or piece of fruit could be poisoned? How many more will be dead by morning?'

Vincent himself was little happier. He was filled with a deep moroseness which lay heavily on his soul as he walked into his hall.

Hawisia sat waiting for him at their table, and seeing him enter she poured warmed wine into his favourite silver-chased mazer and brought it to him beside the fire. He smiled weakly at her before emptying it in one go. She took it from him and refilled it, passing it to him with solemn assurance.

'Husband, you are troubled?' she asked anxiously.

'Troubled?' He stared at her as if awoken from a slow lethargy and despair attacked him with renewed force. He shot nervous looks about him, agitatedly biting his nails. Standing, he strode over to the table and was about to place his mazer on it when the urge suddenly took him to smash it. He lifted it high as if to dash it on the floor in a rage; but as soon as the urge took hold of him, it left him, and he let his hands slowly fall to the table, setting the cup down.

In an instant she was at his side, an arm about his shoulder as he began to sob. 'My love, my darling, what is it? Oh, tell me what has happened!'

He couldn't speak for some while. The words felt as though they would choke him. After so much effort and work, after all his careful planning to recover from the disastrous loss of his ship, he would now be ruined. 'The Coroner came to see me just now.'

'Yes, he was here earlier while I was out. Apparently he was in a foul mood,' Hawisia said.

'Not so foul as when he saw me! He knows everything – how I had Jolly take Ralph's money and jewels, how I had Jolly get the fool to sign his mark on the receipt so that Ralph could be shown to be a thief when the gloves were presented . . . everything!'

Hawisia didn't know what to do or say. She kissed his cheek, murmuring soft words to ease him, but Vincent stood resting his hands on the table-top, his eyes closed. 'We are ruined, Hawisia. There's nothing else I can do.'

'Why? He hasn't arrested you. He obviously doesn't think he has enough proof to present you before the King's Justice.'

'Christ alive, woman, it's not only *him*! Karvinel came to see me as well. He said he would accuse me of being there when Ralph died; said he would allege his clerk saw me there.'

'His clerk is dead,' Hawisia pointed out.

'True, but if he swore it, I could be lynched!'

'A man must be alive to accuse you.'

'But Karvinel could convince others. Oh, Christ!'

'Darling, there is something you could try. I know you had your own men rob Karvinel.'

'You mean my friend in the woods?' He turned to her with a terrible understanding in his eyes. 'You mean pay Sir Thomas to kill Karvinel?'

'Why not? He has robbed the man and fired his house on your orders.'

'I couldn't,' Vincent said. But he knew that he could. His eyes were staring into the distance as he wondered whether this could indeed provide him with a solution. And he knew the alehouse where Sir Thomas would be staying. He always chose the same low dive: the Cock.

CHAPTER TWENTY-EIGHT

Sir Thomas was disgusted by her. When she felt the blade at her neck she had thought he was playing some kind of game, that it was a sign he enjoyed inflicting or receiving pain with sex and she had moaned with desire for him.

He shoved her from him and asked her his questions. She had not been much help. He felt no nearer a solution, an answer as to why his comrade had died. He was forced to the conclusion that it was the whim of a wealthy man, someone who had picked a scapegoat simply because he could. A suspected outlaw would fit the bill – why not make use of him?

Juliana had tried to tempt him into her bed, with a kind of desperate passionless longing. She wanted a man, she said, a strong man who would rescue her from her husband. No price was too high for her freedom. All the man need do was kill Nicholas, the useless fool and she would give herself to him completely.

He had slapped her, hard, three or four times, until her lips swelled and the blood ran, but still she asked him to help her – offering her body, her few jewels, all her money. She repelled him; with her disloyalty and shabby, sordid advances. In the end he left her lying semi-naked on her bed, watching him leave with large empty eyes, as though he was her last hope and prayer and he was leaving her desolated.

It was in the hall that he heard the knock. Instantly he ran to the ladder and slipped down to the ground. Crossing the floor, he peered round the door into the hall. The room was clear, and he hurried to the screens door, looking into the passageway.

The tapping at the door came again and he glanced about him. He had limited options. There were the two doors opposite, leading to the buttery and storerooms, or he could run to the back door. Making a quick decision, he crossed to the buttery and squeezed behind the door. There he waited.

He heard the door open, soft footsteps entering. They passed through into the hall, then out at the far end, going into the solar.

Sir Thomas slipped from his hiding place and was at the front door in a moment, but then he hesitated, seeing a large chest. With a cruel smile, he untied his cloak and gathered it up, setting it upon the chest in full view of Karvinel when he entered. Only then did Sir Thomas open the door and walk into the street.

In the road he saw Hob waiting anxiously, hopping from one foot to the other in agitation, wondering what would happen when the visitor saw Sir Thomas. The knight's smiling face reassured him and he looked relieved as Sir Thomas strode towards him.

'That woman hasn't the brain she was born with,' Sir Thomas said contemptuously. 'But Hamond's revenge has begun. I look forward to hearing how Karvinel responds to finding a man's cloak in his hall.'

'God's teeth!' he continued a short while later. 'What would a man want a gross woman like her for? Give me a lissom wench like your sister. She's much more life in her, more pleasure and amusement. And she has a brain! That fat bitch in there only thinks of herself. She ever looks to the next comfort, not caring what may happen to others.'

It was Karvinel himself, however, whom Sir Thomas wanted to pay for the crime, not Juliana. Before him rose the vision of Hamond swinging from a rope. Hamond had died in order that there should be proof of a robbery. It mattered not a whit that Hamond had been nowhere near the robbery and could not have been involved; Hamond was accused by a merchant and his clerk and that was enough.

But if Hamond had not been there, so the rest of the story was false.

'Why should Karvinel fake a robbery of his own money?' pondered Sir Thomas aloud. 'How would he gain by pretending that his own money was gone?'

Hob skipped at his side as the knight strode to the Cathedral. As they reached the Fissand Gate he suggested self-consciously: 'Because there was more than his own money.'

'Eh?' Sir Thomas looked at him sharply. 'What do you mean?'

'The m-merchant,' Hob said, stuttering nervously. 'He was carrying money for the Cathedral too. It wasn't just his own.'

'What? Who told you this?'

'The . . . the cripple at the gate,' Hob said, terrified of the expression on his master's face.

Sir Thomas stood a moment staring at Hob and then, slowly, he began to chuckle.

Later, much later, in the Cock, in the poor, shabby district of the city, Sir Thomas settled his remaining cloak over the top of the thick blankets to protect himself and Jen against the cold.

'This place is an embarrassment,' he grumbled, pulling her to him. 'I would never come to such a hovel when I owned my own manor. A flea has bitten me!'

'But the manor is gone,' she reminded him. 'And this is better than the mud and cold. Your tent is fine when the weather is still, but when the wind blows . . .'

Sir Thomas cast a sombre eye at Hob, who had begun to snore over at the door. '*Shut up!*' he hissed before planting a kiss on Jen's lips. 'You're right, I suppose. I think maybe I'm too old for the life.'

She stiffened. 'What do you mean?'

'What do you think I mean? I can't keep on striving as an outlaw. It's no life for an old sod like me. No, I have to try to win a pardon. God knows how.'

Jen rolled over onto his chest, staring down at him, her hair falling about their faces. 'You mean that? You'll seek a pardon and settle?'

'That bastard Karvinel must die first. I must repay Hamond's debt, Jen. It's a matter of honour.'

Jen pulled away. 'Don't do that, my lover. If you kill him, they will find you. He's a well-known citizen. They would have to seek you out.'

'I must,' he stated flatly. 'Hamond was my man.'

'There must be another way. Please, there must be.'

He kissed her gently, and she rolled over to lie on her back. They made love quietly, but with a restrained desperation, as if both knew it could be their last night together.

It was dark when Karvinel returned home. He opened the door and tiptoed inside, hoping not to wake his wife. A jug lay on the table in the hall and he poured himself a large cup of wine, standing before the fire, drinking sullenly.

Soon he could start making small payments and investments, he decided. It should be safe enough by then. People would hardly be likely to connect a few small payments to the robbery. Of course he'd have to be careful about the Cathedral. Perhaps he should offer them money for the rebuilding. He would certainly have enough cash when his investments came in.

All that money. He brooded as he sipped, thinking of the two heavy purses he had concealed: one his own, the second belonging to the Cathedral. He had hidden them carefully before pulling at his cloak and tearing at his shirt. Drawing his dagger, he had scratched himself on the chin, the neck and the forearm. Then he had thrown away his knife and walked to the city.

It was a sheer fluke that he had seen the man at the Nobles Inn. Hamond was known about the city. He had a reputation – was the perfect scapegoat. Hurrying to the Cathedral, Karvinel had sought out his clerk and told him his story. He had been robbed on his way back. All his money, and the Cathedral's, had been taken from him, but who would believe him? And now one of his attackers was sitting, bold as brass, drinking in an alehouse.

Peter had been appalled. He had sat white-lipped while Karvinel spilled out his story, and agreed immediately, bless him, that he should support Karvinel's version of events.

With a clerk to back him up, Nick was safe. He went to the Constable and told him about his robbery, and in a short space Hamond was arrested. Cocky at first, he hadn't believed that he would be kept long. He claimed he had been nowhere near the place where the robbery was said to have happened.

But others disbelieved him, especially when a farmer came forward to say that he had seen Hamond in the company of the well-known rogue Sir Thomas. That sealed Hamond's fate. The jury was satisfied that he deserved his end. He was hanged on the twenty-second; one day after Ralph's death.

Karvinel met Peter later that same day, the day the executioner made Hamond dance his death jig. Peter stood underneath the swaying body, gazing up at the dark, blood-engorged face. Peter said that Hamond almost seemed to be watching him accusingly. He had said it with a nervous chuckle, like a man who was too worldly-wise to believe in such nonsense, while Nick Karvinel knew he was scared that the outlaw's ghost might come for revenge. It was partly to soothe him that Karvinel took him to the tavern. Later that afternoon, in the tavern, Karvinel had told him.

He didn't know what had made him admit it. Perhaps he had an urge to share his guilt; or maybe it was the desire to cap another man's story. Because it was there that Peter had told him about seeing Vincent's cart outside Ralph's house, someone filling it with leather. Shortly afterwards Karvinel agreed that sometimes people would act out of character, and had sworn Peter to the secrecy of the confessional before telling him the truth about Hamond's innocence.

Peter had stared at him disbelievingly, in a state of shock. At first he had stammered questions loudly, while Karvinel tried to 'shush' him, to no avail. And then Peter had gone quiet, gazing into his own personal hell, shuddering with abhorrence when Karvinel accidentally touched his arm.

Karvinel had quickly reminded Peter that he had told him under the protection of the confessional, but Peter had curled his lip and withdrawn, not even offering Karvinel a 'Godspeed'.

It was strange how clerical types would behave. Look at Peter that night. Petulant, sulking, turning his back ostentatiously . . .

That fellow Hamond was a thoroughly bad sort – everyone knew that. But perhaps Peter was angry that Karvinel had stolen money from the Cathedral. *That* would explain a lot. In Peter's memory, Karvinel would repay the lot. It was the least he could do. At least he hadn't robbed Ralph as well.

Yes, he would soon be able to afford to repay the Cathedral once a few of his investments came in, he thought, and then he could patch up his problems with Juliana. He wondered where his wife could have got to. The place was silent. She must have gone to her bed, bored with waiting for him to return. He went over to the backyard's door and pissed out. Then he locked up and was about to make his way to the solar when he saw it.

There was a man's cloak on the chest in the screens passage. At first he thought it was his own, but he didn't recognise it; he'd never wear something so shabby and faded.

A horrible thought began to form in his mind. He hated to think that his bitch of a wife could have betrayed him, but her contempt for him over the last few weeks had been visible to all. He grimaced, his expression one of rage and fear; rage at his wife's treachery, that she should dare to behave so, and fear that he might lose her and become the subject of every wit in the city.

He raised the jug but it was empty; he set his jaw and went to the door. No sound. He had intended going up to their room silently so as not to waken her, but now he took his shoes off and went up with particular caution, hoping to catch his wife's lover in his own bed. When he saw her lying there, still fully clothed, and alone, there was a feeling of relief that she was not still entertaining a man, but he was still annoyed with her. He opened his mouth to rail at her, but then a sharp rumbling in his belly made him close his mouth and belch.

A cramp, he thought, nothing more, but there was a presentiment of something evil. He was aware of a coldness, a thickness in the air, and sweat broke out freezing upon his forehead. He was still a moment, confused and forgetting his wife as the pain began, but then he doubled up as the sword-thrust of agony lanced through his gut.

Mouth wide, but unable even to scream, the pain was so intense, he gasped for help from his wife.

But her corpse could do nothing.

Simon awoke with a dull pain at the back of his head. He snapped his eyes shut again at speed and waited for the strong wave of nausea to subside.

This was the trouble with cheaper taverns, he thought queasily. Cheap taverns sold cheap ales and wines. Although both last night had tasted fine, clearly there had been a problem with one or the other of them. Perhaps it was the third jug of wine he had shared with the grizzle-haired host when most of the other folk had left. That must have been the one – the others were fine. And the ale had tasted all right beforehand, as had the cider: a good, strong, tasty brew. In fact Simon realised he could taste it still even now, and the potent flavour was unpleasantly present on the tip of his tongue.

He sat up, puffing and blowing as he tried to settle his gut.

'So you're awake, Bailiff?'

'Ha! I always wake at the same time, Baldwin,' he croaked. 'It takes more than a few drinks to make *me* oversleep.'

'Really? Well, if you can sleep through your snoring, I suppose you can wake refreshed whenever you want,' Baldwin observed caustically.

'Was I snoring?'

'Like a hog. You were so loud that Jeanne couldn't sleep either, but I expect she will tell you all about her sleepless night shortly.'

Simon scratched at his head, one eye shut against the confusing split vision. 'Could I tempt you to a walk before she wakes? I am sure she would appreciate the peace.'

'Hypocrite!' Baldwin laughed and threw a cushion at Simon's head.

'That,' Simon said slowly and with great dignity, 'was not kind, Baldwin.'

'No,' said Baldwin and threw another.

CHAPTER TWENTY-NINE

They walked along Paul Street and into Southgate Street, where they found themselves dazzled by the sun shining straight down the road at them. Simon winced and screwed up his eyes, but Baldwin only slapped his back and chuckled.

At the Carfoix they continued a short distance until Baldwin spied a baker's shop. 'Let us break our fast.'

'Isn't it a little early for food?' Simon enquired tentatively.

'Nonsense. And the bread smells wonderful, doesn't it?'

Simon made no comment, which Baldwin took for acceptance, and the two entered.

The place was already busy, with men and women selecting their loaves from the pile on a table near the unglazed window. At the rear a pair of men wielding long wooden shovels moved loaves about in the large ovens while Mary Skinner stood at a bar and took people's money. There was no mistaking her, not with her raven-black hair. Simon grinned to himself remembering how she had strained and moaned with her man on the evening of Christmas Day, but then the savoury smells of cooking assailed his nostrils and he staggered to the door.

Baldwin went to the counter and ordered a good thick pasty. Paying his money, he smiled at the woman. 'Hello, Mary.'

'Hello,' she answered suspiciously.

'I wonder if you could help me and my friend.'

The older of the two bakers whirled around and stood with his shovel resting butt-first on the ground. 'What sort of girl do you think she is, eh?'

'I am helping the Coroner with his enquiries into Ralph Glover's death,' Baldwin said mildly. 'Of course if you want to conceal anything, I shall simply tell the Coroner. I have no wish to cause any trouble.'

The man glanced over Baldwin, then Simon, then grudgingly nodded. 'Go outside with them, Mary, but stay in sight.'

He managed to convey his deep distrust of the strangers in his tone, but Baldwin ignored him, walking outside chewing on his pasty.

From closer, Baldwin could easily see how Mary could have attracted the glover's apprentice. Slim, with a white complexion, grey, steady eyes, and full, soft lips, she had the grace of a Celt with the calm beauty of a Norman.

'What do you want from me?' she asked, resting on a fence-post.

'We have heard from Elias how he was with you the day Ralph died. We wanted to know whether you had been asked to delay him,' Baldwin said.

'"Delay him"?' she repeated scornfully. 'Why should someone want to do that?'

Simon answered testily, 'So that they could make the poor devil look guilty while someone else murdered his master, girl. Why do you think?'

She shrugged. 'I don't see it's any business of mine.'

'If you weren't asked to keep him here, it probably isn't,' Baldwin agreed. 'But if you *did* help a murderer by keeping the poor apprentice here, you would be guilty of conspiracy.'

'Me? I've done nothing.'

'That may well be true, but if you continue to do nothing, you may be helping Elias to swing. Still, if you're content to carry the responsibility for his death on your conscience, there is little we can do. Come, Simon. We had better go and explain to the Coroner and Receiver that this woman doesn't wish to help.'

'You do that,' she said, unimpressed. 'It doesn't scare me.'

'The Receiver may be interested in the profits of the bakery,' Baldwin mused.

'Well, you tell him how unhelpful I was. We'll see whether he's interested in the bakery, won't we?' she said and returned into the shop as another customer appeared.

Baldwin remained staring after her with a frown of shock on his features.

'What is it, Baldwin?'

'The girl has just answered my problems.'

Simon gazed at him, then back at the shop. 'I don't think I quite . . .'

'She clearly doesn't care for Elias, which after her forni-cating with another man is no real surprise. That means that when she delayed him, we can be sure that it was so that he would be late, *not* because she wanted his company.'

'So we aren't any further forward.'

'Of course we are. We know who the killer was.'

Simon's head snapped round to stare, and once the pain had diminished he gasped, 'Who?'

'Simon, think about it. Adam was poisoned before lunch, by someone who was not in the Cathedral. All the Canons, Secondaries and others were in the Cathedral at Mass. So someone from outside the Cathedral was responsible. Adam's bread had been poisoned. When Peter died, it was because he had eaten something bad – we think his bread. And the bread is made in the morning, then distributed after the dawn Mass. Someone always attends that service. Someone who had a good reason to want Jolinde dead.'

'I really don't see who you're getting at.'

'Probably not, so follow me,' Baldwin said confidently.

His path took them along the High Street, but as they passed by the turning which led down to Karvinel's house they heard a scream. They exchanged a look, then ran together down the lane to the merchant's house.

Outside, a little boy stood shaking with horror while a young woman tried to comfort him, cradling him in her arms.

'My master, my master . . .' he kept repeating.

'It's all right,' she said, while at her side a foolish looking boy stared at the door, shaking his head and weeping.

Simon and Baldwin followed the boy's terrified gaze and walked straight in through Karvinel's door. Nothing in the hall, nothing in the solar downstairs, but from the base of the ladder they could smell the vomit and excrement. Simon curled his lip at the odour and pointedly held the ladder for Baldwin to climb. He was soon back, his face grim and forbidding 'We must fetch the Coroner.'

'I'm here,' Coroner Roger said from the doorway. He clambered up the ladder and while Simon waited below, the two men took in the scene.

'There's no need to guess how they died,' Coroner Roger said.

'No,' Baldwin agreed. 'Both in agony, both contorted, both vomiting and emptying their bowels.'

'Quite. So both were poisoned, although it looks like Nick beat his wife before they died,' Roger said thickly. 'Who did this? And how?'

'I cannot help but feel guilty for this,' Baldwin said heavily. 'I should have guessed what was likely to happen as soon as I had spoken to Jolinde. I should have guessed ... Especially with what my wife told me last night. I should have guessed.'

Coroner Roger eyed him for a moment without speaking. 'You think you know who killed these two?'

Baldwin shook his head regretfully. 'Coroner, I know who murdered Ralph, who murdered Peter, who attempted to poison Adam, and who killed these two as well. I only wish I had been more wise last night. Come. I shall take you to the murderer.'

He turned to the ladder and slowly descended, his heart full of despondency. Like a tapestry, Baldwin knew that an enquiry into a murder would throw up coloured threads which, if arranged correctly, would create a picture that was instantly recognisable. So many of the loose cords had been in his hands the previous night, yet he had not managed to complete the picture until that last comment from the baker's girl. If only he had not been so tired the night before, these two people might not have died.

Walking with the pensive gait of a doomed man, he left the house of death and went into the road. The young woman was still holding the boy, while near her the idiot boy had covered his face with his hands. Behind them a man leaned against a wall, his face shadowed under an overhang. A small gathering of neighbours stood near to hand, murmuring resentfully among themselves.

'Where's the Constable?' Coroner Roger bellowed. A man shuffled forward apologetically. 'Guard this door and don't let anyone in until I return. The Karvinels have been murdered.'

The Constable gaped while the neighbours shook their heads. They would all have to pay a fine for breaking the King's Peace. Baldwin led the way towards the High Street.

'I was confused by the number of deaths,' he told the others. 'It is so rare that you find a series of killings like this. If I had thought about it, perhaps I would have come upon the truth earlier, but I didn't. I allowed myself to be half-persuaded that the glovemaker's death was a mere robbery, a chance theft during which the poor householder died. It is rare to find the murderer in such a case.'

'True. The randomness of the crime makes it all but insoluble,' Coroner Roger agreed.

'Quite so. To be able to discover a murder one needs a reason for a man to kill. One must have a logical, comprehensible motive. So often it is based upon obvious factors.' He paused, stopping at the side of the street while a cart rumbled past. Continuing on his way, he sighed. 'Yet in this case we learned that there were several possibilities: the theft of Ralph's money, the removal of a possible competitor in the race to power in the city, the theft of his stock, possibly the concealment of another crime. And then I was confused by the murder of Peter.'

'We all were,' Coroner Roger aid. 'There was no sense to his death.'

'No. And that was the point,' Baldwin said.

The Coroner threw a look at Simon, who smiled at his confused expression and shrugged expansively.

Baldwin continued, 'Just as it was for the Secondary Adam. Why should another Secondary die? Why should any of them? And then I hit upon the idea that another person was the target for the poison which killed Peter. Now, if someone else had helped, wittingly or unwittingly, to give the poison to Peter, then that person could also be a threat to the poisoner. And so Adam was. He had two jobs in the Cathedral: he made and replenished candles, but he also helped deliver bread in the morning. I think he knows who delivered the bread to Peter.'

'I begin to understand,' breathed Coroner Roger.

'Adam was a specific victim in his own right. A murderer would hardly leave evidence about so clearly without good reason.'

'Ahm . . .' Coroner Roger gave Simon a helpless look.

The Bailiff was not sure either where his friend was leading them. 'Do you mean that whoever poisoned Adam wanted to leave proof so that someone in that room would be blamed with Adam's poisoning?'

'Yes. They probably didn't care who was blamed so long as someone was.'

The Coroner frowned. 'How would a killer know which was Adam's loaf?'

'Adam and the others in Stephen's household sit in order of precedence. It would have been easy. And then the bottle of orpiment was left in the room so that anyone could have taken the blame.'

'And where would the killer have found the bottle?' the Coroner asked.

'Ah, the poison would have been bought from an alchemist. The bottle left in Stephen's room was yellow arsenic, but I doubt that was what poisoned Adam. Yellow arsenic is bright and obvious and anyone would have seen it on – or in – a loaf of bread. Any thief could have walked into the Choristers' hall during the mid-day service to take the little bottle. All the members of the choir would be in the church, so it would be perfectly safe. And I believe that arsenic must be treated to make it especially poisonous. The killer still has the genuine bottle of poison, I expect.'

'So you don't think that Peter was killed because of his clerking for Karvinel?' Simon asked.

'No. I think that Jolinde was supposed to have died. And then Adam was supposed to die because he knew the killer.'

'What of the Karvinels?' Simon asked.

'Who would benefit from Karvinel's death?' Baldwin asked.

'Vincent le Berwe!' the Coroner replied.

'Exactly. Just as Vincent would lose his key enemy by the death of Ralph.'

'There are some others,' Coroner Roger observed.

Baldwin gave a fleeting smile. 'Very well. But Karvinel and le Berwe were the two leading contenders in the city, I think you will agree?'

'Oh, certainly, but there will always be contenders in any city. That doesn't mean that one or other will murder his opponent.'

'No, of course not,' Baldwin agreed.

He had clasped his hands behind his back and Simon could see that he was deeply moved or concerned, although Simon was not sure why. The Bailiff was about to clear his throat and break in upon Baldwin's thoughts when another interruption caused all three to halt.

Jen of Whyteslegh was petrified. She was convinced that she would soon be dead of terror. These three men were among the most powerful and important she had ever seen, let alone spoken to. Such folk hadn't come near her village when she was at home with her parents. There was a worm of fear squirming in her belly as she hastened her steps towards the rearmost man and tugged at his tunic.

Instantly Simon whirled to face her. The sudden action made her stop and put a hand to her mouth as she saw him reach for his sword, but when he saw it was a young woman, Simon stayed his hand and smiled reassuringly.

'You were comforting the child outside the house, weren't you?' he said. His head still ached appallingly, but he felt guilty at scaring the girl and he was determined to put her at her ease.

'Yes, sir,' she squeaked.

'Did you want to speak to me?'

'Sir, I have been told to ask, would you speak for an approver if he can deliver you a murderer?'

Baldwin and the Coroner had stopped a short distance further up the road and they watched Simon as he tried to make sense of her words. 'What do you mean?'

'I have a friend, sir. He has been involved in crimes, but he wants to ask for a pardon. Would you speak for him if he will give you evidence to convict another felon?'

Simon glanced back the way they had come. This early in the morning Exeter's High Street was a bustling mess of humanity, with buskers and hawkers calling out their wares, girls threading their way through the crowd, boys darting hither and thither to offer their services to hold a horse's reins for a period. Somewhere in the seething mass, Simon felt sure that he could feel a man's close inspection. 'Yes,' he said. 'If your friend can help us to stop these murders, I'll speak for him. Let me speak to the Coroner.'

He beckoned and Baldwin and Coroner Roger rejoined him. Roger was unconvinced. 'Why should I allow him to surrender?' he demanded of Jen.

'He has been blamed for crimes he didn't commit – he wants to stop running and hiding all his life. Please, sir, *please*. Let him give himself up.'

The big man puffed out his cheeks. 'Very well, but if the fellow he accuses demands trial by combat, I can't do anything to protect him.'

'I wouldn't expect you to, Coroner,' said Sir Thomas from behind him. 'But Vincent le Berwe paid me to destroy Nicholas Karvinel. That makes him a felon. I think he murdered Karvinel and his wife, Juliana, too.'

'I am afraid I think that there you are wrong,' Baldwin interrupted, 'but I wish to arrest the murderer. Coroner, may we continue?'

'By all means.'

'Are you going to Vincent le Berwe's house?' Sir Thomas asked.

'Yes.'

'Good. In that case I can tell you of all his crimes on the way there. Come – I do not want him to escape. He killed Karvinel and he has stolen my revenge from me. I wanted Karvinel to die for my friend, but now he is already murdered!'

CHAPTER THIRTY

Vincent le Berwe was in his hall when the furious hammering came on his door. He looked up bemused as one of his servants shouted through the panel to demand who was visiting so early. Hearing the bellowed reply, Vincent shot to his feet and called for his bottler, while ordering that the door should be opened forthwith.

'Coroner, and Sir Baldwin. Bailiff Puttock! It is a pleasure,' he said, and then there was a freezing knot in his throat as he recognised the last man.

'Good day, Vincent,' Sir Thomas said, walking inside and gazing about him with interest. 'Receivers do well for themselves, don't they?'

'Are you alone here?' Baldwin asked.

'My wife is at the Cathedral, Sir Baldwin. Why?'

'Because we are here to learn why Karvinel and his wife were murdered,' Coroner Roger grated. 'And we don't want to upset your wife unduly.'

Baldwin smiled. 'Vincent, please be seated. This will take us some little while.'

'Seated? Why? And who is that man? What's he doing here?'

In answer, Sir Thomas pointed at him. 'Coroner, before God, I swear that I know this man. He is Vincent le Berwe, Receiver of the city of Exeter. I met him many years ago when we were both young, he a student, me a youth practising at the warrior's arts. Recently I fell in with felons, and this man Vincent le Berwe persuaded me to help him. He wanted me to ruin his enemy Nicholas Karvinel. To that end he paid me to break into Karvinel's house and steal all I could. Later he paid me to repeat the break-in and fire the place.'

'Thomas! What are you doing? Are you mad?' Vincent demanded, astonished.

'Sir Thomas, did you harm Karvinel and his wife last night?' Coroner Roger intoned solemnly.

It was Baldwin who answered. 'Oh no. Sir Thomas had nothing to do with that, did you?'

The outlaw wiped a hand over his brow. 'No, although I should have. I wanted the bastard to pay for the way he had my man killed. No, I would never use poison. It's a coward's weapon.'

'Who?' demanded Coroner Roger. 'Which man did he have killed?'

'Hamond, the man you had arrested and hanged. He was with me all that day until he went to the tavern for a drink. Neither of us robbed Karvinel.'

Coroner Roger sneered. 'Then who did?'

'No one,' Baldwin answered.

'*What?*' All the men turned to him, the Coroner dumb-struck for the first time since Baldwin had met him.

He smiled. 'That is right. I think when we look through Karvinel's house, we shall find his own money there intact, and we'll probably find the money supposed to be stolen from the Cathedral as well.'

'Why would a man stage a robbery?'

'I think I just gave you the answer: the Cathedral's money. It was a significant sum, far too great a temptation to a man whose own fortunes were so weak. He pretended to have been robbed, then hurried back to the city. There he sought his clerk and told him, I guess, that he had been robbed. Peter was horrified. He agreed to back up Karvinel, even to the extent of identifying a certain felon whom, so they alleged, had been partly responsible for the theft of the money. That was enough to secure the death of Hamond.'

'What has all this to do with me?' Vincent demanded.

'Your responsibility lies with the death of Ralph the Glover,' Baldwin informed him. 'But not directly because you yourself didn't kill him. Just as you didn't kill Peter or the Karvinels.'

'Who did?' Coroner Roger asked impatiently.

'Consider Ralph first. It could hardly have been any of the Cathedral staff who killed him. They were all in the Cathedral at the time. After Ralph left the dawn Mass, they would all have been attending Chapter. What is more, the knife was a slender one, with a blade of only half an inch in width at the base. That is a *very* small blade. And the attacker struck many times, in a berserk manner, which is significant.'

'Of what?' the Coroner demanded, baffled. 'And why kill him? Ralph was a lovely fellow, always kind and honest.'

'He told the City Bailiff that he thought he had learned of a robbery,' Baldwin said. 'He had discovered that Vincent here was stealing from the Cathedral.'

'I wouldn't do a thing like that!' The merchant's cheeks went purple.

'Adam has confessed.'

'The feeble-minded cretin! He hasn't the—' Then le Berwe stopped and shrugged, defeated. 'Well? What of it? I was only doing what any other man would do. It didn't cost the Cathedral much, and I needed the money. My ship sank, you know. I've got next to nothing.'

'So you killed Ralph?' the Coroner said disbelievingly.

Baldwin shook his head. 'Think of the poisonings. What sort of person uses poison? And who was the target? Peter? Or was it someone else: the man living with him – *Vincent's illegitimate son, Jolinde.*'

Simon nodded. They had agreed this before – but what sort of man was le Berwe, to have tried to kill his own son?

'No. This is all rubbish. No, you're wrong,' Vincent said, shaking his head in denial. He half-lifted a hand as if to protest further, but let it fall into his lap.

Baldwin ignored him. 'That must have been difficult for you, Vincent, knowing that your wife had tried to kill your own son. Why? Well, probably because Hawisia is herself pregnant. She would hardly want a competitor to her own child's inheritance, would she? But her plan failed. She poisoned the wrong man. For all her planning, she killed poor Peter by accident. And Jolinde, being a pleasant, easy-going sort of fellow, never even guessed that *he* was the target of the poison.'

The Coroner gaped at Baldwin, dumbfounded. 'A *woman* did all this?'

'That's preposterous!' Sir Thomas exclaimed. 'Hawisia is too highly bred to do such a thing. Perhaps a slattern from a tavern would be capable of it, but a woman like Hawisia?'

Only Simon grunted in agreement as he saw how all fell into place. 'What about the Karvinels? Why should she try to murder them?'

'No, this is mad,' Coroner Roger said, but his tone was unconvinced.

Baldwin continued quietly, assured and certain of his facts. 'Presumably Nicholas knew something. We know that expensive leathers are missing from Ralph's shop. Perhaps Karvinel saw the thief taking them.'

Vincent covered his face with his hands. There were no tears; he was like a man who has found peace at last after a long and terrifying struggle, but his voice was broken, almost sobbing. 'You're right. Karvinel heard that I was seen in the street that morning. I didn't realise what it meant at first.'

'You were in the Guildhall, weren't you?' Simon confirmed.

'Yes. But Peter, *rot* him, told Karvinel I had been there, since he had seen my cart, but it wasn't me, it was my wife. Hawisia came to the Guildhall to see me with one of my carts, saying she thought I wanted it for goods, but I didn't. I told a servant to take it home rather than see her struggle with it.'

Coroner Roger gazed from him to Sir Baldwin. 'I don't understand.'

Baldwin continued. 'Hawisia had wanted to help her husband by removing a threat to him. She thought Ralph

394

was more dangerous than Karvinel and planned his murder to the last detail. She went to his house and knocked, having already ensured that his apprentice would be away. She persuaded Ralph to open his shop for her, and when he had done so, she murdered him, striking him madly, like a berserker. But I think she carried on quite calmly with her plan after that unpleasantness. She was perfectly collected; she took his keys, locked the shop and went to the house, locking that door after her. That was why Elias couldn't get in. She went upstairs and got the money from the strongbox. It was then that Elias arrived. He banged on the door without answer, then went round to the back. While he did so Hawisia unlocked the front door, crept out and unlocked the shop.'

'Why should she do that?' Sir Thomas asked.

'She wanted to make sure that she was not suspected of the murder, so she put something by the body to implicate the apprentice – his own knife and keys. No doubt she stabbed the body first to add a certain verisimilitude to the scene and mark his knife. That was why the Bailiff was so convinced that Elias was guilty. Meanwhile, Hawisia made off, taking the leathers with her. To give herself an alibi, she took the cart to her husband, and then had one of his men push it home for her. Once there I assume she concealed the money and . . .'

'She told me she had sold some jewels to buy me leathers to trade,' Vincent said dully. 'I needed the money. I didn't suspect her then.'

'No, but then you realised from what Karvinel said that she had been there when Ralph died. You realised that your wife had parked the cart there and had stolen the leathers

– and that if she had taken the leathers, she killed Ralph and stole his money as well.'

'Yes.'

'Peter didn't realise that when he saw the cart, it was being pushed by Hawisia. He assumed it was you. But Peter was an innocent, wasn't he? He thought that because Elias had been arrested, Elias must have stabbed Ralph. And he had so much guilt on his conscience after he had aided Karvinel execute an innocent man, helping put Hamond to the noose, that he didn't think clearly about Ralph's death. He just assumed Elias was guilty.'

'Is that why Peter was poisoned?' Sir Thomas demanded. 'Because he saw Hawisia?'

'No. She meant to kill Jolinde, as I said. However, by accident she killed the man who could truly have put the noose about her own throat. It was merely Peter's bad fortune.'

The Coroner was frowning. 'But why should Hawisia have decided to kill Karvinel now?'

Baldwin looked over at Vincent. 'I assume Karvinel threatened to expose Vincent.'

Le Berwe met his gaze. 'You are right. He did so yesterday. My wife suggested, when I told her, that I should approach Sir Thomas one last time and get him to finish off Karvinel once and for all. I told her I couldn't, but she wept and said that she couldn't see me ruined for want of a little help. I tried to stop her but she went off anyway. She said to see Sir Thomas.'

'She never came to meet me,' Sir Thomas growled.

'Vincent never thought she would,' Baldwin said. He faced le Berwe. 'Hawisia knew all about your business dealings, didn't she? And she took great pride in supporting you in both your business and political dealings. Nothing was too much for her to help you, was it? You know full well that she committed these crimes, that she killed Peter and Ralph and tried to kill Adam as well, before last night murdering the Karvinels.'

Vincent did not answer, but his eyes slid away from Baldwin's cold, intense stare.

'Very well. Let us see if we can persuade you to consider your position,' Baldwin continued. 'Hawisia was trying to murder your son when he killed Peter. Did you realise that?'

'I don't think that she would . . .'

'And she certainly murdered your first wife. Christ Jesus, man! How many more people would you have allowed her to kill before you put an end to her atrocious acts?'

Vincent had slowly come to face Baldwin. He stood, gaping with horror, as Baldwin's words sank in. 'No!' he breathed.

'I am afraid "yes",' Baldwin said.

Vincent shook his head, his face slack and expressionless, like a waxen mask which had been left near a fire. He tried to walk to a jug of wine, but stumbled and had to sit on a stool while he poured with shaking hands.

'Are you sure of all this?' Coroner Roger asked.

'It became clear at the baker's just now,' Baldwin explained. 'The girl there clearly didn't care when I said that I'd tell Vincent, although if she had been involved in a crime she should have been worried to hear that the Receiver would be involved. No, she *told* us to tell him! That showed me that she thought she had operated with his sanction. But we already know that Vincent wasn't there that morning. He was at the Guildhall. Except a wife may give orders in her husband's name and many will assume she speaks with his approval. As for using poison, it is ideal for a woman since it can be administered at a distance, and does not involve some of the more risky and unpleasant aspects of murder.'

'And Ralph?' the Coroner asked.

'Was stabbed with a small blade, only half an inch wide. A woman's knife,' Baldwin said dispassionately. 'Just as her berserk attack was typical of a scared woman killing her first victim.'

'Did you know this?' Roger demanded of the silent merchant.

'You only guessed recently, didn't you, Vincent?' Baldwin said softly.

'I didn't guess until last night when she got back. She told me she'd done it all for me, but I couldn't believe her. I honestly couldn't. She told me she'd put poison in Nick and Juliana's wine. All for me, she kept saying. All for me.'

'She is evil, Vincent. She thought to placate you for having tried to kill your son. Where is she? She'll kill someone else if we don't catch her,' Baldwin said gently.

Vincent closed his eyes and tears sprang from beneath the lids. He looked as though he had aged twenty years in the last ten minutes. 'She went to Mass. She's not back yet.'

Baldwin patted his arm, but then glanced through the window at the daylight outside. 'For the first Mass of the morning? Shouldn't she be back by now?'

'I don't know,' le Berwe said and covered his face again.

Sir Thomas was leaning against the wall picking his teeth with a dirty nail. He glanced at Sir Baldwin. 'What is it?'

'This woman is irrational. She sees murder as the only means of controlling events and people.'

Simon was already striding for the door. Over his shoulder he called, 'And two Secondaries are still loose ends to her.'

It was bright and warm in the sunlight and Hawisia felt perfectly composed and calm. The service had gone smoothly for once, the sermon had been comprehensible, and the Secondaries had not dropped the candles or sniggered as they so often did. Today, the twenty-seventh, was after all an important day, for later tonight the boy-Bishop would come into his own.

And everything was going well, too. Thank goodness the Karvinels were no longer a threat. Their menace had been removed from Vincent's life and he could look forward to a secure future. Hawisia smiled. Her man deserved it. She had done it all for him. There were only two items of business left for her to complete.

She had gone to the north tower and offered to take Jolly's loaf to him, bearing in mind Adam was unwell. She carried the bread in her basket now, slightly altered with a few of the drops from her bottle. First Jolly, then she must see Adam again.

The air was crisp and fine. From the precinct she could see the smoke from chimneys and louvres all over the city, rising a short distance and then drifting and falling until it formed a pale grey blanket over the whole place. It was warming and pleasant to see how God embraced the world.

Surely she was in God's hands. At no time had she been in any danger. When that meddling fool Ralph had been about

to tell the City Bailiff of Vincent's little 'arrangement' with
Adam to do with the candles, she made sure to visit him
before the Bailiff. Her luck had held; the baker's girl had
done her job well. Ralph had opened the door, expecting to
see William de Lappeford, and expressed his surprise, but
when Hawisia, at her most charming, explained that she
wanted to buy back some of her husband's cordwain, he had
reluctantly agreed and taken her into his shop.

And as soon as he turned his back in there, she had drawn
her knife and struck at him.

Oh, it had been scary at first. Her first blow had made him
swear, as though he didn't realise what was happening. He
made to turn, so she struck again and again, to silence him
and kill him swiftly. Even when he fell, she kept raining
blows upon his back and then his chest, and after a while she
realised that his breath had stopped. He stared up at the ceiling sightlessly, his shirt stained ruby red.

He was in the way of the door so she had dragged him
away, then took a thin piece of leather and wiped her hands
with it, thinking she should return home now, but just as the
thought came into her head she heard footsteps. Panic took
hold of her – it must be the Bailiff! She frantically sought a
place of concealment, then rushed to the door and pushed it
shut, locking it. But no one tried to enter. She could hear the
dim fool apprentice calling, but then he left.

Relief gave her a new idea. Taking care to see that no one
was about, she slipped out of the shop and into the merchant's
house. Upstairs in the chamber, she saw the money-box.
And, miraculously, Elias's knife and keys. At once she saw
their importance. She could take the money and put all blame
onto the merchant's apprentice.

Swiftly she pocketed the small sack of coins and gems and, taking the keys and dagger with her, she went downstairs. The apprentice was at the back of the house now; she hardly dared to breathe while the latch jiggled up and down. Then she heard him call to his master, over and over. Hawisia knew there was no time to lose. She hurtled through the hall, unlocked the front door, and dived into the shop just as feet came running along the alley beside it. Panting in her quick fear, she heard Elias enter, shouting for his master, and then she knew she was safe for another couple of minutes. She stabbed Ralph with Elias's knife to bloody the blade, then dropped Elias's keys at his master's side, before, with a happy smile, taking an armful of leathers – it was a terrible weight – and staggering with it to the cart outside, throwing them in and covering them with a sheet.

And that was that. She set off with the cart, pushing it down the slight incline to the Guildhall, where she saw her husband, but he was involved in discussions and couldn't waste time with her. Vincent had given her one of his men to take the cart back to the shop. All so easy! She had planned it very carefully, but even she hadn't quite expected to have everything go so smoothly.

The poisoning of Peter was annoying in the extreme. She had delivered the bread, stopping Adam outside the Cathedral on his round, and it had been intended for Jolly, but the Devil had made her stepson give it to his friend instead. Not that it would matter for much longer, she reflected, patting the loaf in her basket. Everyone knew Jolly was her stepson, and no one could associate her with any malice towards him. That made it so much easier, she thought. And in retrospect it was good that Peter had died. He could have been embarrassing after what he told Karvinel.

She was outside Jolly's place now. Knocking, she entered, staring about her at the wrecked walls. It looked as if rabbits had burrowed to find shelter in the floor. Jolly wasn't about when she called – he must still be at the Cathedral helping to tidy up after the service, or perhaps he was in the Chapter meeting – so she put the bread on his table and left.

It was while she was walking along the grassed yard towards the Fissand Gate that she saw them, the Bailiff and Sir Baldwin. She was about to wave to them politely, go to meet them and enquire about Jeanne, when the Coroner loomed up behind them and pointed. All at once their faces turned towards her, and in their expressions she saw only accusation and loathing.

Without a second thought she dropped the basket and fled. She knew the way to the secret passages, for Jolly had shown them to Vincent, and he had shown her, proud of his son. She darted through the workings to the little door and wrenched it open, then hurried down, into the darkness of the city's tunnels.

Water dripped in the blackness. Behind her, light was reflected from the world above, but here was only dark and gloom. Occasional drips were caught in a shaft of sunlight and glistened momentarily like jewels, only to disappear as they fell. She could move quite swiftly here, knowing the direction the passage would take.

How could they have learned of her guilt? Was it something she had done which made them realise the killings were her work? Had someone seen her outside Karvinel's place after she had been in to see Juliana and added her drops to the wine on the table? It was terrible to feel, after so much effort, that her work was all in vain, that all those people had died, their lives snuffed out, to no purpose. It was so *unreasonable*!

A shudder of remorse shivered up her spine as she thought of that poor man Ralph flinching as she thrust again and again. All to help her husband, all to protect him and ensure his safe promotion. All failed; all pointless.

Would it affect him? Yes, of course it would. His career was over. There was nothing she could do for him. Not now. It was too late.

Her mood altered. She was close to collapse, awash with devastation at the realisation that all her plans were destroyed. Where she had intended to serve her husband, all she had achieved was his total ruin. It was dreadful, ridiculous, that a gaggle of busybodies should have been responsible for Vincent's downfall. Why had they insisted upon tracking her down? There was no need.

She heard a stone chink against another. Not behind her but ahead. They shouldn't be there yet – how could they have got in front of her? They must have run like the wind along the High Street. A furtive step slapped into a puddle, and she shrank into a slight depression in the wall nearby, her eyes wide with the fear of the hunted. That was a man's step, surely. It couldn't have been a rat or anything, for a soft, muttered curse followed it. The owner of the voice had soaked his foot.

Reaching for her knife's handle, she slowly eased it free as a figure gradually became visible ahead.

* * *

Baldwin and Simon chased after her as soon as she sped off past the side of the cloisters towards the building works. There they found themselves confronted with an empty space in the angle between the cloisters, the Bishop's Palace and the Cathedral. As they gazed at each other in bafflement, the Coroner ran off to the far side of the Bishop's Palace and stared over southwards towards the city's wall. He turned back with a frown of incomprehension.

'She can't have disappeared,' Coroner Roger panted.

'Certainly not,' Baldwin agreed. 'But where could she have gone?'

Simon peered about the area. There were innumerable doors to lean-to storehouses and workshops built to accommodate the builders. He began to pull at doors, rattling latches and tugging to see whether any were unlocked, but he had the conviction that it was a pointless exercise. If she were concealed inside one of them, she would surely have barred the door somehow.

Baldwin watched him for a moment; he had a feeling that they should hurry, that there was a strong chance of someone else being killed if they didn't find Hawisia swiftly.

Behind him, a small crowd had formed. Hawkers and beggars had seen Baldwin and the others chase after the woman, and several had drifted over to see what was happening. Members of the congregation and choir had joined them, and already there was jostling as Canons and Vicars thrust themselves through. Stephen was the first to reach Baldwin and the Coroner.

'What is all this?' Stephen demanded, gazing from one to the other. 'This is Church land! What are you doing here,

Coroner? You have no rights here, what's the meaning of your intrusion?'

Baldwin cut across the Coroner's explanation. 'We're trying to prevent another murder, man! The murderer came here to hide and we need to find her.'

'Her?' Stephen gasped.

'Wake up, Canon! Who knows this area best?'

'Um . . . I suppose the architect, but he's not here, he's . . .'

'Henry, Sir Baldwin,' came the calm, unhurried voice of Gervase. 'Henry knows all the Cathedral precinct. He has to, from running and hiding from people all the time.'

'Fetch him.'

Gervase didn't move but instead bellowed Henry's name at the top of his voice. There was no sign for a moment that anyone had heard, beyond one Annuellar, who happened to bear the same name, looking up anxiously, but then there was a rush of pattering feet and Henry appeared from the direction of the Bear Gate with what looked like a suspiciously innocent expression on his face. Gervase didn't miss it, but passed the lad to Baldwin without comment.

'Henry, the murderer who killed Peter is here somewhere, but we don't know where. Do you know where someone could hide?'

'The tunnel,' Henry said immediately.

There was a stone in his sandal. Jolinde groaned and sighed, then leaned against the wall with one hand while he fumbled in the dark to untie the thongs about his ankle which bound it. Releasing the sandal, he felt something damp and slippery on the sole and withdrew his hand in disgust as the noisome odour reached his nostrils. 'Dog's turd; oh, God's teeth!'

The shoe fell with a soft 'plop' into a puddle and he peered downwards in an attempt to pierce the murk. 'Oh, God's body – what next?' he breathed, his foot still in mid-air, one hand on the stones of the rough wall.

It was no more than he deserved, really, after spending the previous night with Claricia, missing the night's Mass as he and she made love and slept fitfully, but since the death of Peter he was growing ever more depressed and unconvinced of his potential as a priest. He had taken his father's money, agreeing to try to ruin another man purely to help Vincent; he had forced his friend to join him in robbing a man; he had failed in his oaths by missing services and spent his time indulging his gluttonous whims and in rutting with his woman. Still, she had agreed to wed him once he had left the Cathedral, so this was probably the last time he would come along the tunnel. It was only really from a sense of shame and embarrassment that he had taken this route rather than walking in boldly through the Fissand Gate.

Gloomily he reached down for his sandal and felt his hand sink into a soft, wet muddy-feeling dampness. It could have been anything, and Jolinde found himself hoping very intently that it was only mud.

It was no good. He couldn't keep on living his life in two halves: one that of a serious Secondary, the other that of a secular man who enjoyed the pleasures of the flesh. He must find a new career. If his father would still agree, he could study a while at University, but if he wouldn't, Jolinde would find a living as a clerk, either with another merchant, or perhaps with the Coroner. There were always openings for a fellow who could read and count.

As he came to this conclusion, he heard voices and saw a glimmer of light ahead. The sight made him want to dart back along the passage, but then he realised that with his new resolution there was no point. He would meet them, whoever they were.

Bracing himself and squaring his shoulders, he held his head high and marched towards the light.

There was a flash at his side and he froze with terror as the gleams of light caught a blade that swooped towards him. He screamed, thinking it was some appalling horror from the grave which was setting upon him; he could almost smell the putrefaction of the corpse.

Leaping back convulsively, he saw the razor-edged knife flash past his breast. Before he could say a word, it was reaching towards him again, up to his throat, and he was aware of maddened eyes in front of him. Jerking his head to one side, he felt the swift dragging at his flesh as the dagger sliced through his cheek and on up to his eyebrow. There was no pain, not yet, and he was only aware of a slickness, as if he had broken out into a heavy sweat. Jumping backwards again, he tried to escape the fast-moving blade, but it seemed impossible. His chest was open and unprotected. He saw rather than felt the blade sink into his upper body, grating against his collar-bone, before it was pulled out and came back.

Sobbing with shock and scared beyond his wits, he could do little more than keep moving back, for ever trying to get beyond the range of the knife, but then he was saved by a loose stone. With a muffled cry, he fell on his rump. His assailant hadn't noticed and even as he scrambled to escape, Hawisia fell headlong over him. He felt the dagger pierce his

thigh and clapped a hand to it before she could take it again.
With a strength born of sheer panic and terror, he tugged it
free and stabbed once, twice, three times, and was rewarded
by the twitching and shivering which he recognised as his
assailant's death throes.

It was only then, as her blood seeped over him and her
body gradually became flaccid in death, that he recognised
his attacker from her odour. He could not believe his senses.

CHAPTER THIRTY-ONE

Vespers, Baldwin thought, had to be among the most tedious of all church services. It was invariably later than it should be, because the priests all wanted to let their meals sink down beforehand and would sit around drinking their fine wine while the congregation waited patiently, but at least tonight, on the eve of the feast of the Holy Innocents, there was a subtly different feeling to the place.

The light had long since fled. In the Cathedral there was a thick fug, composed of the smell of sweat and the herbs and spices carried by the richer people in the city to conceal it. Damp clothing gave off various scents: fur smelled of wet dogs, leather stank of burned wood or urine. The effect of these different odours in such a confined area was powerful upon Baldwin. Fortunately, they were driven off by the wafting clouds of pungent smoke which issued from the censers.

All this was normal, but tonight as Baldwin stood in the nave of the Cathedral, his wife on one side, his friend on the other, he could sense that the atmosphere had greatly improved. Only this morning the place had been filled with panic-stricken folk who were fearful of the murderer, and then who wanted to see the body of the dreaded woman who had so unsettled the city. Her body had to be displayed before the Cathedral doors for all to see, because rumours had flown about so speedily, many didn't believe she had died.

Now all appeared serene. The end of Hawisia's short reign of terror had fortuitously coincided with the celebration of the boy-Bishop, and all were keen to enjoy themselves. That was obvious from the cheerful, happy attitude of all the people in this great room.

The mood grew lighter still as the boy-Bishop himself appeared, dressed in his miniature mitre, gloves, and carrying his pastoral staff. He was accompanied by Choristers, all likewise dressed in their silken copes. Once at the altar steps, they faced the congregation and sang the text of the Book of Revelation where it spoke of Herod and the slaughter of the innocent boy-children of Israel.

'*Centum quadraginta quattuor milia qui . . .*'

Baldwin could translate it in his mind: '*The one hundred and forty-four thousand who were redeemed from the earth . . . They now reign with God and the Lamb of God with them.*'

The young voices were shrill, but pure, and as their singing drew to an end, the boys formed a procession and walked slowly through the choir to the screen, offering incense to the Cross and then singing still more prayers. Baldwin found himself relaxing, feeling the worry and strain of the last few days falling from him.

Simon was quiet, he noticed. At the end of the service when they all walked out, Baldwin glanced at his friend. 'Are you all right?'

'Yes, yes. I just want to leave this place, that's all. Get back to my wife and daughter,' Simon said. He stood aside while a young woman pushed to the doors ahead of him. 'I wasn't made for city life. I need space.'

'I can easily understand that,' Baldwin said. There was a tinge of sadness to his voice. There had been a time, when he was many years younger, when he had enjoyed living in a city much larger than this one, but with the passing of the years he had grown to appreciate the peace and relative calm of the pastoral life. In his manor all he need worry about was providing enough food for his table. Matters of politics left him cold, the more so since the destruction of his Order. Oddly enough he found that spending time in a place such as this led him to suspect the motives of all about him.

And not only the motives. There were people who, he was convinced, had misled him intentionally. Intelligent, educated people had deliberately led him astray for their own reasons.

'Simon, Jeanne, I would like to detour a short way before returning to our inn.'

The hall was lighted when they arrived, although it was clear from the face of the bottler who opened the door that the servants and their master had been given leave to go to their beds.

'Please ask if we may see your master,' Baldwin said as the door opened upon the bleary-eyed and bitter-looking man.

411

Grumpily the bottler grunted assent and took them up the stairs to the upper hall. Here they were greeted with warmth, if a little surprise.

'Sir Baldwin! And hmm your good lady wife – Lady ahm Jeanne, is it not? And Bailiff Puttock. Please enter and take seats. Ah, wine. Yes, bring wine, warmed and spiced. You would like warmed wine? Ah, yes, of course.'

Baldwin smiled and nodded and as the Dean bustled around, his head ducking in a curiously birdlike manner, Baldwin sat and observed him. The Dean appeared to notice his close scrutiny and asked, faintly bemused, 'Is there um a difficulty, Sir Baldwin?'

'No. Not now that we have found the killer of the people in the city. All is resolved,' Baldwin said, adding 'Once poor Adam and Jolinde are cured.'

'Yes. One hopes they will soon um recover. The physician seemed hopeful, even about Jolinde.'

They lapsed into silence. All knew how even the smallest nick in the flesh could give rise to appalling infection.

The Dean broke the sombre mood. 'What can I do for you so late in the evening?'

'I wanted to ask why you suspected one of your own staff to be guilty of the murders.'

'What makes you think I suspected anyone, Sir Baldwin?'

'You were convinced that someone from your Treasury was guilty. Naturally you thought it was likely to be a young, callow, untrained Secondary, but you were not stupid enough to think that only a youth would steal. A large sum could be a temptation to anyone, couldn't it? No, you felt anxious that someone else could have been guilty. And so you asked for two unknowns in the area to come forward and seek the murderer. You could only do so when there was another death – of one of the two Secondaries about whom you already harboured suspicions – but you were not so certain that you felt you could take anyone into your confidence.'

The bottler arrived and dispensed wine, but once he had left, the Dean waved a hand airily. 'Please continue.'

'I think that you held suspicions about someone. Someone with access to privileged information, someone with a motive, or perhaps someone who you feel is not entirely trustworthy.'

'Perhaps. But what does this have to do with anything?'

'I would like to know the truth. Perhaps it was because you didn't trust the man's brother? That led you to think that brothers will sometimes behave alike.'

'Ahm, yes. So you have heard about that. But I may not be able to inform you of certain secrets. So much of my life is tied up with secrecy. The confessional, Church diplomatic matters, affairs of state. All these can mean my mouth must, um, necessarily be stilled.'

'Can you give us no explanation, Dean?'

'Perhaps I can give you a slight hint. No more.' As the Dean studied Baldwin, the knight saw his eyes glitter in a friendly manner, and Baldwin noticed how the reticence disappeared, like a ruse thrown away after its deceit had served its purpose.

'Sir Baldwin, ah it is difficult to protect the Cathedral. We monitor everything that we can, with clerks trained in finance to check all our accounts, but it is very difficult when we have such a large project going on. A block of lead is worth a lot of money, but if you have several hundred of them, one can go missing. I was suspicious that money was being filtered out, but I had no idea who was doing it, nor how.

'If you know that the brother of one of your senior dignitaries is a felon, you have to wonder about him when some money goes missing. And if a sum of money is stolen from a merchant transporting it for you, you wonder anew. Especially if only a short time later you hear that a glover to whom much treasure had been given has been killed and robbed. So many coincidences. So much wealth lost.'

'So you expected us to investigate your own Treasurer?'

'No. I wanted to make sure that *all* were investigated. I only hoped you would do so without showing favours.'

'You know that Adam was responsible for selling candles on the side?' Baldwin asked.

'Please do not remind me!' the Dean said and shuddered. 'It is hard enough seeing how he has failed academically and socially without being told of his dishonesty.' He looked up at the window, sadness tightening his features. 'When I look at him,' he murmured, 'I can see, even if from a distance, the beauty of his mother. It will be extremely painful to see him go.'

'So you suspected him of responsibility for these other losses?'

'God forgive me, but yes.'

'How was he granted a position here in the first place?' Baldwin asked gently.

'When he was old enough, the famine was beginning. I had kept in touch with his mother, and she asked if we, ah, could look after him. I felt it was the least I could do. I never thought it would come to this.'

His words made Simon pucker his brow.

'You don't understand,' the Dean smiled. 'It is simple. Adam is my son – half-brother to Sir Thomas's woman and that foolish boy who lives with them. Adam was the first-born. Stephen was a useful go-between some years ago, for there was every reason for him to visit his brother when he still owned his lands, and Stephen would deliver messages for me and bring back her own. And then she married a good man and gave birth to other children – although only Jen and Hob survived. Thus I heard what was happening to Adam.'

'I think I understand. He will leave the Cathedral?' asked Baldwin.

'I cannot allow him to remain.'

'What of Jolinde?'

'He has gone. He had decided to leave before this final disaster.'

'Will Luke stay?'

The Dean eyed him a moment contemplatively. 'When the, ah, family lost everything in a squabble with their neighbour, who happened to be a friend of the King, Luke's mother was already dead. With his father an outlaw, it was, um, natural that his uncle, our Canon Stephen, would protect the child as best he may. And he concealed the true nature of his brother's activities from the child. Why should the boy learn the demeaning truth – that his own father was a felon? If we can, we should hide that shame from him.'

Baldwin smiled faintly. 'The Cathedral seems a haven for many children.'

'There are many innocents whose births are not legitimate,' the Dean answered.

'I see,' Baldwin said, standing. 'Dean I thank you for your patience. Please excuse us if we leave you now.' He drained his cup and bowed.

The Dean rose and nodded, making the sign of the cross, first over Baldwin, then to Simon and Jeanne. 'Go with God.'

The place was filled. Simon was used to such sights. As Bailiff of the Stannaries, he often had to speak to large groups of men and the scene gave him no concern, but Baldwin felt discontented to see so many people all watching him. It was not like being in a court, he felt. There he was aware of his own authority and the aura of the position itself cushioned him from the public gaze, but here, in a strange city, with unknown people staring at him, he felt exposed and threatened.

Henry had the words off pat. He stepped forward and while his friend read out the note of thanks, Henry waited. As soon as the last words were spoken, he took a pair of cordwain gloves, wonderfully stitched and studded with jewels, and passed them to Baldwin. Then there was another short reading, and a second pair were given to Simon, before the boy made the sign of the cross and prayed for them.

Soon the affair was over and Baldwin could breathe a sigh of relief. He and Simon walked away from the public attention while other worthies stepped up to take their awards, and when Baldwin had returned to Jeanne's side, he heard a rough cackle.

'So, Sir Baldwin, are you content now?'

'Coroner, I didn't see you – my apologies. I am very content, thank you. It is enough no longer to be the focus of attention.'

They chatted idly, but there was nothing in their conversation to interest Simon. He had his eye on the Dean, who stood watching Luke and Henry with hawk-like intensity.

Later, when the crowds had thinned and the two men were walking about the city with Jeanne, Simon turned to Baldwin. 'The Dean's son is Adam, so why didn't he confront his boy and ask if he was telling known robbers about Cathedral money?'

'I think he was anxious to be fair at all stages,' Baldwin said. 'He agreed to have the child brought here to be educated, and, to ensure that the boy received the best training possible, he had him quartered with the Treasurer, Canon Stephen. When he began to fear that the thefts were somehow the responsibility of the Treasurer, what could he do?'

'He could have accused the man,' Simon shrugged.

'He could hardly do that, for the Treasurer could retaliate by telling all that the Dean had fathered an illegitimate boy and kept him in the Cathedral for his own satisfaction. At the least you can assume that the boy would have been sent away.'

Simon considered a moment. Then he asked, 'What do you think will happen to Sir Thomas?'

'I think he will be granted a pardon. He is an important enough man, after all. Yes, I would imagine he would be freed. And then he may settle here with his woman.'

Simon nodded. 'And the half-wit with them.'

'Yes, they seem genuinely fond of the lad.'

'Meanwhile Vincent . . .'

'Don't expect me to feel sympathy for him,' Baldwin said grimly.

'It hardly seems fair. The man is ruined, and through his wife's acts, not his own.'

'He was as evil as her in his own way. He may not have dirtied his hands, because he employed Sir Thomas to do his work for him, but that is no excuse. Vincent was prepared to see Ralph broken utterly, just because he feared that a competitor might prove too powerful. To achieve his own ends he destroyed Karvinel. If it wasn't for his own greed and arrogance, Ralph, Peter, Nick and Juliana Karvinel – yes, even Hawisia herself – would probably be alive still. All were killed for Vincent's comfort and avarice. No, don't expect me to feel *sympathy* for him. He is a felon, no better than the worst of Sir Thomas's outlaws. I expect he will swing.'

Jeanne squeezed his arm comfortingly at the tone of cold contempt in her husband's voice.

Simon continued quietly, 'What of Vincent's first wife?'

Baldwin was quiet for a second. 'Hawisia was quick to use poison on Jolinde.'

'So you think Hawisia killed her?' Jeanne asked. 'But she said to me that Jolinde had killed Vincent's first wife.'

'That,' Baldwin said, 'is why I am sure Hawisia did it.'

'Jolinde . . .' Simon continued quietly. 'I wonder what will happen to him?'

Jolinde lay back on the bed in Claricia's room and watched her pour him a large cup of ale. Holding his head in the crook of her arm, she lifted the cup to his lips.

'I really am fine, love. You don't need to do this,' he protested weakly. His speech slurred: after the slash at his cheek, the wound had been wiped and cleaned and plastered with egg-white, but it stung and flamed whenever he moved his mouth too much.

'I want to. You poor love, if you could only see yourself.'
She pulled the blanket a little further up his body so that she
couldn't see the bloodstained bandage over the wound in his
chest. Every time she saw that mark she wanted to weep. An
inch further away, the physician had said, and the boy would
have been dead. One inch!

He saw her expression. 'I love you.'

'I love you too.'

'Is there any bread?'

In the Choristers' hall, the boys settled quietly for the night.
One boy was already snoring, while another, deep in a dream
of his long-dead parents, was quietly weeping in his sleep.

Luke sought sleep but it resolutely evaded him. He rolled
over on his solid palliasse and tugged his blankets and cloak
tighter to him against the freezing chill. Although the shutters were closed, the cold air whistled through the gaps
between the wooden slats and seeped through all the
bedclothes like water.

At least Henry hadn't been so bad on the day, Luke
thought. He had dreaded it, knowing how Henry would crow
over him while he enjoyed his power as boy-Bishop, but in
fact it hadn't been so bad. Henry had not made his life as
miserable as he could have. And when the mayhem began,
Luke had been allowed to play with Henry and his friends.

That had been fun, too! Luke rolled over and rested his
head on his arm, wriggling himself lower under his blanket
as he tried to keep warm. One of the Secondaries had thrown
water from a pot over another, and Henry had seen it.
Instantly he ran for the nearest tavern, where all the Choristers
grabbed pots, pans and cups, gleefully running to the stream

and filling them, before ambushing whomsoever they could. One merchant and his wife had been drenched, as had an Annuellar, but when they mistakenly caught one of the Canons, the game lost its lustre. They all knew Stephen would remember who was guilty and would see to it that their work and behaviour was monitored ever more stringently over the coming weeks.

Luke sighed happily. If he had been boy-Bishop himself he might not have enjoyed it so much. No, thinking about it, he was happy that Henry had won the election.

There was a creak of timber and Luke was just thinking how much this old hall settled in the cold of night, when he heard a muffled snigger and snapped into full wakefulness, just as an entire pot of water cascaded over his face.

'You whoreson, festering, buggering, putrid heap of cat shit!' he screamed as he leaped from his bed. Henry was already at the far end of the room, holding his sides with laughter, and then he saw the light of battle in Luke's eyes, and scuttled from the room.

Soaking wet, Luke chased after him, both silent and determined not to be discovered, two boys full of life: Henry, who would in fifteen years become the Archdeacon of Cornwall; and Luke, who would leave the Church and become one of Europe's leading mercenary soldiers.

In Will Row's alehouse John Coppe raised his pot and Joan tipped more wine into it, smiling down at him. He toasted his dead friends and drank deeply, passing it to her. She lifted it and closed her eyes, finishing it.

'He's leaving the city,' Coppe said after a few moments.

She nuzzled against him, his arm about her shoulders. He smelled homely, warm, sweaty and all manly. 'He can go.'

'Le Berwe had your man killed, though. It doesn't seem right,' Coppe grumbled half to himself.

She pulled away and stared down at him. 'Vincent le Berwe may have told the pirates about the ship, but even if he hadn't, there's still a good chance they'd have got to hear. It's not as if the ship was secret, is it? What happened to you and the others could have happened whether or not le Berwe had dealings with the French, so there's no point worrying about it. And he's wrecked. He'll never have money again, nor position. His wife is dead, and his reputation is gone. I think that's enough revenge.'

Coppe cocked his head. Outside, the wind was picking up and he could hear the shutters rattling in the grooves, while the bush tied above the doorway squeaked and scratched as the dried twigs moved across the painted door. 'Rain soon,' he said.

'Lucky the fire's going, then, isn't it?'

A pounding on the door made both of them look up with alarm, but Joan lifted his arm from her and walked to the door. 'Who is it?' she called.

'The Coroner. Open up!'

She lifted the peg from the latch and pulled the door open, scraping it across the floor. 'Coroner?'

'I've just come from the Guildhall. They wanted you to be given this.'

She took the purse and hefted it in her hand. 'What's it for?'

'A few of the merchants wanted to give it to you and Coppe – to remember your ship and the men who were killed. Look on it as a New Year present.'

421

He pulled his hood up over his head, scowled at her and, before she could utter a word of thanks, he stalked back out into the night.

'God! look at all this,' Joan said, peering inside the purse. 'Do you know what all this money means?'

'What?' asked Coppe, craning his neck to see into the purse.

'It means we can afford more wine!'

And in the Cathedral precinct, in the room Jolinde had shared with Peter, a rat scrambled cautiously across the floor. Tentatively, nose twitching with earnest deliberation, it leapt onto a stool and surveyed the room. The loaf left by Hawisia lay on the table amid a mess of platters, cups and trenchers, but the rat was not discriminating. Anything would do.

It jumped again and was on the table. As it began to gnaw through the outer crust of the loaf, a second and a third rat appeared and followed their leader to the table.

By the time Jolinde returned to pack his few belongings, the rats were all dead.

Michael Jecks

Master of the Medieval Murder Mystery

Discover more about the exciting world of the Knights Templar at

www.MichaelJecks.com

Sign up for the newsletter to keep up to date with latest developments

Connect with Michael Jecks on Facebook

www.facebook.com/Michael.Jecks.author

Michael Jecks
Templar's Acre

The Holy Land, 1291.

A war has been raging across these lands for decades. The
forces of the Crusaders have been pushed back again and again
by the Muslims and now just one city remains in Crusader
control. That one city stands between the past and the future.
One city which must be defended at all costs. That city is Acre.

Into this battle where men will fight to the death to defend
their city, comes a young boy. Green and scared, he has never
seen battle before. But he is on the run from a dark past and he
has no choice but to stay. And to stay means to fight. That boy
is Baldwin de Furnshill.

This is the story of the siege of Acre, and of the moment
Baldwin first charged into battle.

This is just the beginning. The rest is history.

Hardback ISBN 978-0-85720-517-9
Ebook ISBN 978-0-85720-520-9